Guardian Queen

DANA MARTON

Guardian

Queen

DANA MARTON

ISBN-13: 9781940627403

ACKNOWLEDGMENTS

With my sincere gratitude to all the wonderful members of the Dana Marton Book Club on Facebook, especially Hellen Walther, who recommended GUARDIAN QUEEN for the title, and Rose Arey, who suggested the names for Tera's three ships: the *Lance*, the *Sword*, and the *Shield*. And as for the "home team," Diane Flindt, Sarah Jordan, Linda Ingmanson, and Toni Lee—there are no words to express how much your kindness and endless support means to me.

CHAPTER ONE

JOURNEY'S END

"Open your britches, my lord."

Prince Graho's response was a hoarse whisper. "Lady Tera…"

The ship swayed under us, but for the most part only mildly so, the bow easily cutting through the soft waves. Water rushed past the hull—the music of the sea. Our soldiers' swordplay abovedecks added another layer of rhythm.

"You reckon he's a goner?" a sailor mumbled to my right, then grunted when his mates elbowed him to keep quiet.

My people, the Shahala, have a saying: *Truth is the lamp that lights a righteous man's path.*

Truth, however, can also be a ballast around hope's neck.

The men who surrounded me in the ship's dim hold needed hope, so I gave them exactly that. "I'm here now. I can help. All is well."

Truth was, the hardstorms had swallowed two of our five ships. Even the three ships we had left… We had not seen the other two in days. We were lost at sea, running desperately low of food and water.

When Batumar and I had left our island of Dahru to recruit an army on the mainland of Felep, I imagined returning with a liberating force large enough to vanquish the Kerghi mercenaries Emperor Drakhar had sent against us. I imagined our journey would end with victory. Now, with a lot fewer men than we had hoped for, that victory was far from certain. I feared we would end with our heads on Kerghi spikes.

For the moment, I set those worries aside. I faced a more urgent matter.

The last storm had spilled urine from the buckets—some of which had soaked into the wood—but the three dozen Landrian sailors and half-dozen Landrian royal guards around me held their breaths for another reason. Their grim gazes hung on the pain-racked face of their prince as he lay on a worn blanket at our feet, his eyes fever glazed. The light of the oil lamp next to him glinted off the beads of sweat on his forehead.

My heart ached for him. He was a good friend. Batumar and I were only able to bring home our small army because the prince had lent us his ships.

His breathing grew more labored. "Lady Tera—"

"You must allow me to see the injury. No more arguments." I knelt by his side, close enough to feel the heat rising off his body. "If you do not allow me to treat you now, my lord, the pain will only get worse." I pushed on, leaving him no opportunity to protest. "When did it begin? How many days back?"

His chest rose and fell in silence for a while, then he said at last, "After the last storm."

Seven full days.

"We should move him to his sleeping rolls," Durak, the commander of the Landrian Royal Guard suggested, glowering at me from under bushy eyebrows.

Since a broken mast had destroyed the top cabins in the stern, the prince slept down below. Batumar and I slept in another tight storage space next to Prince Graho's. The captain remained in the ruins of his old cabin on top, on principle, even when it rained.

I glanced toward the small storage rooms. "Best to leave him where he is and save him the pain of being jostled."

The prince reached for my hand. "If they help me up, I can walk over."

His fingers curled around mine, his fingernails torn and ragged. The crown prince *and* the admiral of the Landrian Navy, he fought in battle practice daily with his men. He climbed the rigging too, alongside his sailors.

I leaned forward to brush the damp hair off his forehead. "We have more space here than in the storage room. More light too."

The hatch stood open, letting in the late-afternoon sunshine and at least some fresh sea air—not nearly enough, yet more than what we would have anywhere else save abovedecks, and the prince could most definitely not be dragged up there.

"I shall sleep off the fever, Lady Tera." He returned to resisting. "The injury is hardly worth your notice."

I held his gaze and kept my voice firm. "I insist on seeing it."

The men stilled, waiting for his answer, while Durak watched me with undisguised mistrust. He blamed me for dragging Landria into the war and for taking part of the Landrian navy away from the protection of their own shores. The commander took it as a personal insult to his kingdom when I refused Prince Graho's offer of marriage and chose Batumar instead.

The Landrian sailors behind him likely felt the same. They were on this arduous journey at the orders of their prince. They owed me no allegiance. Sparks of tension filled the air, swirling like a swarm of wasps, ready to sting.

"My lord," I began, wishing I had a different truth for him, but I did not. "I believe you have an infection. If the infection is as bad as I think it is, you risk blood poisoning. You must allow me a quick look." I paused, then marshaled my best argument. "We will be reaching land shortly. If you are not able to withstand a battle march, you and your royal guard must remain on the ship."

That threat finally accomplished what cajoling had not been able to gain. At long last, the prince nodded.

Commander Durak shifted closer.

His eyes narrowed, as if to warn that he would be most carefully watching me. He could watch all he wanted. Prince Graho had agreed.

I sent a silent prayer to the spirits, then addressed the prince. "I need to know how it started."

He cleared his throat. "A sliver of wood. As I... My lady..."

Ah. That. I winced, knowing at once what he meant.

A sliver of wood must have dug itself into his skin next to his most sensitive parts, either as he sat on the bucket or squatted over the ship's railing when voiding his bowels. Such injuries happened, especially when the ship pitched.

"When did the fever begin?"

I had first seen him limp some five or six days past. He had squarely refused my help. Then, three days ago, he'd become swollen enough between his legs that I could see the growing lump through his leggings. He had done his best to avoid me, but I had cornered him at last the day before and demanded to know the nature of his affliction.

He had evaded all my questions. Even now, off his feet, he remained silent and would not volunteer further information.

The commander spoke instead, his voice kept low. "He has not been able to climb the ladder to the deck since last night."

That explained why I had not been able to find him among the training men this morning. "When did he collapse?"

"Right before the noon meal."

"You should have come to me at once." I pulled the oil lamp closer to the prince. "Best to have it over with."

3

A moment passed in tense silence, then another, and another. Finally, Prince Graho reached for his sweat-soaked leggings with unsteady fingers.

I held my breath. All around us, men held theirs as they leaned forward, but before the prince could move the fabric aside, his men's attention shifted to something behind me. Heads bobbed.

I stifled a sigh. "Lord Batumar."

I steeled myself for his disapproval as I turned.

The Kadar warlord was built like a fortress: wide shoulders, thick neck, arms corded with muscles needed to swing his heavy sword. The black hair that spilled down his back had silver strands now that had not been there when I had met him. Battle scars he would not let me heal marked his face, one running from his eye to the corner of his mouth. A true warlord, he towered over all of us, and not only because of his stature. He commanded every space he entered.

"Lady Tera." His gravelly voice carried a warning, but his obsidian eyes were filled with warmth as he looked at me. "I wish to talk with you in our quarters."

My heartbeat tripped like some young maiden's in the first blush of love. I too wished to be in our quarters with him. My love for him was endless, yet as a healer with an injured man at hand, my foremost loyalty had to be to my patient. "My lord, I must heal the prince."

Batumar's gaze slid to the fever-ridden man on the blanket and remained there for a tense moment before returning to me. "Can he be healed with herbs?"

He did not want me to use my healing powers. I had put my own health at risk during the siege of Uramit—and countless times before, in truth. I had walked the fine line between life and death more than once. Batumar always protested when I weakened myself by giving my strength to others. But a sennight ago, the ship pitched so badly that the boiling soup scalded the cook over most of his body and face. I did not realize how much the hunger and lack of sleep during our crossing had weakened me. After I healed the man, there was a moment when I thought the burns I had taken on might be too much for my spirit to conquer. Unfortunately, Batumar witnessed that moment. He demanded that I use only herbs for healing for the remainder of our journey.

The prince was not any better, and neither were our soldiers—all protective of me to the point of hiding their injuries. Truly, I wasted half my days hunting down the odd limp or wince or fever-flushed face. Time I could have used for healing!

I drew a fortifying breath, ready to go to battle on the subject. "I cannot tell, my lord, what treatment is needed until I see the wound. All I can tell is that an infection has set in."

I might be in time, or I might be too late already.

4

Batumar scowled. In the dark shadows of the hold, with his scars, with his height and breadth…another woman might have found him frightful. I had seen even combat-hardened men run from him in battle. But for me, he was the light that lived in my heart. As unhappy as I was with his interference, I had to fight the urge to rise and step into his arms.

Prince Graho spoke up then, his voice strangled. "I am fine well, my lady."

Oh, for the spirits' sake! There went all the headway I had made, gone in but a blink.

I pushed to my feet. I'd spent the long journey trapped on the ship with two hundred soldiers and fifty sailors. The only other female on the ship was a tiger. I had had enough of men and their foolish pride. A walk on deck with Marga, breathing fresh air for a while, was what I needed.

I cast the prince as hard a look as I was capable of, then marched toward the ladder—the sailors parting before me. I called back over my shoulder as I went, "I suppose I shall be back tomorrow to cut it off."

Shocked silence.

A weak "My lady" from Prince Graho stopped me before I could place my foot on the first rung of the ladder.

I stopped and turned. The prince held both hands over his private parts, the color rapidly leaching from his face. His circle of guards blanched, more than one moving to protect his own loins.

Then Prince Graho finally said, "If you would help, my lady."

His hands fell away, confirming an ancient truth known to all healers: few things faster convince a man to submit to medical treatment than the threat of losing his manhood.

Avoiding Batumar's gaze, I returned to the prince and lowered myself to my knees at his side once again.

"The sooner we start, the sooner we finish," I told Prince Graho with all the encouragement I could muster.

The prince reached for his britches once again, but Batumar stepped around me, a growl rattling in his throat. "Nay."

I swallowed words more suited to sailors, then looked up at the warlord so he could see the determination on my face. I was not just the woman who had pledged herself to him, but a healer fighting for the life of her patient. Even the warlord better not naysay me. "Aye!"

A full-blown gale gathered in his dark gaze, one that would put the hardstorms to shame. Men shifted away from us and held their breath.

"You wish to look at him *there*?" The warlord's tone turned colder and harder than sword steel.

"If he is injured *there*, looking at his ear will not help him," I pointed out with exaggerated patience.

Batumar glowered.

Why could he not be called away to perform some warlordly task abovedecks? I swallowed an impatient sigh. *Does he still consider the prince his rival?*

I had made my choice between the two men at the port city of Uramit before we had set sail. The warlord knew fine well I loved him and only him. Yet he would not forget that when we had all thought him dead, the crown prince had kissed me and had asked me to be his princess.

The two men had become allies since, but still, every time the three of us were together in a room, the air thickened with tension. Batumar had forgiven, but he could not forget.

"My lord, I must be able to see the injury."

He narrowed his eyes. His scarred chin dipped. His chest—left unarmored even though he had been at sword practice earlier—expanded as he squared his massive shoulders.

The spirits give me patience.

"If I cannot treat the infection now, I might have to *remove* the infected part later."

Warlord or no, Batumar paled the same as the others. And *then* he reluctantly nodded.

The ring of sailors gathered closer around us once again, morbid fascination mixing with horror on every face. Their stained clothes hung too large on their gaunt bodies. With their hair long and faces unshaven, the men more resembled castaways than sailors in the Royal Landrian Navy.

I held up my hand. "Please, all take a step back. In fact, I will need no more than a handful of sailors for help. The rest may leave. And the prince will not need all his guards either. I must have light, and Prince Graho must have air."

Most of the men left, and the rest shuffled back a pace. I shut them out of my mind, shut out the ship and the war. I sent a prayer to the spirits as I waited for Prince Graho to finish unfastening his britches. Then I sent another prayer as, without meeting my eyes, the prince pulled back the cloth fully at last, with a painful grimace.

A few of the guards sucked in harsh breaths, others groaned. Several men turned their heads. One barked like an injured seal.

Even I, a seasoned healer, had to close my eyes for a moment to steady myself.

CHAPTER TWO

PRINCE GRAHO

The prince's loins glowed bright red, his left bollock swollen with pus, thrice the size of normal and ready to burst.

I leaned closer and saw what I worst feared.

Aye, a spot of blackening.

He should have come to me sooner. Anger flashed through me, then sympathy, then worry. Was I too late? I could heal a lot, but I could not resurrect dead flesh.

He held the fall of his britches in a white-knuckled grip. "Might it be set right then with some herbs, my lady?"

His words were as tentative and hopeful as the first warm breeze of spring. And as weak.

I looked him in the eyes. He deserved the truth—all patients did. "No. I am sorry."

His face, flushed with fever before, turned whiter than Landrian lace. While he gaped for words that would not come, Batumar, more warrior than diplomat, put what all the men were thinking into words.

"You mean to geld him?"

I clenched my jaw. "I mean to save his life."

A few of the remaining men backed away another step, but others pushed to the front, darkly curious to see the spectacle.

"Could this not wait until we reach land?" Durak, the commander of the prince's guard, looked ready for murder, his hand creeping toward his sword. He stopped only when he caught the warlord's sharp gaze on him.

7

"No," I said as blades clashed abovedecks and soldiers shouted, hard at battle practice. I shut my mind to all distractions and addressed the prince's guards. "I need fire in a cauldron, boiling water from the galley, and the cleanest strip of cloth on the ship."

I had to move quickly. I would not leave time for anyone to raise objections, least of all the prince.

When I pulled my knife from the small leather scabbard on my belt, a couple of men grunted in alarm at the cold glint of the metal. I offered the blade to Batumar. "If you could shave the spot, my lord."

I thought myself clever, expecting him to object less this way, but the warlord's dark eyes narrowed to slits, and his jaw tilted into the stubborn angle I knew only too well.

I nodded, accepting his unspoken refusal, and shifted closer to the prince. "I shall do it, then."

At once, Batumar's large hand clamped onto my shoulder. "Nay!"

He growled like a distempered tiger and shot a look at the prince that was full of blame for putting me in this position. Then he barked at a young sailor, "You. Fetch my broadsword."

The prince's eyes snapped wide. While his guard moved to protect him, he tried to scramble away on his back like an overturned crab.

"My lord! It is no joking matter." I looked at Batumar with exasperation even as I asked under my breath, "How would you feel in his place?"

At least the warlord had the decency to look remorseful. He cleared his throat. "An ill-timed jest."

The prince gave a strangled laugh then. A heartbeat later, his men laughed too, in quick, unsure, nervous bursts.

Batumar inclined his head to Prince Graho by way of an apology, yet I wondered if he had not made the jest on purpose. He *had* eased the tension.

In any case, I could scold him no further. That brief lightness on his face reached all the way to my heart. He had returned to me a changed man from the torture chamber of the sorcerer of Ishaf. These days, his smiles were rare and all the more precious.

He shot me an apologetic look as well before taking the knife from me. "How much?"

"All of it, if you can."

As the warlord crouched next to the prince, tested the blade with his thumb, then set about his task, the prince did not breathe. He did not so much as blink. Neither did any of his men.

To leave him as much privacy and dignity as I could, for as long as I could, I busied myself with the meager store of herbs that hung from my belt. The long voyage—two full mooncrossings so far, with storms pitching and rolling the ship—had been full of injuries. I had but some rosemary and lavender left.

"Missing something you need, Lady Tera?" the prince inquired weakly.

"Missing everything. But no matter. We shall make do with what we have."

When two sailors arrived with hot water, I added several sprigs to the copper bowl. Both herbs had some mild disinfectant properties, although they were not what I would have chosen for this task. I wished for the essence of moonflowers, the drops of medicine that formed inside the creamy white petals, most useful for open wounds vulnerable to infection.

Two other sailors brought a cauldron with glowing coals and fire, and I set the bowl over the flames until the water boiled again. I grabbed the clean cloth one of the men offered, ripped it in half, then dropped both halves into the water.

Batumar finished shaving the inflamed patch of skin and handed back my knife as he stood. Only then did I return my attention to the prince.

He clamped his teeth together, his gaze determined. Now that we had begun, he was prepared to see this through to the end like a good soldier.

Commander Durak shifted on his feet, his hand hovering near his sword once again. He had pledged his life to protecting Prince Graho, and he stood ready at all times to fulfill that oath. Watching me cut into the prince would be as difficult for him to bear as for the prince to suffer the cut.

I dropped my gaze to the commander's finely stitched sword belt. "The prince will need something to bite on."

Durak offered the belt at once, placing his sword on the planks behind him, out of the way.

"Please hold the oil lamp as close as you can," I told him. "But not over the prince. The ship might pitch."

Durak obeyed without hesitation, and I was glad to see his right hand occupied. This way, should he grow alarmed, he could not grab my wrist as I performed the surgery.

Next, I turned to Prince Graho. "I shall wash the wound. The water will be hot, but not hot enough to burn."

He tried to smile, even as more sweat beaded on his forehead. "I have been missing my long baths at the palace. Nothing better than a morning of pampering at the hands of the bathhouse maidens."

Yes. Well. *This* was not going to be anything like *that*.

I set the blade of my knife on the hot coals to burn away any dirt. I let it cool for a few moments before using the tip to lift the cloth from the boiling water, then I waited until most of the water dripped out and the cloth cooled some. As gently as I could, I cleaned the injured area, even as the prince hissed curses around the leather he now held between his teeth.

I paused to allow him a break, but I could not pause long. "Now I must excise the pus, find the sliver, and pull it from the wound."

Prince Graho blinked his agreement.

With the tip of my knife, I pricked the black spot in the middle of the red swelling. A yellow discharge ran forth, the same as would leave a lanced boil.

A foul, rotten stench filled the air as I watched the pus closely for a wood splinter. The cursed sliver did not leave, however, but remained stubbornly in place. I bit back a groan of disappointment.

"How is it, my lord?" I asked the prince, hoping he would, at least, feel less pressure.

"Good as new," he said around the leather, then clenched his jaw tight as I began to work the swollen flesh with my fingertips until only fresh, living blood flowed.

I pressed until I was satisfied that the wound was cleansed, then I washed off the area once again and dabbed at the wound with the cloth until the bleeding slowed.

"That looked like fearsome hurt," one of the sailors mumbled.

The prince answered with a breathless "It but tickled a little."

"Now comes the easy part," I joked along. "I shall remove the splinter."

I gave no more warning than that, no time for my patient to balk. I eased my finger into the wound, halting not when Prince Graho's back bowed with pain. At first he moaned, then he fell silent as he bit so hard on the commander's belt that the leather creaked in protest.

The men around us watched, mesmerized by the kind of horror that does not allow the witness to look away. Even Batumar remained still and silent next to me.

I prayed to the spirits and near sagged with relief when, finally, my fingertip touched a sharp little point.

"There."

Yet I could not pinch the splinter, not even with the very tips of my fingernails. The sliver of wood had buried itself too deep. To retrieve it, I would have to employ more drastic measures.

"I must cut," I said gently as I withdrew my hand and wiped off the blood. And then I answered the question I knew the tortured prince most wanted to ask. "But not everything. You can still marry a princess. You shall have heirs."

Around us, men drew ragged breaths.

"Aye." Batumar, subdued now, bent to clap the prince on the shoulder. "You will but have a bit more room down there."

Strangled laughter escaped the sailors, but the tension did not lessen this time. All eyes hung on the blade I held in my hand, my fingers tightening as the ship jolted.

The waves were smaller and kinder now than they had been during the storms, but still tall enough to give us a good toss from time to time. I sat back on my heels so I would not fall onto my patient, while Batumar strode to the ladder, put a foot on the bottom rung, and called up, "Hold the ship steady!"

"Aye, my lord!" The deep voice of our captain responded from above.

When several heads appeared in the opening, Batumar waved the curious soldiers back. "The Lady Tera must have light."

The heads disappeared. Batumar returned to us to crouch at the prince's head and hold down his shoulders. Two of the prince's guards dropped to their knees on either side of him to hold Prince Graho's hands out of the way, pinning his wrists to the blanket. Two other men moved to hold his feet. I could show no hesitation. No time now for anything but full confidence.

I held the knife over the fire again. "I shall be as quick as possible."

Prince Graho's complexion turned green, his gaze focused on the blade. Batumar's expression was encouraging, if grim. Many of the men around us were as pale as if they too were sick.

As I removed the knife from the flames, the prince squeezed his eyes shut. I waited until the blade cooled. And then I cut.

The sailors gasped and cursed. Prince Graho screamed around the leather in his mouth, his body bucking off the floor. Batumar wrestled him back down, but the prince only relaxed, his muscles turning slack, when he lost consciousness.

Sweat rolled down my temples. I held the future of the Landrian throne in my hands. *Help us, kind spirits.*

I sliced the thin skin up straight, slid two fingers into the opening, and popped out the swollen, infected ball of flesh—half furious red, the other half nearly all black. Cutting had been the right decision. Another day's wait, and I would have been too late.

I could not draw the blackening from the prince's body, not even if he and Batumar agreed to the use of my powers. I could heal nearly anything, but blackening had to be cut out before more and more of the body deadened and the illness killed the patient. I refused to lose the prince to blood poisoning.

I paused long enough to draw a full breath, then, holding the knife steady, I removed the deadly threat from the prince's body with one last sharp slice.

Once again, I let the flowing blood cleanse the wound. Then I thrust the knife back into the fire, heated the blade to red, and cauterized the main blood vessels. I washed the wound with herb water before stitching the skin closed, leaving a hole where any pus and blood could seep out for the next few days.

When I finished, I sat back on my heels, as drained as if I *had* given my own strength to the prince. "The worst is done."

All around me, shoulders slumped with relief.

I wished for ruhni powder and shlunn hulls, but settled for packing a freshly boiled and cooled piece of cloth against the hole in the prince's skin. I wrapped another strip around his groin to hold the first one in place. He did not awaken, thank the spirits.

"You need to wash his face with cold water, keep a cold cloth on his forehead, and make sure his fever does not worsen," I told Durak. "If it does, strip him naked and wrap his whole body in a cold, wet blanket."

Two sailors hurried off to fetch water.

"I shall be back often to check on the prince. But if he calls for me when I'm not here, you must find me, day or night," I ordered his royal guards as I stood at last.

"Aye, Lady Tera," Durak answered, his voice rough, his gaze haunted, as if he had just returned from bloody battle. He looked at me with grudging respect instead of the disapproval I had grown used to since I had rejected the prince's courtship.

I nodded at him, then raised my voice to make sure it would carry. "The prince will live."

Prince Graho groaned in his oblivion. I hoped he heard me.

As I watched him, my hand strayed to my empty herb belt. I needed more cleansing herbs for the days to come. And herbs against infection. Feverfew too, if the wet sheets proved insufficient to bring down the prince's fever.

Help us, kind spirits.

We needed to reach land.

One of the prince's guards crouched next to me to clean up the remains of the surgery: the blood and the pus and the blackened piece of flesh. I thanked him, even as my lungs begged for fresh air. I picked up my knife, cleaned it, sheathed it, then headed to the worn oak ladder that leaned against the open hatch above. I limped for a moment, my legs half-numb from kneeling.

Batumar followed me, lost in thought. I remained silent as well, watching where I placed my feet on the rungs. Then we reached the deck, and I could not have said anything if I tried, for the sailor in the crow's nest up the mainmast began shouting.

"Land!"

CHAPTER THREE

LAND AT LAST

I had seen battles that produced less clamor. A flock of seabirds circled above us in the air, but their cries drowned in the noise of men climbing up the ladder behind us. The soldiers already on deck rushed to the railing, loudly guessing what land awaited ahead.

The sudden shift of weight rocked the ship, until Temro, the barrel-chested captain, began shouting from the helm, "Pull back, ye motherless bastards, curse yer eyes!"

His four-pronged black beard fell to his chest, each prong representing one of the four directions of the compass, each wrapped in a length of blue leather cord to symbolize that the captain had mastered the seas and could take his ship anywhere he wanted.

Batumar drew me through the throng of excited men, shielding me with his wide shoulders. Then, when we reached the railing, he moved me in front of him. Far on the horizon, the sun was setting over a dot of land, bathing it in an orange glow, as if both land and water were burning. I could not tear my gaze away.

"No matter what island it is, they will have news of the other islands of Mirror Sea. They might know how Dahru fared in our absence."

Batumar responded with a heartfelt "Aye."

I had met the warlord after tragedy had taken most of his family, but he had four living daughters, all matched to warlords far from Karamur, the Kadars' capital city. And he had only recently found his indomitable mother. The last we saw the Lady Leena, she was leaving on a pilgrimage to the sacred springs to thank the goddesses for returning her son to her. We had been worrying about our loved ones, and more than a little.

"The island of Rabeen!" Captain Temro's booming voice reached us from the helm.

My heart danced around in my chest like a drunken sailor. Rabeen was an outlying island, a market island in the Strait of Ghel, the most commonly used entrance to Mirror Sea. *The way home.*

A cry of celebration went up from the men, followed by more back clapping than at a wedding. If anyone bumped into me, I cared little, but the warlord placed a hand on the railing on either side of me to protect me from the jostling crowd. No matter what went on around us, I was always his first thought.

"Blow the horn!" the captain called up to the crow's nest. "Thrice repeated!"

A horn blared, letting our other ships know—if they were close enough to hear—that we'd sighted land. But even after our horn sounded the second time, no response came.

I turned my head enough to look at Batumar. "I wish we had a way to know how the *Sword* and the *Lance* fared."

We had sailed from the harbor of Uramit with five of the finest Landrian warships, each manned by fifty Landrian sailors and carrying two hundred soldiers. Our flagship, the *Shield*, a handsome six-sail carrack, had been accompanied by four square-sailed caravels.

One caravel sank the day we entered the hardstorms. Another we lost halfway through the storms. Only two caravels trailed our flagship out of the graveyard of the ocean, the *Sword* and the *Lance*, but we lost sight of both in a blind fog shortly after. I prayed to the spirits daily to keep them safe.

"If Lord Karnagh and Tomron did not lose their ships in the hardstorms, they will not lose them on calm seas." Batumar's gaze was steady, his voice sure.

All the leaders of our army had begun the journey on the flagship. We used the first two days of our voyage on the *Shield* to strategize, to plan how we would approach our island once we reached it, how we would lead our combined armies.

We stopped at an uninhabited atoll before entering the hardstorms, the deadly gales that left the wild ocean near impassable. Lord Karnagh, along with the other Selorm lords and their battle tigers, moved to the *Sword*, one of the four smaller, square-rigged caravels. Tomron, whom I had appointed the general of my army, boarded the *Lance*.

Batumar and I should have separated and gone to the last two ships to lessen the risk of losing too many of the leaders if the flagship sank, but

Prince Graho had insisted that I remain with him on the flagship because the carrack was the largest and the safest of our five vessels. Batumar, of course, remained with me. He rarely let me out of his sight. In truth, I did not want the warlord out of my sight either.

"The last we saw the *Lance* and the *Sword* they were weather-beaten." I'd been praying for them every spare moment I had.

"But still seaworthy, no fatal damage to sails or rigging," Batumar said. "They weren't taking on water."

He was right. The caravels would catch up soon. I would have to trust that the spirits heard my prayers.

As we stood at the railing, Marga squeezed through the throng of men to join us, rubbing her head against my arm. The tiger prowled the deck for most of the journey, watching for jumping fish in calm weather, growling and snapping at lightning during the storms. She hated the belly of the ship. Now she leaned her weight against Batumar, trying to push between us. The warlord responded with tightening his embrace around me.

"We shall spend the night at sea and sail into port at first light," he called to the captain.

Captain Temro responded with a crisp "Aye," and shouted to his sailors to roll up the sails.

Then Batumar turned to one of the Landrian Royal Guard who had come up from the hold behind us. "Make sure we have a full guard tonight."

"A full guard, Lord Batumar." The man hurried off to organize the shifts.

"Rations lifted!" The captain's deep voice rang out over the ship.

The mass of men around us greeted this news with yips and hurrahs, shoving away from the railing at last.

I was smiling just as wide as they were. *Dried fish tonight. Tomorrow a feast.* We were saved from starvation. We could resupply on Rabeen.

I tipped my head to rest it on Batumar's shoulder.

"You look happy." He brushed his thumb along my jaw. "Thinking about standing on firm land again?"

"I'm thinking about fresh fruit, and bread drizzled with honey." My stomach growled.

The warlord licked his lips. "Roasted meat with steamed chaka roots."

I was laughing as I turned back to the sea. *Land. Rabeen.* So close to home now. *We made it.* I swam in a sea of indescribable relief.

When Batumar asked, "Should we return below?" I shook my head. *Not yet.*

I needed to keep an eye on the island, needed to assure myself that it was real. So we stayed at the railing and watched the dark strip of land in the twilight.

Summer arrived while we had battled the storms, the breeze warm. Hope bloomed in my chest, a stubborn little flame. We had survived the hardstorms. *Twice.* Once on our way to the mainland, and now on our way back home. We had at least one ship, filled with soldiers. True, we had suffered heartbreaking losses, but we had *not* lost hope. And Batumar and I still had each other.

He remained silent behind me. Perhaps he was thinking similar thoughts and was giving thanks to his Kadar gods and goddesses.

I began another prayer of thanksgiving myself, then, as the sun dipped below the horizon and the island disappeared from view, I turned in the warlord's arms. His gaze roamed over my features. His arms tightened around me as he nestled me against his hard body. I buried my face in the warmth of his neck, and he rested his chin on the top of my head. We stayed like that for a few moments, entangled in each other, before we pulled apart to return belowdecks at last.

We climbed down through the hatch in the stern, straight to the galley to collect our food: flatbread and salt herring, with a handful of raisins as hard as peppercorns.

A couple of men broke out in song and dance, right there in the small galley—a wild sailor dance that imitated the ship's pitching. We could hear others doing the same abovedecks.

An old Landrian seaman who'd never before missed a chance to cast me looks of disapproval stood up from the three-legged stool in the corner and ambled over to me, holding out his dirt-crusted, sweat-stained hat. "'Ere ya go, m'lady. We'as collected a small gift as our thanks for your 'elp of our prince."

The hat held enough raisins to fill a milk pitcher, likely the whole crew's share.

Before I could thank him, he gave a sharp nod, pivoted on his heel and stomped off, leaving me with the gift in my hands. The rest of the sailors in the galley flashed gap-toothed smiles, looking at me as if I was suddenly one of them.

Batumar and I ate our meal together, then I took my leave of the warlord and headed to Prince Graho, while Batumar went off to issue orders for our landing the next day. My brain buzzed with expectations. *Tomorrow we land. Tomorrow we land!*

The prince waited for me awake, in good spirits himself. Two of his royal guards stood on one side of him, Commander Durak on the other. The guards moved aside to make room for me.

A weak smile turned up the corners of Prince Graho's lips as I sat next to him and lay my hand over his. "You saved my life, my lady."

"I could draw the pain."

"No." He circled my wrist gently with his fingers and pushed my arm away. His stubborn gaze warned against argument.

The commander cleared his throat. "Should we move him to his sleeping rolls now, Lady Tera?"

I considered the matter with care before I responded. "I do not want his wound to tear open. You can try moving him up to the deck tomorrow, if he feels better. Some fresh air would not be amiss. But only if you can carry him up the ladder without jostling him overmuch."

The prince scoffed and stuck his bristled chin out at a jaunty angle. "By tomorrow, I shall climb the ladder myself."

I patted his hand and did not naysay him. If manly vanity spurred him to heal faster, I would not hold him back.

"The men say we reached Rabeen." He paused. "Do you think I will be able to go ashore?"

"We shall see," I said, instead of *impossible*.

I asked his guards to wash him in cool seawater once again, careful to keep it away from his bandages. I left half my raisins for him and his men, then I moved along to make my rounds, looking for any injuries among the crew and soldiers. When I ascertained that no one else needed my healing skills that evening, I headed to my sleeping roll, yawning as I went.

This time of day, I could see little of the room, but enough moonlight filtered through the porthole that I did not walk into walls. We had few candles left and only a smear of lamp oil. I would not waste any.

I set my half a hatful of raisins atop an upended barrel in the corner, then undressed to my undergarments. In the hardstorms, if we capsized, a waterlogged dress would have pulled me down into the depths of the ocean. I had come to enjoy sleeping unrestrained so much that I kept the habit even after we reached calmer seas.

I'd barely lain down atop the blankets before Batumar entered. He carried a bucket of water in one hand and a lit candle in the other.

"We can buy more candles on Rabeen tomorrow." He set the bucket in the corner and the candle next to it. He unfastened his sword belt and hung it from a peg, then sat on the floorboards by the bucket, leaning his back against the wall, his legs stretched out in front of him. "Go ahead."

I stripped, then washed my body that had been tired but a moment ago, yet now gained new life from Batumar's nearness. I rinsed my shift, wrung it out well, then pulled it back on. The material was light enough so it would not be damp long. We were far enough south so that even the nights were hot.

Not as hot as Batumar's eyes while he watched me, but near. His gaze burned through the semidarkness.

When I returned to our blankets, no more than a few steps in the small cabin, he blew out the candle, then knelt by the bucket and washed up. He still would not let me see the scars on his body, the wounds he had suffered at the hands of the Sorcerer of Ishaf. He would not let me heal them either.

He washed his shirt, then came to me at last, the damp linen clinging to his shoulders. He lay next to me, on his side, facing me, watching me. This was always the best part of my day: spending the night next to Batumar, just the two of us. I liked listening to his even breathing in the dark and to his heartbeat when I slept with my head resting on his chest.

"How fare the troops?" he asked.

"No serious injuries other than the prince. I only wish the men would come to me more readily with their ailments."

He reached out and wound a lock of my hair around his finger. He caressed that lock with careful reverence as if touching exotic silk. "They are battle-hardened soldiers. They will not cry for help over a skinned elbow, my Tera."

"They might not hold back so much if you did not glower at them every time one asked me for healing," I told him. "How goes the training?"

"Instilling true military discipline takes more than a few mooncrossings. Once we are back home, once we regain our lands, I shall build up a proper army. And I will encourage all the other warlords to do the same." He paused. "When the war is over," he asked, shifting closer, "what would you wish to do?"

I did not have to think long about my answer.

"I shall plant the largest garden of healing herbs in the world." I had dreamt that up during the hardstorms to calm my fears. "I want to start a school for herbal remedies: teas, tinctures, poultices, and the like." I was excited just thinking about mortars and pestles. I could smell the sweet chamomile and pungent sage already.

While Batumar worked on keeping us safe, I would work on teaching people how to heal themselves. I could see myself walking through the endless garden, a babe on each hip, explaining each plant's uses to any who wished to learn.

"I shall heal all who come to me," I told the warlord. "Like my mother did. I will spend my days not in a Pleasure Hall, but in a Hall of Healing, where the rows of rooms hold not concubines, but the sick. I wish to become Tika Shahala—a healer of the highest order—as was my mother, Chalee."

Then, after a satisfying day, I would lie in Batumar's arms each night, talking quietly as we were at this very moment.

Perhaps he was thinking something similar because his face softened in the moonlight that fell across the bed. He leaned toward me, brushing his lips over mine.

My breath caught. My body came alive and begged for more.

Yes. This. This was what I hoped for and planned on doing once we gained our precious peace. But as I pressed closer to the warlord's hard body, a distant, faint horn sounded in the night.

We both froze and held our breaths. Then Batumar rose, walked to the porthole, and opened the round window wider. We listened.

The distant horn sounded again.

I scrambled to sit, wild hope leaping in my heart. "Which ship, do you think?"

"Lord Karnagh's."

Yes. As the horn sounded for the third time, I recognized its distinct, deeply resonant timbre.

Our own horn answered from abovedecks—sharper toned and much louder. Then yet another, different horn blew, high-pitched and piercing, the sound even fainter than the first.

"Tomron!" I grinned into the night as a happy clamor buzzed on the other side of our door. "We have the *Sword* and the *Lance.*"

Joy filled me, replacing endless days of worry. With three ships, we should have enough fighting men to push the enemy off our island. I sighed with pure happiness. Mostly because of the ships. But also because Batumar lay back next to me and bracketed my face with his large warrior hands.

CHAPTER FOUR
RABEEN GAINED AND LOST

Batumar claimed my mouth and kissed me as if he had all the time in the world, as if the war was already won and we were home, happy and free. He kissed me as if the whole world wasn't falling apart around us. He made me forget who we were, where we were. I enjoyed every moment of that kiss. Then the kiss ended, and I laid my head on his chest.

"I wish it were morning already, and we were pulling into harbor," I said after a few moments.

"Let us hope that our good fortune will hold," Batumar responded.

"Good fortune?"

"After a journey as difficult as ours, it would not be unusual for half the men to be dead or dying. On this ship, at least, we still have near all our soldiers and sailors."

Near, as nine had been washed overboard by ravenous and merciless waves.

Batumar's lips touched against my brow. His hand caressed my cheek. When I tilted my head up, his lips meandered down my temple, then over to the corner of my lips. And then his mouth claimed mine again.

He pushed me onto my back and came up on his elbow next to me, nuzzled my ear, then neck, and then his large hand slid lower, nothing between the heat of his palm and my skin but the thin fabric of my shift.

My blood raced. My heartbeat drummed a slow, drunken rhythm. My body awakened.

"I wish to see you safe on Rabeen," Batumar said in a rough whisper against my lips.

I blinked at him, feeling as if I had been doused with a bucket of seawater. He wished me to stay on the Island of Rabeen while he waged war against the Kerghi invaders on Dahru.

I put my palms on his rough cheeks to make sure he paid my words full attention. "I will not separate from you." He was precious to me, body and spirit. "You are my heart."

He gathered me closer. "As you are mine. In truth, I hate every moment when you are out of my sight."

"We sailed together from home. Let us then finish this journey side by side. I will not stand in a port and watch you sail away into danger."

Memories flooded me as I said the words. Memories so old, I had not thought about them for a long time. "When I was a child, my mother sailed away to heal Barmorid, then High Lord of the Kadar. I never saw her again. She died on that journey and never returned."

Batumar held me, kissing my cheek and rubbing my back.

After a moment, I added, "Even had you not asked me to join you on the journey, I could not have let you sail to the mainland without me." I sighed. "I went with you and lost you anyway, when I thought you drowned in the sea. When I lost you, I felt as if I lost my heart." I paused. "No. I will not be left behind."

"I expected you would say that." He kissed me once more. "But I had to try."

His large hand caressing my skin filled me with pleasure. He laid kisses on my lips, on my chin, trailing them in a meandering line down my neck. Then his lips found my breasts through the barely there fabric. Soon he had me mindless, my body straining toward his.

"Batumar…" I wiggled to shed my worn shift.

My breasts were freed first. A soul-shattering groan left his lips at the sight, although truly, he could not have seen much in what little light the moon provided. His arms shook from the effort to hold back as he supported himself above me. But he did hold back—as he had held his desire back for far too long now.

"At the abandoned metropolis, whose name history has forgotten," he said in a tortured tone, "I held you in my arms in the ruins when you lost our babe. You nearly died."

My breath caught. "You remember?"

While he had survived being tortured by the sorcerer of Ishaf, he had few memories of those dark times, or the days that followed.

"More than before," he said darkly. "But still only flashes."

From the look on his face, he had filled out the gaps between the flashes of this particular memory with his worst fears.

"Batumar—"

He was withdrawing already, dropping to the blankets next to me, his breathing ragged. He rolled onto his back and drew me into his arms, until my head rested on his shoulder once again. When I placed my hand on his chest, over his rapidly beating heart, he covered my hand with his own.

"I will not risk your life for my own selfish pleasure," he said. "We still have much warring ahead of us yet. I will not risk another babe."

I groaned in protest but argued with him not. He would not hear me now. I settled for what I could have and relished the comfort of the warlord's embrace, but even that pleasure lasted only the blink of an eye before someone rapped on the door.

"I beg your pardon, my lady." The thick wood muffled Commander Durak's voice. "Prince Graho is burning up with fever."

Batumar kissed me one more time, gently and with an ocean of love, before he unlocked his arms to let me leave.

"Coming!" I grabbed for my clothes in a hurry, my body aching for the warlord, my mind worried for the prince. I left our room, still working on my buttons.

I was careful not to step on any sleeping soldiers as I hurried forward. The commander escorted me with an oil lamp, although I would have found the prince without light, following the sounds of struggle.

"I must reach them in time!" the prince yelled at his men, who held him to the floor so he would not hurt himself thrashing. "Release me!"

"I need a bucket of seawater," I called as I neared.

Water drawn from the sea was colder than our fresh water that had been collected from the last heavy rains and had been sitting in barrels up on the deck for days.

Durak held the lamp up so I could see, and I sank to the floorboards next to the prince. I placed a soothing hand onto his burning forehead. "You must stay still, my lord."

He opened his eyes but could not focus them on my face. They remained dazed, then, in an instant, they filled with urgency.

"I must reach them before they are hurt." The prince gripped my hand. "I cannot be delayed."

"They are safe. You already saved them. Rest."

He was speaking of the kidnapped children of his kingdom. I had met him on that very same journey.

The prince finally halted his struggles and seemed to fully see me at last. "I found them?"

"And returned them to their parents," I assured him.

His tortured body relaxed. He drew a calmer breath, then another. But, too soon, the urgency flashed back into his gaze. "And the ships sinking? Had I dreamt that?"

"Nay," I told him with a heavy heart. "We lost two of our fleet. Only the *Shield*, the *Sword*, and the *Lance* remain."

He closed his eyes, then moaned as if he saw our dying men behind his eyelids. He had called those captains and those sailors to his service and had many friends amongst them.

The guard who had left but moments ago hurried back to us with a bucket of water, sloshing some in the process. "Fresh from the sea, my lady."

I grabbed Prince Graho's discarded shirt from the floor and soaked the stained linen, then washed his fevered skin to cool him. Over and over again.

Marga stuck her head down the hatch with a soft chuff, wanting to know what I was doing. I sent a soft chuff back, then *all is well* in spirit song. Since the tiger had saved me from drowning during our voyage to the mainland, she kept a guardian's eye on me. *All is well. No danger.*

She watched me for another breath, then disappeared from the opening.

My mother had taught me how to talk to animals in spirit song, a language of one living being to another. Some of the best Shahala healers could do it, so attuned they were to the spirits of others. Animals, with their quiet minds, could hear—if not the words, then the intention behind the words. People could not. People's minds were always loud and busy worrying about something.

I washed the prince one more time, then finished my ministrations by piling the cold, wet cloth onto his forehead. He fell back into restless sleep, his eyes darting this way and that under his eyelids. He did not wake when I checked his wound—as red and swollen as expected.

"He will be fine well," I told his men. "He is but exhausted from fighting the fever."

I stayed with him.

Men snored around me. Waves lapped against the *Shield*. I could hear the boots of the night guards slapping on the deck above as they walked the ship.

I said a prayer of thanksgiving.

"Thank you for saving the *Lance* and the *Sword*. Thank you for bringing us to land. Thank you for keeping the prince."

* * *

Morning light and Batumar found me dozing as I still sat at my patient's side. Prince Graho rested peacefully at last. Not even the captain shouting orders above or the ship lurching forward awakened him.

The fever had left his battered body, thanks to the spirits.

Batumar's frown softened when he looked at me. He pulled me to my feet and brushed some stray strands of hair out of my face, his gaze searching mine. "I wish you would concern yourself with your own rest as much as you concern yourself with the welfare of others."

I rested my face against the curve of his neck and closed my eyes. "We land today."

"Aye." He held me tighter, murmuring his words into my hair, "How fares the prince?"

"He will live," I said louder than necessary, so I would be heard by all the men who were preparing for their morning.

We left Prince Graho to rest under the watchful eyes of his guard and went up on deck. I drew the fresh breeze into my lungs as I stretched my aching limbs, looking for the *Shield* and the *Sword*. I wanted to see if the caravels sustained further damage since we lost sight of them, but they were too far. They *were*, however, sailing under their own power—neither towing the other—a good sign. As sunshine warmed my face, relief warmed my heart.

I grinned at Batumar. "We have three ships and the men they carry."

Before he could respond, Captain Temro greeted us, striding forward from the stern, the four leather-clad prongs of his beard slapping against his barrel chest.

"My lord. My lady." He flashed a smile filled with crooked teeth. "A good morning, indeed."

"Are the caravels damaged?" the warlord asked him, glancing at the looking glass in the captain's hand.

"Some torn rigging and tattered sails, my lord, but nothing that could not be repaired in a quiet harbor given half a chance."

"A good thing, then, that a quiet harbor is lying straight ahead."

"Fortuitous, indeed."

Soon the two men were deep in a conversation about shipwrights of which I understood less than if they spoke in a foreign language.

I left the men to their discussion and hurried to the prow, hungry for another glimpse of Rabeen. When I had first woken at dawn, I had been afraid I had only imagined that strip of land on the water. But no, Rabeen was still there, waiting. I smiled into the morning while, behind me, the captain shouted, and more sails unfurled.

My gaze searched the island that was growing on the horizon. I hoped we would find Rabeen safe and untouched, even if I had no fond memories of it. The island's merchants were rich, yet the streets were full of little children maimed to make them better beggars. Rabeen's slave market was an abhorrence that both angered and offended me, as I was certain it angered and offended the spirits.

On our last visit, Batumar and I had sworn to do something about that. Now we were here with an army. But as we neared land, I saw no sign of life, no merchant ships in the harbor. Unease skittered up my spine.

I was searching for movement so intently that several moments passed before I realized that Batumar was standing next to me with the captain's spyglass. He had the copper tube trained on the island and was looking as carefully as if he intended to count all the apples and figs in the market stalls. Then again, maybe he did. We *were* desperate to resupply our ships. But as he kept looking, he lost the lightness our two lost ships' reappearance had brought to his face.

"What is it? What do you see?"

He handed me the looking glass without a word.

"Bad news?" My heart sank as I fitted the copper tube to my eye.

The spirits help us. And help us better than they had helped Rabeen.

The last we had seen the island, it had been a busy market, teeming with life. Now everything stood in ruin. No colorful flags snapped in the wind. The merchants' tents had been trampled, their houses demolished. The sole ship in the harbor was a burned skeleton. No wonder I had not seen the white of sails.

The sight of the destruction made my stomach roil. As cold, invisible fingers squeezed my heart, I handed the looking glass back to Batumar. "I can see no movement at all."

They can't be all gone.

"We will find out what happened when we land. There are always survivors after a battle, especially on an island." He tried to encourage me. "Some men might have been out fishing when the enemy arrived. Some who were left for dead, lived. Some hid themselves."

Rabeen destroyed. My mind had trouble catching up with my eyes. I turned back to look again. On the mainland, I had seen multiple sieges—from both sides of the fortress walls. I saw now what I had not noticed upon my first visit here: Rabeen had no towers, no ramparts.

"The island was wholly defenseless!" The words slipped from my lips, an accusation.

Batumar took my hand. "Its treaties were its defenses. What few pirates sail Mirror Sea have an agreement with the Merchant League of Rabeen. The pirates have always bought and sold goods here. They would have no reason to sack the island. Neither would the surrounding kingdoms. They gain much income from the market. Rabeen has always stayed safe, protected not by walls, but by alliances."

He let my hand go so he could raise the spyglass once more and scan the land ahead. "Enemy ships could be hiding on the other side of those cliffs, soldiers waiting in the ruins, ready for our landing." He lowered the copper tube and captured my gaze. "I would have you stay on the ship until we ensure that Rabeen is safe."

"Must we truly argue about this again?" I set my jaw. "I will not cower on the ship while I send men into danger."

He watched me for a moment before he nodded, worry giving way to pride in his gaze. "As you wish."

He brushed a kiss over my lips before he left to organize the landing. I stayed in the prow and kept searching for signs of life on the island as we approached. Nothing moved. A forest of small masts caught my eye. I did not remember Rabeen having that many fishing boats. Then again, they could have been out at sea.

Birds circled in the air above the masts. Not seagulls. Something larger, darker…

Carrion birds.

A shudder ran through me. I had seen enough carrion birds in the aftermath of battles to never want to see another.

As we neared, I could see what drew the birds to the harbor. The small forest of what I had thought were fishing boat masts were no such thing. They were all gallows, and on them hung at least a hundred men.

Cold spread through my chest, such cold that my heart felt frozen and brittle. Dread flooded in like ice water, filling me to the brim as if I were an empty waterskin. In the full heat of summer, I could not stop shivering.

Neither could I stop looking. Beyond the gallows, on the ground everywhere lay more of the island's dead, mostly men, stacked in piles. The few women were older, past childbearing age. The Kerghi hordes preferred taking the children and young women as slaves.

Nothing moved other than the birds.

A terrible fear fell on me, like a house collapsing, burying me in the ruins. As if rocks sat on my chest, I could not breathe. My blood thrummed a panicked rhythm in my ears. A desperate prayer flew from my lips. "Kind spirits, if there is anyone here who can be saved, let us find them."

* * *

We reached the harbor midmorning and dropped anchor.

Only a handful of structures remained standing, the island little more than rubble. Captain Temro communicated with our two other ships through horn signals, ordering them to stay at sea for now. Should we be attacked, the caravels would remain safe.

"The Kerghi did this," I told Batumar when he appeared next to me a little while later. "But how? The ones who came through the Gate of the World on Dahru have no ships."

As some walled cities had gates, so did our island, a wondrous portal left to us by ancient men whose knowledge we had lost. One could travel through such Gates to another island, or even to the mainland, provided that one's destination also had an ancient Gate. Most Gates opened to but one place, but the Gate on Dahru was the Gate of the World. It made passage possible to all other Gates. I was convinced that was the reason for our enemies wanting our island above all others.

Yet even the khan could not send ships through a Gate. All the surviving Gates were on land.

"Think you some Kerghi sailed through the hardstorms from the mainland?"

"If we can sail through the hardstorms, so can the enemy."

As the wind turned, the unforgettable battlefield stench was so strong that I had to draw the collar of my light summer cloak over my nose. The destruction was overwhelming, disheartening. And all those dead bodies dragged to the harbor...

I drew a shallow breath. "This feels like a message."

Batumar's gaze grew pensive. "Almost as if our enemies anticipated our return."

As our men prepared for docking, they too kept glancing at the island. The carnage must have reminded them of the homes they had left behind, the families they had lost. They worked in silence, the only sounds the ones the sailors made tying up the sails. Near me, a young soldier who'd just come up from the hold paled at the sight of the gallows.

Did he wonder if he was looking at his own fate?

Was he?

He, and all the others, had left the safety of Uramit to follow *me*. I had brought them here. I had never felt more keenly the weight of my responsibilities than at that moment, with the sight and smell of a conquered Rabeen in front of me.

The prince was an admiral. Batumar was a warlord. Tomron was a general. Lord Karnagh led the Selorm warriors and their tigers. But it had been *I* who had called all these men to battle. I, Tera—a *healer*. What did I know of battle strategy?

Yet I had to lead. If I had doubts, I must not show any. Spreading doubt in wartime was deadlier than spreading the plague.

I must lead or we would perish, and evil would reign.

On the wind came a whisper, my mother's last message to me.

Spirit, be strong. Heart, be brave.

CHAPTER FIVE

THE CHRONICLE KEEPER

I was about to step on the plank to go ashore with Batumar when Durak's shouts reached me from midship.

"Wait! Lady Tera!"

The panic in the seasoned commander's tone made me turn back. One look at his anguished face had me running toward him, armed soldiers jumping out of my way. When I reached the hatch, I scrambled down the ladder so quickly, I nearly tripped.

The royal guard surrounded their prince, holding him down once again. This time, he was not fighting them in a fever dream. He was convulsing.

"Prince Graho?" I dropped to my knees and felt for his scorching forehead, pushing wet cloth out of the way.

He did not respond. He was past knowing anyone was with him.

"When his fever returned, we wrapped him in a wet blanket as you ordered." Durak's expression tightened with worry. "It does not help, my lady."

I had checked on the prince but a short while before. He had been feeling better. But now... His fever spiked too suddenly and higher than was safe. I reached for him with the intent of drawing the fever from him into my own body, then stopped. I might yet be called to heal more grievous injuries today. Batumar was right. There were always those who survived. There had to be some even on Rabeen, at least a few dozen, terrible infections from battle weapons, and many broken bones. Burn wounds too—there had been fire. The prince had but a fever.

"I need one of the empty water barrels from abovedecks," I told the two royal guards on my right.

As they ran off, I turned to the guards on my left. "Start bringing buckets of seawater."

The barrel arrived first.

"Pick up the prince and put him in," I ordered the men, then, as a dozen buckets of seawater were delivered, I had his guard dump the cold water right on the prince. They doused him until the barrel was filled to the brim and the prince shivering.

"The Lady Tera assisting me with my bath. And what does Batumar have to say about that?" he joked weakly when he finally revived.

"He is too busy inspecting Rabeen. How do you feel?"

"As if death swallowed me down, then vomited me back up. I think I gave him a stomachache."

He was gaining back his sense of humor—a sign of recovery.

I stayed with him until the fever left him once again, until he was dressed in fresh clothes and returned to a dry blanket. Only when he dozed did I return abovedecks, hurrying to the prow to see where Batumar went.

Marga padded up and placed her plate-size front paws on the weatherworn railing next to me. Her whiskers twitched at the smell of blood and bodies, yet she did not leap into the water to swim to land. She stayed to protect me.

Four dozen soldiers remained on board with near four dozen sailors to defend our ship should we come under attack. The rest of the men had disembarked and were spreading out, inspecting every possible nook where the enemy could be hiding. Batumar was leading eighty or so soldiers toward the market.

The men moved forward with their weapons held ready, without hesitation. Where Batumar led, they followed. He was born to lead. He drew every eye and gained the confidence of fighting men without effort.

The warlord's gaze cut back to me, as if to assure himself I was still on the ship, still safe. Then he signaled to the men to move forward. The soldiers dispersed in pairs, soon disappearing beyond the charred remnants of the dockside warehouses.

I did not dare leave the prince, no matter how much I wanted to join Batumar on land, so I did the next best thing. I borrowed the spyglass from the captain again and climbed to the empty crow's nest atop the mainmast.

Blue ocean stretched to the east, the white sails of our two other ships remaining a safe distance away. As the captain had said, they did not appear irreparably damaged. One of the tight knots in my stomach eased.

I turned the looking glass on the island. Batumar appeared, then disappeared among the ruins. The soldiers moving on the abandoned streets and over the fields were all our own. I saw no sign of the enemy.

Bodies lay everywhere. I lowered the looking glass and squeezed my eyes shut, but saw the dead still.

There must be survivors. Maybe hiding in the orchards on the far side of the island. There are survivors, and we will find them. We will find them, and...

"My lady!" The shout woke me.

The sun was nearing its zenith in the sky. I peered down from the crow's nest at Batumar. "I fell asleep."

"You slept precious little last night. I am glad you had some rest at last."

I was not. So much time wasted!

"The enemy left no troops behind," the warlord said as I climbed down to him, my legs and arms stiff, spyglass tucked into my belt.

When he could reach me, he lifted me away and held me against him for a couple of heartbeats before he set my feet on the deck. His hands lingered on my waist. His thumbs caressed me—a gesture of affection invisible to the men around us.

I looked up into his scarred face. "Survivors?"

His eyes were filled with love, but his tone carried sadness. "Two."

I gripped his arms. "On the whole island?"

"A young woman and an old man. They need your help. I checked on the prince. He is well. He can spare you for a while."

"Let us hurry, then." I handed the spyglass to the nearest sailor with instructions to return it to the captain. "And bring me a small cauldron on your way back," I told the man.

I had my knife and my flint. I had, in the very same pouch hanging off my belt, a needle and a small spool of thread left. Herbs I had none. I had used the last bit on the prince.

The *Sword* and the *Lance* were docked next to us, one caravel on each side of the flagship. I had not heard them drop anchor. Nor had I heard the captains shouting orders. My sleep in the crow's nest must have been fair deep.

I glanced from one ship to the other as we crossed the deck of the *Shield*. "Lord Karnagh and Tomron?"

"Disembarked already. They are searching for food and water with their men."

"How have their crews fared?"

"Both caravels lost men to the storms, but even after accounting for all the losses, we still have five hundred soldiers combined."

Hope filled me. *Five hundred might just be enough.* I smiled at Batumar, and he returned the smile, brushing my hair from my face in a gentle caress. He claimed my hand, and my heart thrilled as always at his touch. My happiness did not last long, however.

We reached the plank, and the sight of the dead, the aftermath of battle, tore at my heart. And that was before the debris floating in the narrow strip of water between our ships and the wharf caught my attention. *Oh merciful spirits.*

Not driftwood but small bodies bobbed on the water, some caught on the rocks—babes so small that they could not have been weaned from their mothers' breasts yet. Anguish ripped into me so hard that I lost my breath. My gaze sought Batumar's. "How could they?"

He put his arm around me and gathered me against his side. I wanted to bury my face into the comfort he offered. Yet I had brought men and ships here. I needed to lead them. I could not hide my eyes.

I pulled away from the warlord and looked at the small bodies to remind myself what we were fighting for. "Why?"

He responded, but in a tone that said he wished I had not asked the question. "The Kerghi can force the young mothers onto their ships more easily if they allow the women to hold on to their babes. Yet suckling babes are naught but a nuisance to slavers."

I could see it as if I had been there. Once the captured women were aboard, the Kerghi had ripped the babes from their mothers' arms and tossed them overboard. The cries of the seabirds above sounded like the screams of women echoing in my ears.

I put one foot in front of the other, willing myself to move forward. We walked off the plank and onto land, Batumar by my side, his sword free of his scabbard, his gaze scanning the harbor for any hidden danger. Marga trailed behind us, her thick tail swishing in the dirt. She sniffed at the dead, but as hungry as she had to be, she let them be for my sake. When, at last, she bounded ahead, Batumar's gaze followed her.

"She will do fine," he said. "She can hunt rats."

I winced. I did not want to think about rats. I could see signs all around that they, along with the carrion birds, had already violated the bodies. As if that wasn't enough, an army of flies buzzed in the harbor, the sound stomach-turning. And so was the smell.

I drew shallow breaths. "Before we leave here, we must bury the dead."

"Burying this many would take days." Batumar's voice carried quiet frustration laced with regret. "We do not have enough provisions to stay. We have not, so far, found sufficient food stores. We must go on."

Everything in me protested. Grief weighed me down, as if someone was packing boulders onto my back, adding one for each body we passed, until I could not look at one more merchant, one more fishwife, one more babe.

I had to turn my mind to other things or drop to the ground right there and scream until I too was dead. "Have our men found nothing to eat, then?"

"What meat and fruit the attackers left behind has rotted," Batumar said. "What few sacks of grain they missed have burned with the stalls. The Selorm lords are checking the orchards."

We had three ships full of men. We needed more than a few bushels of apples.

"At least we can refill our water barrels." I glanced back toward our small fleet. "Why are the men not bringing them?"

Before Batumar could respond, I remembered the battles we had fought on the mainland where I learned more than I ever wished to know about warfare. "Bodies in the wells?"

"Aye."

Tossing the dead into the wells was a common military tactic. The decomposing bodies spoiled the water for anyone who came after the battle moved on, for those who would want to rebuild.

"How long can we last without water?" I looked up but found no cloud in the sky—all clear. Even the wind stood still, promising no rain.

"The men are still looking," Batumar said. "They might yet find something drinkable."

We walked north past the market, past the two-story brick houses where many of the merchants had their homes above their shops. Their servants and the island's farmers lived farther from the harbor, most in modest mud huts. These too had been burned. Here too bodies littered the ground.

"How did all this happen?" I asked. "When?"

"I have not questioned the survivors yet. I came to fetch you as soon as word reached me that the man and woman were discovered and were in need of help."

As we hurried on, I spotted the bodies of Kerghi mercenaries now and then, mixed in with the dead of Rabeen. The mercenaries no longer had weapons; their swords and lances had been stripped from them after death.

For the most part, the Kerghi hordes had no uniform. Yet I could easily tell the killers apart from their victims. The Kerghi were covered in battle scars, but even beyond that... The evil that drove them to slay nations, the evil that lived in their hearts, showed on their faces even in death. Darkness still echoed in their blankly staring eyes and made me shudder.

Batumar and I moved in silence like spirits, down crooked streets filled with death, until we reached barren rock. Only as we crossed the tops of the rising cliffs did I realize that the island was not as easy a target as I had first thought. On this side of Rabeen, at the cliffs, enemy approach would be near impossible. The only way up from the narrow, rocky beach was a crumbling footpath. Any invaders would be easily knocked back.

"This way." Batumar led me down the stone steps.

About halfway to the water, on a long ledge that followed a sharp outcropping of rock, we came to a skeletal woman. Two of our soldiers guarded her from a distance.

Her clothes torn, she had wedged herself into a crevice at the far end of the ledge. The crevice was the height of a grown man and equally wide, but only half as deep. Other crevices lined the rock wall, similar in size, rough-hewn but evenly spaced, clearly man-made. They had small holes in the stone up the sides, some with iron hinges, as if at one time the crevices had doors or bars.

The woman snarled at us like a cornered animal. She had a sword, probably taken from one of the corpses in the market. Dirt streaked her face. No tears, though. Either she was past weeping or too dehydrated to cry.

"Where is the man?" I asked Batumar as we walked closer. "You said a man and a woman."

"He is farther inland."

He would have to wait, then. I hoped he wasn't too badly injured.

I stepped past our soldiers and waved them back still farther, then shook my head at the warlord, telling him without words not to come any closer as I approached the fear-stricken survivor.

"I mean no harm." I realized I said the words in Kadar, the language I had been speaking with Batumar, so I quickly repeated them in the language of merchants. "I mean no harm."

The woman's pale eyes were feral, her dusty hair a tangle, her simple clothes of rough linen torn and blood splattered. She might have been a cook or a maid. Her skeletal arm supporting the heavy sword was sagging with exhaustion. As she shifted, I caught sight of a festering wound on her thigh.

I moved toward her, one slow step at a time, smiling, keeping my hands visible so she would see I had no weapon. "Are you in pain? I can help. Can you tell me what happened here?"

Her wild eyes showed no sign of comprehension.

"It might be days before she recovers enough to be able to answer our questions," I said to Batumar in Kadar.

I stopped out of reach of the woman's blade and held my flask out for her. "Water. Please take it. You need to drink."

She only wedged herself more tightly into the far corner of the crevice and held her weapon higher, her eyes darting from me to Batumar, then skipping to the soldiers at our backs.

"Return to the top of the cliffs," Batumar quietly ordered the men, and then he too drew back a few more steps, but the woman did not relax.

"I am Lady Tera, a Shahala healer." I kept the smile on my face. "I travel with an army to chase the Kerghi hordes back across the ocean."

She watched me, unmoving.

"We sail for Dahru," I told her. "I would that you come with us. To stay on Rabeen is sure death. There is nothing left."

Her gaze cut to Batumar, then back to me once again. She did not move, but she blinked a few times as she thought over my offer. She looked utterly terrified and exhausted, and as if she did not entirely trust herself to make a decision.

Then Marga caught up with us, bouncing down the path in giant leaps before padding toward the woman to sniff at her.

"No, Marga!" I tried to stop the tiger, but I was too late.

The woman held the sword out in front of her like a lance. With a fierce scream, she rushed forward to fight the tiger, and I caught a glimpse of a small girl who, all this time, had been hidden behind her mother.

"Stop!" I jumped between the tiger and the woman. Marga would not have attacked her first, but the tiger would defend herself if attacked.

They mean no harm. They are scared, I told Marga in spirit song and begged her to calm.

Even as I threw my arms around her thick neck to hold her back, Batumar roared, "Tera!" and leaped to catch the desperate survivor whose sword missed my neck by a hairsbreadth, and only because the warlord grabbed her arm in time.

Marga tensed and growled at the sudden burst of violence, so I kept my arms around her, whispering soothing words into her ear and letting my eyes tell Batumar that I was all right.

He did not look reassured. He looked as if he was silently pledging never to allow me to leave the ship again and considering locking me into the storage room for good measure.

By the time I calmed the tiger down, the warlord had disarmed the woman. He held both of her wrists in one hand, but gently so, careful to cause no harm, no matter how she screeched and fought.

Then, worried for her mother, the young girl attacked Batumar with a sharp cry, a stone held tightly in her little fingers.

I shoved Marga back when she growled again. "Go catch some fish."

The water was not far below us. I did not think she'd had the time to hunt for rats yet. She had to be hungry.

I had to shove again before she left, even as I leaped forward to catch the girl for fear that she would fall off the narrow stone ledge.

I need not have bothered. She stood frozen in place with wonder at the sight of the tiger obeying my command. The child and her mother both looked at me as if I were a sorceress.

"A Selorm battle tiger," I explained as Batumar released the woman at last.

He kept her sword, stepping back again to give her space. She was no danger to us disarmed and had been little danger even with the sword she barely had the strength to wield. Finding herself free and empty-handed, she immediately picked up her child and darted back into her crevice.

"We will not hurt you." I moved closer, then crouched within reach to hold out my water flask again.

The woman snatched the water from me in a blur of movement. She set her daughter down and let her drink first before quenching her own thirst, her gaze flitting between the warlord and me.

She did not drain the flask but saved some and handed it back to her daughter, who finished the water to the last drop, then held the flask out to me with hesitation. The mother snatched the flask and tossed it to me instead.

"How long since the battle?" I asked her.

She shook her head.

So, long enough for her to lose count of the days.

"Do you know of any others who survived?"

She shook her head again, and this time, a sharp sob escaped her. Tears filled her eyes and rolled down her gaunt face. Her knees trembled as if her brave attack on the tiger had used up her last remaining strength.

My heart clenched, filling with sorrow for her and her child.

"Will you let us help? Will you come with us? We have some food on our ship." Not much, but enough for the two of them. "I have raisins," I told the little girl and watched her wary expression turn wistful.

We waited while the woman came to accept that she could not stay here on the barren ledge. Then we waited while she accepted that everything she had, everything she loved, was lost. We waited until she wiped her eyes with the back of her hands. And then she finally nodded.

She stepped forward, but her knees folded at last. Another sob escaped her as she fell. On the ground, she tugged the little girl into her arms and wrapped her body protectively around her child. The girl peered at us from behind her mother's arms like a baby bird from a nest, scared and curious in equal measure.

I spoke to them both and talked the mother into allowing me to treat her festering wound. I thought about using my power to close the gash at once, but I feared it might yet convince her that I was a sorceress. I wanted her to trust me more, not less. I asked Batumar to bring me some seawater, and while he was gone, I drew the infection from the woman's body so slowly and carefully that she did not even notice.

When I had my water, I set to repairing the injury the old-fashioned way, starting by cleaning off the dried blood. The salt in the water had to burn, but the woman barely flinched. She gritted her teeth as I cleansed the wound, then stitched it closed. I cut a strip from my own cloak to bandage it.

When I was done, the warlord called the soldiers back from the top of the cliffs. "Take this mother and child to the flagship. Give them food and water."

"Go with the men," I told the poor woman. "Rest on our ship. I will find you and bring you healing tea." I hoped to find some herbs on the island before we returned to the *Shield*.

As the soldiers moved forward, fear rounded the woman's eyes, but she was too weak to protest, let alone fight off the men. The burly soldiers scooped them up, then carried them off as easily as a farmer might carry a couple of wineskins to a feast. The woman looked near panic, but her daughter settled in, content with her fate.

Batumar tossed the Kerghi sword into the sea, while I started up the path to the top of the cliffs. He followed, putting his hand at the small of my back for support, as if needing to make sure that I was there and hale and had not been harmed. I knew too well how he felt. I had lost him once and had him returned to me as a wraith. I touched him often, in myriad small ways, to make sure he was with me.

After a moment, he began drawing distracting little circles with his thumb. When I stumbled on a loose rock and tipped backward, I came to rest against his hard chest, and his arms came around me to hold me in place. His warm lips nuzzled my neck.

"My lord," I gasped out a weak protest. "This is hardly the time or the place." Yet I did not truly wish him to stop.

"You spent the night with the prince," he grumbled. "And the morning."

I sighed. "And with his royal guard."

"Do not remind me."

He growled, his hot breath tickling the sensitive skin under my ears, the sound vibrating inside me. After he'd lost his voice from torture in Ishaf, the first sounds he had been able to make were growls and mumbles. He had communicated with Marga the best, mimicking the animal. He could still growl like a tiger, although his voice had much recovered.

Recovered, as in I healed it bit by bit, without his notice. He had forbidden me to waste my strength on healing his scars, but had not specified his voice, and so...

He kissed the side of my neck.

A soft shiver ran down my spine. "I meant to point out that I was hardly *alone* with the prince."

Batumar glanced up the path. As soon as the soldiers reached the top of the cliffs and hurried away toward the harbor, the warlord turned me and kissed me, fast and hard.

"I love only you, my lord," I said when I regained my ability to breathe.

"I am but an old warhorse," he said, his tone dark. "Covered in scars."

I shook my head and began walking once again. "Which you refuse to let me see."

His tone suddenly hardened. "Half the army is in love with you. From the young men to the grizzled warriors." He groaned. "Nay, make that the whole of the army."

"They appreciate my healing skill. They are soldiers. They feel safer knowing I will be going with them to battle."

I stopped to peer back at him. He knew my heart was his. He had never been the prince's greatest admirer, but even so, his words felt to me out of character. As was his stormy countenance. His shoulders were stiff, his stance combative. Suddenly, he looked on the brink of violence.

I stilled. "Batumar?"

He caught himself and shook his shoulders as if shaking off snow from his winter cloak. "Forgive me, my Tera. I do not know what came over me." He looked around. "This place has an odd..." He smacked his lips thoughtfully. "Taste."

I quieted my mind. Then I felt it too. Not a taste, closer to a smell. Sulfur? Something dark clung to the cliffs like invisible mist. Unease washed over me. Despite the noon sun, I shivered.

Batumar drew his sword as he passed me and led me to the top. "The old man the soldiers found is somewhere on the other side of the cliffs."

Some of our men were searching through rubble, others hurrying toward the far end of the island, and about half a dozen standing in the middle of a field, their heads together.

"You think they found another survivor?" I asked Batumar.

"If they did, they will come for us."

He was right. I put them from my mind and moved along, following the warlord.

We found the old man we sought lying under a dindin tree in the middle of a field, talking with one of our soldiers. But before we could reach him, another soldier cut across the fields and drew the warlord aside for a report. Nothing in the soldier's expression alarmed me, so I hurried forward in case my healing was urgently needed.

Marga caught up with me once again, dripping water. The tiger paid no attention to the two men by the dindin. On the other side of the field, an olive orchard stretched into the distance. The movement in the orchard held her full attention.

"Is that how it is, then?" I watched the Selorm lords and their tigers among the trees. "Fine well. Go ahead."

Marga bounded off in their direction. She had a fondness for Tigran, Lord Karnagh's battle tiger. They appeared to have a bond.

The old man under the tree watched her go with relief. He was thin, but not as thin as the woman and child we found. Judging by his richly embroidered sateen robe, he was a well-to-do trader. He had likely started out with a belly, in much better shape than the other two survivors.

As I drew near, I glanced up at the tree next to him. The gnarled branches were bare now, but probably still held some fruit when he had first sought shelter here. A juicy dindin or two a day—the fruit resembled fist-sized, hairy melons—had kept him from dehydration.

"Greetings." I inclined my head to show my respect, but even as I did so, I was already examining the bloodstain at his midsection where he was pressing both his hands against an injury. "I am Lady Tera. I am a healer. May I help you, Grandfather?"

I noted the intricate symbols embroidered onto the golden-brown silk edging of his kaftan. A well-to-do trader for certain. Maybe even one of Rabeen's Elders.

He confirmed his high status by saying in a slight accent I could not place, "I am Boscor, leader of the Rabeen Merchant League and Keeper of the Chronicles. Greetings, Lady Tera."

Relief surged through me. He did not appear as distressed as the mother and child. Boscor could answer questions. He could give us something we needed even more than food and water: news of the enemy.

CHAPTER SIX

THE BLUE DWARF

"Lord Batumar, warlord of the Kadar," Batumar said as he walked up to us. He cut straight to the point. "When did the attack happen?"

"Lord Batumar?" The chronicle keeper stared for a couple of startled moments as if seeing a spirit. "Some seven days back, my lord." He moved to rise but gave up with a grunt of pain. "Boscor, at your service, my lord. Leader of the Rabeen Merchant League and Keeper of the Chronicles."

"What fleet carried the Kerghi to your shores? Whose ships?"

Boscor cleared his throat, watching Batumar with uncertainty. "The Kerghi sailed on Kadar warships."

My heart sank.

"How many ships?" Batumar demanded without pause, as if unsurprised by the man's answer.

"Four, my lord."

"Carrying how many of the Kerghi?"

"I do not know. I hid as soon as I realized the harbor was under attack. I did not see them all come to shore."

The warlord and I exchanged a look. The last we knew, our ships were safely docked in the largest Kadar harbor, Kaharta Reh, under Kadar command.

The chronicle keeper added, "We did not realize, until too late, that we were under attack. We never expected... We had treaties in place with the Kadar!"

Batumar nodded. "Know you the new High Lord of the Kadar? Who is he?"

"We had news that the Kadar warlords held an election, as you were thought dead, and Lord Samtis was chosen. I am most glad to see you hale, my lord," the chronicle keeper rushed to say. "And you, my lady."

I knelt by the man's side to take a closer look at his injuries. As he moved his hands away, I saw at once why he had been left behind for dead. He had bled even more than I had first thought, the kaftan soaked through on his abdomen. "Do you know if the Kerghi took the entire island of Dahru? Did the Kerghi overrun the Shahala lands?" I asked, then gestured at his wound. "May I?"

An injury to the bowels would have killed him by now. At the very least, he would be at death's door from infection. But, as he pulled his kaftan apart for me, I saw that the blade that had reached him had not been buried in his guts. *Thank the spirits.*

"I know not about the Shahala, my lady." Boscor winced as I probed the edge of his wound. "I am sorry. The last I heard, Lord Batumar pushed the invaders back into the mountains. We thought we were safe. Then, suddenly, the Kerghi were here, in our harbor. In our markets!"

I glanced at Batumar.

"So the Kerghi came down the mountain," he said. "In search of food, most likely. They could not take any of our fortified cities. But they took Kaharta Reh, or at least the harbor, and gained control of our ships, then sailed straight to Rabeen for its market, which they knew to be poorly defended."

"How would they know anything about Rabeen?"

"The pirates who dock in our port sometimes sail to the mainland," Boscor put in.

True. We had sailed on such a ship on our way to Ishaf.

"Do you think the Kerghi came for provisions, then they sailed back to Dahru and went back up the mountain?" I asked Batumar.

"They could have."

I wanted to believe that with all my heart. I wanted my people the Shahala to have been skipped over, not to have experienced devastation akin to the devastation of Rabeen.

"I think you might be right, my lord," Boscor put in, giving me hope. "I think they came straight for us. Had they attacked any of the other islands, we would have heard, and we could have prepared. We could have hired mercenaries of our own." He hesitated before adding, "My lord, I am not certain, but... You understand I know very little Kerghi. It's only that the language is somewhat similar to Riblian..."

"Did you learn something from the enemy?"

The chronicle keeper nodded. "As soon as I realized that we were under attack, I hid myself with our most ancient scrolls in a secret closet at the council hall. I thought I might be able to save the treasures of our past, but then they set the building on fire, and I had to run. Yet while I was hiding…a captain looted the hall with his men. He said something about claiming Rabeen from the Kerghi khan for his services."

"Rabeen is not Khan Verik's to give." Batumar's tone hardened. "The khan is but Emperor Drakhar's dog. The Kerghi hordes are but the emperor's mercenaries."

Emperor Drakhar wished to rule the world. The Kerghi hordes were among the many mercenaries in his service. They just happened to be the ones tasked with invading the islands of the Mirror Sea, including our home island of Dahru.

"From what I made out," Boscor said with care, "the Kerghi khan thinks to break with the emperor and rule the islands of the Mirror Sea himself. He plans to make Karamur his capital."

My hands fisted at the thought of our fortress city, the seat of the Kadar High Lord, ruled by the Kerghi khan, our people becoming his slaves.

Not now, not ever. Not as long as I breathed.

"Did you overhear anything else, anything more?" Batumar demanded.

"No, my lord. I am not even certain of this much. I was worried about the chronicles. And, as I said, I do not understand the Kerghi language well."

While two soldiers ran up to us and distracted Batumar with the latest report, I probed the chronicle keeper's wound. "How were you injured?"

"A Kerghi mercenary tried to run me through with his sword." Boscor's voice filled with undisguised outrage, as if he thought his title and high standing on the island should have protected him from such a common fate at the hand of a common soldier. "He would have if I did not trip and fall, twisting away."

I could see where the blade had gone in, slid sideways into fat, glanced off his rib, and poked out through his side. No sign of infection. The gash, however, was not near as well healed as it should have been after seven days.

"I kept reaching for fruit," Boscor said in response to my frown. "I fear I have torn the wound open more than once."

I did not want him to lose more blood, yet he was not in any imminent danger from his injury. So, to spare myself an argument with Batumar, I treated the chronicle keeper the same way I treated the woman at the cliffs, cleaning the wound first with boiled water, then stitching it closed. He would need a poultice to ward off infection and speed healing, and I hoped I would have the necessary herbs before the day was out. If not, I could still use my powers. For now, I just needed to cover up the injury to protect it from dirt and flies. As the chronicle keeper's rich robe was too fine to cut, I sliced a long strip off my own cloak once again for a bandage.

"You shouldn't have, my lady. Thank you, my lady."

I noted his slight accent again. "On what island were you born?"

"I came from the Kingdom of Orh, back when I was a young man, to expand my father's spice business. I stayed on Rabeen for my beautiful wife." His face clouded. "Gone these past ten years now."

The chronicle keeper's eyes filled with tears. "She died in bed, in peace, without having to witness the destruction of her beloved island, and I am glad for it. I wish the gods granted me the same mercy."

"What gods are worshipped on Rabeen?" I asked as I worked.

My people, the Shahala, believed in spirits. The Kadar sacrificed to their god of war and his concubines, the goddesses. Numerous other gods were worshipped on the islands of the Mirror Sea.

I had seen no temple on the island, nor had I thought to ask about Rabeen's religions the first time I had been here. But if they had a hidden chapel somewhere, we might yet find more survivors there. "Have you a sanctuary?"

Boscor shook his head. "When I first arrived here, most everyone worshipped at a temple ruin of the ancient god Kratos that stands near the foot of the cliffs. His altar is under water now."

Kratos. I shuddered at the name, even as Boscor continued.

"The people here have always been a mix—like any market town—gathered from all over the islands. Few gods are overlooked in our ceremonies. These days, we cast our sacrifices into the sea from the top of the cliffs."

I finished bandaging him. "You may move, but move carefully."

"Yes, my lady. Thank you, my lady. Have you found many others?" he asked as I washed his blood off my hands. "I called for help during the first days, over and over, but nobody came."

"A mother and her child also survived," I told him, and explained how they were found at the cliffs.

Boscor frowned. "In a sacrifice hole?"

"On a narrow ledge."

The lines on his forehead deepened. "The cliff was the back wall of the old temple once. You must have seen the rows of crevices."

I nodded, thinking again how evenly placed they were, in such orderly rows. "I wondered about their purpose."

"In ancient times," Boscor told me, "followers of Kratos kept human sacrifices locked in those holes behind iron bars, dozens in every temple, to be given to the god on certain holy days. They did not sacrifice slaves or foreigners. Such would be an insult to the god. One offered up blood of their blood."

I shivered, staring at the man. "Their children?"

"The closer the blood, the greater the sacrifice, the more devout the family. They brought their sacrifices the first of the holy year, then every time anyone came to worship, they saw whose sons and daughters were in the sacrifice holes, waiting to serve the god with their blood. There could be no doubt which were the most pious families."

I could not comprehend the horror.

Kratos had taken my child, but the unborn babe had *not* been given willingly. Before the memory could crush me, I recalled Boscor's earlier words and hastened to ask, "And now? You said people throw their sacrifices from the cliffs."

"Goats, my lady," he reassured me with a tired smile. "Rabeen no longer keeps with the old ways."

I gave thanks to the spirits.

Boscor, on the other hand, appeared less pleased. "What did you do with the mother and child found in the sacrifice hole, my lady?"

"They were taken to our ship."

He nodded slowly, lost in thought for several long moments. "It is said that once someone enters a sacrifice hole, they belong to the god. No man can remove them but for the purpose of sacrifice."

The midday sun beat down on my head and back, but a cold shiver crawled up my spine.

"The old god..." Hesitation crept into the chronicle keeper's tone. "They say he does not like being denied a sacrifice. If he is angered..."

I knew full well Kratos's angry side.

"He is a god of darkness. We shall be gone by nightfall." I tried to reassure myself as much as the chronicle keeper with my words.

"To Dahru, then, across the sea?" The chronicle keeper's pinched expression relaxed. "Kratos does not rule the waves."

I was not so certain. I would never forget how a watery grave nearly took Batumar from me.

"I would have you carried to our ship," I told Boscor, "so I can fully repair your wound there once I have the necessary herbs. Will you come with us?"

I could not imagine remaining on the island as it stood now, but I had seen men and women hold on to the ruins of their former lives, to destroyed fortresses and burned fields, clinging to memories when nothing else remained. As our army had cut through the mainland and grown in number, man after man joined us, but as many if not more remained in their war-ravaged villages, determined to rebuild. I had grown to understand that some men could leave the lands they were born to, but others were rooted too deep.

The chronicle keeper struggled to sit up. "I would thank you if you took me with you, my lady. My home and store are gone. The scrolls, Rabeen's chronicles of which I was keeper, are burned," he said in a tone as bitter as if the enemy had made him eat the ashes and he could still taste them in his mouth.

He cast a glance at Batumar, who had dismissed the reporting soldiers and was listening to us once again. "My lord, I can pay for the journey." He shifted to his side and began digging in the dirt with his bare fingers. "A moment, my lady."

Soon the rim of a large bean pot was revealed. When the chronicle keeper showed us the mass of gold coins within, my mouth fell agape. He might not have been able to save the scrolls, but he had saved some of his treasure. He must have come here—the dindin tree to mark the spot—hidden the gold, then was cut down before he could run and hide himself.

Batumar called back the soldiers who had just left us. He ordered one to dig up the pot and carry it back to our ship, then ordered the other one to carry the chronicle keeper. "Set him up on deck, somewhere in shade. And make sure the man receives food and water."

"Aye, my lord." The soldiers obeyed, one dropping to his knees to begin digging with his dirk, the other one bending toward Boscor.

Once the chronicle keeper had been carried off, the warlord turned to me. "Shall I escort you back to the market, my lady? Shall we search it for herbs?"

"And maybe more." I tilted my head. "If one merchant hid his treasure when he saw the enemy approach, might not others have done the same?"

To defeat the enemy, we needed a strong and well-fed army. We could not resupply on Rabeen, but we had to resupply somewhere. Which meant we needed funds. War required coin above all else. This I had already learned on the mainland.

Batumar caught my meaning. "Shorak," he addressed the soldier who finally freed the buried pot. "I need our men to look under the floorboards in all the merchants' houses. Search every building for hiding places no matter how small, even if too slight to hide a man. This time, look for hidden coin. Pass the word."

"Aye, Lord Batumar." The man hurried off with the gold, calling to the group who were still talking under the trees a short distance from us.

"We sail from here to Sheharree and resupply there," Batumar said to me then, his words bringing an instant smile to my face.

Sheharree was a Shahala port on the island of Dahru, a city of my own people. I hoped against hope that my people were safe and the mercenaries who destroyed Rabeen had not pillaged the Shahala lands. "Do you believe the city is free?"

"If it is not, we will need to find another market on another island. Either way, we must resupply before we engage in battle, before we sail to Kaharta Reh."

"Do you think the enemy is still there? Might they not have gone back up the mountain?"

"If the Kerghi took the Kadar fleet, they likely took the port city where the fleet was stationed," the warlord said with reluctance. "And if they took the city, they would want to hold it. We are most likely to find the enemy there. Or, at least, the port is as good a place to start looking for the main enemy force as any."

I could not argue with his logic.

"We shall know more once we reach Sheharree," he added. "They will have news from up north. It will save us from having to sail our ships blindly into Kaharta Reh. When we first meet the enemy, we must be prepared."

We had begun walking back toward the harbor, but a strange sound made me stop.

"Anything the matter, my lady?"

I wasn't sure. "Did you hear anything?"

The warlord stilled, listened. "The wind?"

I heard the faint moan again. "Something else."

Goose bumps rose on my arms. All around us, the landscape stood empty, except for the retreating soldiers' backs.

Yet the breeze brought another soft moan. Batumar must have heard it this time, because he whirled around as if to determine where the moan came from so he could step between me and any possible danger.

"Aaah." Louder now. From a small pile of rocks at a short distance to the east of us.

Another survivor! I ran toward the spot. Whoever was making the noise sounded like he was in pain.

In but a blink, Batumar caught up then caught me, slowed me. As we approached—more carefully now—the sound became more otherworldly, as if echoing up from the bowels of the earth. Only when we were nearly on top of the rocks could we see that we found an old abandoned well, its stone rim crumbled by the ages. We peered down together, squinting side by side into the darkness.

A moment passed before my eyes adjusted to the lack of light. And then I saw someone lying on the bottom of the dry well—a little boy.

"A child!" I squinted harder. *A blue child?*

Of course, not blue! The color had to be a trick of the shadows in the well. Then another, more important, detail snagged my attention. The angles of his arms were wrong as he lay.

His bones are broken. No doubt his injuries had trapped him on the bottom.

"Do not fear," I shouted down. "We shall bring you up."

Instead of another moan, a very adult, bitter laughter bounced up the stones. As the boy struggled to rise and more of the light hit him, I could discern at last that although the size was that of a child, the exact shape was not. Also, I had been right about the color.

We found not a blue child in the well, but a blue dwarf.

CHAPTER SEVEN
THE DWARF IN THE WELL

The warlord watched in silence as the dwarf struggled.

I placed a hand on his arm. "We must bring him up."

"Must we?" he said under his breath and glanced back toward the top of the cliffs, then down the well again. His next words came with obvious reluctance. "I felt something at the cliffs as we came up the steps." He frowned. "When we stood on the top of the rocks."

"As did I." I did not feel the strange sensation here, however. I was near certain it had come from Kratos's ruined temple, but I did not want to say the name aloud. No sense in calling that which one does not want to appear.

The dwarf below us was standing at last, panting.

My fingers flexed on Batumar's arm. "My lord, he is a victim, the same as the others."

The warlord's expression remained unconvinced. He shouted down the well, "Are you a sorcerer?"

The Kadar despised sorcerers of any kind. Centuries past, Noona, the dark sorceress, had come close to wiping out their entire nation. Then also, when we had first arrived at the mainland, the sorcerer of Ishaf had nearly stolen Batumar's very spirit. Neither of us would forget that for as long as we lived.

The warlord looked more like his old self with every passing day, but sometimes I wondered whether he had inner wounds that he kept hidden from me as he hid the outer ones, whether he had fully recovered. I kept my hand on his arm to remind myself that he was alive, that he *had* truly come back to me.

The dwarf watched us from the bottom of the well, squinting against the light. "Were I a powerful sorcerer, my lord, I would not be stuck here."

Batumar considered the man's response before asking, "Have you any weapons?"

The dwarf's laughter was as bitter as it was weak, so thick with despair, it twisted my heart. "Had I a sword or even a paring knife, I would have long since killed myself."

I believed him. A leathery black wing lay next to him on the ground. The rest of the bat was gone, and I had little doubt where it went. Still, a single bat was no great feast. The dwarf had to be half-mad with hunger, thirst, and pain, and the knowledge that no rescue would be coming. He could not have predicted our small armada sailing out of the hardstorms, not in a hundred years. He had likely spent the past several days preparing for a painful death.

His pitiful state must have finally moved the warlord as well, because he called down the well, "I will bring you up."

"I should go down, my lord," I offered. "I could heal him where he is, then we could both climb back up."

"I do not trust him enough to have him alone with you, my Tera."

The room on the bottom of the well was not sufficient for the three of us. If I went down, Batumar would have to stay where he was.

"The man is injured," I protested. "He is hardly a threat."

"I am unwilling to take a chance."

Batumar removed his flask, then unfastened his sword belt and laid it on the ground, but he did not completely disarm. The daggers he carried in each boot, he left in their place. And truly, nearly every part of the warlord was a weapon. I had watched him take down many an enemy bare-handed.

He found a spot on the well's crumbling lip that would hold him, swung his legs over, then turned toward the stones of the well, searching for a foothold. He never paused, but began his descent. I had no doubt he could stand his own against the dwarf, even if the dwarf did have bad intentions, but I disliked the way the dark hole swallowed Batumar regardless.

I leaned over the rim and watched him lower himself handhold by handhold. The stones were dry, no wet spots anywhere nor any moss growing. The well must have run out of water a long time ago. If the island had seen rain in the past few days, it could not have been much.

Batumar moved with power as he climbed, but not with an easy grace. The sorcerer of Ishaf had broken his bones. Even though the breaks had healed, the warlord's body was not the same as it had been before.

As he neared the bottom, the blue dwarf shuffled out of his way. Then the warlord landed at last, and the two men measured up each other. They hesitated, as if unsure what to do next.

Oh, for the spirits' sake. Clearly, with broken arms, the dwarf could not hang on to Batumar's neck and ride up on his back. *I should have gone down the well.*

Before I could tell the warlord just that, he found his own solution. He sat on the ground and spread his cloak out behind him. "Sit in the middle."

The dwarf did. The warlord gathered the corners of the cloak and tied them diagonally across his chest. When he stood, he had the dwarf on his back in a bundle. *Cleverly done.* Not that I was going to say that to Batumar.

The climb up was even more ungainly than the climb down. Yet the dwarf's weight slowed the warlord little. In but a few moments, they were out of the well, the dwarf on the ground where I could unbundle him from the warlord's cloak at last.

"Stay still." I did not want him to injure himself further.

He obeyed, moving not a muscle while I inspected him in the sunlight.

He was younger than I by at least a few summers, his hair short and black, his eyes dark amber. He stayed flat on his back, squinting hard against the sun. Tiny runes covered what skin his clothes left bare. Blue tattoos decorated every visible spot—from his eyelids to the pads of his fingers. Where his short hair parted, I could see runes tattooed even on his scalp.

For protection? Some of the tribes of the Outer Islands believed in the protection of sacred words and texts.

"You must be parched." I grabbed Batumar's flask from the ground, uncapped it, then held it in front of the blue man's mouth.

He held his arms immobile, but his head tilted up, and his cracked lips closed around the opening. He swallowed loudly and greedily, without spilling a single drop, sucking at the flask even when it ran empty.

Once the dwarf was satisfied that he had extracted every last drop and his eyes grew a little more used to the bright light, he pulled back and examined us in return. He inclined his head as best he could from his prone position. "My lord, my lady, I am in your debt."

"I am the Lady Tera of the Shahala," I said, and when Batumar remained silent, I added, "And this is Lord Batumar of the Kadar."

The warlord already had his sword belt fastened, his right hand resting on the pommel.

The dwarf kept a wary eye on him but did not scamper back. He understood that should Batumar decide he was one of the enemy, there would be no escape.

"Would you share your name?" I asked when he did not volunteer one.

His gaze cut to me, and he flashed an apologetic smile. "I do not have a name, my lady."

What should we call him, then? We could not leave him here, and if he was to travel with us on our ship, we could not be addressing him as Lord Dwarf. *If* he was a lord. His clothes—boots, britches, and a tight, sleeveless tunic—were all inexpensive and utilitarian black. Even the bulky ring on his left hand was made of steel and carried no gemstone. *Where did he come from? What island? What nation?*

Batumar interrupted my thoughts. "He is an assassin."

I stared. I had never seen an assassin before. The Shahala, a nation of healers, had no dealings with such men, and the Kadar preferred to fight man-to-man, face-to-face.

Assassin.

Instinct pushed me to step away, but I stayed my ground. I remembered how people feared me when they'd thought me a sorceress. The assassin had made no move to harm us. I did not think he could if he wanted to. Not until his arms healed.

"How came you to Rabeen?" Batumar asked in a tone that turned the question into a command to answer.

"I ran away from my master." The dwarf closed his eyes for a breath and sighed. "I planned to join up with pirates."

Batumar did not move his piercing gaze from him. "You changed your mind and decided to remain on Rabeen instead?"

"I was merely waiting for a pirate ship to come into harbor. The Kadar ships came instead, four of them, but they did not carry Kadar warriors. The men looked to be Kerghi mercenaries." The dwarf's face twisted into a grimace. "I was at the docks and expecting no trouble. I was one of the first ones they caught."

"How many were they?"

"Hundreds, my lord."

"Why did they spare your life?"

"I told them when a blue assassin is killed, all his brothers come together to hunt down the killer."

"Is that true?"

"No, my lord." The dwarf deflated. "There is no brotherhood among assassins."

Batumar's questions did not relent. "How did you come to be in the well?"

The dwarf seemed to shrink, if possible. "The Kerghi set me free so they could make sport of hunting me. I was never a fast runner, but I nearly reached the olive orchards when they caught me and tossed me into the well, thinking to let me die slowly."

A moment of silence passed before he added, "After three days, when I knew I would never be able to come up, I drank the poison in my ring."

My gaze fell to the bulky steel ring on his left hand.

"How are you not dead, then?" The warlord's tone dripped suspicion.

"I was trained from an early age to tolerate poison, digesting a small portion each day, my lord," the dwarf said miserably. "Still, I had nothing else. I tried the only thing I could." He shook his head, his amber eyes haunted. "The potion only made me suffer."

As I was not sure what to make of his tale, let alone his profession, I focused on his lack of name. "What do people call you when they talk to you?"

A hard smile turned up the corners of his lips. "An assassin has no friends. And my enemies never see me," he said by rote, as if repeating a mantra.

I suppose the fact that we saw him meant we were not his enemies—a comforting thought. But not having a name on a voyage that lasted several days would not do. "Had you no name as a child?"

He looked at the dirt in which he lay. "Urdy," he said at last, in a heavy tone. Then he sighed again. "A good assassin would have forgotten that."

"I am a healer, Urdy," I forged ahead confidently on the tail of my small victory. "May I see your arms?"

He nodded.

While I examined the breaks, Batumar kept questioning him, but Urdy knew no more about the Kerghi invaders or the state of our island of Dahru than Boscor the chronicle keeper had.

Urdy's left arm was bent at a nasty angle, a large bump under his blue skin. The right arm was worse, the bone sticking out. I winced, thinking about the pain he had suffered for these past seven days.

He misinterpreted my reaction for squeamishness and tried to shift away. "A lady should not have to see such ugliness. I'm sorry."

I put a hand on his shoulder to stop him.

At the same time, Batumar said, "Worry not. She is the least squeamish of all the ladies in the world. Only yesterday, she gelded a man."

I thought Urdy might have paled under all his tattoos. He definitely pressed his legs tighter together.

I cast Batumar a reproaching glare, but the warlord widened his eyes with false innocence. Then, when I lay my hands on Urdy's arm to soften then reknit the bones, Batumar shook his head. If I wanted Urdy on our ship, I would do better to allow him to heal the natural way. Batumar would consider the assassin less of a threat without his full strength.

As I pulled my hands back, Urdy said, "'Twas worse yesterday. I had maggots in the wound." His glance darted between me and his injury. "I ate them."

I sighed. "That might not have been best done. Maggots clear away the rotted flesh. They would have helped."

With his eyes downcast and chagrin on his face, he mumbled, "I was hungry, my lady."

I could certainly understand. I too had known hunger. "Our men are gathering what food might be found on the island. We shall be happy to share. Will you travel with us to Dahru?"

"If you allow me, my lady. My lord," he added, casting a questioning and not altogether hopeful glance at Batumar.

The warlord flashed me a look that said he was doing this for my sake and my sake only, then he shouted for a soldier to help Urdy to the ship.

"If you would, my lady." The dwarf hesitated. "You offered healing. Would you set my arms here?"

"If you can wait but a little longer, I might find some herbs to numb the pain of the treatment. I mean to search the market."

"I would rather have it over with." He paused again, and I understood that he worried about being jostled as he was carried to the ship. "If I had only one broken arm, I would have set it already."

I believed him. He looked that determined. I shifted forward. "Let us begin."

Urdy inclined his head with a look of gratitude, then drew a deep breath. "Which side first, my lady?"

"Worst comes first."

He thought for a moment then flashed a relieved smile. "If I lose consciousness, I shall be spared the pain of the second procedure?"

"Exactly so," I told him.

Urdy glanced at Batumar. "I like the way the lady thinks."

The warlord quirked an eyebrow. "See that you do not like too much about her."

The assassin winked at me, but did so while dipping his head, so the warlord, standing over us, would not see.

I bit back a smile. "Brace yourself."

"I am always braced for anything, my lady."

I supposed he was if he could swallow deadly poison.

I pulled my knife from its sheath, then began my work, cutting away the dead skin, while the warlord kept questioning the dwarf, who responded between grunts and gasps. Then came the setting, and then the stitching and the splinting. He swore once, under his breath, but he did not faint.

When I finished, Batumar had one of our soldiers take Urdy to the *Shield*. But even as the dwarf was carried away, the warlord stayed by my side, never taking his mistrustful gaze from the assassin.

CHAPTER EIGHT

MUTINY

Some of the soldiers were slow to return to the ships.

The men milled in groups of a dozen here, two dozen there, exchanging meaningful looks and whispering. I did not like the way they avoided my gaze. Batumar and I had been through a mutiny on a pirate ship the first time we crossed the wild ocean. It had not ended well.

Standing at the farthest point of the wharf—well away from the dead and the flies—I could no longer see the warlord. He had escorted me back to the harbor after we had gathered as many herbs as we could from trampled kitchen gardens and also looked through the spilled goods on the ground at the market. The warlord had carried my bundles back for me, then left me to see to our sailors and soldiers as they were returning to their ships.

I handed out herbs for dysentery, set a wrist broken by rough seas, and cleaned cuts received in battle training. Then, my healing work done, my concern turned to the men gathered at a distance, talking intently with each other.

I looked for Lord Karnagh but could not see him, no matter how much I craned my neck. Then I caught sight of Tomron at the other end of the harbor, coming from the city, and I sent a soldier to fetch him. Tomron had been with me from the beginnings of our army, brave and steadfast. I watched him as he hurried to me, limping. He was Batumar's age, built with muscle atop muscle, his nose nearly flat. He had once told me that in his youth, he used to fight for coin in taverns.

He bowed when he reached me. "Lady Tera, I am glad to find you well."

"And you, Tomron?" I glanced at his leg.

"Barely a sprain." He flashed a wry smile as he shook his head. "I survived the hardstorms, then injured myself jumping from plank to shore when we reached safe harbor at last."

"I could make a poultice."

He declined with thanks, and I understood. He did not wish to appear weak in front of his men, running for help with something so minor. He would tough out the pain. I did not try to convince him otherwise. We had some days left yet before reaching Dahru. His sprain would heal before we had to go to battle.

"One of the Selorm lords found an unspoiled well at the far end of the olive orchard," he said with a wide smile. "I sent half of our sailors off with the empty water barrels."

The news cheered my heart. "I wish we found more food."

His smile widened. "Our Landrian archers killed a herd of wild goats on the steepest cliffs on the north side of the island. The goats fell into the sea from the cliffs, but the tigers fetched them for us, my lady. Selorm battle tigers are good swimmers. The men are field-dressing the goats as we speak. We should see them soon, returning with the meat, enough to feed all of us well for three days, or six with strict rationing."

I could have embraced him for that news. Then the soldiers loitering ashore caught my attention yet again. "Have the men become dispirited in the crossing?"

"Some. Aye." Tomron's expression hardened as he followed my gaze and looked at the largest group of men who had their heads together. "They wonder if we might not be better off staying on the island."

I absorbed his words in silence.

"The storms and the loss of the other two caravels shook them," he added.

"As did finding the people of Rabeen massacred, I suspect."

"The dead brought back memories, for certain. Our men have seen their own cities laid to waste just so. They wonder if our numbers are enough to fight the enemy. While here... If we built fortifications, we would have a fair chance of holding the island."

"The market city was prosperous before its destruction," I agreed. "No reason why it could not be prosperous once more. New wells could be dug. We could live on fish until the fields Rabeen's farmers planted in the spring would be ready for our harvest in the fall."

Tomron glanced toward the men once again, a frown creasing his brow. "Few of our army are trained soldiers. Most are farmers and merchants who joined up because Emperor Drakhar's armies razed their villages and cities on the mainland."

I understood, I truly did. I wished to sail to Dahru to confront the enemy, to fight for my homeland and for my own people. Our soldiers, on the other hand, were going to battle, risking their lives, for strangers and countries they had never before seen. The thought of remaining here—with the fruit orchards and olive groves—had to tempt them.

I drew a ragged breath, the vision of our army disintegrating on Rabeen's rocks slamming into my chest like a battering ram.

* * *

"My guards tell me Rabeen could be made defensible," Prince Graho said when I went below to check on him and shared my concerns about the mood amongst the men.

Four royal guards stood by his side. They had washed him of the sweat of fever, combed his hair, and dressed him in fresh clothes. The sun was at an angle so that its rays reached the prince. I did not pull him into shade. Sunshine had its own healing powers. His eyes were clear. His fever was gone. The breeze outside pushed fresh air down into the hold, the heat not uncomfortable.

"Your britches, my lord. I brought a poultice. We found some herbs at the market that will help."

He did not fight me this time, but he did look away from me as I began to change his bandages. These his men had not touched, on my orders.

I washed the wound in herb water, then prepared the poultice, looking for infection or any spots of black near his injury, but found neither. He had minded my instructions to keep the wound clean and do nothing that would strain him.

"Where is Commander Durak? Back on the island to gain more tactical information?" I asked to distract the prince. "Just as well. I do not think he altogether approves of me."

"If he's said anything…"

"He does not have to. His hard looks say aplenty."

"He is a hard man. Have I ever told you he was a childhood hero to me?" Prince Graho's eyes lit with frank admiration. "In his youth, in his first battle, after an enemy lance ran through his chest, he was left for dead on the battlefield. They say he came to at twilight, to rats chewing off his ear."

"That would explain why he only has the one." I laid the poultice in place.

"As enemy soldiers sorted through the dead," the prince said, "stripping them of weapons and valuables, Durak overheard them talking about a surprise attack at dawn. He broke off the lance's shaft and crawled to my father's camp to warn him, the foot-long metal tip still stuck between his ribs."

I was beginning to understand why Durak was the commander of the prince's guard. "And would he too prefer to stay on the island?"

"With our three warships, we can repel the enemy should they return." The prince paused, but only for a moment. "Rabeen has but two major harbors. The narrow beach is on a shallow inlet. The enemy could only come ashore there if they grounded their ships. The rest of the shoreline is mostly cliffs. With what force we have, we could stop any invaders from putting troops ashore."

As an admiral, his first thought, of course, was naval defenses.

I was grateful for his experience and knowledge, and yet... "The enemy *did* put his troops ashore."

"And how many soldiers do you think, my lady, Rabeen had for its defenses?"

"Too few, according to Batumar." I had to agree. I could not remember seeing the slightest hint of an army the last time we had been here. "Rabeen was a market, not a military installation."

"There you have it," Prince Graho said with satisfaction. "We, on the other hand, have ships well manned by sailors used to war, and over five hundred soldiers."

We both looked up as Tomron hurried down the ladder, his boots slapping hard onto the wooden rungs. While I waited for him to reach us, I addressed the prince again. "Would you stay, then? Give up now, when we are so close?"

Prince Graho's pallid expression turned uncertain. "It might be better for some to live than for all to perish."

I could not deny the wisdom of his words.

"And you?" I asked Tomron who came to a halt next to us and was trying not to stare at the prince's injury.

While I grabbed a roll of clean linen and began the careful work of swaddling my patient, Tomron said, "Where my Lady Tera leads, I follow, even into the jaws of death and down his slimy throat. And then I will cut his belly open." He rattled his sword. "And I will set my lady free."

Gratitude flooded me. My general was normally more taciturn, but mayhap he knew I needed to hear his words of allegiance. "Thank you, Tomron."

Prince Graho gave a bitter groan. "I should have said what he said."

I finished with his bandages and patted his shoulder. "You are not in your best form. But by tomorrow, you will be your valiant prince self again. We will win this war, and there will be songs sung about your prowess."

His troubled gaze cleared. "One of those long ballads?"

"Definitely so."

Tomron's lips twisted into an amused smile at our banter. Then his expression grew serious. "My Lady Tera, we best get the men back on the ships without much delay."

The tension in his tone worried me. Bidding the prince to rest, I pushed to my feet and walked to the ladder, but I stopped with my foot on the bottom rung.

"How bad is it?" I asked, and made sure my voice did not carry.

"Time is of the essence," Tomron said under his breath.

The first person I saw when stepping on the deck was Batumar, thank the spirits. As soon as he spotted me, he strode straight toward me, his expression carrying enough thunder to have men move out of his way. His shirt and britches were covered in dust. He must have gone back to Rabeen to help our men sift through the rubble.

"There you are." He stopped in front of me, his gaze softening for a moment, but only a moment, before he said, scowling, "I do not like the looks of the men." He glanced over his shoulder. "I would give much for a few hundred true Kadar warriors. They would not be having battle jitters."

Twice as many men loitered in the harbor than before, no longer performing tasks but remaining on shore regardless. I would have to bring them back on board and quickly, before even more joined them. The more they talked out there, the more they would convince themselves to stay.

I considered standing in the prow of the ship as I addressed them. Then I decided to go among them instead.

"If you wish…" Batumar began, but I shook my head.

I could not leave the task to Batumar, even though I knew with certainty he would remove any burden from my shoulders to help. If I wanted the men to fully commit to fighting this war to the end, I had to remind them that I was fully committed to leading them.

My mind churning, I left the ship once again. Instead of walking on the stone ramp, I climbed the rocks that separated the harbor from the market. I was close enough to the men to be heard and high enough to be seen.

Now, I thought. *Now I must win them.*

"Men!" With rows of bodies on the gallows providing the background, I addressed our troops, my voice flying out over the rubble. "You stand here not only as soldiers. You stand here as fathers, brothers, and sons."

I gestured at the dead. "You have seen your families massacred. You have seen your homes burned. Yet you remained strong. You survived. And soon will come the time to rebuild."

They nodded in agreement, their faces hopeful. They expected me to suggest that we all rebuild here.

Instead, I posed a question. "When a man's house is on fire and his bed is burning, does he replace the bed before putting out the flames?"

Their expressions turned puzzled then thoughtful. Understanding began to glint in eyes here and there.

"You have lost much," I said. "Most of you have lost everything. What would you not do to erase those losses? What would you not do to bring back your parents, your brothers and sisters, your wives, and your children? Would you not do *anything*? Are you willing to do whatever it takes, no matter the price?"

Voices rose in the crowd. "Aye!"

The men watched me intently now. Many of them knew me as a sorceress. I knew some expected me to suggest magic. I went on quickly to dispel such false hope.

"We cannot undo the past. Yet together, we have the power to save the future. One day soon, you will have homes again. You will have wives. You will have children. But they will only be safe if first we defeat this enemy. We must clear them out of the islands of the Mirror Sea, or we will never have safe homes here. If we do not defeat the Kerghi hordes, what happened to your homes before will happen again. What happened here in Rabeen will come to pass once more."

The men stood still and silent.

"Today, together, we decide what world we make for our future children—mine and yours. Will we huddle on this island, hoping to evade the eye of the enemy for a time? Will we live in false hope? Then, when they come, for they surely will, do we allow the enemy to take once again all that we hold dear?"

"Nay!" came the response, most of the men shouting now. "Never again!"

"We will defeat this enemy! We will push them into the sea. We have come this far. We will make the islands of the Mirror Sea into a place where our children live safely and free. What would you do to save your sons yet unborn?"

All the men screamed, "Anything!"

"Are you men who will hide on a rock? Or are you men whose names future generations will know and respect? Will your name be lost to history, or will you be legends? Will you fight?"

"AYE!"

I drew my lungs full. "Then let us go and fight!"

"AYE!" The men cheered. Some threw their caps into the air; others waved their swords over their heads.

I watched them, my heart racing with a savage pleasure.

As they clamored to get back on the ships, I gave thanks to the spirits. Only then did I see Batumar standing a short distance behind me with Tomron and Lord Karnagh. They had lent me their full, unquestioning support in front of the men.

Two warlords and a general. Yet they looked at me as if I were a queen.

"My lady." They bowed one after the other.

Batumar beamed with pride and love. As Tomron had pledged his loyalty to me in the hold of the ship, Batumar pledged it with every breath he took.

Lord Karnagh, warlord of the Selorms, stepped forward. When we had first met, his hair had been a striking lion's mane. The thick, twisted locks still fell below his waist, but they had turned near silver during the winter he had spent at the Beast Lords' Chapel, fighting death.

He gifted me with a warm smile, his battle tiger, Tigran, by his side, and, of course, Marga next to the male tiger. "A speech fit for a war queen."

He was a friend, and I had missed him these past couple of mooncrossings. "How did you fare through the storms, my lord?"

He made a dismissive gesture with his left hand. The right arm of his brown leather doublet hung empty. By the time I had found him at the chapel, near death, he had cut off his infected sword arm to save his own life. The worst injury for a warrior born for battle, but he would not let it stop him.

"The storms tossed us some," he said simply, a man who had stared death in the face more than once, "but we made it through with most of our men. We are ready to fight."

He flexed his left arm. "I have been practicing."

Our two tigers circled us, chuffing at each other with affection.

Lord Karnagh watched the animals with undisguised pleasure. "Do you know Selorm tradition, my lady?" He went on without waiting for my answer. "From a litter of battle tigers, the sire always receives one cub, preferably male."

"No litter is expected." Marga and I spent enough time together that I would have felt the new life growing in her.

Lord Karnagh would not be discouraged. "Soon," he said, and patted Tigran's massive shoulder, as if urging the tiger to do his duty.

We climbed off the rocks and headed back to our small fleet, trailing behind our soldiers as they boarded. The scent of goat stew wafted from the galleys and filled the air. Our cooks had been busy.

Lord Karnagh strode to the *Sword*, Tomron to the *Lance*, while Batumar and I returned to the *Shield*.

Even as the men ate, the captains drew anchor. As our ships left the harbor, Batumar went below to confer with the prince. I remained in the stern and watched the wharf behind us with its forest of gallows. I said the Last Blessing over the massacred, then swore to the sky that I would never forget Rabeen and its dead. I prayed to the spirits that Dahru had not suffered the same devastation.

The last I saw of Rabeen was the cliffs, gilded in the rays of the setting sun. I watched the waves crash into the rocks where the ancient god's temple stood submerged in water. I could not see even the tip of a single pillar, yet a cold shiver still ran down my spine.

I turned toward the open sea then and pushed away all feelings of unease. We were returning to Dahru. *Home.* We were bringing five hundred soldiers. And when the Shahala healers joined us, our five hundred would count as twice that number. The healers would be able to heal those injured in fighting and quickly return them to the battlefield.

Thank you, kind spirits.

Marga padded up next to me and rubbed her bushy head against my side.

"We will free Dahru," I told the tiger, my heart filled with hope. "We will make a new start. You will see. Only a little longer, and we will reach home. We will face our enemies. And we will win."

CHAPTER NINE
HEART BE BRAVE

"An earworm," I told the soldier who sat on an overturned bucket before me on deck the following morning.

"I thought so, my lady." The grizzled warrior nodded. "It screeched all night, leaving me no sleep. Gives me a fierce headache."

He had been rubbing his forehead and sticking his finger into his ear every time he took a break from morning practice. The way he winced made me suspect the worm, but, of course, the man would not come to me. I had to go to him.

"You must have picked it up on Rabeen. I am going to pull it. Tilt your ear to the sky."

He did as I asked. "Will it hurt?"

"Not nearly as much as if I left it in." If it was a yellow-ringed worm, it would eventually burrow into his brain. But even if it was the slimmer black earworm, it would start eating the man's eardrum eventually.

"I need hot oil," I told the soldier next to me. "Bring some from the galley."

Lucky for us, we had found a few dropped and rolled-away flasks of olive oil in the ruins of the market of Rabeen.

"I will also need a bucket of seawater," I told the nearest sailor, and he ran off to fetch it.

The two men came back at the same time. I accepted the oil first, still in its flask and boiling hot, as if the cook had simply held it over the fire. Holding the metal flask with the rag the soldier used to carry it, I stuck it into the bucket of seawater to cool it a little. When I was sure I would not burn my patient, I poured as much as I could into his ear, then quickly handed off the flask to the nearest man.

The worm took no time at all to show itself, flat head first, which I pinched, yanking. *Yellow-ringed worm.* Longer than my middle finger. Oh, how it screeched! The sound only stopped when the cursed worm bit me, winding around my finger as if it would never let go.

I plunged my whole hand into the bucket by my feet. The worm squirmed right off my finger then, trying to escape the salt that burned its skin—only to sink deeper into the water.

"Over the side!" I shouted, and one of the braver sailors grabbed the bucket, then ran off with it.

"Toss the whole bucket!" I shouted after him.

Ringed worms were quick. I would not want it to end up in his ear.

I did not relax until I heard the splash, and neither did the men around me.

"Thank you, my lady." The soldier in front of me rose, rubbing his ear.

I nodded, then called, "Next!"

Another soldier sat, cradling his right arm with the left.

"You should have come to me right away," I scolded him as I grabbed his elbow and shoulder to rotate his dislocated shoulder. "I want everyone to come to me when they are hurt, instead of trying to protect me. I am a healer."

Judging by the swelling, he had hurt himself at the beginning of training, at dawn, and now it was midmorning.

He swallowed a groan as I popped the joint back into place. "Yes, Lady Tera. We but wish you'd save your strength for battle. For when it really matters."

"This matters."

"Of course, my lady."

I shook my head, fair certain that he would hide his future training injuries just the same, then I moved on to my next patient and the next.

The sun was high in the sky by the time I returned belowdecks, carrying a bucket of fresh water. I checked on the prince. No fever. He had royal guards aplenty to see to his needs, so I carried the water to the mother and child whom we had settled into the prince's unused room.

As I opened the door, I caught the woman jumping to her feet and shoving her daughter into the farthest corner. She stepped between us for good measure. Her gaze darted to the bucket, staying for a second, then moving on with disappointment, as if she had not assessed it for its content but whether it could be easily used as a weapon.

I made sure to smile. "I brought water. How are you faring?"

"When we reach port, will you sell us at a slave market?" she demanded.

I put the bucket between us and slowly sat on the floor with my legs crossed, making no gestures that could be interpreted as threatening.

"We are headed to Sheharree, a Shahala harbor. You must know that my people, the Shahala, keep no slaves."

She watched me with distrust. "The Shahala keep no army either."

"'Tis not a Shahala army."

"Whose army is it, then?"

"Mine."

Her eyes widened, but in another moment, they narrowed again with suspicion. "The Shahala have no warrior queens."

I smiled. "I am neither warrior nor queen."

Her little girl peeked from behind her mother, looking light enough to take flight. Her matted hair was so dirty, I could barely tell the color.

"I am Nessa," she peeped up for the first time.

"Greetings, Nessa. Did you sleep well?"

As the girl nodded, the mother relaxed a small measure. "I'm Ina. M'lady," she added.

"Did you lose your husband in the attack, Ina?" I asked gently.

Anger filled her eyes instead of tears. "He was but a goatherd, m'lady. They didn't need to kill him none."

The mother and child eased forward from the corner at last, and I thought they might yet sit with me and tell me more of what had happened on Rabeen, but Marga pushed her bushy head through the door, and Ina and Nessa drew back with identical screams.

I rose to nudge Marga back.

"The water is yours," I told Ina before stepping after the tiger. "If you need anything else, send someone to find me."

Not that she would. She would neither leave the room nor talk to one of our soldiers willingly. I would come back and check on them later.

Marga and I walked to the storage room I had been sharing with Batumar for most of the journey. Now a soldier stood guard in front of the door, which meant Urdy was still in there. I had once again spent the night by the prince's side, as his fever had spiked shortly before midnight. Batumar had shared our storage room with Urdy, for the warlord would not let the dwarf out of his sight.

I shot the guard a questioning look.

"The dwarf is not to leave the room today." The man shifted on his feet. "He is not to have visitors either, my lady."

I did not have to ask on whose orders.

I did not challenge the poor soldier, who was clearly uncomfortable, but continued on to exchange a few words with Prince Graho, then hurried down a narrow passageway to grab two bowls of leftover goat stew from the galley before I went to find Boscor on deck.

"The wound is much better, Lady Tera," the chronicle keeper assured me after thanking me for his meal. "You have worked a miracle."

His eyes were clear, no flush on his cheeks, his wound pink, not red. *No fever. No infection.* I had treated him the night before with my newfound herbs.

"The pain should lessen each day as you heal more fully," I told him.

He must have been hungry, but he ate with no hurry. In fact, he took the time to say a silent prayer first, bowing his head. He had a quiet dignity that reminded me of the old Guardians of the Forgotten City, whom I greatly missed.

I stayed to talk with him and eat my meal in his company, my gaze wandering to the men who were back at swordplay after their midday break. Our storm-tattered sails sagged in the weak wind, the masts creaking as if even the timber was tired of the long journey. Yet the soldiers threw themselves into training harder than ever.

"How fare the mother and child?" Boscor asked.

"Resting." At least, I most sincerely hoped.

"And the crown prince of Landria?" Boscor winced as he asked. "I overheard talk of his surgery."

"Recovering as we speak." The wind blew tendrils of my hair into my face. I pushed them back. "You could keep him company. He is impatient to rise and join training, but it would be best for him if he stayed put for a while longer yet."

The chronicle keeper shook his head. "My opinion on going belowdecks holds. Climbing the ladder would hurt too much. And I am not having myself carried down on a soldier's back. I would prefer not to be dropped. I do not wish to add a broken neck to the list of my injuries."

He had said as much the previous evening and had spent the night on deck. As the night had been clear and he had not been in the way, nobody objected.

He finished his stew and placed the empty bowl next to himself. "I am most glad that the gods favored me by putting me in your path." He folded his hands over his belly, linking his fingers. He cleared his throat, and watched me with hesitation before saying, "But, my lady, are you certain about the assassin?"

Oh. Was the assassin's presence the true reason why Boscor would not go belowdecks?

"With both his arms broken, he cannot do much harm to anyone," I told the chronicle keeper.

Boscor nodded but did not appear relieved. I had to remind myself that he was not a military man. I had been surrounded by soldiers for so long, I had grown used to the fearlessness with which they viewed the world. I could not expect the same from everyone I met.

"You must be eager to see your home again, Lady Tera," the chronicle keeper commented after a little while, his tone heavy with melancholy. He must have wondered if he would ever return to Rabeen.

"I fear for our people," I confessed. "I cannot stop worrying about what might have happened on Dahru while we were gone."

The lines on Boscor's face deepened as he squinted against the sunshine. Sympathy filled his voice. "Rabeen darkened your hopes."

"Aye." The aftermath of the massacre…I could not push the images from my mind. They tore at my spirit.

Think not of darkness. Think of hope.

We were so close to home. *Nearly there.* We had food and water once again. And no ship-killing gales. Sailing Mirror Sea could not, in any way, be compared to sailing the wild ocean with its hardstorms.

"Your island has its Kadar warlords and their keeps and castles," Boscor encouraged. "Dahru is not near as defenseless as Rabeen was."

"When we left Dahru, its defenses had already been breached by five hundred Kerghi mercenaries who came through the island's Gate," I reminded him, drawing my cloak tighter around me against the strengthening wind.

He drew up a graying eyebrow. "Do you think more have come through since?"

I shook my head. "At the cost of his life, the old Guardian of the Gate closed the Gate. When we left to gather this army, the enemy sat on the mountain behind their makeshift fortifications, and the defenders of Karamur sat behind the city wall, the two armies equal in force."

"And neither could attack the other, because to do so, they would have to move out into the open and expose themselves, put themselves at a disadvantage." He scratched his chin thoughtfully. "So, you set out to increase your numbers and tip the scales."

Such a simple plan. I swallowed my last spoonful of stew as I nodded. "Karamur is protected by five hundred of our soldiers, and we bring five hundred more."

"How did you ever reach the mainland? Only the pirates brave the hardstorms."

I allowed a small smile. "We sailed with the pirates. Under assumed names. We met Prince Graho on the way. He was traveling in disguise himself, as a merchant."

Boscor listened with rapt attention as I regaled him with the full journey. "My lady, I must write this down. The tale must be saved for prosperity. It belongs in the chronicles."

"Let us survive this war, and then we shall write about it," I promised.

This he accepted, humming and nodding, as if already planning how to lay out the chapters.

"We might have brought an army," I said, setting my empty bowl aside, "but pushing the Kerghi off the island will still be a bloody battle. They are soulless mercenaries, hardened by decades of fighting, merciless. And who knows, they might have broken the stalemate and overtaken Karamur by now. The Kadar might not have troops in the fortress city anymore. At the very least, since the Kerghi captured the Kadar fleet, it is very likely that they had taken Kaharta Reh. There is battle aplenty before us, and we know so little. I am weary of the killing and death." I paused, then added, "If I had the power to vanquish one thing from all the world, it would be war."

Boscor looked back toward Rabeen, although the island had long ago disappeared in the distance. His eyes grew unfocused. "Then you must vanquish fear."

"Fear did not destroy Rabeen."

"Fear is the father of hate. We hate what we fear," he said as he turned back to me. "And hate is the father of violence. We want to destroy what we hate."

"Can we not love each other?" I thought for a moment. "If fear is the father of hate, is courage the father of love?"

"Understanding is the mother of love. To seek to understand others is the beginning of loving them, of having compassion for them. Love is the mother of courage."

I was not certain about that.

He must have read the thought on my face, for he asked, "My lady, have you read *The Book of Siege*?"

"No, Grandfather."

"The ancient tome is at the library of Karamur." He sighed, probably thinking the enemy might have it by now. To his credit, he decided not to discourage me by voicing that opinion. He tilted his head as he watched me. "Still, you must have heard of some of the famous sieges."

"Dining in the High Lord's hall, I could not have escaped the retelling of such had I tried."

He smiled. "What stories do you remember?"

"The story of Emila, Queen of Mistron. When the siege of Mistron Castle grew desperate, she exposed herself on purpose to the green plague. Then she stole out of the castle in the middle of the night and allowed the enemy to capture her."

I tried to remember the rest of the tale. "The Gradnian king raped her before giving her to his men. He died a week after she did. And then his sons, and then half his army. The other half returned home and carried the plague with them. The Mistronians waited until the plague spent itself, then took Gradnia. The Mistron King renamed the Gradnian capital Emila, in his queen's honor."

Boscor nodded with satisfaction at my familiarity with the story. "Might you remember any other tales?"

Sails billowed above. Our ship sailed on smooth water, the sailors moving around us in no particular hurry. The world seemed at peace. I embraced the moment, for I knew too well how brief such peace was, how fleeting.

I hugged my knees, turning my face into the wind. "I know the story of the siege of Ramlan. When the siege force set a fire in front of Ramlan's gate to burn down the fortress, a hundred of the fortress guards jumped from the wall on top of the fire to smother the flames with their own bodies."

As Boscor smiled, encouragement warming his eyes, I remembered yet another famed siege.

"Lord Karnagh once told me a Selorm tale. When Lord Meber of the Selorm and his people were near starved in a siege, some of the people of the city volunteered to be cut down to feed the battle tigers with their own bodies. With the tigers' renewed strength, Lord Meber marched out his gate and swept away the enemy."

Boscor asked, "And do you think, my lady, that Queen Emila was courageous in exposing herself to the green plague, then allowing the enemy to capture her?"

I did not have to think. "Most courageous."

"How about the hundred guards who jumped into the fire from Ramlan's walls?"

I had fallen into fire from the wall of Karamur. I remembered the pain well. My fall had been accidental. To do that on purpose…

"Aye," I said. "The guards were courageous."

"How about those who sacrificed themselves to feed the battle tigers?"

"Aye." A shudder ran through me, my gaze cutting to Marga as the tiger stood by the railing. She was watching fish jump from the sea, her tail twitching.

Boscor asked, "And what made these men and women act the way they did, with so much courage?"

I suddenly understood his meaning. "Love for their kingdom and people. Love for their families."

The chronicle keeper nodded. "In all the tales of all the courageous acts I have ever heard, the most courageous people always acted out of love. Neither hate nor greed can ever give a heart such strength. So, I say, my lady, that love and courage are most closely related."

I thought of Ina, hiding in that crevice on the cliffs, starving and nearly too weak to stand, but still jumping in front of the tiger to protect her daughter.

From love comes courage.

I breathed in the salty air and thought about how much I loved

Batumar, and our people, and the men on the ship who had pledged their lives to our cause.

My strength renewed.

"Heart be brave," I whispered into the breeze.

CHAPTER TEN

FROM RABEEN TO SHEHARREE

I was still sitting with Boscor when Urdy ambled over and sat down next to us with a nervous smile.

"My lady. Master Boscor."

I had been changing Boscor's bandages, but now I checked around for Batumar. I did not want him to see Urdy with me and misinterpret our proximity.

The warlord had two of our men bring Urdy up from the hold earlier, then deposit him well out of arm's reach from us. They had not done it gently. Nor had anyone shown the slightest kindness to the dwarf since.

I saw several men bumping into him on purpose as they strode by, jostling his broken arms. Others gave him wide berth. The sailors, a superstitious lot, made signs with their fingers to ward off evil every time they passed him.

If Urdy had not arrived on the ship at Batumar's order, I was certain by now he would be on the bottom of the sea.

The assassin's attempts to befriend our soldiers and sailors at every chance did not help matters. His offers of help to braid rope with his toes were rebuffed with curses.

I met his wary gaze. "I was going to see to your arms next."

He relaxed at my words. Had he thought I would send him away?

Boscor, on the other hand, stiffened. The chronicle keeper drew back, casting Urdy an uneasy glance. "They say, my lady, that you only see a blue assassin when you are about to die, a heartbeat before your death. It is a queer feeling to be so close to one."

An expression of defeat clouded Urdy's face. "I am not a very good assassin."

I moved closer to him so I could check whether the wrappings on his splints had loosened and needed tightening. I probed his arms from wrist to shoulder. He winced but did not complain. So much gratitude shone in his eyes as to make me feel embarrassed.

"How did you come to your profession?" I asked. "If you don't mind telling."

He hesitated before responding. "A *morden* came to our village. He wanted to buy small children." Pain flashed in his eyes. "My father brought me forth, saying the man would find none smaller than I."

"Mordens train assassins," the chronicle keeper put in, his tone carrying distaste. "They have rival schools on the smaller, nameless islands on the edge of the ocean."

At my questioning look, he added, "The chronicles are full of dire warnings about the Islands of Assassins. I never thought I would see one of their kind on Rabeen."

"I but meant to travel to the mainland with some pirates," Urdy mumbled.

He had explained his presence on Rabeen before, but only now did I think about what it truly meant. I had believed our crossing of the wild ocean to be a rare thing, the possibility known to few. But maybe a lot more people than I had thought knew about the crossing, a lot more people than I had thought braved the storms.

"I did not realize how many ships are crossing the hardstorms these days." Unease filled me. For centuries, isolation had been our greatest protection. "Do you think," I asked the chronicle keeper, "that the hardstorms are weakening?"

"Most certainly. They are nothing like the storms of my youth. But the wild ocean is still not nearly safe enough for merchant ships. The loss of valuable cargo is too great a risk. More pirate ships cross these days, though, for certain." His gray eyebrows pulled into a disapproving frown. "I heard rumors at the slave market that Emperor Drakhar will soon be sending slavers."

I shuddered. Leave it to the emperor to use every opportunity for his dark purpose. May the spirits defeat him.

"Why, do you think, are the hardstorms weakening?" I asked. "The emperor has a powerful sorcerer at his side, or so they say. Has the sorcerer brought about the change?"

"I could not say, my lady."

Urdy shifted on the boards. "I do not understand wars."

He was watching the soldiers train. "Why go to the trouble of a bloody battle when one man can poison half an army in a single night? A drop of the venom of the silver scorpion into every boot, absorbed into the skin as feet sweat. Or a handful of *porrem* seeds cooked into a spicy soup that disguises the taste. Or the odorless and tasteless saliva of the rekk lizard. A few drops can poison an entire well and not kill the men until the next day, so thousands can drink before they realize anything is amiss."

I stared at him, appalled.

The chronicle keeper frowned as he shook his head. "Are those not the secrets of your morden? I thought assassins tell no tales."

Urdy winced with embarrassment as his gaze cut to us. "As I said, I am not a very good assassin."

I was about to comment, but movement on my right caught my eye, and I turned in time to see Prince Graho's head pop up from below. He climbed up to the deck with care, two of his guards close behind him. They followed the prince as he limped over and slowly lowered himself to the planks between me and Urdy.

His skin was pale in the sunlight, his face too carefully schooled. His fever was gone, but the site of his surgery must have pulled and hurt with every step.

"My Lady Tera."

"Prince Graho." I smiled at his foolish bravery.

Boscor cleared his throat and shifted to sit up straighter.

"And this is Master Boscor," I said, taking the hint. "Leader of the Rabeen Merchant League and Keeper of the Chronicles."

"Former Keeper," Boscor corrected, but seemed pleased that I had used his full title. "Now a grateful refugee." Then, the smile sliding off his face, he indicated the dwarf with his head. "Urdy. Assassin."

"Runaway Assassin," Urdy amended.

The prince took a good long look at him, and the look was not friendly.

Batumar strode over, grumbling under his breath, "Why is it that every time I see you, you are surrounded by men?"

"Mayhap, my lord, it is because I am the only woman on a deck full of sailors and soldiers."

His gaze sharpened as it landed on Urdy. "What business have you with the Lady Tera?"

"My lord," I interjected. "I need to see to his injuries every day."

Batumar's obsidian gaze returned to me, frustration filling it first, then heat, as if he was thinking about throwing me over his shoulder and carrying me off to his sleeping rolls. Then he drew a full breath, and his eyes cut to the prince over my shoulder. Wordless communication passed between them. It lasted but a few heartbeats, then, with a brief nod at us, Batumar returned to practicing with the men.

Prince Graho sat straighter. He glared at Urdy until the dwarf moved a little farther from me. The prince even fixed the chronicle keeper with a hard look, as if Batumar had given my safekeeping into Prince Graho's hands for the time being. Maybe he had. I did not protest. Such trust from the warlord would restore the prince's confidence and manly pride, which, I suspected, had suffered from recent events.

Prince Graho indeed stuck by my side as I worked my small healings that amounted to little more than righting sour stomachs with herbal teas and treating training injuries. The healing claimed my time, but not my full attention. The closer we reached to home, the more worry filled my mind.

I implored the spirits without ceasing: *Let us find our people safe.*

Then, finally, late in the afternoon, a shout rose from the crow's nest once again. "Land!"

I had been about to seek out my dinner, but instead, I rushed to the prow of the ship. I squinted so hard, my eyes hurt, until I could finally make out enough of the landmass ahead to know that we indeed reached Dahru, the south end of the island, the Shahala port city of Sheharree.

Thank you, merciful spirits!

The beauty of our verdant island squeezed my heart. Dahru was a jewel, an enormous emerald floating on the perfect azure sea. A mosaic of fields lay past the harbor city, then began the gently rolling hills with their flowers and birds and tall numaba trees. Far in the distance, our majestic Mountain of No Top watched over our home with its snow-frosted peaks.

As my gaze slid to the north of the harbor, toward my mother's beach where I had grown up and first dreamed of becoming a healer, Batumar came over and claimed my hand, solace in his touch, questions in his eyes.

I shook my head. I did not want to visit my old home. I did not come here to reminisce. I came to save our island.

The warlord kept my hand even as his gaze turned back to the harbor. His posture stiffened. And then my smile too evaporated. We were close enough now so even without a spyglass I could make out the details of the single large ship in port.

I gasped. "A warship!"

CHAPTER ELEVEN

RAIN OF FIRE

"A Kadar ship," Batumar said, his voice tight and the words clipped. The wind whipped his light summer cape. Yet while the cape flitted behind him, the man himself appeared unmovable, as solidly rooted to the deck as our mainmast.

When I had first met him, he had looked exactly what he was—the most powerful warlord of the land. And now... So much more. A hero from myth, a weapon forged in fire.

My gaze lingered on the determined set of his jaw for another moment before returning to the city. Behind the warship, the harbor was just as welcoming as I remembered. *Too trusting*. No defensive walls of any kind blocked the view, no gates, no fortifications. In fact, from this distance, Sheharree's harbor looked a lot like Rabeen's.

My people had no need of fortifications in the past, and I prayed to the spirits times would return when men could live this freely again. For now, I held my breath, fearing for the Shahala, who laid themselves so open to the sea, utterly defenseless.

"The question is, is the ship under Kerghi command?" Prince Graho asked as he limped up to us. He inspected the harbor through the captain's looking glass, then scoffed. "Worse defenses than Rabeen. I would not have thought that was possible. Are defensive structures out of fashion in this part of the world?"

"The Kadar side of the island is fully fortified, my lord," I told him.

"You will like the fortress city of Karamur. But the Shahala are a people of peace."

In a just world, my people should need no protection. Before this war, I would have told the prince and Batumar how inhospitable walls were. I would have been proud that my people were open and welcoming, proud that we valued knowledge above strength. But after having seen what I had seen in this war... A lot of what I used to believe was now in question.

"You must wish to take a closer look." Prince Graho handed me the looking glass.

The buildings still stood, as tightly packed as they ever had been. Sheharree being a southern city, the houses were built tall and close together so the streets between them would receive as much shade as possible. Rabeen's streets had been twice as wide to allow for the transportation of goods and livestock that went in and out of the markets in an endless stream. Most of Rabeen's trees—except for the orchards—had been cut to make room for more market stalls. In Sheharree, every public square was thickly planted, as were many of the rooftops. While Sheharree did brisk trade, its markets were certainly not on the scale of Rabeen's.

"No merchants ships," I noted, and my stomach clenched as I thought of Rabeen's empty harbor. That empty harbor had meant... *But it does not have to mean the same here!*

Yet Sheharree always had its fair share of ships. As a child, I had never been to the docks with my mother without seeing at least a dozen sets of sails. She used to trade her healing services for exotic herbs brought from distant lands. Oh, how I had loved the harbor then—the sights, the sounds, the crush of the crowd. Now its unnatural stillness filled me with a dark sense of foreboding.

I handed the looking glass to Batumar.

He gentled his voice as he said, "We must assume that Sheharree has fallen."

I had thought I was prepared for whatever might face us at the end of our journey. I was not. Images of the piles of dead on Rabeen overwhelmed me. I was not certain I could bear to see the Shahala so destroyed.

If only we had come sooner. If only we had more ships... If only we had more men...

At least no forest of gallows waited for us here. Yet desperation cleaved my heart in half. "If the Kerghi sacked Sheharree, why would they leave a ship? They left none to hold Rabeen. They loaded up what they could and sailed away."

"Rabeen was but a market," Batumar said. "They took what they needed. Nothing left there to guard. Here, the city still stands."

Understanding dawned on me. "The Kerghi khan wants to make Dahru the seat of his new empire. So sparing Sheharree made more sense than reducing it to ruins."

The warlord nodded.

I was glad that all the buildings yet stood. Of course, that the city was not in ruin did not mean my people had not been massacred.

"They left only the one ship here," the prince said as Batumar inspected the coastline. "We do not know where the rest of their fleet is. The single ship could be a trap. We sail into port to fight it, then the rest of the fleet appears at our backs."

Dahru had a ragged coast, dotted with lagoons and inlets, plenty of places for ships to hide. More ships could be but waiting for a signal. Except...

"They do not know that we are coming," I told the prince. "Why would they have a trap waiting?"

"In any case," Batumar lowered the spyglass, "we must land. We did not fully resupply on Rabeen. We must purchase food for our army here. Our ships cannot sail to Kaharta Reh with hungry men. Our army must be strong enough to defeat the Kerghi horde when we find them."

"Aye," the prince agreed, but still looked troubled. Turning, he called to the captain. "We will stay the rest of the day out at sea."

Better to face the enemy in the morning rather than at night. We had taken the same precaution at Rabeen. I silently prayed to the spirits that there would be no other similarities.

"For now," the prince said, "let the people in the harbor think that we are but a ship passing by."

He was firmly back in charge, moving more easily now, not fully recovered but making fast progress. I kept offering him my healing powers, but he still refused them. He wore his sword belt once again. I pitied the commander of his guard if he thought he was going to keep the prince from fighting once we landed.

Shouts rang out as Captain Temro ordered the ship to adjust course and sail out of sight. We had been coming in at an angle, so a slight adjustment would remove us from the horizon in short order. We would be glimpsed, then lost again. Our horns signaled to our two caravels trailing us at a distance to stay farther out to sea. This way, they would not be spotted from land.

While Batumar and the prince discussed strategy, I kept watching the city. I hoped for a hint of a white Shahala robe, but I did not catch a single glimpse. I told myself we were too far out to be able to see people. They were *not* all dead. Then, as our ship adjusted course, the harbor disappeared from sight.

I hated, hated, hated to leave. We had traveled across the wild ocean, through harsh and war-torn lands, and now we had returned. We were home at last. I wanted my feet planted on Dahru's soil without any further delay.

"Just a little longer." Batumar caught my mood as he often did. His gaze filled with understanding as he turned to me. "Tomorrow," he said, "we shall find out how our people fared in our absence."

"Tomorrow." Impatience burned through me.

For certain, I would have been a lot more grateful for being able to spend a night in peace if I had known all that awaited us the following day.

CHAPTER TWELVE

BATTLE FOR THE HARBOR

Our mainmast was on fire, moments after the enemy realized that our ship carried soldiers. It was barely past daybreak, the *Shield* only halfway to harbor.

At least the *Lance* and the *Sword* were yet undamaged. The two caravels stayed out of the reach of the fire arrows, but close enough to reach us in time if our ship capsized and we needed saving from the water.

"Hold still." I was treating a burn wound, doing my best to help a squirming sailor.

"It is unfortunate we can't respond to fire with fire in full measure." Boscor ducked as the enemy loosed another volley of flaming arrows. He was kneeling by my side, in the cover of our water barrels, helping with the wet rags.

The arrows hit, I drew my patient's pain, and he loudly offered his gratitude as he hurried back to his work, yanking burning arrows from the deck and handing them to the few archers we had onboard.

I drew a deep breath and sank back to my heels, giving my body a moment to handle the pain of the burn I had just taken upon myself. "When we left Uramit, we stocked our ship for land battle," I told Boscor as his gaze followed the man. "We did not anticipate finding the Kadar fleet in Kerghi hands."

"And you were not able to fully supply on Rabeen." Boscor's tone was apologetic. "My lady, are you well?"

"Soon enough." My gaze dropped to his abdomen. "I could heal you too. The battle has begun. I will be healing all day. I will be depleted no matter what. One more won't matter."

He hesitated but a blink before he drew back. "Thank you, my lady. But the warlord is right. Save yourself for the fighting men."

Batumar strode toward us, as if he had heard his name being spoken. He gestured toward the enemy ship, handing me the looking glass he carried. "Look at the city."

I fitted the copper tube to my eye, my attention catching on the enormous enemy ship turning toward the *Shield*. "Is it preparing to ram us?"

"Aye."

I could now clearly see the lettering on its side. "The *Barmorid*."

The Kadar named their warships after their High Lords. Barmorid had been the High Lord before Batumar. He had also been my father, although my mother had never told me. I had not found out the truth of my parentage until after her death. By then, Barmorid too had died, before I had a chance to meet him. I had too many questions and nobody to answer them—the least of my problems at the moment.

"Look at the city, my Tera," Batumar urged.

I aimed the copper tube at the jumble of white buildings past the harbor and gasped when I saw people at long last. Then I could finally make out their familiar clothes, the customary Shahala thudrag and tunic.

"My people live! I can see them."

The warlord's hand came to rest on my shoulder. "The Shahala are not fighters. When the enemy came, the locals likely offered little resistance. I would wager there was no widespread battle on the streets."

Good. Smart. I wanted my people to live. Yet I had been at war long enough to feel a twinge of embarrassment that the city had given up its freedom without a fight. The warrior nation of the Kadar would have fought to the death.

I used to think the Kadar bloodthirsty barbarians. And now...

Now my heart belonged to a warlord, and I led an army. As I watched the port coming closer and closer, once again I felt as if I stood not by the railing of the ship, but on a dividing line between cultures and beliefs, straddling two worlds. Or as if I were two Teras—one a healer, maybe a little naïve even after all this time. And the other...a woman who would do whatever it took to save her people.

"Tera!" The warlord ripped the top off the nearest crate and held the lid over my head like a shield just in time to save us from the next wave of flaming arrows.

I ducked and caught sight of Urdy scampering down into the hold for safety. *Don't fall.* But he seemed to manage, even with broken arms. "I will have someone take you below," I told Boscor.

"My lady, I would rather wait out the battle on deck."

I glanced toward the stern. "The captain's cabin is the only cover, and it offers little protection. The roof is fair ruined."

"Still, if the captain would allow me…"

I could see the truth in the chronicle keeper's eyes. When the Kerghi had set the council hall of Rabeen on fire, he had been hiding in a secret closet. He could easily have been trapped and burned to death. With fire arrows flying above us, he was afraid of being trapped down below. Soldiers could carry him down, but if the battle did not go well, if the ship caught on fire and began sinking, in the chaos would anyone remember to bring him up again?

Prince Graho ran up to help, and the warlord handed our makeshift cover to him. "Protect the Lady Tera."

The warlord's gaze cut to mine and held for a moment. He knew as well as I that the prince was not ready for battle. Prince Graho would never have withdrawn to the safety of the other side of the ship for his own sake. He would, however, take me there to save me.

We scrambled away under the protection of the crate top and the shields of the prince's guards, who were running to us from every direction, Commander Durak in the lead. They reached us not a moment too soon, for we barely entered the dubious protection of the captain's half-destroyed cabin when yet another volley of arrows hit our ship.

"Here!" Boscor called us to the safest corner, with the most roof left over it.

Outside, another one of our sails caught on fire. Sailors scrambled for buckets, but the flames spread too quickly. Then Captain Temro's voice rang out over the chaos. "Cut away the sails!"

Even as fire licked the ropes, men raced up the rigging and hacked away at the burning canvas. Soon both sails were cut free and the wind blew them into the ocean, clear of the ship.

Something crashed onto the top of the cabin and my heart jumped into my throat as I whirled to look through the large gap.

Marga. "You scared me."

The tiger roared, pawing at the wood, thinking I was trapped in there. She was going to break me free.

Another volley of fire arrows hit. One flaming missile flew right by her head.

"Marga!" I reached my hands toward her, and she obeyed, leaping down to me, even as a burning, broken beam fell from the ceiling, barely missing her.

When flames danced across the floor, Marga snapped her teeth at them, and I threw my arms around her thick neck so the distressed animal would not swipe at anyone. Far too many of us were crammed into the small space.

I hummed my spirit song to her. *All is well. It will be over soon. Stay.*

I did not want her to bolt, nor did I want her out in the open, exposed to the arrows.

I caught Prince Graho looking toward the nearest hatch, the one that led down to the galley. If he had any dreams of taking us down there, they were cut short. Even as we watched, the hatch doors were slammed shut so no fire arrows could fall down into the hold when the next volley came. A heartbeat later, a burning chunk of rigging plummeted from above, right on top of the doors.

Captain Temro ran past, shouting orders. Secondary sails unfurled. Our ship raced forward.

"Faster!" our captain shouted. "Pull! Turn!"

The prince grunted with frustration next to me, his feet poised to rush out, his hand reaching for his sword, then stalling. He would remain to protect me.

I placed a hand on his hip. When his gaze cut to me, I pleaded, "You must be fit for battle."

He hesitated, then his head jerked once in agreement. And I healed him at last—as much as I was able.

Most of my healing worked by drawing an injury into my own body, then letting my healing spirit repair it there. A burn, a cut, a fever I could take. A broken bone I could soften, then knit together by following the pattern of my own good bones. But the prince's injury I could neither take into me, nor follow the pattern of my own body to repair. Our parts in question were mismatched. I could but take what remained of the infection and draw his pain, this last a temporary measure. As long as his flesh wasn't fully healed, the pain would return. Yet what little I was able to do helped. His tightly drawn eyes relaxed.

"Go!" I shouted over the din.

"Are you certain?"

"They need you more out there than we need you in here."

He was through the broken doorway before I could finish, calling back an order for his guards to remain with me. Commander Durak followed him anyway. I insisted that the rest of them go as well. The prince sent four of them back.

I watched him catch up with the captain, the two in heated discussion, then the captain shouted, making changes. Just in time. We nearly crashed into the Kadar ship as we pulled up alongside it.

The ships scraped along each other. I lurched, grabbing on to Marga for support, and managed to stay on my feet. Our men on deck rushed to the enemy ship to throw their hooks and planks. I watched the ones who hung back, injured. Many were burned, their shirts melted right into the skin on their backs.

My healing power rose, and I felt it arc from my body. It had happened before—at the siege of Karamur for the first time. Mostly, my healing required closer proximity, my hand on my patient. But during the siege, and a few other times since, I had been able to heal from afar.

As much as I had grumbled at Batumar for insisting that I use only herbs during our ocean voyage, now I was grateful to him. My powers were strong and ready.

I took away the agony of the injuries first, dropping to my knees when it became too much. I refused to stop. I repaired burn after burn, man by man, until the blood in my veins turned into a river of pain.

I thought the Shahala might help from the harbor once they sensed my power. At the siege of Karamur, they had been able to join in. But the enemy must have trapped them in their houses, because no help arrived this time. We would free them and soon, I swore to the spirits.

While I healed, our sailors lashed the two ships together, and our soldiers rushed forward to board the *Barmorid*.

Our soldiers fought hard for every foothold. The enemy gave little. From time to time, I even thought it might be the Kerghi who would conquer *us*, but each time, we prevailed. The endless days of practice during our voyage paid off in full. For most of our soldiers, this was their first naval battle, but they fought well.

Men from both sides were cut down and fell into the water. Those of ours that I could reach with my power I did, healing them enough so at least they could swim.

I was stanching a heavily bleeding head injury when a shout rose, drawing my attention to the wharf where Kerghi soldiers clambered into boats, paddling toward us to kill us in the water once our burning ship sank. It did look like it might. Most everything on deck seemed to be burning. Our sailors rushed to put out the flames, but they fought in vain. The flames were winning. Smoke began to fill the cabin.

Marga paced, wild-eyed, shaking her head over and over, trying to shake the smoke from her nostrils. The tiger was near fearless, but she hated fire. She roared when the back of the cabin suddenly collapsed outward and fell into the water below with a splash we could hear even over the battle din.

I shoved her toward the opening. "Go! Jump! Fight!"

She hesitated to leave me. Then I pushed harder, and she loped forward at last, splashing into the sea. In but a moment, shouts of alarm rose from the men below. Then a scream.

Marga was fighting. I could not cower in the cabin any longer either. The fire arrows had stopped, and, in any case, the burning cabin no longer offered protection—just the opposite.

I had healed the worst of the injuries for now. Other tasks yet waited. I gathered my strength, then pushed my way through the Landrian guards, shouting, "We need to fight the fire!"

They had no choice but to follow as I grabbed a bucket and headed to the nearest water barrel that held the last of our precious sweet water. If we won the day, the barrel could be refilled. If we lost, the lack of water would not matter.

"My lady!" Boscor called, standing in the doorway, but I had no time to reassure him.

The guards would not leave me. They helped me instead. Time stopped as we battled the flames, coughing from the smoke and sweating from the heat. But we made progress. We triumphed over the fire.

Marga too had done well. By the time I looked over the railing, wiping soot from my face, only a handful of enemy boats remained in the water. The tiger had been busy turning them over.

Our caravels were catching up with us and joining the battle. Our archers were picking off the enemy survivors who still struggled among the waves. Now and then, Marga swooped in and grabbed one by the neck, then shook the man until his spine snapped.

She knew how to fight, how to kill without being distracted. She did not stop to eat from the prey but moved on to the next enemy and the next. The blood of battle tigers ran in her veins.

Once Lord Karnagh's ship reached us, he gave the command, and the Selorm tigers too jumped into the water. They finished off the last of the enemy, then swam for shore to clear a foothold for us there.

By the time our troops disembarked, the ground they reached was red with blood. The tigers were tiring, but the soldiers from our caravels were fresh. They pushed the enemy back from the harbor, little by little.

Batumar fought in the middle of the battle, his great sword dripping crimson, his tall frame and wide shoulders standing out among the other warriors. He was like an avenging god come to fight among mortals. I checked on him from afar from time to time, but stayed on the flagship, setting bones, stitching up wounds, stopping men from bleeding to death.

Only when I had seen to the worst of the injuries on the ship did I rush to disembark. More of our men needed my help on land.

Prince Graho caught up with me. His clothes were splattered with blood, but I saw no new injury on him save for a cut on the back of his hand, which was shallow enough not to need immediate assistance.

"You must stay on the wharf, my lady." He stepped in front of me to block my way. He took Batumar's request to protect me seriously. "We might have to withdraw to the ship if the battle turns."

I skirted around him and kept going, heading for the nearest man on the ground. "I have full confidence, my lord," I called over my shoulder, "that you will not let danger reach me."

He argued no longer but sent forth two of his men with "Find our wounded and bring them to the Lady Tera right here."

He sent another two men to fetch clean well water from the section of the city our men had already taken, and any clean cloth that could be used for bandages.

The moans of the injured and the cries of the dying surrounded me. I barely noticed as the noise of the battle moved farther from the harbor. The royal guards brought more and more men to me. Prince Graho inspected them first and led me from one to the next, in order of greatest need.

He even patched up some lesser injuries himself, once water and bandages arrived, and barked orders to his guards to do the same. He had seen me work often enough. Now he showed his men what he had learned. His wound must have pulled and pained him once again, but he refused to allow his injury to hold him back.

Soon Shahala healers appeared to help, a handful at first, then a few more, coming in a slow trickle. They lent me their potions and implements freely. All of us worked together. The simple joy of being with my own people once again renewed my strength.

Marga found me too, padding across the field of bodies, sniffing but not touching. I sent her toward the narrow beach next to the harbor to keep her away from the dead and the dying. She could fish in the shallows to fill her stomach.

I healed the injured through the afternoon, working myself into sweaty exhaustion, until Batumar appeared before me at long last at twilight, wearing blood-soaked armor and a darkly satisfied expression.

He smiled that rugged, scarred warlord smile of his that always set my heart aflutter. Then he pulled me up from my knees and into his strong warrior arms, and the look in his eyes changed to one of hunger. He was often…*ravenous* after battle.

His obsidian gaze held mine as he said, "We have the port city."

I searched his face for any sign of pain, running my hands over as much of him as I could reach. "Are you injured?"

"Nay."

Thank the spirits. "Have we lost many?"

"We had the numbers for a speedy victory. Our losses could be much worse."

"What of the enemy?"

"Slain."

"All?"

"Save a few we left alive for questioning."

I shook my head, regret and chagrin stiffening my muscles. He knew this was not my way. I wished always to offer terms of surrender.

"The decision was made." His tone was heavy and hard. "We cannot take prisoners with us into the next battle, nor can we leave them here behind our backs."

The decision was made. He meant Lord Karnagh, Tomron, and himself—three warriors making a warrior's decision.

"If we wish for a different world, must we not make different decisions, my lord?" I asked. "Look at what men who commit senseless murder wrought on Rabeen. The new world we will build must be better."

His gaze would not leave mine. "You cannot win a war with kindness. You have seen this and worse on the mainland."

I shook my head to shake his words from my ears. I believed with all my heart that kindness could not only survive but triumph under even the worst circumstances.

"I thought we would... When we reached home..." I released the pent-up air from my lungs and softened in his arms again. He had won the city. He was hale. Sheharree was free. Now was not the time to quarrel.

"Are we safe here, then?" Prince Graho limped over and broke the momentary silence. "What about enemy reinforcements? Should we not prepare for the possibility?"

"Since none appeared thus far, it is doubtful that they have a great number of troops anywhere near," Batumar responded, letting me go and turning to the prince. "Sheharree is the largest Shahala city, the largest port. The enemy would have put their main southern force here. If other troops are strewn across the Shahala lands, they are smaller bands. Should they arrive, we shall stand against them. But I do not think any of the enemy got away to give warning to the rest."

I spotted Tomron striding toward us, covered in blood. I hurried to meet him halfway. "Are you injured?"

"Kerghi blood for the most, my lady. I need but a good bath to wash it off." He looked at Prince Graho and Batumar behind me. "The city delegation is at the harbor's entrance. They wish to speak to us."

To offer us an official Shahala welcome—including the traditional feast.

I could barely stifle a moan, so much did I wish for a meal. Dinner and a bed on solid ground tonight sounded like a dream—a bed that would not toss under me with every errant wave.

Before I could say anything, Tomron added, "Lord Karnagh sends a message. He is holding some beggar who is demanding to see the Lady Tera. He claims to be the Guardian of the Gate. Lord Karnagh says the youth is likely addled in the head."

Batumar caught up to us, and I shot him a hopeful glance. "To have the Guardian with us... But how could he have reached the island?"

Last we knew, the young Guardian had been trapped on the mainland. When his father had sacrificed his life to close Dahru's Gate, the son had been visiting the Gates of other realms, learning, as had been his duty.

I wiped my hands on the bloody rag that hung from my herb belt. "I must speak with him."

"As you wish, my lady." Tomron sent one of his men to Lord Karnagh, then hurried off to organize the harbor's defenses.

I might have been exhausted to the bone, but Tomron's news went a long way toward restoring my spirits. I smiled at Batumar. "The Guardian of the Gate might be here on Dahru."

Where we were too, home at long last. I pictured our three well-armed ships sailing into Kaharta Reh. We had a chance. We had the element of surprise on our side.

Sheharree was already free. We had won our first battle.

Now we would replenish our food and water. Now we would fill the empty spaces on our ships with Shahala healers to aid us in our battles up north. Now we would fight for freedom for all our people.

Now we would win.

CHAPTER THIRTEEN

SHEHARREE

Blood had dyed my pale brown dress a hundred shades of red, from fresh crimson to dry brown. As happy, excited, and impatient as I was to meet with the Shahala Elders, I wished to clean up beforehand. Except, on the ship, I would have only a bucket for cleaning. In the house of our host, I would be able to have a true bath in a wooden tub. My aching body begged for warm water, enough to cover every patch of my skin.

I sank into the fantasy for a spell, then let it go and resigned myself to cold seawater in a bucket.

"We best clean up before we meet with anyone," I said to Batumar, then turned to Prince Graho. "We shall not make the Shalala delegation wait long."

While the prince sent a message with his guard, Batumar and I walked back to the *Shield*. His black boiled-leather breastplate did not show stains, but it did show myriad scars where swords had tried to cut through to his heart. I walked a little closer to him, close enough so our arms would brush against each other.

"You are beginning to think like a war queen." He smiled as we walked up the plank. Exhaustion deepened the lines around his eyes, but he was clearly satisfied with the day.

So was I, even if we were not finished yet. "We need a tight alliance with the Shahala. We need them to trust us, to believe in us, believe that we can take back the island. They need to see leaders and power. I hope to take at least a hundred healers north with us and have our ships fully resupplied."

"Some of the Shahala farmers and merchants might join our army," Batumar said. "Our soldiers were farmers and merchants once. If a farmer can wield a sickle, he can wield a sword. And merchants carry swords already, to fight off robbers."

I shook my head. The warlord did not know my people as I did. "The Shahala will not join us in the fight. They will help with healing." And I was grateful for that. "But they will go no further."

We crossed the deck and reached the front hatch that stood open, then climbed down below.

I walked into our room first, glancing back at Batumar. "Where is Urdy?"

Batumar scowled. "Ran off already, from the looks of it."

I stripped off my blood-soaked dress. "Wherever he is, I wish him no harm."

"The question is, my Tera, does he wish *us* harm?" Batumar dropped his leather armor into the corner, where it fell with a hard clatter onto the worn wood. "Emperor Drakhar's spies in Uramit no doubt informed the emperor when we set sail from the mainland. And then we find an assassin on the very island where we are most likely to come out of the hardstorms. An enemy ship is anchored in the very harbor on Dahru where we would be expected to go next. All by mere chance?"

"How could the enemy know how long it would take us to cross the storms?"

"The pirates know the hardstorms. It is not that difficult to make a pirate talk. They are happy to take coin."

I was not convinced and let my expression show it. Batumar did not press his point. Neither of us had any proof one way or the other.

We washed hurriedly, while I stole glances at him to assure myself that he truly was unhurt. He had a fresh shirt on before I could catch a glimpse either of his chest or his back. I did see plenty of bruises on his arms and legs, not to mention fresh cuts on top of his old, white scars.

"If you even think about calling those bramble scratches injuries," he warned, "I shall be offended."

I rinsed my hair in the bucket, then combed my fingers through the strands. "You could be sensible, my lord, and let me disinfect them. Even a very small injury can cause a dangerous infection. Prince Graho can vouch for that."

The warlord hesitated for a moment. As he loosened the neck of his shirt, the teasing glint disappeared from his eyes. "Maybe some herbal wash, then, before we bed down tonight."

I bit back a smile. "Very well."

I headed to the door, but he caught my wrist and pulled me against his hard chest. That look of ravenous hunger returned in his gaze. With his free hand, he reached under my chin and tipped my head up. "Do you know what I find most healing, my Tera?"

"Camel urine mixed with powdered goat eyes?" I asked with all innocence. "A wisewoman in Uramit told me it cures near anything."

The warlord claimed my mouth with a warning growl. *Ah.* My eyelids drifted closed, but not before I saw his eyes crinkle with laughter.

He might only have meant to show me the dangers of teasing a warlord, but his kiss stole my breath, my thoughts, my heart. By the spirits, how I wanted this war to be finished.

As if he heard my thoughts, he eased back, promising in a rough tone, "We are back home. We will retake the island. We will live in peace again."

I lay my head against his shoulder and gave thanks to the spirits that we still had each other. I knew how easily Batumar could have been one of the bodies left on the battlefield. He always rushed into the thick of the fighting. On the mainland, I had seen him take on two, even three, of the enemy at once. He gave no thought to his own safety, only to the safety of his men and winning.

I wrapped my arms around him and raised my lips for a second kiss. His fingers tangling in my hair, he responded with heat in his eyes and a carnal smile. And perhaps we would have done more than kiss if Urdy had not walked in at that moment.

The assassin immediately drew back, looking everywhere but at the two of us. His face darkened a shade, as if he was blushing under all that blue ink. "Forgive me, my lord. My lady."

While I wondered whether assassins blushed, Batumar stepped toward him. "Where have you been?"

"In the galley." Urdy inched back and cast a nervous glance toward the other storage room where Ina and her daughter Nessa hid from the world. "The little one was hungry. I could hear her crying through the wall. I went to ask the cook for a biscuit."

My gaze dropped to his empty hands as I came up behind Batumar. "Did you find anything?"

"Yes, my lady. I brought her two apples. I stayed awhile. All the battle noise scared the girl."

The fighting abovedecks must have scared Ina too. The mother and child had been through a bloody battle on Rabeen and seen their entire island demolished. They must have found the day's violence—and the chance that we might lose—terrifying.

I glanced toward their door. I wanted to go to them, but we could not keep the Shahala delegation waiting without giving offense.

"Maybe you could return to them and entertain Nessa with a couple of tales," I suggested to Urdy. "Of happier times," I quickly added.

Urdy cast me a dubious look, and it occurred to me that having been raised at a school for assassins, he might not have seen a lot of happy times. Nor could he talk to the girl about his work.

"Do you remember any of your mother's stories?"

"Vaguely." He scratched his chin. "I remember one about a three-legged rabbit and a fox who could sing."

"Sounds perfect for Nessa."

Urdy cast a worried glance toward Batumar. "With your permission, my lord?"

The warlord nodded, and then off we went, leaving Urdy to his task.

I braided my damp hair as we walked off the ship. Batumar walked with the sure steps of a warlord, his heavy boots thundering on the plank. I followed with more measured steps, careful not to trip on the hem of my most regal dress—red sateen edged in gold, one of a dozen garments the merchants of Uramit gifted me with for liberating their city. Red and gold were the colors of the House of Batumar.

When I finished with my hair, I searched the harbor. "Do you see Marga?"

"The last I saw her, she was off with the Selorm battle tigers."

"Let us hope she stays there. If she returns to the ship, she might scare Ina and her daughter." I was glad Urdy was with them.

Men passed us, carrying the dead—both ours and the enemy's. I was so preoccupied with thoughts of meeting the Shahala Elders, some time passed before I realized the dead were being carried onto the *Barmorid*, the Kadar warship we had retaken from the Kerghi.

I stopped.

Batumar stopped with me and followed my gaze. "We will send them out to sea, then set the ship on fire."

"Why not send them on the *Shield*? Our sails are damaged." So was the deck and the railing, although that damage was mostly surface charring.

"The *Shield* is still seaworthy." Batumar glanced back at our flagship. "Now that we are in port, the sails can be replaced. Our Landrian sailors know their own ship, but not the Kadar warship. In a battle, their knowledge of the ship might make all the difference. Now is not the time to switch."

When his attention returned to the *Barmorid*, it lingered. But then he turned fully away from the water and toward the city. "War is full of sacrifices. Once we win the war, we can rebuild the Kadar navy."

We began to walk again. More lifeless bodies were carried past us, making me think of Rabeen and the dead we had left behind there without a proper funeral. *Once an island of merchants, now an island of vultures.* I thought of the dark presence at the temple ruins at Rabeen's cliffs. A cold shiver ran up my spine, as if that presence reached out and drew a talon over my skin.

"We do not have enough sailors to man a fourth ship." Batumar kept talking. "Nor can we allow the *Barmorid* to fall back into enemy hands. We will face more battles up north. I would not want the Barmorid to reappear behind us under enemy control once again."

I caught the regret in his tone. The last time he had been on Dahru, he had been the High Lord of the Kadar, with the Kadar fleet under his command.

So much had changed in so little a time. For a moment, I could not catch my breath. The stakes were so high. With only three ships and fewer than five hundred men, were we equal to the challenge before us?

We were *not* alone in this, I reminded myself. We were in Sheharree. My people the Shahala would join up with us. We would leave the harbor stronger than we were when we had reached it this morning.

I cast a last glance at the *Barmorid*.

For a moment, looking at my father's name on the side of the ship, he felt more real to me. And for that moment, I felt the same regret that I had caught in Batumar's tone. Yet I understood that, as he had said, the ship was only one of the many sacrifices we would have to make.

"Sometimes I forget that I am half Kadar," I told Batumar. In my heart and mind, I was a Shahala healer, nothing more, nothing less, the only thing I had ever wanted to be.

The warlord claimed my hand. "As long as you do not forget that you are wholly mine."

* * *

Prince Graho and Lord Karnagh waited for us at the entrance to the harbor, the two in quiet discussion.

The prince wore his best royal garment. I had not seen him come onto the ship. His guards must have brought his clothes to him to save him the walk.

Lord Karnagh too had changed, into clean britches and a green velvet doublet embroidered with Selorm battle scenes and tigers. The empty sleeve hanging by his side did not make him any less dashing.

Only Tomron was missing. He would not join us until he'd fully secured the harbor. He was most thorough with his duties.

Lord Karnagh saw us coming first and offered a look of apology. "We had the youth who claims to be a Guardian, but he disappeared. Everyone who saw him and can identify him is out searching for the man."

I swallowed my frustration while he added, "We will find him, my lady."

I had no time to explain how important the Guardian was to our cause, for the Shahala delegation arrived and stopped to wait for us on top of the wide stone steps that separated the harbor from the city proper.

Like ancient statues they were in their long white robes that barely moved in the wind. The only difference between their garments and those of other Shahala men was the wide strip of red embroidery around the neck of the Elders' robes. The embroidery showed the sacred symbols of our people—representing each of the nine original tribes.

The men all had long white beards that rustled with each gust. The women too were old, grandmothers many times over. They inclined their heads without smiles.

Surprise slowed my feet. In the Elders' stiff stances and even stiffer expressions, I detected a range of emotions—from resentment to outright anger. I had expected a warm welcome and gratitude for the liberation of the port city. I had expected offers of food and accommodation for our army.

I was still frowning when we stopped at the bottom of the wide staircase and returned their bow. The harbor's famous ninety-nine limestone steps stood between us as each group measured up the other.

At least two hundred townspeople turned out to watch the proceedings, gathering behind the Elders. As my gaze slid over them, the familiar features of one of the men caught my attention.

Despite the short beard that was a shade darker than his blond hair, recognition flared. "Koro!"

In but a blink of an eye, countless memories flew back to me: long talks, longer walks, climbing trees together on the hillside.

Koro's eyes widened. The delegation waited with decorum, projecting an air of authority, but Koro broke away from the spectators and skirted around the Elders before descending the steps at a run, his arms opening as a stunned smile split his face. "Tera? Tera!"

He shook his head in wonder as he reached me, then laughed as he picked me up and swung me around. I had to brace myself on his shoulders, laughing with him. Here was my childhood friend, alive and well.

He set me down at last but kept staring at me, searching my face. He held me tightly by the arms, as if to make sure I was real. "Tera, it is you. Thank the spirits!"

He was far from the boy I had left behind. He was a grown man, a large man, handsome, his brown eyes dancing as he looked me over.

"Are you well? Your family?" I asked. His father had been one of the richest merchants in the city. "Your ships are not in the harbor."

Koro's face clouded. "All lost. The Kerghi took everything of value. They killed my parents when my father would not surrender the keys to his warehouses. I escaped because the healers hid me as one of their own. I have been pretending to be a healer's apprentice since."

I reached for his hand—as I had done countless times in our childhood—and squeezed it. "I am truly sorry."

I was saddened by the news and yet overjoyed at seeing Koro once again. A moment passed before I noticed the shadow that fell over us.

Batumar.

The warlord uttered not a single word, yet somehow that silence was more threatening than his tiger growls. I pulled back. Koro reached after me, oblivious to danger, his gaze riveted to my face. Batumar shifted closer.

Oh, for the spirits' sake!

As I tried to think of what to say to defuse this new—and most unnecessary—tension, Prince Graho stepped in, clasping Koro's arm and pulling him away from me, introducing himself. "Prince Graho of Landria."

Koro inclined his head. "Koro, my lord."

"Lord Batumar and *his* Lady Tera," the prince nodded toward us.

Koro kept smiling as wide as would fit on his face. "I know Tera well. She and I were intended." His gaze found me again. "I held on to your bride price long after you disappeared. But that too was taken by the Kerghi. I never forgot you. Not for a day."

Batumar held still, the way Marga held still before pouncing on her prey.

Prince Graho put an arm around Koro's shoulders and smoothly drew Koro back up the stairs with "I hope there is a meal prepared. We are all famished. Even on the other side of the world, I have heard tales of Shahala hospitality."

Lord Karnagh went with them, walking on Koro's other side, glancing back at Batumar with humor glinting in his eyes.

Batumar's gaze followed them for a while before he turned to me. He offered me his arm. He walked up the steps with me, but his eyes said he wished to return me to the ship.

We did not get far before Koro realized he was getting ahead of us, and he turned around, taking a few steps back. "Tera, I barely dared hope to see you again. I know it has been a long time since we were intended for each other, but..." He swallowed, his eyes misting over.

When he looked as if he might embrace me again, Lord Karnagh nudged him forward. "Best keep your distance, young man. She is more dangerous than she used to be. She broke my bones, she did."

Prince Graho, never to be outdone, added, "She cut off my..." He flashed a look loaded with meaning.

He kept talking into Koro's ear until they reached the Elders. Koro glanced back at me again, this time with impossibly wide eyes.

I bit back a tired laugh.

Batumar was less than amused. "Who is the ill-mannered pup?"

"An old friend. He is a good man. A kind man."

"As long as he knows if he calls you his *intended* one more time, I intend to cut him in half."

Before I could talk Batumar out of murder, Marga and Tigran came bounding up to us, sniffing toward the strangers. The tigers must have caught plenty of fish in the shallows. Their bellies were near dragging on the steps. In addition to filling up, fishing had also washed the blood from their fur, for which I was grateful.

I patted Marga's shoulder. "Thank you for your help in battle."

I could swear her maw stretched into a satisfied smile.

The Shahala did not draw back in fear as we approached bracketed by two tigers. My people had an affinity for animals, and an understanding of them. They merely kept a deferential distance.

The Elders bowed once again as we reached them.

Batumar inclined his head. Prince Graho returned the bow in measure. So did Lord Karnagh.

I bowed the deepest, to show proper respect. "May the spirits heap their blessings upon you and upon your people."

"The spirits favored us greatly by bringing you." They greeted us as was customary for a traveler. "May they watch over you every step of your journey."

Their words were as sweet to my ears as honey drizzled over breakfast cakes. I smiled at the pure pleasure of hearing the language of my childhood. *Home.* I was truly home at last.

Gormil, who had often sought my mother for advice on rare injuries, stepped forward. His face crinkled with the many lines that marked his age. "Blessed be the spirits for your return, granddaughter. We feared you perished."

His words were welcoming, yet his tone sounded reserved. Was he troubled over our losses? We had been prepared for worse. We had *been* through worse. But I would have time over our meal to recount the tale of our long journey. For now, I said, "Blessed be the spirits for protecting Sheharree and her people."

The wrinkled faces before us clouded.

"All could not be protected," Gormil said, then forced a more polite expression once again. "Come eat with us and rest, and tell us all you can, for we are eager to hear how you have come to be at our shores and why."

Yet his tone did not warm. I glanced at Batumar. If he noticed anything amiss, he did not show any sign. I followed his example and asked no questions.

The delegation led us to the Square of Gathering, where even more people waited. Our warriors drew many curious glances. Yet, oddly, the mood of the crowd was less than celebratory.

The towns we had liberated on the mainland always greeted us with cheers. I was embarrassed that my people did not, for I knew how much our soldiers had sacrificed to be here.

Koro turned back to me with another wide smile. "Tera, do you think—"

Prince Graho and Lord Karnagh distracted him. Then, before he could speak to me again, we reached the House of the Elders.

The House of the Elders, in the middle of the Square of Gathering, had but one room, large and round. The Elders held meetings, resolved disputes, and dispensed advice here.

People crowded into the room behind us. The space stood open to all, at all times. Such was the way of the Shahala. We did not need inner chambers and secret rooms. My people preferred to do all things in the open.

We sat at the Elders' table in the middle, the wood worn from centuries of use, the cut a round center slice from a numaba tree, as thick as a man's wrist and richly carved with blessings. Koro did not sit with us, but stood with the crowd.

The nine carved doors that represented the nine Shahala tribes allowed in a cross breeze that carried the familiar scents of my childhood. The south end of the island had myriad flowers that grew nowhere else but here, their sweet aroma underscored by the faint, salty scents of the nearby sea.

The flat pebbles of the floor came from the quarry in the woods where, a lifetime ago, Koro and I had often played. The white columns that held up the round roof had been carved out of the limestone of the very hillside that protected my childhood home from the desert winds.

Everywhere I turned, every detail whispered *home*. Yet I could not sink into the comfort of the thought.

Men and women gathered around us. Some I recognized by sight if not by name. A few stared; others avoided my gaze. I knew some of my people had disapproved when they had heard that I, daughter of Chalee, Tika Shahala—the highest order of healers—had become the Kadar High Lord's concubine, but after the siege of Karamur where the Shahala had helped the Kadar, I thought the old resentments of our people had disappeared. Yet I could feel tension in the air.

"I fear all will not go here as we expected," I whispered to Batumar under my breath.

CHAPTER FOURTEEN

SEEKING ALLIANCE

"How do the Shahala fare?" Batumar, sitting on my right, asked the Elders, and the room around us quieted.

Gormil answered, his tone measured, almost ceremonial. "As you know, my lord, when at first the Kerghi came through our island's Gate, we lost a great many of our number. But even more of us found shelter and safety in Kadar strongholds, for which our nation is most grateful to yours."

Batumar nodded. "Yet you left the protection of our walls. You would have been welcome to stay."

Gormil's posture stiffened. "Once the siege of Karamur was over, we thought the most severe threat to our lands ended. Our people wished to return home, where the spirits of our ancestors live."

"And ignore the five hundred enemy soldiers barricaded around the Gate?" Batumar's voice held no censure, only puzzlement. He was a military leader with a military mind.

"Aye, my lord. We thought the enemy would remain behind their makeshift fortification until spring, and then the Kadar would march up the mountain and defeat them."

The muscles in Batumar's face tensed. "We did not have the numbers." He paused before he asked, "Have you news of the far outposts on the edge of the desert?"

He was asking after his daughters. I held my breath for the answer.

A puzzled frown pulled Gormil's gray eyebrows together. "Those are in

Kadar territory. We know little of them."

Batumar showed none of his disappointment but moved on to a question to which Gormil would more likely know the answer. "How many Kerghi soldiers sailed on the *Barmorid*?"

"Two hundred or thereabout." The Elder fell silent. His cheeks, papery from old age, flushed. He shifted. "You must think the number none too great, but they were trained fighters, well armed. Our people could not stand against them. Those who resisted were cut down. Some ran into the forests and hid. A great many surrendered. We believe in the preservation of life above all."

"How were this many of the Shahala spared?" I asked, grateful that the enemy did not follow their usual tactics.

"The Kerghi saw our healing powers at the battle of Karamur." Pride crept into Gormil's tone. "Through their new khan, Verik, I believe word has reached Emperor Drakhar's ears, and the soldiers were given orders to keep us alive and leave us in our homes. This way, we can keep serving all who need us."

My blood chilled.

Keep us alive and leave us in our homes.

Not to serve all who needed them, however, but to serve Emperor Drakhar. The Shahala would be enslaved just as much as all the other conquered nations. And what would happen when the emperor realized that not all Shahala had healing powers? What would happen to the merchants and the teachers, the shopkeepers and shoemakers?

I drew a deep breath. "We have it on good authority that the new Kerghi khan wishes to break with the emperor and create his own empire. He wants to make the islands of Mirror Sea his and Dahru his seat. If the Kerghi succeed, the emperor might not be long in charge. And if the Kerghi fail and the emperor destroys the insurrection against him... What will you do when he has you transported to the capital of the empire to serve only him and his nobles?"

Gormil shook his head with impatience. "Emperor Drakhar is the greatest might in all the lands. He is not an uncivilized ruler. He has his own physicians in his cities, whom he holds in high regard. He is a learned man. I heard said that his castles are filled with art and all manner of inventions from all around the world."

"All stolen!" The words burst from me on a wave of frustration.

"How fare the other Shahala cities?" Batumar asked, no doubt holding the map of the island in his mind, ready to mark off enemy positions.

I fell silent, ashamed of my useless fight with Gormil, ashamed that Batumar had thought to ask about my people first.

"The traveling traders brought us news," Gormil said, then listed the handful of major ports. "Each is under the power of an enemy captain, with a small contingency of warriors. Most of our villages inland have not been overrun."

Prince Graho leaned forward. "Do the Kerghi have warships in every port?"

"No, my lord. Not to my knowledge. Only the *Barmorid* here. But ours *is* the largest Shahala port."

Batumar flashed me a meaningful look that said he did not believe the Kadar ship in Sheharree was a coincidence.

"Will you liberate all our cities, my lord?" Gormil asked, his face a careful mask.

Batumar responded with a heavy "Nay."

Prince Graho, on my left, appeared torn. He opened his mouth as if to make a case, but then he shook his head. "We must not delay. We must not give the enemy time to discover that we are here. Best would be to sail as soon as we can and take them unawares."

Gormil did not beg for help or protest our unwillingness to give it. Instead, he appeared relieved.

"You could free your cities yourselves," Prince Graho suggested. "You outnumber the invaders."

"Healers do not fight," Gormil shot back immediately, voice thick with disapproval.

He does not want us to free those Shahala cities, I thought as I reached for a cup of water. Gormil wanted no more war. He felt safe under the emperor's protection. The Shahala would survive, and for Gormil, that was enough.

I drew a deep breath. "We wish to take healers with us to aid us in battle, as many as would volunteer."

He avoided my gaze, looking at the other Shahala instead. "We are not to leave our homes. On the emperor's orders."

"You are content to live in captivity?" Lord Karnagh inquired, his tone puzzled, bordering on condemnation.

Gormil sat up straighter, his demeanor very much that of an Elder, a leader of the community, a man who spoke with the full authority of the nation.

"Our people the Shahala come from nine tribes, each named after a founding father," he began, raising his voice now so all in the room could hear. "We are the Roosha, the Torno, the Shelba, the Mortir, the Zetra, the Fertig, the Lormen, the Tuzgi, and the Pirta. Once, we lived on a faraway island, surrounded by greedy and immoral kingdoms. When those kingdoms angered the spirits beyond forgiveness, the spirits brought down the very sky upon them. Only the Shahala escaped, with the help of the spirits. We came through the crumbling island's Gate to Dahru, an uninhabited island at the time, where we made our new home. To live in peace forever." He emphasized the last words.

97

The Shahala around us murmured in agreement. Batumar raised an eyebrow at me. Whether the Shahala or the Kadar had first come to the island was a centuries-old contention between our people.

"When we received this new home from the spirits," Gormil went on, "our ancestors pledged to avoid all the ways of evil, all greed and violence. Our lands have not seen war in hundreds of years."

Because the Shahala had made an alliance with the Kadar, I wanted to say. The Kadar were a warrior nation and protected the island for us. Our years of peace had been paid for with their blood.

Gormil was not finished. "This past year, our healers helped the Kadar during Karamur's siege. We participated in war. And now we have foreign soldiers in our cities."

The Shahala Elders around the table muttered about offended spirits while Gormil concluded his speech with "We will heal all who come to us for help, but we will not go to battle alongside any army."

The rest of the Elders murmured their support, and so did some of the common people in the room.

Batumar looked at me, anger shimmering in his eyes. I gave my head a slight shake. I did not want him to argue. We could not force the Shahala to be our allies if they did not wish it.

Yet I was heartbroken at their refusal. All that time we'd been gathering an army on the mainland, I'd never once thought we would have to fight alone in this war.

I could see the anger in the tight set of Gormil's lips and shoulders clearly now. As understanding dawned on me at last, I folded my hands tightly together on my lap, cursing myself for having been blind.

I had seen our arrival to the city as a liberation. But my people considered the Shahala lands sacred, home to the healing spirits of their ancestors, lands that should be kept pure from greed and war and blood. Yet today, in the port city, we had massacred men. Batumar said it himself: we had given no quarter.

The Shahala in me, all that I had once been, wanted to apologize. But I also led an army, and I had a difficult time accepting that Gormil did not grasp what stood at stake should we lose.

The arrival of dinner cut off further conversation, and perhaps just as well. What more was there to say?

A handful of women served us. I turned my attention to them and the simple wartime fare: a little meat with a lot of mashed turnips. Not the traditional Shahala feast, but I was grateful for what we were given. The Kerghi soldiers who had been stationed in the port city lately had probably requisitioned the best food for themselves already. I imagined the men and women of Sheharree did not have much left to share.

Batumar must have realized that as well, but still he said, in a tone that brooked no resistance, "We *will* gather supplies before we sail. And pay for them."

Gormil carefully inclined his head. "We will find enough provisions to last you until you reach the next harbor."

Food might be in short supply, but he understood that we were the army in the port now and could take what we needed, even if he disagreed.

My stomach twisted. The meal sat in a clump in my stomach. The Shahala Elders viewed us as little better than the Kerghi hordes. They wanted their precious peace above everything.

Peace over freedom. Had they always been this way? Had I been simply too young and naïve to comprehend it?

I understood at last that when I was healing the injured soldiers on the wharf earlier in the day and the Shahala healers did not come at once but only showed up later, they did so not because the enemy had trapped them in their houses. They stayed away because they did not want to declare for either side before the battle was decided.

I spoke up. "We will also need all the healing herbs you can spare."

Gormil hesitated for only a moment. "Of course." Then, perhaps to distract me from asking for more, or perhaps from true curiosity, he asked, "Would you tell us of your journey?"

A voice called from the back of the crowd. "Some say you came through the hardstorms. Did you go through the storms to the mainland, then? The army you brought are all foreigners."

Batumar's gaze hardened, as if he was on the verge of pointing out that while those foreigners had fought today for Dahru, the Shahala themselves had not.

Since *that* was a discussion best avoided, I launched into our tale, and, as the others ate, I recounted our long journey. Batumar, Lord Karnagh, and Prince Graho seemed content to let me speak.

I was recounting the destruction of Rabeen when one of our soldiers ran in. "Three of the enemy prisoners escaped!"

The soldier was allowed through at once. He dropped to his knees in front of me, breathing hard, lowering his head as if for the executioner's axe. "A boat slipped out of the harbor, heading north, my lady."

Prince Graho jumped to his feet, then groaned and braced himself on the table against the pain from his wound. "Send the quickest skiff in the harbor after them."

The soldier dipped his head deeper. "The prisoners stole the last skiff in the harbor. Twice as fast as any of the small vessels that remain. We sank most of the boats while fighting the enemy."

Gormil was on his feet and moving to the prince. "My lord, may I?"

Prince Graho nodded and thanked him. A fleeting touch was all it took. The lines of pain cleared from the prince's face. He was healed.

Batumar pushed his chair back as he also rose. When he glanced at me, his expression said he did not think we had much hope of catching the escaped Kerghi.

Yet we had to try. We had to apprehend the men.

In the next battle we would have to fight, the element of surprise was the only advantage we had.

CHAPTER FIFTEEN

KORO

While I thanked the Shahala for their hospitality, Prince Graho hurried off to see if he might yet find a fast boat somewhere, or one with only minor damage the shipwrights could quickly repair. Lord Karnagh went with him. Batumar and I stayed a few more moments to talk to the Elders about the supplies we would need, then we hurried after the others.

We barely left the Square of Gathering when Koro pushed through the crowd.

"Tera!"

Batumar's chest rumbled.

"Koro can help me bring the survivors of Rabeen ashore," I told the warlord, stopping to wait. "They will be safe here in Sheharree when we sail off to battle. The Shahala will see to it that they are fully healed."

Koro caught up with us before the warlord could respond. "I would be happy to help the Lady Tera, my lord, any way I can."

Batumar glanced between us then pulled me into his arms, kissing me most soundly, taking me by surprise. The warlord was not normally given to expressing his affections in front of others. But this time, he stopped only after he turned my knees to the consistency of fish jelly.

"I will see you shortly, my Tera," he said in a brusque tone before striding off with a last look at Koro—a look that said if Koro put one foot wrong, he was going to find himself breakfast for tigers.

"I have heard tales of him." My old friend's gaze followed the warlord for several moments. "I did not think he could be more frightening than the tales. Yet you seem content to be by his side."

"He is not as harsh as he appears." At least, not to me. His enemies certainly had reason to fear him.

In the old days, I would have taken Koro's hand. Now I resisted the familiar gesture and simply started toward the ship instead.

"Come. I shall tell you everything." And as we walked, I did tell him the full tale, my life as it had been since I had been sold into slavery, ripped from our Shahala shores. How Batumar found me and how I became his concubine.

As Koro and I climbed the ladder down into the hold, he looked down at me over his shoulder and gave me a pained smile. "The warlord has your heart."

"He does."

"They said you were dead," he said as I stepped off the ladder. "Lost. You and the High Lord both. But you returned with ships and men, with Lord Batumar and the crown prince of Landria. With the Selorm lords and their tigers." He smiled again, this time with melancholy, stepping down next to me. "Once, we climbed trees together. And here you are now, a legend."

While he had lost his parents, the family business, their trading ship, everything. He had once been the son of a wealthy trader, his life mapped out before him. He had been ready to follow in his father's footsteps, as I had been ready to follow in my mother's. Yet the spirits had arranged for us different futures.

I did take his hand then. "I am no legend. But we *will* free our people."

His face flushed with frustration. "I have no sword to offer."

"Offer then to care for the survivors of Rabeen. I ask of you only that. We brought two men and a woman with her daughter."

He squeezed my fingers. "You have my pledge, Tera. I will care for them."

We reached the storage rooms, and I knocked on the first door, calling out before entering.

Ina still drew back and kept her daughter close, but her stance was not as defensive as before. She was no longer balancing on an imaginary line, on the sharp edge of a decision between fleeing or attacking.

She had not yet lost her gauntness, but she had washed her clothes and her daughter's in a bucket at one point. Their hair was combed now and braided. They no longer looked as desolate as when we had found them.

"This is Koro, an old friend, a good man whom I know well," I began my introductions. "Sheharree is free. You would be safe if you stayed here. Koro has offered his help."

Ina's gaze traveled down Koro's long robe that clearly marked him as something other than a soldier. Then her gaze returned to his face, and she watched him as if she wanted to see inside him, while Koro simply smiled, unmoving, unthreatening. His kindness sat plainly in his eyes. He tried neither to convince the woman nor rush her.

"What would I do here?" Ina asked.

"I am a healer's assistant," Koro said in a friendly tone. "You could do the same, growing and sorting herbs. I could show you how, if you wish."

"We would be fed? There is food here?"

"Not much now, but the Kerghi hordes came after the spring planting. The seed was in the ground, so they could not take that. We will have a harvest come autumn." He watched as Ina drew her daughter close, indecision still the ruling emotion on her face, and he added, "There is a hall for women who assist with the brewing of medicine. The vats have to simmer days on end. If you can help with that, you and your daughter could stay there."

Ina had more questions, and Koro—soft-spoken, patient—answered all of them.

Nessa piped up too. "Do you know if there is a dolly for me to play with where we are going?" she asked in a breathless tone, looking at Koro shyly, with mostly downcast eyes. "I lost my dolly when we were running from the soldiers." Her face turned pinched. "'Twas a corncob doll. She had blue eyes like mine."

"I do not know how to make one, but I can bring you a basketful of corncobs and cloth for a dress," Koro said, and that was the right answer.

Nessa's expression softened into a small smile.

"Will you stay, then?" I asked Ina, because it seemed important that she would follow her own will. Mother and daughter were walking into a new life. They had to choose to build it.

"We will, my lady." She blinked rapidly, then gave up holding back the tears and wiped her eyes instead with the back of her hands. She sniffed, inclining her head in a quick bow. "Thank you for bringing us here."

We went in search of Urdy and Boscor next. Sailors rushed around us, repairing the ship and preparing it to sail in the morning. A multitude of torches lit up the *Shield*, pushing back the darkness.

We found the two men together, Urdy having just brought the chronicle keeper some drinking water. Boscor accepted the tin cup, but with a narrow-eyed look, not bothering to hide his reservations, as if he fully expected poison.

When Koro offered his hospitality to the pair, Urdy immediately objected, drawing himself as tall as possible. "What days I have left, I would spend it in your service, my lady. I owe you my life. I shall not shirk such a debt."

"You owe me naught, Urdy," I told him, despairing. "And you will have a long life yet. There are many healers in the port city here. You will be fully healed tonight."

"I live only until the assassin master finds me." He sounded certain. "I am a runaway assassin. The morden will not let me live. I brought shame to his school and his reputation."

As I watched the tight set of his eyes, I understood that he felt safer with us, under our protection. And I knew that, no matter what Batumar might say, I could not turn Urdy away.

"I owe you my life as well, Lady Tera," Boscor spoke up next with a quiet dignity. "I am too advanced in age to serve you well, but allow this old chronicle keeper to witness the battles ahead. I lost Rabeen's scrolls. Recording the liberation of Dahru and the vanquishing of the Kerghi will erase some of my shame. Allow me this favor, my lady. Allow me to witness and record and go to my grave knowing a small measure of peace."

His losses were written on his lined face and spoke to my heart. Yet while Urdy was a trained assassin, Boscor was but a merchant and a chronicle keeper. A chronicle keeper he might be, but chronicles were written *after* battles, in quiet rooms. He had no place on a battlefield.

"We go into mortal danger," I reminded him.

"Lady Tera…" For the first time, the haughty demeanor of the Leader of the Merchant League of Rabeen disappeared, and he was as close to begging as I had ever seen him.

I gave a small nod. "As you wish."

"Thank you, my lady." His voice thickened with gratitude and relief.

I glanced over at Koro, who was entertaining Nessa by balancing a tin cup on his nose. Nessa's eyes were round with wonder, while Ina's hands fluttered by her side. She was leaning forward, as if ready to grab her daughter back at the slightest sign of danger. But at least she did not attack Koro when he tossed the cup to the girl and Nessa caught it with a surprised squeal. If anything, as Nessa tried to balance the cup on her own nose, Ina's expression softened, if only for a moment.

Koro's gaze cut to me. *Shall we?*

The four of us walked off the ship together, while Boscor and Urdy stayed behind. Urdy sat down next to the chronicle keeper. Boscor shifted away from the assassin, but he did drink his water.

At least fifty of our soldiers guarded the harbor, scanning the night sea. Ina shot them a wary glance as we walked off the ship, then her gaze moved past them, at the city that looked magical with the moon and stars above, and the light of oil lamps flickering in every window. I could only imagine what that meant to her. *People, community, protection.*

She moved forward hesitantly, toward the lights, Nessa by her side.

Koro was in no rush to leave. His lips curved into a bittersweet smile. "In another life…" He paused, shook his head. "I missed you, Tera."

"We will free Dahru." I gave him a quick hug before drawing back. "In the spring, bring Ina and Nessa to Karamur to visit. I think Nessa would like to see the fortress city and the High Lord's castle."

Ina's husband had been a goatherd. I doubted they had been outside of Rabeen before this.

Koro's gaze turned to the mother and daughter, lingering on Ina. "She is not broken. She has strength in her eyes."

I grinned. "You should have seen her take on a tiger. You had better watch yourself with her."

My friend's expression held nothing save admiration as he looked after the woman for another moment.

We said our farewells, and I watched them go, Nessa in the middle, her little hand firmly in her mother's. Their close link reminded me of mine with my own mother, Chalee. I'd still had her at that age. Longing filled my heart for her love and wisdom. I had learned much since her death, but still I wished for her advice. Of all the people I had ever known, she had the purest heart.

I wished Ina and Nessa well and asked the spirits to keep them together for a good long time. Just before they disappeared from sight, Nessa gave her free hand to Koro, who took it without pause, as if walking hand in hand with the little girl was the most natural thing in the world.

Anyone walking past them would have mistaken them for a family.

"I am glad the pup gave up on trying to steal you from me," came Batumar's raspy voice at my back.

I shook my head, but I was smiling. "Koro is a friend."

"I saw the truth in his eyes when he rushed down those harbor steps to greet your arrival." Batumar slipped his arm around my waist and gathered me flush against his chest. "You are mine."

"Should I embroider the words BELONGS TO LORD BATUMAR onto the bodice of my dress while we sail to Kaharta Reh?"

"That would be best," he said in all seriousness.

I groaned at his response, but stayed in his embrace, looking toward the city.

"Are you sad to see them go?" the warlord asked. "They will be safe here. From Kaharta Reh, we shall go to Karamur and cut off the head of the snake. The fighting should not return to Shahala lands."

I filled my lungs with cool night air and put my hands over his. "I was thinking... I would like to have a daughter one day."

The warlord's agreement was a deep rumble as he turned me in his arms to face him. His rugged face held undisguised love and need. "Aye."

A daughter with Batumar's obsidian eyes.

My breath caught at the image that readily appeared in my mind.

I wanted a daughter to teach as my mother had taught me. Except... My mother had left me too early, with too many lessons untaught.

"When this war is over," I told the warlord, "I shall write a scroll full of advice for what daughters we might have."

He searched my gaze. "What kind of advice?"

"*Do not go on a long sea voyage with hundreds of men and a possessive warlord* will be the first on the list."

Laughter brought light to Batumar's face as he lowered his lips toward mine. He gave me a soft kiss at first, then his mood turned in an instant, and I was pressed against his wide chest while he kissed me harder.

"Lady Tera!"

Batumar gave a murderous growl. I very nearly growled with him. But instead I stepped back, searching the harbor for the man who called my name.

A moment passed before I spotted the scrawny beggar elbowing his way through our men. He had the look of a war refugee—clothes threadbare and torn, and none of it clean. Gaunt he was, a man who knew hunger.

Two of our soldiers moved to stop him, but I called to them to let him through, my heart leaping with joy as I recognized him. He did not wear the Guardian's usual brown robe but the garments of a simple peasant, tan britches with a tan linen shirt, his dark hair longer than I remembered.

I'd met him but once before, in the Forgotten City, when he had interrupted his travels and study of the Gates to be with his mother on her deathbed. We had spent only a short time together, but we had become good friends.

His face lit up with a smile as he broke into a run, opening his arms, losing all the decorum Guardians normally displayed.

As I knew I would be thoroughly and tightly embraced, I warned Batumar, "The young Guardian of the Gate is like a brother to me."

Humor lit up the warlord's eyes. "Are you implying, my lady, that I am a jealous beast?"

Relieved that I did not have to worry about Batumar unsheathing his sword, I hurried into the Guardian's arms and did greet him like a long-lost brother.

"The spirits be praised!" His gaze darted between Batumar and me. "I thought we lost you and the warlord. The darkest rumors—" He bit off the rest. "Yet others said you came south, so I followed, hoping to find you here. When I saw Sheharree occupied..." His expression turned from elation to grief.

"How come you to be on Dahru?" I stepped back. "Last we knew, you were trapped on the mainland."

"I was traveling across Felep to learn as much as I could about all the working Gates, and even visited a few ruined ones." The Guardian paused, his shoulders collapsing. "I was in Canvar when I felt the Gate of the

World shudder on Dahru."

"Your father closed it to stop more enemy warriors from reaching our island."

The Guardian gave a sober nod. "Ours is a powerful Gate. The most powerful of all. The only Gate of the World."

From the way he said the words, I knew that when he felt Dahru's Gate tremble closed, he had understood that closing the Gate of the World required great power, more than a mortal man could survive. He had known then that his father had given his life.

I had grieved the old Guardian at the time, and now I grieved him anew. And I grieved for his son, born to duty, his life thus far spent on learning. He'd had few opportunities to truly get to know his father, and now it was too late.

"You must have found it difficult to be trapped on the mainland." Away from his home, and away from the Gate his duty demanded he should guard.

"Aye." The single word sounded tight with pain.

"But you found a way to return," Batumar said in a tone of frank approval.

"Not long after I arrived at Canvar," the Guardian told us. "Emperor Drakhar's army took the city. I fought and was struck down. I woke buried beneath the bodies left on the street. In the moonlight, I exchanged my clothes for those of a farmer who lay dead atop me, then I dragged myself to the city wall, hoping to recover enough by morning to flee."

I smiled at him with all the relief in my heart. "I am glad to see you did."

"Regaining my strength required a few days, my lady. In the meanwhile, I heard that the emperor had a sorcerer by the name of Drav, who was trying to open Dahru's Gate of the World using the Gate of Canvar. The sorcerer bound a Guardian from the eastern lands to his will by bending the man's mind." The young Guardian shuddered, and I saw fear in his eyes for the first time. "I wanted to stop them. I did not want my father to have died in vain."

"What happened?" Batumar asked, his tone heavy, as if he already knew the answer.

"I reached them just as they opened Dahru's Gate of the World," the Guardian said. "I came through the Gate of Canvar to Dahru with the first wave of mercenaries as one of them, wearing stolen armor. I thought I might yet be able to close our Gate of the World again from our side. I am of the island. This Gate is mine." He shook his head. "As I tried, the sorcerer felt me and sent his men through to capture me."

"And then?" I asked with a fearful heart, thinking of what the sorcerer of Ishaf had done to Batumar.

"They pressed me to disclose the whereabouts of the Forgotten City of my people," the Guardian said at last. "They also demanded that I tell them of any weakness in the defenses of the Kadar's fortress city of Karamur, so that the Kerghi might breach the walls."

"Have the Forgotten City and Karamur fallen, then?" Batumar asked, and I held my breath.

"They were both free when I left," the Guardian responded. "I did not give the enemy what they sought. But the cities might have fallen since I last saw them. The Kerghi hordes were coming through our Gate as fast as they could. And the Kerghi captains were willing to do anything to discover our weaknesses."

His voice cracked on the word *anything*.

My heart squeezed. *They tortured him.*

"Are you in need of healing?"

He shook his head with a half smile. "I was healed by the first healer I met once I reached the Shahala."

"Has the sorcerer come through the Gate to Dahru? Is he here?" Batumar asked.

"The last I knew, he was still in Canvar."

"How did you escape his men?"

"The Guardian of the Cave came for me. The enemy held me captive in a small cave near the Gate. Armed guards stood at the opening. I was staring at the back wall, begging the spirits for a way out, when a gap appeared in the stone. The Guardian of the Cave stood in the gap, reached out, and pulled me in. We walked clear through the rock and came out the other side."

Batumar looked mystified, but I had no doubt it had happened exactly that way. I had seen the Guardian of the Cave open passageways in rock before. I had walked through them myself.

The young Guardian of the Gate smiled again. "The Guardian of the Cave closed the gap behind us. I wager those guards are still wondering how I escaped. I hope they think I turned into a bat and flew right over their heads."

I smiled with him as he continued. "The Guardian of the Cave said you sailed through the hardstorms. But other rumors said you came to the Shahala. I thought maybe you meant to sail through the hardstorms, could not find a way through, and came here instead, so I headed this way."

"We did sail through the storms to the mainland," Batumar told him. "And we brought back an army."

"So I see, my lord." The Guardian's voice filled with wonder. "An army and three fine ships. All good news, and I have some more of my own." He smiled at me. "What Kadar and Shahala the Kerghi captured have not yet been sent through the Gate of the World. The last I saw them, they were kept in an enclosure on the mountain, near the Gate."

My heart gave a hard thud. "For how long? How much time do we have to save them?"

"I am not certain, my lady. But if I understood right, the sorcerer's hold on Dahru's Gate is not perfect. He is sending troops through from Canvar, and he can only send so many each day. Once he sends enough for Kerghi victory, he will come through himself. Then, from this side, he can send slaves back. He can only control the side of the Gate where he stands."

"Do you know when he plans on coming?"

"I know the Kerghi wanted to send their captives through in time for the Day of Enit."

Enit was the god of trade and protector of markets, his day the biggest market day on the mainland. It fell on the same day as the Shahala Harvest Feast. Which was...

My heart raced as I counted. "In a fortnight?"

Too soon. A fortnight could not possibly be enough for us to reach Dahru's Gate. And once we lost those captured men, women, and children... How would we ever find them again, scattered as they would be across the world, sold as slaves?

Batumar questioned the Guardian some more on all he had seen after coming through Dahru's Gate, until one of Prince Graho's guards found us with a message from the prince. The harbor held nothing fast enough to catch the skiff the Kerghi prisoners had taken, but Prince Graho did send a boat after them. Mayhap luck would be with us and our men would catch the escaped Kerghi.

I bade the young Guardian to rest on our ship, then Batumar and I took our leave to confer with Prince Graho and Lord Karnagh, sending word to Tomron to join us. Everything we had to do, we had to do in a hurry. We would sail at first light. We had lost our one advantage, the element of surprise. The less time we gave the enemy to prepare for our arrival, the better.

The fate of all our people depended on the upcoming battles. The islands of the Mirror Sea would be either ours or the Kerghi khan's. We would be either free or slaves.

CHAPTER SIXTEEN

KAHARTA REH

By the time Prince Graho told the captain to pull up anchor the following dawn, our damaged sails were replaced and our food stores replenished, all our water barrels filled. I had one more task to accomplish, however.

I strode over to Boscor, laid my hands on him, and sealed his wound, taking his injury into my own body. The Shahala had not come onto the ship, so all this time, he had still been suffering. I had meant to bring a healer to him and Urdy, but our time in Sheharree had gone differently than I had anticipated.

The chronicle keeper gave a sharp gasp at the tingling sensation of the pain leaving him. "My lady…"

Urdy climbed up from below and ambled over, his steps speeding when he saw me stagger momentarily. "Lady Tera…"

I laid my hands on his arms and softened his bones.

He sat on the boards with a heavy thud, staring at me as I knit the ragged edges together, pouring my strength into him even as I drew his suffering. I was strong enough to take it, but with the pain came something dark, something unexpected. By the time I realized this, it had spread through me. *Poison.*

The heavy sludge in my blood knocked my feet from under me, and I half sat, half collapsed next to Urdy.

The poison he had taken to escape the slow death of being trapped in a well might not have killed the dwarf on Rabeen, but it had stayed in his blood and would have killed him little by little. He had trained himself to be immune—almost, but not entirely. I had no resistance to the toxic brew at all. I could not even discern the ingredients, the cold feel of them unfamiliar.

I had already used most of my healing powers on the sailors' burns the day before, then on the worst of the injured soldiers in the harbor before the Shahala healers reached us. Now I paid the price.

"My lady?" Urdy's eyes snapped wide with wonder and horror. Mayhap I was the first Shahala healer he had met. He seemed to only now realize that this was how true Shahala healing worked.

He dropped to his knees in front of me, yanking the splints from his arms, twisting the limbs to test them, then bowing his head to me. "My lady, I am not deserving."

Boscor was by my side. He reached for me, fatherly care in his eyes. "You must rest."

I had to agree. "For a short while."

Sailors rushed around, going about their work, oblivious to the fact that—for the moment—I balanced on the edge of death.

Boscor put a hand under my elbow. "My lady, allow us to help you to the prow and find you a quiet spot out of the way."

The prow would have to do. I could not go below. I did not trust myself on the ladder.

Marga sensed that something was amiss and padded over, sniffing at me. I leaned on her with one aching arm while I pressed the other against the invisible wound in my belly. Boscor and Urdy assisted. When we reached the prow and I lay down, the tiger curled around me, nudging my head with hers until I laid my head on her rib cage. She licked the side of my face with a low rumble, satisfied to have me in her care.

Boscor hurried off for water, and when he brought me the cup, I drank. Then I lay there, trying to catch my breath. The two men sat across from me, watching me with worried expressions.

I coughed. "I need only a little rest."

Boscor closed his eyes, his lips moving slightly as he began a silent prayer. Marga made a rumbling noise in her chest, almost like a purr, to soothe me.

"My lady...forgive me..." Urdy's tone was pained and desperate as he stood again and began to pace.

"I shall recover. Tell me what you will do after the war ends." I needed distraction from the pain.

"Now that I have been through my first sea battle, I do not think I am cut out for piracy," he said. "But I did like making Nessa laugh. Once the war is over, I might join a traveling circus." His gaze met mine. "Being blue like this, I do not have many choices. I suppose I could sign on in a mine and spend my days down below in darkness, but I think I prefer the circus."

His resignation to never being accepted by others hurt my heart, and the whole rest of my body was hurting plenty already. Yet I had to acknowledge that Urdy might well be right. Neither the sailors nor the soldiers had warmed to him so far. None would talk to him save to disparage him.

"I have some skill with knives." He flashed a self-deprecating smile. "I could try knife throwing."

I nodded, not wanting to think how he had gained that skill.

"I am fair good with ropes." More frustration crept into his expression as he sat back down. "No good with a garrote, though. One must have the height for it."

"And if the world were different?"

"If I were not blue, not a dwarf, and not trained as an assassin?" He gave a heartbreaking sigh. "I would be a minstrel, tall and handsome, singing songs of love to the ladies in some kind king's court."

"Do you sing a lot, then?"

"I sang in the well and liked it. Before that..." He sighed again. "Assassins are supposed to be quiet."

I wanted to ask him to sing for me, but I did not wish to draw Batumar's attention to us until I recovered.

"Are there many schools for assassins?" I tried to imagine a people so different from mine, dedicated not to healing but killing. And in organized schools! Even we healers did not have that. Older healers simply took young ones as their apprentices. I had been taught by my mother.

"Only three around here, all on the Outer Islands. The Blue School, the Black Rock, and the Pit."

"Pit?"

"The school is inside a dead volcano. To honor their god, they mostly kill with fire, smoke, and boiling."

I winced. *Do not think about it.*

"And the Black Rock?" I asked quickly.

"On the far side of Black Rock Mountain. Black Rock assassins are hired when information is needed from the victim before the killing. A Black Rock assassin will become whatever his target needs him to be. A lover for a woman desperate for love. A father to a young ruler who recently lost his. A best friend. A protective guard. When the dagger goes for the heart or the poison cup is offered, it is held by someone most familiar, someone least suspected."

I shuddered, yet I could not help asking more. "And the Blue School?"

"We are the unseen."

I remembered Boscor having said something similar, that people only saw a blue assassin but a moment before their death.

The chronicle keeper opened his eyes, his prayers finished. "More water, my lady?"

"Yes, please."

As Boscor walked off toward the barrels, I wanted to ask Urdy more about the Blue School, but I caught sight of Batumar striding toward us with thunder on his face. I tried to rise but slid back and remained where I was. I would need a little more time yet.

The warlord towered over me when he stopped, putting himself squarely between Urdy and me, his expression tight, a muscle ticking in his jaw. He said a single word through gritted teeth. "Why?"

Urdy jumped to his feet and slid between us. The top of his head reached only the warlord's waist, yet he stood his ground. "The blame is all mine, my lord." He bowed his head. "So should the punishment be."

Batumar glowered at him.

I smiled at the blue man's courage. "There will be no punishment, Urdy. But thank you for your protection."

Batumar cast me a hard look that said he would decide what would or would not happen next. Then he returned his attention to Urdy, and I knew a roar was coming.

I hurried to say, "I would talk with Lord Batumar alone."

Urdy turned to me and bowed so deeply that his forehead nearly touched the boards. "As my lady wishes."

As Urdy left, Batumar shook his head. Then he repeated, "Why?" His gaze fixed on mine.

"I did not realize Urdy's body still held the poison." I brushed my hair out of my face. "But even if I did... I would not have left him to die." I still ached all over. My voice was weaker than I would have liked as I went on. "To win this war, I know I must become more than I have ever been. But I cannot deny what I have been, what I still am—a healer. I cannot become the warrior queen everyone wishes me to be."

His dark expression softened. And then he bent down and lifted me into his arms.

Marga growled her discontent but stayed where she was, only casting a reproaching look at Batumar for taking me away from her.

The warlord grumbled as he carried me to the hatch. "The chronicle keeper and the assassin should have stayed with the Shahala. Gormil could have healed them."

I held on to his neck as he climbed down the ladder, and to turn his mind to different matters, I asked, "Do we sail straight to Kaharta Reh?"

"Yes. We shall go around Feor."

Kaharta Reh was the second southernmost Kadar city. Below it, Feor sat at the very edge of the border, a much smaller port town.

"The Kerghi will not have a significant force in Feor," Batumar said. "If they have taken the town, they have left it in ruin and moved on. Any time we waste in Feor will only give the enemy troops in Kaharta Reh more time to prepare for our arrival."

Batumar caressed my arm absently as he carried me to our storage room, the soft, loving gesture going a long way toward easing my pain.

"Kaharta Reh is likely lost. If the enemy has our Kadar ships, it most likely means they have taken the city." He laid me down onto our sleeping rolls. "I do not expect Lord Tahar still lives."

The possibility of Lord Tahar's demise grieved me precious little. I had not forgotten the days I had spent as a slave in his possession. But I had friends at the House of Tahar, people with whom I had served. I said a brief prayer for them as I lay weakly in the warlord's arms.

"Do you think, my lord, that the Kerghi have taken the entire Kadar fleet?"

"Aye. The Guardian said our Gate has been opened. The Kerghi can have no shortage of men. But I do not expect them to let the ships idle in Kaharta Reh's harbor. They would be scattered by now, gone to the other islands, if not attacking them, then at least mapping their defenses in preparation for attack. We will not have to face the full fleet all at once."

Batumar's words should have calmed my fears, but they did not. All I could think of was that Dahru's Gate stood open—more and more Kerghi troops coming through every day—and that the Shahala healers would not help us in the coming battles. Yet we had to win, and in a fortnight at that, or our people would be taken off the island and sold as slaves.

The warlord and I both fell silent, each thinking about the coming day. The task before us seemed unsurmountable.

Then he pressed his lips against my temple in a soft kiss, and little by little, I relaxed into his embrace. Abovedecks, the captain was shouting the order to loosen the sails. We were on our way.

I moved my head to lie over the warlord's heart. "I've missed this."

"As have I. I will not spend another night without you. The assassin can sleep in the crow's nest for all I care."

I sighed. "He is disliked by the men. They say he will bring bad luck."

"He might." Outrage crept into Batumar's tone as he added, "The dwarf says I snore."

When I did not respond, the warlord tilted my head up with a finger at my chin so he could look into my eyes. "Do I?"

I kept my expression the very picture of stunned surprise. "He dreamt it for certain."

* * *

We reached Kaharta Reh six days later, faster than I had anticipated. When I had been taken there two years ago in the belly of a slaver, the journey seemed to last an eternity. This time, I sailed standing tall in the prow of the ship, the crown prince of Landria standing on my left and

Batumar on my right, and a Guardian, not to mention an army, behind me.

All very encouraging *if* a dozen warships were not waiting for us in the harbor.

"Must we engage them?"

"There are not that many places to come ashore between here and Karamur," Batumar said in a heavy tone. "If we bypass this harbor, the ships will follow us to the next one. Other ships are waiting there most likely. We will be trapped between two forces."

Before I could respond, he added, "It is only a quarter of the Kadar fleet."

"And still too many for us to challenge outright." Prince Graho paced, his gaze fastened to those ships, his expression grim.

"Know you a strategy for three ships facing a dozen?" Batumar stood with his feet apart, facing the enemy head-on as always. If the overwhelming force concerned him, he showed it not.

The prince stopped and rubbed his chin. "Battle strategy is created for roughly equal forces. Navies do not fight under odds as poor as this. Battle is engaged if there is a hope for victory. When one is obviously outnumbered, it is better to withdraw from the field of battle and sign a treaty."

I fought against the discouragement that tried to gain hold of my heart. We were not only vastly outnumbered, but also outmaneuvered. The Kadar ships had warning, so they had time to line up in a semicircle that could easily close around us if we sailed into the trap facing us.

The embrace of death, I thought and shivered.

Batumar offered encouragement. "The Kadar warships are wider and heavier than our Landrian ships. They will be slower."

The prince grinned at the warlord. "Are you admitting the superiority of the Landrian navy to those Kadar washtubs, Lord Batumar?"

"Best hope those washtubs do not sink us today."

"Have you heard of the rebel wars of Wyrn, my lords?" Boscor said behind us.

I had not realized he was there.

He had washed the blood off his richly embroidered kaftan and was freshly shaven, his hair combed. He no longer looked like a victim of war, but every bit an important official. He stood several steps away, at a respectful distance, and came closer only when I gave him a welcoming smile and Batumar nodded.

"Of the Wyrn wars, yes," the warlord said, his brow furrowed. "But not in great detail."

Boscor preened. He had been an important person on Rabeen, yet on our ship, he'd been reduced to a convalescent refugee. Now, he clearly enjoyed being able to contribute his knowledge. "They are in the chronicles of Rabeen, for one of the rebels who later became a slave ended up a servant of the previous chronicle keeper and related the events to his master."

We looked at him with expectation.

"For the first year of the rebellion," he said, folding his hands over his belly, "the insurgents were winning. Three thousand ill-equipped rebels against the king's thirty thousand trained soldiers." He paused before adding, "Wyrn was much larger back then than it is now. The kingdom broke up when the king died and the princes came to power."

I found the thought comforting, as that was my secret hope for Drakhar's empire. Emperor Drakhar was an old man by all accounts, with over a hundred sons from his countless concubines. I hoped someday soon they would be fighting each other to the death for his throne and leave the rest of the world in peace.

Prince Graho shifted with impatience. "A fascinating history."

"I apologize, my lord." Boscor cleared his throat, his expression saying the prince was but a young pup and should listen to his elders. "I *am* coming to a point."

The prince raised an eyebrow, while Boscor went on with his tale.

"The rebels took nearly the whole kingdom before the rebellion was put down. They did not use the kind of military strategy taught in books. They used rebel tactics."

"Which would be?" asked the warlord, his gaze fast on the chronicle keeper.

Boscor offered a sly smile. "Trickery."

"I learned battle strategy from the War Master of Landria," the prince said. "Do you think your *tricks* are better? Master Maion taught all the best admirals."

"With all respect." Boscor bowed. "Admirals know but one thing, how to lead one large force against another. We do not have a large force. And yet…"

"And yet?" The prince's tone was more than skeptical; it was dismissive.

"A single candle can burn down an entire castle," Boscor told him.

The prince watched him for a moment. "All right. Tell us about rebel trickery."

So Boscor recounted what he remembered of the Wyrn wars from the chronicles, how the rebels marched on top of a hill in a circle, forming a never-ending loop to fool their enemy into thinking the rebels numbered in the thousands when they had but hundreds. How that night, they lit a thousand fires, even if they had no men to sit around them. How, on a different occasion, they allowed themselves to be captured so, from the inside, they could take a fortress with walls they never could have scaled.

We listened to those stories and more, for Boscor knew many. Then we spent the better part of the day planning, while the enemy let us sit in the water undisturbed.

"Why are they not attacking?" I asked the warlord as we headed belowdecks at dusk.

"Their ships are slower. If we flee and they have to give chase, they will be at a disadvantage."

Prince Graho, coming down the ladder behind us, added, "They fully expect us to surrender in the morning."

CHAPTER SEVENTEEN

ALL SHIPS LOST

"Nock."

"Draw."

"Ho-o-old."

"Loose!"

Our archers released an impressive volley of fire arrows at first light, signaling our intent to wage serious battle. Tomron's unit had cut enough saplings from the Shahala woods before we left to have an arsenal. We had a full barrel of oil and our old, torn sails cut up for rags. The archers had spent the past six days putting it all together. Their true arrows were carefully made in a meticulous process and would have been a waste for this purpose.

The Kerghi responded in kind, fire raining on us once again from the sky.

Our ships fought hard, careful never to get close enough to be boarded. We fought as people ready to fight to the death but who also wanted to prolong that end as long as possible.

Only when the half circle of enemy vessels began closing around us did we pull back. But even as we did, the Kerghi captured our flagship, the *Shield*.

The *Lance* and the *Sword*—smaller and faster—raced out of reach. The much larger, slower Kadar ships could not catch us. They gave up once we sailed out of arrow range. They knew we would return. They expected us to sneak back again in the middle of the night to liberate the *Shield* and our men.

Batumar, the prince, and I were on the *Lance* by this time, having switched commands. Tomron led the flagship, with a hundred volunteers onboard. They were the ones trapped in Kaharta Reh's harbor.

As dusk fell, Batumar, Prince Graho, and I stood once again by the railing, waiting at a distance that still allowed us to see the shore. The young Guardian was not with us. He had gone to the *Sword* to stay with Lord Karnagh. Should our caravel be sunk, that would at least leave the Guardian and the Selorm warlord to attempt the island's liberation.

Marga lay at my feet, tapping her tail. She disliked being crowded, and the *Lance* was filled to the brim, since we were carrying extra soldiers. We left only enough men on the *Shield* as were needed to fool the enemy. I laid a hand on the tiger's head, shifting closer to Batumar at the same time. "The Kerghi will not kill the captured men, will they?"

"For now, they will use our soldiers to lure us back," he promised.

We waited, all hands on deck, all eyes riveted to the harbor that was less and less visible as the sun slipped behind the island. We kept waiting, even after the last rays of the sun disappeared.

Then, at long last, a different, flickering light appeared on the horizon. Little by little, the light grew, as a new sunrise, but at the wrong time of the night and in the west. Soon, towering flames lit up the entire harbor.

"A quarter of the Kadar fleet gone," Batumar said, his tone grim and heavy.

Regret thickened the prince's voice as he responded, "It had to be done." As the son of a seafaring nation, he would never rejoice at the sight of good ships burned. He did offer a note of hope. "The fleet can be rebuilt."

I silently prayed to the spirits to protect our men who had volunteered to be captured. And also the ones who had been hidden in the *Shield*'s hold to start a fire once our flagship was anchored in port next to the Kadar ships.

Since the ships were tightly packed into the harbor, they rapidly caught fire from each other. A strong southern wind carried the sparks from sail to sail.

Then the wind changed. We held our breath as stronger and stronger gusts blew from east to west, from the sea toward the city. The fire turned brighter and brighter.

Next to me, the railing creaked under the warlord's grip. "The market stalls are aflame. The warehouses will be next."

Boscor's suggestion worked only too well. By morning, fire might take everything. Losing the ships was one thing. Losing the largest Kadar port city was another. I had suffered greatly during the time I had spent in

Kaharta Reh, yet never had I wished it destroyed. I watched the destruction in anxious silence, my heart breaking at the sight.

Merciful spirits, I begged, *please save the innocent.*

Boscor told us the old stories from the chronicles. Batumar, Prince Graho, and Lord Karnagh had come up with the plan. Tomron and his hundred had volunteered. But *I* had sent them. *No one else but I.* The final decision had been mine.

"If the fires burn out by dawn, we take the city then," Batumar told us, then turned and walked the length of the ship, calling out to the men to go to their rolls and grab some rest before the next day's battle.

The *Lance* had only the captain's cabin abovedecks, which we left to the ship's captain. We slept on the bare deck, among the soldiers we had brought over from The *Shield.* I needed to see the stars. I needed to look at them and think about how they had watched us from the beginning of time, how even now they saw the entire world. I needed to feel that there existed more in the world than this war, and maybe some of that *more* was good. I gave a heavy sigh.

Batumar enfolded me into his arms and kissed the top of my head. "The emperor's war had a beginning. It will also have an end."

All those steadfast points of light in the endless dark sky helped me believe that. I pressed tightly against the warlord's wide chest.

* * *

Dawn came too soon, the excitement of battle filling our men as they prepared. I felt no such thrill. The dread of losing more lives settled on me instead. I might have led an army, but I was no general. While Batumar and the prince sharpened their swords, I prayed for the spirits' favor.

Our first difficulty of the day became apparent as soon as we reached the blackened harbor.

"There *is* no harbor," I said as Batumar found me in the prow. "No docks to pull our two caravels against." I paused. "I suppose we can drop anchor, then row onto shore in boats."

"The boats would have to make several trips," Batumar said. "If any enemy archers are hiding among the ruins, the first wave of our troops would be massacred by the time the next wave arrived to reinforce them."

My gaze moved to the tall stone walls that had protected the city for centuries but were now collapsed in two places. "Look." I pointed. "Our fire could not have done that."

"The Kerghi must have breached the walls when they took the city."

Mayhap they had found that easier than breaching the massive city gate—poles as thick as my waist held together by wide strips of metal. The last time I had seen it, the wooden gate had stood as tall as a ship's mast, guarding the entrance of the city, wide enough to allow four ox carts through side by side. Now the two wings hung from their hinges, charred and stilted.

Behind the gate, the city still burned in places, the streets filled with smoke, yet farther in, most of the houses seemed to be still standing. Outside the gate, on the other hand, the wooden structures nearest the harbor had all been reduced to ashes.

"The ruins might hide soldiers, but they cannot be hiding a great many, and they will have to stay in place to keep in cover," Prince Graho said, coming up behind Batumar.

As our ship neared the remains of the harbor, the warning call of a war horn tore through the morning, then another and another, coming from the city. The enemy was most definitely waiting for us. After a few moments, an otherworldly animal call answered the horns.

The sound was one to put fear into the hearts of men, but my heart swelled with joy instead. "What are the manyinga doing in Kaharta Reh?"

"They might have been hidden here by our warlords when they realized the island's Gate was open once again and enemy troops were coming through. Or..." Batumar shook his head instead of finishing the sentence.

Or, I thought, *Khan Verik might have sent the manyinga here to ship them to the other islands of our Mirror Sea, so his Kerghi soldiers could ride the beasts to battle.*

Except, now we were here, and we would save the herd.

The stables stood at the east end of the harbor. I could see the long flat roof from our ship, the wooden roof shingles scorched but not burnt. My chest swelled with hope. The herd could have been slain. I did not care for what purpose the Kerghi had spared them, only that they had been spared.

Prince Graho turned to shout to the captain. "We must run our ships aground on the beach!"

My breath caught. Running the ships aground would mean we would lose the last two ships we had. We would lose *all* our naval capabilities.

As the captain hurried over, the prince pointed at a narrow strip of sandy beach next to the harbor, where small fishing boats sat both in and out of the water. They had been far enough from the warships to have been spared by the flames. "We can run the ships aground side by side there, then disembark all at once."

Batumar nodded. "Amass enough soldiers on the ground to protect the rest until all our forces can land."

The captain stared at the shore, his expression suitably grim. "Running a ship aground is not without its own risks."

"Can you do it?" I asked the man.

He patted his beard, his brown eyes stricken as if his heart was breaking. "Aye."

"Send horn signals to the *Sword.*" Prince Graho issued the order.

I looked from one man to the other. "Will the enemy not catch then what we are planning?"

"Landria has not fought any naval battles with the Kerghi before now," the prince told me. "They do not know our signals."

As the captain returned to the wheel, I swallowed my regrets, and they sat in my stomach in a heavy lump. Today, we would lose our remaining ships—the ships that had carried our troops safely through the hardstorms. Any battles we fought from now on would have to be fought on land.

I watched with an aching heart as the sailors adjusted our sails. Soon the caravels' prows pointed at the shore like arrows ready to be let loose. Then we charged the beach.

"Brace!" Prince Graho called out as we reached the sandy shoals.

The timbers shook, the ship tilted, and I lost my footing. I windmilled my arms to grab on to something, anything. Then Batumar caught me.

By the time he righted me, our men were throwing rope ladders over the railing and climbing down, while others dropped into the shallow water at the ship's midsection and waded to shore. The Selorm tigers were hitting the waves with loud splashes as they jumped from the *Sword* next to us.

The first of our forces were on land sooner than I had expected. Volleys of arrows came at us. Our archers responded until all quivers ran empty. Then our forward force charged ahead, ready to fight man-to-man, for the enemy was pouring out of the city, leaving their charred cover.

Batumar hurried down the ladder before me, then jumped, too impatient to climb all the way. When he held out his arms for me, I let go and dropped into them. *Kind spirits, keep him safe today.*

Prince Graho and his royal guards landed next to us. He immediately ordered two of the nearest men to stay with me: Lison and Fadden. For once, Batumar nodded his thanks instead of bristling, then ordered two more men to my side, Hartz and Atter. When the warlord and the prince at last ran off to join the battle, Marga went with Batumar.

I was moving away from the ladder when a young man fell from above and hit the sand next to me with a thud. He rolled out of the way, gasped, then lay flat on his back. He had the prince's coloring—blue eyes, blond hair. Probably a Landrian.

"Just had the air knocked out of me, Lady Tera," he said when I reached for him. He colored with embarrassment as he scrambled to his feet. "I lost my footing."

When I helped him up by the arm, he hissed. I saw the problem at once. "Your shoulder is dislocated."

"No time for that now. At least it is not my right arm." He moved to rush into battle, but I held him back.

"I can set it. It will take but a moment."

He gave a quick nod, so I put one hand on his shoulder, another on his elbow, manipulated the joint to the right alignment, then pulled hard, down and forward.

As the shoulder snapped back into place, the young man bit back a groan but was running off already with a "Thank you, Lady Tera."

Urdy and Boscor found me and stayed close to me and my guards. Our small group followed the fighting at a distance. I healed our men but was careful not to take on too many injuries, not to exhaust myself too soon. I helped only enough to get them back on their feet, enough so they could lift their swords once again. I had no time for poultices or to start a fire to boil water to disinfect wounds, nor did I have fresh water to boil. I would do all that once the battle was over, I promised each and every man I treated.

From the corner of my eye, I caught Urdy cutting an enemy mercenary's throat now and again among the men on the ground. I did not stop him.

Our soldiers fought more fiercely than I had ever seen them fight. We had no choice now but to win. We could not withdraw onto our ships and sail away. We had to win, and we had to reclaim the manyinga. We had to ride the great woolly beasts to Karamur, the fortress city, and engage the main force of the enemy, then close the island's Gate before more Kerghi could come through and overwhelm us completely. Before the sorcerer came through and began sending our captured people to distant slave markets. *That* I would not allow, no matter what I had to do to save them.

Unfortunately, from what I could see of the battle, we did not appear to be winning.

CHAPTER EIGHTEEN

BACK AT TAHAR'S HALL

The last rays of the setting sun painted the horizon red, as if on their way to a feast, the god Rorin's concubines in their blue-purple cloud gowns had walked through a river of blood.

Crimson stained my own gown as well, and not merely the hem. The tide of the battle for Kaharta Reh had finally turned, and the harder our men fought, the more injuries I had to heal.

Our soldiers advanced through the city, while I advanced from the beach to the paved part of the harbor, for the sand always managed to find its way into the wounds. I stayed there instead of following our troops farther, past the charred stone wall and the giant broken city gate, where they fought from street to street. As we had done in Sheharree, a handful of the prince's men brought the injured to me. They even set up a small fire with a cauldron of water, which helped a great deal.

I glanced up to see how many more men were waiting for my healing when I saw a group of our soldiers shove a Kerghi in front of them, coming from the city toward the harbor.

"Who is that, do you think?" I asked Boscor, who had not left my side but spent the day assisting me with herbs, hot water, needles, and string.

The injured man under my hands responded, "My lady, he is the Kerghi commander."

"Where are they taking him?"

The young man shrugged and turned his gaze from mine.

"You should not watch, my lady," Urdy said gently, at last returning. He had gone off in search of clean cloth for bandages, and now he spilled an armful at my feet, on top of my cloak that I had set on the ground to keep my healing supplies clean.

I had been kneeling next to my patient to pry the arrow from his thigh, but at Urdy's words, I stood to see the Kerghi commander better. My back needed stretching anyway. I had been kneeling and bending over injuries for most of the day.

I rolled my shoulders and watched as our soldiers marched the enemy commander to the harbor's flag post that the fire had left unharmed—the wood was encased in studded copperleaf. Even the golden flag of the emperor waved untouched at the top. Since the flagpole stood on a mound and the pole itself was taller than our ship's mainmast, taller even than the stone walls, that flag could be seen from most of the city. I had seen Lord Tahar's flag fly up there aplenty during my days of slavery.

I squinted to better see the men at the flagpole. "Why are they bringing a Kerghi instead of Lord Tahar's flag?"

Neither Boscor nor Urdy nor my patient responded.

So it took me by surprise when our soldiers made quick work of the Kerghi commander. They ran him up the flagpole and hung him by the neck. As he kicked, then went still, I held my breath.

This is war.

I could do nothing for the Kerghi, as I could do nothing for our people whom the Kerghi killed. All I could do was help the living. So I returned to healing, working as quickly as I could, for there seemed to be an endless supply of injured soldiers to heal.

They gave me news on our army's progress, so I knew when the east end of the city was cleared, then when the last Kerghi troops huddled in the warehouses of the west side refused to surrender and instead fought to the death.

One man bleeding from a chest wound told me that, seeing their leader's fate, the last of the enemy warriors fled up the coast. He grunted with disappointment as he finished with "Prince Graho told us not to chase them."

"It is better that you rest. The troops are exhausted." And so was I. Indeed, by the time I closed the deep gash over his ribs, I could barely stand.

I stretched and drank from the flask on my belt, while he moved on with his thanks. I drew a deep breath, then made the next one shallower, for the air was filled with the smell of blood and spilled guts. Some of the injured men had died on their way to me, but were left with me regardless. Such was the faith of some of our soldiers in me, they thought I might yet be able to bring back even the dead. I hated to disappoint them.

While I rested for a moment, wiping the sweat from my brow, Boscor kept bandaging wounds, instructing Urdy how to go about helping him. When I smiled at the chronicle keeper, he simply said, "The chronicles I studied all my life contained a number of medical texts."

At hearing this, I grieved their loss nearly as much as he did.

My guards too were helping with the injured at my direction. They worked a short distance away—far enough to have sufficient room, but close enough to come to my aid should I call them.

We were almost finished. I had closed the most grievous wounds, and I could close the rest without my power. I could use ninga beetles. I knew exactly where to find those—in the creek at the end of the fields behind the House of Tahar.

I headed just that way when I was steady enough at last to walk. I left Lison and Fadden with the injured men, along with Boscor and Urdy, taking only Hartz and Atter with me. They were both good men, toughened by war. Atter was missing both ears. He was a man afraid of little. Both he and Hartz had faced death with me more than once on the mainland. In one of our very first battles, Hartz had taken a lance in his side. I had no doubt they would protect me if the need arose for protection.

"Are you certain, my lady?" Atter looked as if he would not mind confirming my order with Batumar, sounding painfully uncomfortable that he had to argue with me. Both he and Hartz had been farmers before the war. Neither was used to questioning a lady.

I smiled at him to set him at ease. "The city is ours. I expect I will be safe, and, in any case, I hardly need an entourage to collect a bucketful of beetles."

I needed to go to the House of Tahar for other reasons as well. I wanted to arrange shelter and provision for our troops, and this was where I was most likely to find both. Tahar's compound stood far enough from the harbor to escape the inferno of our fire.

We hurried down narrow streets stained with blood and littered with bodies, then stopped before a familiar hammered-iron door that guarded the entry of the largest cluster of buildings on the street. For a second, I could but stare at the worn metal of the door through which I had been thrust into slavery. There had been a time when I had not thought I would leave the House of Tahar alive.

A dark shroud of memories wrapped around me, tried to suffocate me. I shook off those memories and nodded to my guards. They banged on the door, but it did not open.

I would not be afraid and would *not* be thwarted. "Lift it off its hinges."

They did, stepping inside with their swords drawn. I was not far behind.

At first glance, the house seemed empty, but as we moved forward, servants peeked around doorways that led farther in, sticking their heads out, then drawing back. I did not recognize any of them.

"Where is Lord Tahar?" I asked the closest one, a bent-spined crone who was slower to withdraw than the rest.

She kept her gaze to the ground, her trembling hands clutching her apron. "Beheaded by Rapter, the Kerghi commander, the day the commander took the city, my lady."

I could not say I mourned the man.

A younger servant took a tentative step away from the protection of the doorway where she had hid. "'Tis the House of Rapter now." She shifted on her feet, her gaze darting to my guards.

"Not anymore," I informed them. "The Kerghi commander is hanging from the flagpole in the harbor. Kaharta Reh is Kadar once more."

They did not rejoice. None of them was Kadar. They had the curly blond hair common in the northern countries of the mainland. They had probably been brought through the Gate.

The emperor liked carrying away his captured slaves, replacing them with others who had no connections to or knowledge of the land. It made an uprising less likely. The unfortunate men and women would be unlikely to rise up to take back a strange country. Running away too was more difficult when the servant had no network of friends to help, no knowledge of what landscapes waited ahead.

I moved forward, assessing the damage to the building and finding little. The Kerghi commander had probably saved it for himself during the initial invasion. I was glad the fire hadn't reached it.

"This will serve as our quarters," I told my guards. "You can put the front door back on its hinges."

I needed a safe place tonight. I meant to heal the rest of our injured men. We needed to take as large a force north with us in the morning as possible.

"Prepare what food stores you have and hold nothing back," I instructed the servants. "What we do not eat, we will take with us on the morrow. When we leave, you may come with us or stay. We go north, to retake Dahru's Gate. Once the Gate is ours, you may return to your homes, if you wish."

I moved on, meaning to cross the Great Hall and come out in the courtyard, then cross the fields to the creek, but I was only halfway across the cavernous space when the back door opened.

Kumra swept in, her daughter Keela following close on her jeweled heels.

The air became trapped in my lungs as I watched them. I felt as if I had fallen from a great height, like the young man I had treated in the harbor after he'd fallen from the ship. As if I too suddenly had something dislocated.

When I had been a slave at the House of Tahar, Kumra had been Lord Tahar's favorite concubine. She had tortured me when she was in a good mood, and nearly killed me, more than once, when she was not. She'd hated me from the moment she had laid eyes on me, for I possessed something she did not: healing skill.

I had not expected to see her here with her daughter. The last I had heard, Lord Tahar had banished both of them from his House for their scheming. They must have returned after his demise and found favor with the Kerghi commander, for they were both dressed in gowns near as resplendent as in the old days. Kumra wore a blue silk richly embroidered with silver, while Keela wore green sateen decorated with seed pearls. The gowns had a foreign cut, the waistline not at the waist, but higher, right below the women's breasts. Neither of them wore a belt of protective charms in the Kadar tradition. They had adjusted to their new lord's customs.

They both recognized me, mouths falling agape one moment, and then the next, that old hate sparked anew in their eyes. The house guards must have gone off to fight on the street, or Kumra would have called for them by now. Only by their absence was I spared.

"What are *you* doing here?" She spat the words, her gaze cutting to my very present and towering guards, then back to me. "Batumar has perished. You have perished with him."

I forced false cheer into my voice. "We but sailed through the hardstorms to bring home a liberating army."

A long moment of complete silence stretched between us, the servants watching wide-eyed, barely daring to breathe.

"You lie." Kumra's expression shimmered with rage. She looked as if she would like nothing more than to fly at me and claw my face. Her gaze darted to my guards once again as she seethed. "Captain Rapter would *never* surrender his city. He is a strong lord, and Khan Verik is even stronger. He is to come here and soon."

Triumph glinted in her eyes. I had no doubt she meant to seduce the new khan and had visions of sitting by his side on some golden throne in Karamur. She did have a skill for manipulating men.

"Captain Rapter is dead," I told her. And since I no longer had to explain myself to Kumra, I did not give her any details. "Make sure a room is prepared for Lord Batumar and me. And for Prince Graho of Landria."

Keela's eyes rounded comically large as she gasped next to her mother. "A prince?"

I ignored her. "Lord Tahar's private quarters will do."

"The three of you?" Kumra's expression turned sly.

"Also Lord Karnagh. And two more men will stay with us as well."

Kumra looked as if she were choking on her own spit.

"More lords and princes?" Keela asked, her voice thick with hope.

I flashed her a cold smile. "A chronicle keeper and an assassin. They both pledged themselves to my service."

Her face froze, and so did her mother's. If Kumra had hoped to get to me in the middle of the night, I dashed those hopes most thoroughly.

Yet I could not rejoice in their shock, nor could I spare thought for revenge. I had an exhausted army to care for. "Most of our army will remain in the harbor and the city streets to secure Kaharta Reh. Food needs to be sent out to them. Others will rest at Warrior Hall. Make sure it stands ready to receive them."

The two women stood as motionless as the wide stone columns behind them, as if unable to catch up with the sudden change in their fortunes. I doubted anyone had ever given Kumra an order in her life. I did not have the time to wait for her to adjust to the notion.

I swept past them with a "You best hurry. There is much to do before my men get here."

I was glad that Hartz and Atter followed close behind, protecting my back.

Since we had to pass by Warrior Hall, I looked in there and found it a filthy mess. Once I stepped outside, what few servants I found hiding in doorways I sent there to clean. I did not trust Kumra to carry out my earlier instructions.

On a premonition, I hurried to Maiden Hall next, across the yard, and found the door locked. Hartz and Atter made quick work of it, splintering the wood under their boots.

The smell hit us first before our eyes could comprehend the horrific sight. Then our ears were assailed by the cries of the unfortunates.

The round space was filled wall to wall with haggard women and children, unwashed and bruised, tied with ropes in groups of sixes and sevens. Now these were Kadar. Farmers' daughters by the looks of them, recently captured from their villages farther inland. They were prepared for transport, to be sent up to the holding pens on the mountain, to be sent through our Gate to the slave markets on the mainland.

"Cut them free," I ordered, but Hartz and Atter were moving already, even before I uttered the words.

"The city is free and so are you." My voice shook with anger. "Go find food in the kitchen. There is a creek at the end of the field if you want to wash. After that, if you wish to help and are able, do what you can to take care of the liberating army. Help in the kitchen and with serving the food would not be amiss. If you are injured, come to Pleasure Hall."

I pointed at the door on the opposite wall. "If you see any injured soldiers, lead them there as well. I shall be there later to heal all who need assistance."

Staying here made more sense than returning to the harbor. At Pleasure Hall, hot water and clean cloth would be available in abundance. Our men could bring any injured soldiers to me here.

As the women cleared out, I carried my gaze around the empty hall, seeing for a moment my first night here, and my good friend Onra. We had both escaped slavery. We had both ended up in Karamur. She married a kind baker. With all the hope in my heart, I hoped she was safe.

I said a quick prayer for her, then down to the creek I went with Atter and Hartz, and we at last filled a water jar with wriggly ninga beetles. Atter carried them back for me, keeping a hand over the jar's mouth so the shiny, black-winged insects would not escape.

As I opened the door to Pleasure Hall, for a moment I feared I might find more slaves warehoused in place of concubines, but Pleasure Hall stood empty. Only two chambers showed signs of recent occupation: Kumra's old chamber and another, which I suspected belonged to Keela now. I did not want to think about both mother and daughter serving the Kerghi commander's bed, so I put the thought from my mind, then went off to find a servant.

"Start cutting up what clean linen you can find for bandages. I will be healing the injured in Pleasure Hall. Make sure everyone knows that the injured men soon arriving are to go there."

The girl blinked uncertainly but did not dare naysay me. The authority in my voice must have convinced her, because after another moment, she bowed and hurried away.

"I need you to return to the *Sword*," I told Atter then. "I need more healing herbs. They are in burlap bags in the captain's cabin. Bring everything. And pass the word that I am here."

Atter left with a small bow and an "As you wish, my lady."

I went to the kitchen next, with Hartz, to seek Talmir, my old friend, who had been the cook the last time I had been here.

"It is sad to see the fields trampled," Hartz said, looking past the buildings as we walked.

"What did you grow on your land, back before the war?" I asked him.

"Mostly wheat, my lady," he responded, then added proudly, "I also bred mules. Finest mules in the country."

We entered the kitchen, but Talmir was not there. Nor could the new cook tell me what had become of the man who had previously prepared the meals. I gave orders for our dinner, making sure the cook understood that neither Kumra nor Keela were allowed around the food that would be served to our army.

On my way back to Pleasure Hall, I kept an eye out for the hateful concubine and her daughter. I preferred to have them where I could see them. I had no doubt that they were already plotting behind my back.

CHAPTER NINETEEN
OLD ENEMIES

For the first time in my life, I sat at Lord Tahar's table for the evening meal. When I had been a servant here, carrying trays and pitchers, never could I have imagined that one day I would sit in the place of honor.

Batumar and Prince Graho sat at the head table as well, along with Boscor, Urdy, Lord Karnagh, and Tomron.

"Those of us who survived being captured with the *Shield* were locked up with the manyinga," Tomron was saying in response to a question from the chronicle keeper.

"Thirty-five men." The words fell heavily from my lips, stones dropping into dark waters. Thirty-five survived out of the hundred who had volunteered. We lost too many brave soldiers. I was humbled by the willing sacrifice of every one of them.

"We resisted to the last moment," Tomron said, "so the enemy would not suspect a trap."

Prince Graho rose, cup in hand, to offer a toast. "We had a long day. We fought a bloody battle—"

"Do not forget herding the manyinga together!" The shout came from one of the back tables where our captains and commanders sat.

Since the room could not hold all our men, the rank-and-file soldiers ate at the trestle tables set up in the courtyard or on their bunks inside Warrior Hall. All but those on guard duty.

"Even if I could forget the herding, I will never forget the smell," the

131

prince rejoined.

The men laughed. Apparently, the Kerghi had not been fastidious when it came to mucking out the stables. They had taken our animals, but had not taken good care of them.

The manyinga were twice as tall as a horse and ten times as stubborn, but could carry more weight than a team of oxen. We needed them to carry our provisions north with us. Finding them was a true boon and a blessing from the spirits.

"We won," said the prince with a smile, servant girls watching him moon-eyed from the doorways. "And we will keep on winning. Our army might be small, but it will not be conquered. Our soldiers will not be taken for slaves. When, at the end of our victory, we disband, we will be free men of free countries!"

Cheers rose from all around, the captains stomping their boots in approval.

The kitchen servants hurried in with food, their expressions cautiously relieved. As our troops had not turned to rape, the women accepted at last that they would not be harmed and were truly liberated. Among them, I recognized more than a handful of Kadar women from the group we had freed from Maiden Hall.

I had expected Kumra and Keela to demand seats at the head table, but when they had come to me before the feast, they begged to be allowed to serve. The sudden change in them was too drastic to be trusted.

"Forgive us." Kumra had inclined her head to me and pinched her daughter when Keela was too slow to do the same. *"You have the unwavering protection of the greatest Kadar warlord, Batumar. You have powers not given to ordinary women. The rest of us must survive on our cunning. We are at the mercy of men who are stronger than us many times over. Do not cast us out. Allow us to serve."*

I did allow them, but only to clean. So now they stood by the wall, their shapeless dresses made of drab linen, their expressions contrite. They were waiting for the feast's end so they could help the servants clear the plates.

A red-haired servant girl brought us pink *runt* root in sugar sauce, ladling a generous portion on each of our plates. The captains watched with interest as the head table got served first. They had not likely seen sweets like this since the war had begun or maybe not ever. I doubted many of them had ever before sat at a true lord's table.

The runt root, oh, that was nicely done—happiness on a plate. The sweet smell brought back my childhood, my mother stirring the sauce over the fire, smiling and singing. Saliva gathered in my mouth as the plate was set in front of me.

I had the spoon halfway to my lips when Batumar's hand stayed my arm.

I followed his gaze. He was watching Urdy, who had gone still in the process of inhaling the sweet aroma. Then the assassin and the warlord exchanged a quick glance, and Urdy lowered his spoon.

"You, girl." Batumar pointed at Keela. When she hurried over, a smile spreading on her face, he handed her his plate. "Eat this."

While I set my spoon down, premonition sending a chill down my spine, Keela's eyes lit up. She thought she found favor with the warlord and would have a new protector in him. She immediately lowered herself to the ground and sat behind Batumar, at the lord's feet as would his concubine, and began to eat.

I pushed my plate away. Poison had ever been Kumra's weapon in the past. I had forbidden her from going near our food, and had even set a guard on her to watch her. I should have had her locked up. But she'd pleaded so sincerely for forgiveness, and I'd had so many other things on my mind…

My gaze sought her out at the back of the room. She was withdrawing step by slow step, slinking away among the serving women.

Batumar's cold and commanding voice stopped her. "You. Come here."

A handful of his captains stood and moved to block the doors, understanding that something was amiss. Swords rattled as hard hands descended on their pommels.

Kumra walked forward, head down, the very picture of obedience.

Batumar handed her my plate. "Let me see you eat this. All of it."

She gripped the plate in a white-knuckled hand while lifting the spoon to her mouth with the other. Both mother and daughter ate in silence. Neither showed sign of poisoning. I relaxed, waiting for the warlord to tell them they could stop.

I was watching Kumra take yet another spoonful of pink root when Keela gave a sharp gasp behind Batumar. As I turned to her, she looked at me, her eyes wide with fear, her hand pressed to her stomach. Her chin wobbled. Her chest heaved, as if she could not quite catch her breath.

"Poisoner." Boscor gasped the word.

Keela shook her head wildly, already beyond speech.

The clatter of her plate and spoon falling onto the stones rang through the suddenly silent hall. Foamy saliva began dripping from her mouth. Then the foam turned red with blood. She coughed and gasped, collapsing on the floor onto her side, her gaze cutting to her mother, pain and shocked betrayal in her watering eyes.

Batumar turned in his chair, the legs screeching against the stone floor, overpowering for a moment the choking sounds Keela made. My heart beat to the same rhythm as her rapid gasps.

Kumra dropped to her knees then, drawing everyone's attention, perfect tears of contrition rolling down her cheeks, her plate falling from her trembling hands and spilling its remaining contents at her dainty feet.

"The plot was hers, my lord." She would not even look at her daughter. "I could not stop her. Have mercy!"

At the flick of Batumar's wrist, two of our captains strode up behind Kumra and yanked her to her feet. Then, at Prince Graho's nod, Durak, the commander of his guard, took the prince's plate and walked around the table with the glistening delicacy.

"Let me go!" Kumra balked at last, struggling against the men who held her. "I am innocent!"

"Hold her tight," Batumar snapped in a tone that could have frozen a hardstorm in place. His chest heaved with fury, his dark gaze as sharp as his sword, impending violence shimmering around him.

As our men obeyed, Durak forced the syrupy runt root sauce into Kumra's mouth, every drop of it, regardless how hard she fought. When she tried to spit, Durak sealed her mouth with one hand, then held her nose closed with the other until she swallowed, gasping for air.

I moved to rise without even knowing what I meant to do next, but Batumar put a hand on my thigh and pushed me back down, kept me in my seat.

His cold, forbidding gaze turned on me. "Our people must know that our justice is swift."

Prince Graho, on my other side, said in a softer voice, "The people must know that we will protect them from *all* enemies."

Boscor fidgeted next to the prince. "They brought their punishment on themselves, my lady."

Batumar let me go. I could have risen then, but I did not.

Durak released Kumra at last. She no longer tried to beg. With hate boiling in her eyes, she spit poison at me.

I wiped the spit off my cheek with my sleeve and watched as her eyes rolled back into her head. As her legs gave out, as the men let her go and she folded, I watched her convulse, then I watched her go still, her mouth frothing with pink, then blood red. I watched justice being served.

When I at last carried my gaze around the room, I found a great many eyes on me. These were my captains, my army, and they looked to me. They needed to see me strong and unshaken.

I hardened my heart as I stood. I steeled my voice. "Death to Khan Verik and all who serve him!"

A deafening cheer rose in the room.

I meant the words. Aside from the threat to my own life, I could have lost Batumar tonight. Our army could have lost its leaders. As I looked out over the room and the people within, I knew that I was ready to do whatever it took to fight whoever sought to harm me and mine.

I sat, and Batumar reached for my hand on the table, rubbing the pad of his thumb over my knuckles, a look of love and approval in his eyes.

"How did you know the poison came from Kumra?" I asked him under my breath. When I had lived at the House of Tahar, I had heard tales of Kumra poisoning others, but I did not think Batumar was familiar with her past.

"I watched her face," Batumar said. "And then too, the servants serving in the Great Hall...our arrival turned their lives for the better. For Kumra and her daughter, it turned for the worse."

The two lifeless women were carried out. After that, Urdy sniffed and tasted all our food. He assured us that he knew the smell of all poisons and had been sampling them for so long, he was immune to most. Once he was done, he proclaimed that everything but the runt root's sugar sauce was safe.

The men ate with caution first, then more heartily. They were no strangers to violent death. Neither the attempted poisoning nor Kumra and Keela's demise shook them. The conversation resumed, the battle for the city retold over and over. At the conclusion of each tale, we raised our cups to victory. Soon the hall filled with cheers and laughter.

Even I relaxed, buoyed by the day's successes. Hope bloomed in my heart once again. We *would* win our countries back.

"I like that smile." Batumar leaned over. "What are you thinking about, my lady?"

"Captain Rapter, the city's Kerghi commander is hanging from the flagpole. Kumra and Keela are being lowered into the mass grave dug for the Kerghi soldiers. One by one, our enemies are being vanquished. We will not stop until our lands are liberated."

"Spoken like a war queen." Batumar grinned. Then he grinned wider.

The playful look in his obsidian eyes made my heart beat faster. "And what are *you* thinking about, my lord?"

"Before the feast began, I ordered the servants to clean Lord Tahar's bedchamber and find some fresh sheets. I will have you tonight, all night, all to myself, in a real bed. I confess to being unable to think of little else but that."

* * *

After the feast, I walked back to Pleasure Hall with Marga and two guards—Atter and Hartz—the tiger pushing between the men and me as we went. I absently patted her head, my mind on Batumar. I looked forward to the day's end, when I could finally settle into the warlord's arms.

Prince Graho departed with Tomron to inspect our troops and search out what weapons and food they could find to take north with us the following day. Lord Karnagh strode off with the Selorm lords and their tigers to see if the tigers might yet discover some enemy still hiding in the ruins. Batumar went with Urdy to interrogate a handful of captured soldiers. Urdy spoke better Kerghi than I did.

I had healed scores of soldiers before our meal, but more injured men had been found and brought from the battlefield. I needed the work. I needed to restore life after having to watch the taking of it all day.

Work I got, more than I had anticipated. Pleasure Hall had filled with bleeding soldiers in my absence. Their injuries were grievous and needed as much of my power as I could give them. When Boscor sought me out to offer his assistance, I gratefully accepted.

There were so many cuts, soon we ran out of ninga beetles. I sent Atter again to bring more from the creek. He knew by now what to look for. Soon after he left, I used up all the cold water in Pleasure Hall's tall jars, so I turned to Hartz.

"I need you to bring me clean water, by the bucketful. Grab what servants you come across on your way to the creek and tell them to help."

"I cannot leave you alone, my lady."

"Kumra and Keela are dead. I have no other enemies here. I have the tiger and Master Boscor for protection. I shall be safe. Please go and bring water." I fixed him with a hard look. "As fast as you can."

Hartz followed my orders, but his tight expression as he left said he did not like them.

I moved on to the next person, not a soldier but an injured child, one burned in the fire the night before. She was stripped to the waist, angry red blisters covering her chest and stomach. Tears ran down her sooty face. She was surrounded by three similarly injured women.

"Who is this child's mother?" I looked from one to another, then the next, but they all shook their heads.

"The Kerghi killed her mother," the oldest of the women said.

I focused on the little girl, on her uncombed hair and slim frame. I could count her ribs through her ruined skin. "I am Tera. I will help you feel better. What is your name?"

She watched me with distrust, but, after a moment did open her mouth to answer. Of course, Marga had to pad closer to us just then. The girl snapped her mouth closed, drawing back, eyes going wide and filling with fear. Marga nudged me from behind, then thrust her giant head through under my arm to sniff at the burned flesh. I pushed her back.

"The tiger is my friend. She will not harm you," I promised, but the girl scrambled out of reach and wedged herself between the women, who were themselves pulling back.

Marga lost interest in the girl and began pacing the empty space that opened up around us, shaking her head and huffing, clearly bothered by the thick smell of blood in Pleasure Hall.

"She is just hungry." I tried to explain, but none looked reassured at my explanation. In hindsight, perhaps those were the wrong words to say.

I reached out to rub Marga's shoulder as she passed me. "Let me see about finding you something to eat."

I turned back to the child, who was now crying, her fearful gaze riveted to Marga. I could work my healing more easily if I calmed her first.

"I will take the tiger out, then I will come back," I promised her even as I drew the worst of her pain. When I returned, if she'd settled down by then, I could begin repairing her skin.

I needed a short break, in any case. I had already taken on the pain of many, and there were still dozens more waiting. Burn wounds required a lot of healing power. The transfer of pain was sharp and real, and I had worked on a great many burn wounds that day.

As I stood, dizzy for a moment, Boscor moved to come with me, but I shook my head. "See if you can ease her fear with one of your stories."

Marga was nudging me once again, so I put a hand on her giant head and scratched behind her ear. "All right. We shall go to the kitchen and find you some leftovers."

I wanted to make sure she would get nothing that Kumra and Keela could possibly have touched. I also did not want some scared servant to throw something at the tiger and startle her into an attack.

"The kitchen is close by, in the next building. Finding Marga a meal will not take long," I promised Boscor before we left him.

When I found the cook, I asked him for meat.

"I am sorry, my lady." The man bowed his head, casting worried glances at the tiger by my side. "Meat has been in short supply in the city for some time. Perhaps bones?" he rushed to suggest. "I saved them for the soup tomorrow, but if you wish—"

"Bones are fine for her as playthings, but they do not provide enough sustenance. Have you any chickens?"

"Only the egg-laying hens," he said with reluctance. "We are most dependent on them."

"I shall need a dozen."

These the cook unwillingly gave, butchering them quickly and carrying them behind the kitchen for Marga while we waited.

More time than I had anticipated passed by the time I was walking back to Pleasure Hall, leaving a happy tiger behind with a pile of poultry. Boscor would have had time for a dozen tales or more. I hoped he'd put the girl to sleep. I could heal her so, and she would wake healthy.

I was about to step into the main building when a distraught voice called from behind me. "Are you the Lady Tera?"

I turned to find a boy of maybe ten summers running toward me across the dark courtyard, tears washing his face. His drab clothes were stained and torn; his mousy hair hung in tangles.

"Are you the Lady Tera?" he begged the question once again as he stopped at a respectful distance and bowed.

"I am."

"It's Prince Graho, my lady." The boy was breathing hard from his run, gasping for air, barely able to finish. "At the harbor. Please hurry!"

CHAPTER TWENTY

NEW ENEMIES

I rushed to the panting boy. "Has there been more fighting?"

Had I been mistaken to think the battle was over? Had our men come upon enemy soldiers hiding in the burned warehouses?

The boy's eyes were wide with bewilderment. "I do not know, my lady. He is in the harbor. Please, hurry."

I looked toward the creek, hoping to see either Hartz or Atter returning. I could not spot either.

"Boscor!" I shouted. The windows were open; he might yet hear. I did not want to waste time by running off to find him.

I had no time to wait for him either, I realized then, and headed in the direction of the harbor. The boy scrambled to lead me.

We were halfway across the yard when Boscor called after us. "There you are. I was coming to find you, my lady. The child is asleep. Where are you going?"

"I will see to the girl later. Prince Graho is hurt."

The chronicle keeper broke into a run. "Are the prince's guards with him? Speak, boy," he snapped.

The boy whimpered, tears clinging to his eyelashes, looking from Boscor to me, then back to the chronicle keeper. He was scared out of his wits, no doubt from the night of fire, followed by a long day of battle, and now all the dead lying in the streets.

"I was out looking for my brother when a man came running and said to bring the Lady Tera and quick from the House of Tahar," he told Boscor as the chronicle keeper caught up with us. "He might have been a guard."

Boscor grabbed the boy's shoulder. "Show us where he is."

The boy pulled from his grip and took off in the direction he had come from. We followed close behind while I checked my belt, glad for my numerous bunches and bags of herbs. I had rolls of bandages tucked up my sleeve. *But oh—*

"My knife!" I left it at Pleasure Hall.

"I have it," Boscor said, right behind me.

I let him keep it for now as we hurried on. Truly, if Prince Graho was as badly hurt as I thought he might be, I would simply use my healing powers. Whatever the price, I could not let the crown prince of Landria, my friend, die here.

The boy led us past the burned harbor, past our beached ships. When I glanced back, I could no longer see the charred and collapsed wharf. The jumble of half-collapsed fishermen's huts we were walking through blocked the view. The huts stood deserted, a small army of dark ghosts in the night.

"Why did the prince come down here?" I asked Boscor, just as I finally spotted Prince Graho lying on the sand, catching a glimpse of him through a gap between rows of destroyed shacks.

Three men huddled around the prone form at the edge of the water. I thought I recognized Durak as one of them, the commander of the prince's guard, by his wide shoulders, but I could not make out his face.

Boscor thanked the boy for his help, and the boy ran off, calling for his brother.

I broke into a run too, toward the group on the beach, seeing nothing but that deathly still form on the sand. I jerked back violently as Boscor caught me by the wrist.

I twisted to look at him. "What is it?"

When he silently pulled me back into the narrow gap between two rows of huts, I went without hesitation. I trusted he had a reason. Yet as I scanned the night, I saw no danger, nothing alarming. Even so, a cold shiver ran down my spine.

"What is it?" I asked again, this time whispering.

The chronicle keeper did not let me go. His fingers were suddenly an iron manacle around my wrist. My knife flashed in his other hand.

"Boscor?" My mind tried desperately to catch up with what was happening.

His expression hardened. His familiar, kind face turned into that of a stranger. "I am afraid, my lady, your journey ends here."

I could make no sense of the words, yet I knew he meant me harm. The shock was so great that I could not even push out the single word, *Why?*

He read the question in my eyes and answered anyway. "The Great

Khan wills it so."

I blinked at him, so stunned, I even forgot to struggle. "Are you the khan's man? But on Rabeen…"

His gaze remained cold, all warmth and friendship thoroughly gone, his bearing suddenly that of a much younger man. "I am the khan's assassin."

My heart lurched. A host of questions assailed me, but I understood that there would be no time to ask them. And if the spirits granted me any time at all, I would not waste them on questions. I had a more important task to accomplish. "Let me heal the prince first. Please."

"The princeling will have to take his chances."

His voice had no inflection, his eyes held no emotion. Boscor my friend was gone. I did not know the man who stood before me.

Something Urdy had said a while ago came back to me and made sense suddenly. "Black Rock?"

Anger sparked in Boscor's gaze. "The damn dwarf." And then he added in a low voice filled with exasperation, "Assassins tell no tales."

I racked my brain for what Urdy had told me about Black Rock assassins. They were hired if information had to be gained before the assassination. They became whatever the victim needed—they gained trust first, to gain the information.

I have been missing the old Guardians who had each been like a father to me. So, to get close to me and gain my confidence, Boscor had become a friend and something akin to a father figure.

Boscor's fresh wound when we had found him made more sense now. He had not ripped his injury open while reaching for dindin fruit.

"You cut yourself when you saw our ship sail into port."

A wry smile spread on his face. "Last I heard, you were healing all who came before you. I did not expect to find you reformed and my wound left to poultices."

He always stayed on deck on the *Shield*, never went below. To stay away from Ina and Nessa? Because they could have told me he had nothing to do with the Merchant League of Rabeen or the chronicles? He had been safe with Urdy. Urdy was new to the island. The dwarf could not reveal him for an impostor.

Anger began to gather in the pit of my stomach. "How did you know we were coming at all?"

"Drav, the emperor's sorcerer, saw it. Emperor Drakhar sent word to Khan Verik."

"What knowledge did the khan ask you to gain from me before you killed me?"

"Khan Verik wants to know if you can be pressed into his service. The emperor has his sorcerer. Rumor has it that you were revealed as a sorceress on the mainland."

Understanding dawned. "The khan wants his own empire. He wants his own sorceress to stand against the emperor's sorcerer."

Boscor's knife hand moved, and my free hand snapped to his wrist on instinct to hold him off.

"Last chance to swear fealty. But I do not think you would serve the khan," he said as the knife slowly moved toward my throat. "Am I mistaken, my lady?"

He was much stronger than I. I could not hold his hand still, could only slow him. "You are not."

"I thought as much. And so Khan Verik's question is answered. If you cannot be turned into an ally, you are a threat. You *are* the leader of an army."

The blade reached my neck and pressed against my skin.

As I stared into Boscor's face, his expression returned to that fatherly look I had come to know. "I will make it quick and painless. The khan has given no instruction to that end. I can do as I wish."

Was he delusional enough to think he was doing me a kindness?

Marga! I called for the tiger through spirit song. *Marga! Quick!*

I listened with all I was for her roar, a sign that she heard me, that she was on her way.

I heard nothing but the waves crashing against the shore somewhere behind me.

Batumar! Batumar! But Batumar had always been deaf to the spirit song. It worked much better on animals than it did on people.

Think. Delay.

"Why did you help us last night? You gave us the idea for burning the enemy fleet."

"The khan paid me for your life, not for me to win him this war. Your life or to deliver you to him willing to serve." He paused. "I did not like his fleet. I did not like thinking he might sail those ships to Black Rock someday." Boscor held my gaze. "Let go of the knife. I would make this easy for you and without pain. In truth..." He sighed. "You have earned my admiration, my lady. I have killed many men, most of them worthless, a few less so, but you... I would follow you were I not an assassin."

"Wait!" I would not let go of Boscor's wrist. I fought him with all my strength, stalling for time. "How did you know so much about the chronicles of Rabeen?"

"Of the chronicles of Rabeen, I know nothing. But Black Rock has a very large library," he said with honest pride. "Black Rock assassins are learned assassins."

"Oh!" I gasped as a thought barreled into my mind with the power of a tidal wave. "The man my mother married... Jarim. Was he...?"

The emperor had sent Jarim to kill my mother and kill me in her womb.

But Jarim had fallen in love with her. He decided to wait until I was born and kill only me, then stay with my mother to console her. Except, every time they came together, my mother left a little of her goodness behind in the man. When I was born, he let me live. I had grown up knowing him as my father. I had not learned the truth until after my mother died, after Jarim sold me into slavery.

"A Black Rock assassin whose name has not been spoken on the rock in decades." Boscor scowled. "He failed most disgracefully."

My mind reeled. Question after question tumbled through my brain. Yet I could not dwell on the past, not with a blade at my neck.

Marga! I called again, but the tiger did not call back.

The spirit song worked only when we were near each other. She was behind the kitchen back at the House of Tahar. *Marga!* I tried again anyway.

"I will not beg you for my own life," I said to Boscor, "but I will beg once again for the prince's."

Even as I spoke, I tried to reach Prince Graho with my healing power, but I could not. I could not even sense his pain. My powers were weakening faster than I had thought. I should not have been surprised, not after I had spent the entire day and most of the evening with healing.

I opened my mouth to keep begging, but even as I drew a deep breath, the blade pressed harder into my neck. I swallowed in panic, my throat dryer than the sand beneath my feet.

My arms shook. I scrambled to find something to say that would stall Boscor for another moment. Movement flashed to my right, before I could find the words. Almost at the same time, Boscor released the knife, the cold metal sliding off my chest before it fell to the ground at my feet.

I was not sure if the surprised grunt was his or mine. Then he whirled, shoving me to the ground in the process, and I caught sight of a dagger sticking out of his forearm. He pulled the blade from the wound and threw it at his attacker in a single motion.

A small shadow darted between two huts.

Urdy.

I scampered back, thinking only to get away from Boscor. The dwarf flew forward. He had rearmed. He had a dagger in each hand, the tips as thin as needles.

Watching the two assassins was like watching tigers fight each other. They came together in a crash, in a burst of violence that stole my breath. Everything happened too fast. In a blink, one of the needle daggers was sticking out of Boscor's left eye, the khan's hired assassin sinking to the sand. One heaving breath was all he had time for before life left him. He lay on his back, one hand over his stomach, almost in the exact position he'd been in when Batumar and I had found him on Rabeen.

Urdy did not get to have a last word either. By the time I turned to him, he lay still on the ground.

My heart raced as I rushed to him and put my hands on his shoulders to shake him. "Urdy!"

A knife was buried to the hilt in his heart. If only I felt a blinking flame left inside him, I could have saved him. But I sensed not even a tiny spark of life. Boscor's first throw had found its target. Urdy had been fighting with the blade embedded, knowing he was already dead. Yet he had fought for me.

He still had one of his daggers. He had died like a warrior, weapon in hand.

Tears splashed from my eyes onto his blue cheek that looked black in the dark. I brushed the drops away. "Thank you for being my friend." I closed his eyes. "You were a very good assassin."

I wanted to stay with him, but I could not, so I wiped my tears, then left the huts and the dead, hurrying toward the men farther down the beach. I would grieve for Urdy later. I would send prayers for him to the spirits. He would be buried with honor, on a hillside, I would see to it. But right now, I had to save the prince.

If I was not too late already.

"I am here!" I called to the men once I reached close enough that they would hear me over the crashing waves.

They looked up, relief evident in the slumping of their shoulders. One gestured frantically for me to hurry.

My gaze fastened to the dark shape lying at their feet. *Deadly still.* My heart pounded hard enough to hurt.

No! Not Prince Graho. I ran faster, stumbling on the sand. *Not this time. Not another friend. Not the prince.*

CHAPTER TWENTY-ONE

KIDNAPPED

Even as my heart raced, something on the sand behind the crouching men caught my attention.

The single mast was oversized for the small fishing vessel that lay at an angle, half pulled onto shore. I stared at it hard through the darkness as I hurried forward. "Is that the skiff that escaped from Sheharree? Did the prince find the escaped Kerghi soldiers?"

Had the Kerghi killed Prince Graho before his guards could catch up with him?

I turned my gaze back to the royal guard, waiting for their answer. The three unfamiliar soldiers wore Landrian blue but had the olive complexion of the Kerghi. I stopped and took a quick step back, then another.

The man nearest me shifted to the side as he rose, and I caught a full glimpse of the body on the ground at last, indeed lifeless. He was not the prince, yet familiar, even with wet sand on his face.

Durak. The commander of the prince's guard. I gasped as I saw the dark line of blood on his neck where a knife had severed artery and tendon.

A trap!

I turned and sprinted back up the beach—no easy task on crumbling sand—but the strangers seized me before I could take a dozen steps. As I opened my mouth to scream, one clasped his large hand over my face. Before I could catch my breath, they tied me, gagged me, tossed me to the bottom of the boat, then covered me with burlap.

My capture happened in less time than Boscor and Urdy's fight among the shacks. *This is how fighting goes,* I thought, my mind numb. This is why soldiers train so much and prepare, so they can fight back but in a blink.

I only ever entered the battlefield in the aftermath, to heal. I had seen men fight, and I knew the thrusts of the swords were rapid, but watching was nothing compared to being in the middle of violence.

My fate was sealed before I could even think. Before I could acknowledge being scared out of my wits. Then I did panic.

Marga! I need your help. Marga! Please hear me!

I struggled to no avail. Too soon, we were on the water. The boat rocked as, one by one, the men jumped in. I fought to sit up, but they pushed me back onto the bottom, then placed their waterlogged boots on top of me to keep me down.

Seawater soaked through the burlap that covered me, then through my clothes. I shuddered with cold and despair. I tried to scream around the gag, but no sound escaped.

"You think she's 'nough?" one of the men asked.

"More 'an nuthin'," another answered. "We need coin."

"We go to the khan with news we lost the city, an' he'll chop off our heads," said the third. "Bringin' him a bit o' fluff will not stay his fury."

"She's sum'on' important like, you mark me words."

"She was with them lords, fer certain. Aye?"

"Still say we shoulda nabbed one of 'em lords."

"You seen the size of 'em?"

"Not too late to dump her in the sea an' run off."

"Run off where, ye boil on a Weranian witch's arse? Khan Verik has the island. He made the fortress city his seat. We have a fishin' boat that'll likely sink from the first big wave. We none of us are sailors. Ye know which way is home?" He snorted. "I thought so, ye pile of buzzard shit."

The third man stayed silent. Was he too thinking about drowning me? Would he speak up and decide my fate?

I held my breath, waiting. I was not nearly as grieved by the threat of a watery grave as by the knowledge that the enemy had indeed taken Karamur, the seat of the Kadar High Lord. And while their khan sat safely behind those walls, more Kerghi poured through Dahru's open Gate day after day.

The hope burning in my heart died, as if smothered by the burlap that covered my face.

Our island was well and truly conquered.

We had arrived too late.

* * *

The skiff sailed through the night, until the men pulled onto a small abandoned beach the next morning. We stayed long enough only for two of them to head into the forest and scavenge for food while the third stayed with me and the skiff. At least he pulled the burlap off my head so I could breathe more easily.

I squinted against the sunlight. The sail was not black, as I had thought the night before, but smeared with mud so it would blend into the night. I could see the man too, more clearly for the first time. He was the rough sort, scarred and mean eyed, some of his hair missing at his temple where a sword must have shaved off his scalp in a fight. He kept watching me, and I did not like the cold, calculating look in his eyes.

I was relieved when the scavenging men returned at last with eggs, mushrooms, roots, and berries. Of course, they shared only among the three of them, giving me none. With my stomach a tight knot from anger and fear, I could not have eaten in any case. I did, however, have another need.

My bladder was near bursting, but, with the gag still in place, my mouth full and sore, all I could do was moan my distress. Whether they understood what I wanted or not, they ignored me. They pushed the boat back into the sea, and soon we were riding the waves once again, as fast as our single sail could carry us.

They did not cover my head again. After a while, they even let me sit up, carefully surrounding me so I could not throw myself over the side. The only small relief was that my hands were tied in front of me and not behind me. From time to time, I bent to the bottom of the boat to splash water on my face. Each time, without letting them see, I drank seawater around the rag in my mouth.

By midmorning, I was soiling myself. By midday, I was retching over the side of the boat. They did remove the gag for that. By that night, I was shaking, my muscles cramping, my mind hazy with delirium. I welcomed it all. The sicker I looked, the better.

We did not land again until the middle of the night. This time, they let me crawl across the narrow, rocky beach to the edge of the forest and squat there. The three men stayed several steps back.

"Better here 'an in the boat." The half-scalped mercenary's tone dripped with disgust.

My back to them, I peered ahead in the moonlight. Before me spread a stand of oaks, the undergrowth mostly weeds. I thought of Kumra and her poisons, whether there existed a way for me to escape the Kerghi.

One against three. Yet the chronicles spoke of worse odds at the siege of Mistron, or even the battle Lord Meber won when some of his men volunteered to sacrifice themselves to feed the battle tigers. I thought of Queen Emila, who exposed herself to the plague, then went among her kingdom's enemies and devastated their forces with the disease.

I would have done that to defeat the Kerghi and save my people. If only I had a plague handy.

The spirits must have guided me, for I spotted a small clump of black nettle just then, its dark, oily leaves standing out against the lighter green of grass. I could not create a plague, but maybe I could fake one, the spirits willing.

I kept my back to the men while I picked a handful of nettle leaves, shoved them into my mouth, chewed them, then spit them into my palm. As I stood and turned to my captors, I rubbed my hands over my face, as if exhausted and faint, neither of which I had to pretend. Then I began shuffling back toward the water, skirting the men, who were still relieving themselves.

The itching attacked me first, then the burning, as if I'd accidentally splashed lamp oil onto my face and it caught on fire. I could feel the blisters rising. My mouth felt as if I had eaten an entire hill of fire ants. I rubbed my hands over each other, then I scratched my neck. Everywhere I touched, everywhere the oil reached, my skin rebelled.

About a dozen steps from the boat, I collapsed.

The youngest of the three men—the one with barely a shadow of a beard—strode over to kick me in the side. "Up!"

The others came too and reached out to grab me, but as I turned my face into the moonlight, they halted.

"What ails 'er?"

The young mercenary took a hasty step back. His voice was less than steady as he asked, "Have they brought the plague, then?"

"Dinna see none of 'em like this."

The scalped man walked around me in a wide circle. "Could 'ave kept their sick on the ship, aye?"

"Get in the boat!" the young mercenary snapped, backing away, his voice underlined with cold fear.

I crawled to the edge of the water, where I collapsed again.

Eyes closed, I let the sea wash over my face. I held my breath as the waves came in, then breathed as the waves went out. The cool water should have felt a relief to my burning skin, but instead, the salt stung my blisters. My whimpers were the truth, no pretense.

"Put 'er in the boat," the scalped man ordered.

The other two took only one step closer.

"You certain?" the young one begged, his breathing harsh.

The other one swore. "If we take 'er to the fortress city an' spread the plague…"

"She'll be dyin' before we get there," his young friend added. "Won't see sunup, I bet me sword."

"Best leave 'er 'ere. The tide's comin' in. It'll drown 'er. The waves will wash 'er away."

Silence stretched as the scalped man watched me. He had murder in his gaze, but he did not want to come any closer to me, not even to run me through with his sword.

I closed my eyes and did my best to look to be dying. Seabirds cried in the air above me as if calling out the news of my death. That might have helped.

At long last, the sound of splashing reached me. The men were pushing the boat back into the water.

I opened my eyes to a crack. The boat sat bobbing in the waves. The sail unfurled, but they did not turn it into the wind. They waited.

The tide came in and washed over me. I let the waves suck me in, draw me off the beach. I let my water-logged clothes draw me under. Then I swam around a large rock that protruded from the water and clung to its side, lifting my face so only my nose stuck out, barely enough to draw breath between each wave.

When the tide rose, I moved higher too. Again and again. My clothes dragged me down, but I fought them even as cold seeped into my bones. The salt stung my blisters so much, I cried under the water.

When the sea covered the rocks at last and I had nothing to hide behind, I cautiously stuck my head all the way out, fully breaking the surface.

The black sail was some distance away. Two of the men were looking forward. One was looking back. I ducked under the water again.

Not until I could no longer see the skiff did I crawl ashore, hoping my dark clothes would not be visible on the dark rocks of the beach even in the moonlight. I crawled to the edge of the forest, then collapsed on my back and coughed up enough salt water to fill a small bucket. When I was done coughing, I smiled.

I was half-drowned, my skin still threatened to melt off my bones, but at least I was free. At least the sand in the seawater had scrubbed the black nettle oil off my skin, so the blisters would likely not spread any further.

Rain began to drizzle from the sky.

Thank you, kind spirits. I tilted my face up to wash off the salt water that still burned my scrapes and cuts. I welcomed the rain, even if it meant that I could not start a fire. I might not have dared in any case, for fear of being seen. The skiff was gone, but other enemy troops might be near.

Even as I thought that, I heard a rustle in the woods. Someone walked in the deep shadows my gaze could not penetrate. The rustling sound came again. Closer. Whoever it was, was coming straight toward me.

CHAPTER TWENTY-TWO
A NEW PLAN

The dark shape shuffling in my direction would have reached to my waist if I were standing instead of pressing myself into the ground. *Some kind of an animal.* It moved slowly. Stalking me? Dry twigs snapped beneath its feet. *Something heavy. A tiger?* Yet it did not have the shape of a tiger.

Round. Short feet. Moonlight glinting off not fur but…a shell.

I breathed a sigh of relief.

Greetings, Grandmother, I welcomed the giant turtle with spirit song.

She looked as magnificent as a queen, her mossy shell her royal cloak. She slowed to look at me as she passed by me.

She was large enough to carry me on her back, and for a moment, I considered whether I could ask her to take me up the coast, closer to Karamur. But I was too exhausted to hang on to her in the cold water. A strong night wind blew from the east, whitecaps dotting the choppy sea. I still felt half-drowned, weak from hunger, and the salt water would have been too painful on my blisters. I kept healing them, but black nettle blisters kept coming back and back, that was the curse of the plant.

The turtle moved on. I watched it crawl across the rocky beach, then into the waves, majestic to the end.

The wind never eased. I shivered through the night. In the morning, I moved out from the shelter of the trees so the rising sun could dry me. I ate clams, then a single red crab, sucking out his raw white meat and swallowing it without much chewing, since the inside of my mouth was still blistered.

I had to decide whether to follow the coastline back to Kaharta Reh, or cut through the forest to find the North Road that led to Karamur.

Batumar and our army were in Kaharta Reh, but they might be gone by the time I backtracked. He would search for me, but he could not stop the war for me. They had to keep moving. They had to reach Karamur as quickly as they could. News of our arrival would find Khan Verik soon. We could not give him too much time to prepare for battle.

If I cut through the forest, I had a chance of meeting up with Batumar. Of course, if he was not on the road at the time and place I reached it, I would have no way of knowing if he was behind me or ahead of me. In addition, the enemy probably used the same road—the main road through Kadar lands. If the Kerghi captured me, I might not be able to escape them again. And a final consideration: the woods were full of predators.

I *could* walk north on the shore, but any passing ship would see me.

Before I could puzzle out the right course of action, a spot of white on the gray sea caught my attention.

A sail.

I looked again, my heart beating a wild rhythm.

Two sails! I pressed myself flat into an indentation on the rocky beach and watched as two boats sailed up from the south, closely hugging the coastline. Single-sail fishing boats, four men in each. They were watching the shore, even the two men who handled the sails. They were all clearly fighting men, armed with broadswords and bows. Some of them were dressed in Landrian blue, but I did not let that fool me again. I stayed low to the ground and watched, prepared to let the boats pass, but as the sail turned and sunlight hit the face of the man in the prow of the first boat, my breath caught.

I was on my feet in a blink, waving and shouting. "Hartz! Hartz!"

The boats turned toward shore almost at the same time, the men waving back and shouting, "Lady Tera!"

I led them to the part of the rocky beach where the enemy had come ashore the day before, a narrow stretch with some sand that would not break the bottom of the boats. Then they were on firm ground and running toward me, smiles on every face, which soon turned to concern.

Hartz winced. "My lady. What happened?"

Atter, Lison, and Fadden all looked horrified and worried as they formed a protective barrier around me. "Are you ill, my lady?"

"Black nettle."

"Thanks be to the gods."

"Lady Tera!" The four men from the other boat caught up with the crew of the first and joined the protective circle.

They were of the prince's guard. I knew them all by name but not much more than that. Valen, the one with the long scar on his cheek, seemed now to be their leader. He was a man passionate about all he did. I had heard him entertain the others in the evenings with outrageous tales of his prowess in battle as well as in the beds of countless Landrian women.

"Lady Tera…" His gap-toothed smile too turned to horror as he took in my injuries. "Is that the plague?"

"Black nettle. Three Kerghi mercenaries took me from the beach in Kaharta Reh. I pretended to fall ill with the green plague, and they left me here for dead."

Valen's expression changed from worried to impressed.

"You should have seen me earlier." I smiled, ignoring the pain. "You might not have brought the boats ashore."

Atter replied in all solemnity, "Even had you the green plague, my lady, we would not have abandoned you."

I believed him. Atter, Hartz, Lison, and Fadden had been with me almost from the beginning.

"Marga noticed first that you were missing," Hartz said. "That tiger raised a right ruckus, she did. She tore up and down the beach, then jumped into the water, swam in so far, we thought she would drown. She was half-dead when the waves washed her back ashore."

"Did she recover?" Marga was as dear a friend to me as any man or woman.

"Aye, my lady. But she is on a tear and make no mistake. Nobody dares go near her."

"Batumar will calm her." I had no doubt he could. Marga liked him almost as much as she liked me.

Hartz grimaced. "The warlord is near as bad as the tiger."

"Worse, my lady," Valen put in. "And Prince Graho not much better."

"Tomron took your disappearance hard too." Hartz spoke again. "As your general, he blames himself for not protecting you well enough."

"I had protection. I sent them off. Tomron is not to be blamed." I paused as I looked south. "The army is not waiting for my return, is it?"

"Nay. The warlord said the enemy was taking you either to the Gate of the World or Karamur, if they held the city. He ordered the army to move out at once, taking the manyinga with them, going up the North Road."

I hated saying the words, but they had to be said. "Khan Verik does have Karamur. He holds the fortress city."

The men's expressions clouded. They had been through enough battles to know that defeating an enemy protected by fortress walls would be a hundred times more difficult than engaging them in battle out in the open.

Hartz found his words first. "We must take the news to Prince Graho and Lord Batumar. Our orders are to take you to the North Road as soon as we found you."

The thought of joining Batumar filled me with longing. I wanted to march alongside our army. And yet...

In a few days, we would all be standing outside Karamur's walls, preparing for a siege. Our army had provisions, but we had no siege engines. And with more and more Kerghi pouring through Dahru's Gate daily, we would be badly outnumbered. Worse, we would be caught between the enemy forces in the city, and those coming down the mountain, fresh from the Gate.

How many of our people inside the city walls were still alive? Were some in the dungeons? The Guardian had said the khan kept all his captives by the Gate, ready to be transported off the island. Yet there must be a few Kadar who remained within the walls. If only I could reach them. If only they could help us from the inside. I could see no other way that we might succeed.

We had come so far, had sacrificed so much already. I could not bear the thought of failing now, of dying in sight of the walls of Karamur without ever being able to enter our city.

The only possible solution that came to mind weakened my knees. I shivered as I turned the idea in my head this way and that. Dark fear filled me like thick fog coming off the sea. A plan formed slowly, a plan that might not work, that might yet bring me death, but nevertheless, a plan.

Spirit be strong, heart be brave.

"I shall not go to the North Road," I told the men, ignoring my doubts as I ignored the pain of my blisters. "One boat shall take me up the coast. Atter, Lison, Hartz, and Fadden."

As they lurched into protest, I continued. "The other boat shall be left behind here, its crew marching to Batumar on foot to let him know you found me and I remain well. Tell the warlord the Kerghi now hold Karamur. Tell him that I shall meet him there. I shall pass through the mountain." Then, since Valen and his men were foreign to the island, I added, "Once you enter the forest, keep straight west."

"My lady, the warlord..."

"My lady, the prince..."

"My lady, our orders..."

They all protested. But they did not naysay me in the end. They considered me the leader of our army. I silently swore I would never take them and their loyalty for granted.

"Aye, my lady," Hartz said at last.

Valen gave a quick bow. The men acquiesced.

I smiled my gratitude. "Let us hurry, then."

The crew of the second boat—the prince's men—grabbed their provisions and headed into the forest at once with Valen in the lead. Hartz, Lison, Fadden, and Atter pushed our boat into the water, and we climbed in. I was soaked to the waist once again. For once, I did not feel the cold. My mind was thoroughly occupied with other matters.

"The prince was hale the last you saw him?" I asked as we cleared the breakers. "I was lured to the beach with a tale of his grave injuries."

"The prince is hale, my lady. But Commander Durak is dead. As are the dwarf and the chronicle keeper," Hartz said, adjusting the sail.

I leaned out of his way. "The Kerghi killed Durak. Boscor was the khan's assassin. Urdy saved my life."

Stunned silence followed my words, the only sound the waves slapping against the boat.

"How far up do we go?" Lison asked while the others stared, then offered me food and water, along with a dry blanket.

"We go all the way to the northern tip of the island," I told him, falling on the chunk of cheese and bread. "To Barren Cove."

"A Kadar port? If it is taken, we might be able to sneak in at night. We are but a small boat."

I kept chewing as I looked to the north, into a gray, threatening mist. I swallowed, then looked back at Lison. "We go to a hidden cove of pirates."

CHAPTER TWENTY-THREE

THE CAVE

The spirits sped us along. The wind stayed steady, no storms on the horizon. The only difficulty we met along the way was passing Wid, late in the evening.

"The northernmost Kadar port," I told the men, wrapped tightly in a blanket against the wind. "This is where the skiff would have brought me had I not escaped. Then from here, they would have taken me to Karamur, the rest of the journey over land."

We lay low in the boat, our sail darkened with mud, a trick I had learned from my kidnappers. The wharf was crawling with Kerghi, the enemy loading their spoils of war by torchlight. We watched them and the dozen Kadar warships in harbor, hulking, giant shadows in the night.

We gave the harbor wide berth but did not dare sail far out to sea. We had to keep the shoreline in sight. We did not want to sail past Barren Cove. I worried about that all the way until we spotted the great white cliffs the following day.

Birds circled high above, the bay empty, the narrow beach not much more than rocks and scraggly weeds. At the farthest end, a stream cascaded down, splashing into the sea.

I breathed a sigh of relief. "No pirate ships."

"My lady," Atter argued once we disembarked and I pointed out the cave opening high up on the cliff, the Mouth of the Mountain. "You cannot mean to climb up there."

"I climbed down once. Lord Batumar and I did together."

"With ropes, my lady," Hartz protested.

They had heard the tale. During our long march through the mainland, every part of my journey had been told and retold many times—to distract ourselves from impending death and all our other miseries.

"It cannot be done." Atter backed up Hartz. "The climb is too dangerous."

Lison, however, merely shrugged. "A hard climb, make no mistake, but it will not put me off. I was a roofer before the Kerghi came."

Fadden, the youngest of the four, agreed. "Not near as chancy as climbing the mainmast in a gale, and I did that enough when we came through the hardstorms."

Little did they know that the climb was not even the worst part of what awaited us. I had to tell them all of it. *Time to finish the tale.*

I turned to them and made sure to look each in the eye, one after the other. "The caves are dangerous. Some of caverns are filled with sulfur, and the ones that are not..." I drew a deep breath. "An ancient god dwells within." I would *not* say his name. "He is not a kind god."

"You escaped him once. We shall escape him again," was Lison's immediate answer.

I smiled at him before turning to Hartz. "I shall take Lison and Fadden with me."

Because I did agree with Hartz and Atter on one thing: this was not a climb for men unused to climbing. Both Hartz and Atter were farmers before the war. Sending them up the steep cliff would be the same as sending them to their death.

"Where you go, we go," Atter protested immediately.

Hartz would not be outdone. "Our orders are not to let you out of our sight."

I could not let them sway me. "I am changing those orders. Lord Batumar could not have foreseen this. We adjust our battle tactics to the battlefield. Is that not how we have always fought?"

Both were scowling, hardly convinced.

"I need you here, at the bottom of the cliffs," I told them. "My plan is to get into Karamur unseen. I shall find a way to open the portcullis in the night for our troops once they arrive at the city walls. But should I fail, I will need to escape this way. I need you to keep the escape route open and safe. The enemy might know that we are here. They might come after us. The emperor has a sorcerer in his service who saw us arriving at Rabeen. The sorcerer might well see us arriving here and send other men."

At that, Hartz and Atter agreed to my plan at last and swore to hold the small beach at all cost. I thanked them, then moved on to the next step.

"We need driftwood. And strips from our sail to wrap around the end.

We need a couple of fatty little fish for the fish oil so we can make torches."

Hartz's expression lightened. "Those we have, my lady."

He hurried back to the boat, dug around among the bags on the bottom, and produced nine fine torches indeed.

I thanked the spirits for saving us the precious time. The sun was dipping behind the cliffs already.

"We best climb if we want daylight for our ascent."

"The wind works in our favor." Fadden turned toward the sea. "Coming from the east."

An east wind meant that we did not have to wait for the gusts to die down. Had it been a sideways, buffeting gale, ascending would have been a challenge. But a steady current of air rushed from the sea to slam into the cliffs. The wind would push us against the rocks and help us cling to the surface.

I tied my cloak into a bundle on my back to carry my share of our supplies. Fadden, Lison, and I were taking all the food the men had brought in the boat. Hartz and Atter convinced us that they could fish for themselves.

I pinned my gown up to my knees in the front, then climbed first, never looking down, my gaze searching for the next handhold and the next. I did not check on Fadden and Lison behind me but kept track of them by their grunts and heaves. I let my mind float back to my childhood when I climbed the numaba trees on our hillside every single day.

When I reached halfway up, I stopped to rest on a wider ledge. Only then did I cast my gaze below. "How goes it so far?"

Below me, Fadden scoffed. "At least the cliffs do not sway like a ship on the waves. 'Tis easier than climbing twisting rigging, my lady, for certain."

I turned to continue up, glad not to have my cloak freely hanging on my back. It would easily catch the wind and act like a sail, pulling me off the rock face.

Here the ascent proved more challenging. Again, I kept my gaze on the next handhold, ignoring the bleached bones in the crevices, the remnants of ancient sacrifices thrown out the Mouth of the Mountain. I knew when Fadden and Lison reached the bones—could hear them murmur prayers for protection to their gods.

Sweat trickled down my back. Every time I had a hand free, I wiped it on my dress, then dusted it with what dirt I could find in the crevices. I called down, advising the men to do the same. A wet palm could cause any of us to slip and plunge into the depths.

Then I almost did plunge, reaching for a blind grip and encountering a hidden seagull nest, its feathery inhabitant taking noisy, frightened flight. My heart beat as fast as the outraged bird's wings.

I paused to catch my breath.

"My lady?" came from below.

"I am fine well." To prove my words, I continued to climb, hand over hand over hand, until I reached the mouth of the cave.

The damp, blind darkness that stretched endlessly in front of me filled me with relief and dread in equal measures. I pushed to my knees, then turned back to wave at Hartz and Atter, who stood sentinel at the foot of the cliffs. The two men waved back, a gust of wind swirling their capes around them. I could not make out their faces, but their movements were tense, as if they already regretted agreeing to my plan.

Lison reached the mouth of the cave next. I helped him up. As soon as he was on flat ground, he murmured another prayer to his gods, even if he did not look entirely sure if his Selorm gods would be much good in the belly of the earth on Kadar land.

"A day or two, then?" he asked, peering into the black cave. "Then we are out in the light again?"

"Inside Karamur, the fortress city," I assured him as Fadden appeared.

Lison helped his friend up, then we sat right inside the opening to eat and drink, enjoying the last bit of sunlight we would have for a while. We did not talk. Lison and Fadden asked no questions. Perhaps they did not wish to show worry in front of me.

After we rested, we tied up our bundles again, leaving out three torches. We lit them with flint and steel. The two men also kept their swords to hand.

"Ready?" I asked.

"Aye." Their responses were sure and instant. "Aye."

Aware, more than ever, how lucky I was to have guards as loyal as these two brave men, I said a silent prayer to the spirits, then led the way forward.

The air tasted like blood and fear. The darkness that waited for us ahead made me shiver. For I knew it was not an empty darkness.

CHAPTER TWENTY-FOUR

BATUMAR

The manyinga beasts grunted their complaints as the unrelenting march in the summer heat wore them down at last. Their shaggy brown fur made them more suited for the northern tip of the island.

"Looking at them, one would not expect them to moan and groan like old women," Baran said, riding on Batumar's side. He was one of the original six, the first group of warriors who had joined Tera's cause on the mainland.

Batumar did not remember meeting him. He had been a *hollow* at the time, without awareness or reason, kept alive only by Tera's nearness.

"The manyinga prefer Karamur halfway up the mountain," he said. "They like the winter snows the best."

"Do they not mind having to dig for frozen grass under the ice crust, my lord?"

"They use their trunks. They mind neither ice nor snow. They enjoy the cold."

Yet the manyinga could not have wished for Karamur half as much as Batumar did as he watched them, trying to judge if he could have any more out of them that day. The great beasts were hearty animals, but their strength was not limitless. They still marched, but they marched under protest. They should have been allowed to drink and graze at midday, should have been allowed to rest.

The ragtag army too needed respite. The soldiers on the manyingas' back were lucky, and so were the ones who rode the fifty horses Batumar had found in Kaharta Reh. But there were hundreds more men forced to march on aching feet. Batumar turned forward in the saddle. He was willing to sacrifice the manyinga—and every man—to have Tera in his arms once again.

He could almost hear her saying, *The day is about to turn to dusk.*

Yet what did dusk matter? He wanted to reach Tera as fast as possible.

You will keep going and march through the night? she would ask if she were here.

And he would say, *Aye.* If his manyinga collapsed, he would walk, and if his feet wore off, he would crawl.

You cannot lay siege to Karamur on your own, she would point out next. And, damn it all, she would be right. So, Batumar rose in the saddle at last and turned back once again to the long column of animals and men following him.

"Halt!" He shouted the single word and hated it with every fiber of his being. Every step he would not take toward Tera tonight hurt him, a pulsing pain drumming through his blood.

The other leaders of the army passed his order down the line like an echo.

"Halt!" From Prince Graho.

"Halt!" From Tomron then.

"Halt!" From Lord Karnagh, whose men and tigers were bringing up the rear. He tried to keep as much distance between the tigers and the horses as possible.

As the order to stop was passed down the line, some of the men dropped into the dust where they stood. Others pulled off the road and sat in the shade of the trees. Vast forests edged the North Road on both sides, blocking any breeze that might have brought relief.

Baran glanced from one green wall to the other, shifting in his saddle. "Enemy troops could be hiding but a hundred steps in, and we would not see them."

"The scouts would have warned us." Batumar too watched the forest. "And we have all the Selorm tigers."

"The tigers will not smell much with all the sweating men and manyinga," Baran replied, but then relaxed anyway. "At least they will hear better once the army settles for the night. And the tigers can see as well at night as any man during daylight."

Batumar scanned the woods for Marga's yellow hide, but she did not appear. "Marga has been gone since this morning."

"Probably caught a deer and fed. She's sleeping in the shade of some bushes. There's no rushing a tiger."

Batumar nodded. Maybe better to have Tera's tiger at a distance, in any case. She had been too quick to growl since Tera had gone missing. She had even taken to snapping at the manyingas' heels.

Marga will catch up with us when she is ready, Tera would say if she were here.

Batumar looked up the rising road that pulled him forward. No one else seemed to feel the urge to hurry. Behind him, empty water flasks clinked as the soldiers pulled them from their belts, eager for a break. He glanced back, catching a few unfamiliar faces.

Some sixty Kadar warriors joined them before they left Kaharta Reh, men who had been hiding alone and in small groups, biding their time to strike back at the Kerghi. The battle for the harbor had brought them out into the open.

Batumar was glad for every new man.

"There is a creek up ahead," he called out. He knew the North Road as well as he knew his own sword. He was home, on Kadar land. And yet he was brooding. He knew he was, but he did not care.

During the past long months spent at sea and on the mainland, not a moment had passed that he had not wished to be back here. But now, even being home ceased to matter. Tera was not with him. His heart had been ripped out of his chest. There could be no *home* if Tera was not there.

What cared he for the road? What cared he for the forest? He would burn the entire world to get her back. She was the light in his soul. Without her, nothing mattered.

Taken.

Marga had led him on the scent trail. They had found Boscor and Urdy among the fishing huts, both slain. Then Commander Durak, down by the water's edge, the sand all torn up—signs of a brutal struggle. Tera was gone. It flayed Batumar's heart, black fury consuming him as he had roared her name to the waves. He had sworn not to rest until he got her back. But the army did need a break.

"Take them," Batumar told Baran, pointing at the men who had been walking next to his manyinga. "And tell the forward scouts that we are stopping for the night."

The half-dozen soldiers—covered in dust and sweat—had been heading for the shade, but as Baran slipped from his beast and issued a command, they turned back and marched off without complaint.

"Set guards!" Batumar called out the next order before he too slid to the ground and stretched his legs, then unfastened the two buckets hanging from his manyinga's side and strode into the forest.

"Valen!" he called out when he spotted the man, one of Prince Graho's, by the creek. "Come tell me again how the Lady Tera seemed when you last saw her. Repeat for me every word she said."

Valen hurried over. The man was a head shorter than Batumar but built for battle, with a compact, wiry build that made him an efficient warrior. An old scar puckered his cheek. He had a gap in his smile where his two front teeth had been knocked out by a sword pommel. When it came to a fight, Valen would give everything he had. He was the type always to run into battle at the front of the line, the very reason he had been sent in the boat after Tera.

"We thought the beach was empty as we sailed by," he began. "But then she jumped up from the rocks and waved."

Batumar filled his buckets as he listened.

She could jump. She could wave. She could talk. The last the men had seen her, she had been hale—save some blisters from black nettle.

The tension in Batumar's chest eased, but only a little. He set down the buckets and filled his flask. "Tell me more."

He knew he sounded like a child demanding his favorite bedtime tale, but he needed to hear the words.

Valen obliged him, the two of them heading back to the road with water. The soldier finished with "We all wanted to go with her and told her so, my lord. But she insisted that the four of us carry her message to you."

The day before last, when the four Landrians had walked out of the forest, Batumar wanted to run them through with his sword for leaving Tera. He had calmed since and could see the wisdom of her plan, so now he simply nodded.

He was putting the buckets of water in front of his manyinga when Baran and his six came running around the next bend in the road, Kerghi soldiers right on their heels.

"To arms!" Batumar called and unsheathed his sword. He swore as he ran forward. Marching the troops until they were utterly exhausted had been a mistake. "To arms! To me!"

Half the army was down at the creek. The ones on the road were the ones too spent to make it to the water. Yet he could hear metal singing as swords flew from their scabbards, and he knew men were scrambling to their feet behind him to follow him into battle.

The fight broke out too fast for the archers to nock their arrows. The two forces came together in a ground-shaking clash, the soldiers launching themselves at the enemy. Batumar looked neither left nor right but at the Kerghi commander before him—a mountain of a warrior with a large iron nose ring.

"Here is where you die," he told the man.

The commander's arms were nearly as thick as his thighs—he had the look of a man who had spent time in the gladiator pits of the mainland—but Batumar would not think that he was outmatched. He thought only that the bastard stood between him and his Tera. And he would not be allowed to remain there.

Each time their swords met, Batumar felt as if the bones in his arm would shatter. He had met few men in his life who could match him for size, but this one towered over him by a full head. The man's black boiled-leather armor was reinforced with metal disks. If it was a memento, brought with him from his gladiator days, it was the right one to keep. Batumar could not slice through. His blade merely threw sparks as it met the metal. He had to pull back to stab. Yet the other man's arms were longer. It took a reckless lunge to cut the commander's throat at last.

Batumar did not wait for the man to hit the ground. He leaped forward to the next Kerghi mercenary, and then the next and the next. When a sword sliced his right arm open, he went on fighting with his left.

CHAPTER TWENTY-FIVE
TERA

For a while, the passage through the mountain remained straight, without side channels, no need to guess if we picked the correct direction, no need to worry about having to backtrack. Our only trouble came from bats, rats, and snakes.

Our torches scared the bats, and they near took off the tops of our heads as they swarmed for the exit. The snakes we could avoid for the most part, as they were pale so far into the cave and easily seen in the light of the flames. The rats were brazen. They smelled our food and tried to climb our legs to get to the bags. We fought them off, but not without being bitten and scratched.

Then we were too far in for animals, but here the ceiling began to lower. First we hunched, then we dropped to our hands and knees, then we crawled on our bellies, suffering more scratches yet, the stone floor uneven.

Suddenly, the bottom of my feet heated. This I did not remember from my previous passage with Batumar—whom I missed a thousand times more than I missed the sunlight. At first, I thought the heat a trick of the mountain, then realized the true cause and called back, "Lison! You are setting my boots afire."

"Sorry, my lady." He stopped moving immediately to allow more distance between us.

Behind him, Fadden cursed him for a fool.

Soon we reached the first of the side channels. I remembered the right turn and took it. For the next turn, however, I hesitated and had to look closely at the stone before making my decision.

"You memorized the entire passage, my lady?" Fadden asked from the back.

"Not quite. Vooren, one of the stewards of the High Lord's castle, brought Batumar and me through. He knew the way. His grandfather had been through the caves and tunnels and left the true path marked."

Each time the old steward had taken a turn, he had marked the wall with a print of his bloody hand. If he continued on that way, the sole print remained, an indication to us to follow. If the way had turned out to be a dead end or unpassable, the man had returned and placed a second print diagonal to the first before searching for a new path. So at each opening, if a single print showed, I took the path. If double prints showed, I went past the fork in the tunnel.

I paused to explain this to the two men behind me, hoping to ease their minds, but their expressions did not appear in any way relieved in the flickering light of the torches. They clearly preferred the open land to crawling about in caves. If I ever had to do this again, I was going to bring miners with me rather than a roofer and a fledgling sailor. Although, I wished from the bottom of my heart that I would not have to pass this way ever again.

We moved along as quickly as the path allowed and stopped only when our torches flickered out at last, first mine, then Fadden's, then Lison's. We had no way of knowing whether day or night ruled outside, but we decided to rest. We ate and drank again, then settled down for the night.

I dreamt of Batumar, his strong arms around me, his warm lips on mine, only awakening to Lison lighting his second torch. I felt refreshed. Mayhap morning had come, mayhap not. It did not truly matter.

"Let us move on." I wanted to see Batumar outside my dreams. I lit my own torch, then peered behind Lison. "Where is Fadden?"

"He was gone when I woke, my lady. He has probably gone to do his…" Lison looked away then cleared his throat. "Morning business."

Which I also had to do, so I moved back until I found a suitable crevice where I could relieve myself, then kick gravel over my leavings.

I returned to Lison, and we waited in the flickering light of our torches for a while. Then we shouted. "Fadden! Fadden!"

No response came.

We waited a good long time, but Fadden never returned.

"Think he is lost, my lady?" Lison's voice filled with tension.

The same tension stiffened my muscles. "We should go find him."

"He knows the signs to follow." Lison stepped into my path. "He will catch up. My lady, we should not delay."

I could not deny the truth of his words. And yet…

I filled my lungs with stale, musty air. "Fadden!"

The single word echoed down the narrow passage behind us. I had no doubt it carried far. If Fadden was anywhere near, my voice should reach him, and, in turn, his own response should reach us as well. But as the echo slowly died away, no answering call came.

Lison and I waited another moment, then another and another. Then we move forward in silence, our hearts heavier than our bundles—although we did leave Fadden's share of the food behind, should he find his way back.

I walked more slowly than the day before to give the man a chance to catch up. Lison and I stopped sooner for our midday meal than we had to. We spent more time on eating the small meal than we should have. But Fadden never reached us.

Once we could wait no longer, we packed up our bundles and moved forward again, then turned down a new passageway in the rock. Here, I could smell the distant stench of sulfur.

"Remain close," I whispered to Lison, gripping my torch tighter.

I said no other words for a while, nor did he, as if he too, sensed that silence was best for this part of our passage.

I felt as if invisible eyes were watching me from up ahead, barely out of reach of the light my torch threw on the walls. I was peering forward, trying to see what waited for us, my attention so focused on the darkness that I did not notice when Lison fell back.

I was about to turn into yet another new tunnel when I realized I was no longer hearing his footsteps behind me. I spun at once. He was not there. Nor was he anywhere near. I could not see the light of his torch, and the passageway was long and straight behind me.

He had been with me at the last turn, of that I was certain. But after that... *Where could he have gone?*

"Lison!" I whispered his name. Mayhap his torch had gone out and he was not as far behind as I feared.

No response came.

"Lison!" I shouted.

Nothing.

I sat and waited, the light of my torch a fragile dome protecting me from the darkness and what might lurk ahead. My heart beat against my rib cage. Blood rushed so loudly in my ears, I might not have heard Lison now even if he walked up to me.

He did not.

The flames flickered, reminding me that I had but one torch for each day I had to spend in the cave. If I waited here too long, I would have to finish the journey in complete darkness. And I would not be able to find the exit, if I could not see the handprints.

I called for Lison one more time, said a prayer to the spirits for both him and Fadden, then stood and moved forward with a heavy heart. At every noise—made by my own feet dislodging some small rock—I jumped. Up until then, I had only to watch for danger ahead. Fadden and Lison had my back, they would have alerted me if danger threatened from that direction. With their loss, the passage seemed even more frightening, in part at least because I had only the light of one torch now instead of three.

I hurried. I watched for the signs that showed the right path. Yet I still lost my way.

I kept looking for the bloody handprints, but I could no longer find any, had not seen any for a while. Should I backtrack? The path still angled up. I had to go up the mountain to Karamur. I prayed I was moving in the right direction.

I walked until I tired, then I walked some more, until the torch flickered out at last. Only then did I stop for the night, if indeed night had descended outside. I wished for Lison's and Fadden's steady breathing. I could hear nothing other than my own panicked gasps for air.

I thought I sensed movement ahead, then suddenly behind me. Then something touched my face, and I shrieked, only to find that a lock of hair had slipped from my braid.

My eyes closed, but I could not fall asleep.

For a while, I prayed to the spirits for their protection, then I thought of Batumar, hoping thoughts of him would calm my fears. But calm would not come, nor sleep, so I hunted for my flint and lit my last torch. Then, comforted by the circle of light around me, I did sleep a little.

When I woke, I called for Lison and Fadden again, in vain. Where were they? I could not bear the thought of them lost in the mountain, yet I could not go back for them either.

The path ahead of me still inclined upward. I walked on.

Spirit be strong, heart be brave.

Spirit be strong, heart be brave.

By the time my stomach growled for its midday meal, I knew I was hopelessly lost. I had not seen any signs since the day before. And even if there were some waiting for me ahead, it would not matter now, for as I sat to eat, my last torch sputtered out. I was all alone, in the thickest, most complete darkness in the world.

CHAPTER TWENTY-SIX

BATUMAR

"I swear the damned road stretched since the last time I came this way. How can it be that we are still not at the end?"

Batumar rode at the head of the long column of soldiers, in the saddle of the horse he'd traded for his manyinga so he could lead a quicker, leaner advance force. His right arm hung useless by his side. He paid no mind to the pain. He thought of little but reaching Karamur in time—before Tera exited the cave and walked into the castle. Before the enemy could capture her.

The gods help him, if anyone harmed her—

"How is the arm, my lord?" Tomron asked, riding alongside with a pierced thigh.

"It would be better if the Lady Tera was here," Batumar responded.

Riding behind him, the young Guardian of the Gate, who was now missing a finger, inquired, "You would let her heal you, then?"

And weaken herself? "Nay," Batumar said and nearly smiled. He simply wished her at his side. Everything was better when Tera was with him. He needed her, and so did the rest of the men.

Somewhere behind him, well out of sight now, rode Prince Graho with a broken collarbone, leading the bulk of their army—some four hundred soldiers. Lord Karnagh brought up the rear. He had suffered no injury in the last battle, but he was missing his sword arm already. They had not a whole man among the four who led the troops up the North Road.

At least the army had grown yet further. A group of forty or so roving Kadar warriors joined them after hearing the last battle. They had been living in the forest, attacking smaller Kerghi units who passed by.

Batumar shifted in the saddle. "The Kerghi we cut down will not be the last group of mercenaries we will meet on the road. There will be more and more clashes the closer we come to Karamur."

Which was why he had made the forward force a formidable one-hundred men. Instead of the entire army stopping daily for skirmishes, his one hundred rode ahead. They would clear the road of any enemy troops, so the main body of his army following later could march on uninterrupted.

"We lost only a dozen soldiers at the creek," Tomron commented.

"Winning a battle is not the same as winning the war." Batumar kept his gaze on the winding road. "A dozen clashes where we lose a dozen men each, and we have lost a third of our army."

He watched for the scouts who were riding yet farther ahead. He needed to be better prepared for the next attack than they had been for the last one. But the clamor, when it sounded, came from the rear.

Tomron twisted in his saddle, wincing as his thigh muscle pulled. "Three riders on Shahala horses," he reported. "Should we stop?"

"I will not waste time. But go see what they want."

"Aye." Tomron turned his horse around and rode off at a gallop.

He returned but a short while later, with three men. Batumar held back a groan as he recognized Koro among them, the young man from Sheharree who had insisted he had once been Tera's suitor.

Batumar supposed some maidens might find the youth handsome, but he was no rider. He was breathing hard, as if he had run a race.

"Lord Batumar." Koro stopped to gasp for air and to wipe the sweat from his forehead. Something akin to triumph glinted in his eyes. "I brought the Shahala healers."

Batumar looked over the pair of exhausted Shahala who had come with Koro. "Two of them?"

They were covered in dust and sweat, but did wear the healers' white robes. Each had a burlap sack of herbs tied to his saddle.

Koro sat up straighter. "Twenty."

Twenty was not a bad number. "And what did the Elders have to say to that?"

"They did not approve. But the younger healers wanted to come nonetheless." Koro cleared his throat. "Only most of them are not as learned. Some are still apprentices."

Batumar shook off the distemper that had settled on him at the sight of the man earlier. "The healers are most welcome and most appreciated." And then, he tacked a "Thank you," to the end.

There, Tera would be proud of him.

Koro relaxed in his saddle. "They are working their way up the main column already, plying their skills on the injured. These two came with me as we heard some of the men in the forward force were hurt."

The two healers began with Batumar and Tomron right then, working quickly, while Koro's gaze searched the group.

"Prince Graho said the Lady Tera has gone ahead to Karamur."

"She has," Batumar told him and left it at that.

"Is that safe, my lord?"

"The Lady Tera makes her own decisions." Batumar let his tone harden.

"Of course." Koro tugged on the reins of his horse until it danced back.

As the healers moved on to see to the rest of the soldiers, Batumar stretched his arm. *Good enough to swing a sword.* Koro deserved his gratitude. "You may ride at the head of the column with me, if you wish."

"Thank you." The young man inclined his head. "But I will ride back and help." And off he went, his horse's hooves raising a cloud of dust behind him.

Batumar shook his head. Then he shook it again when he caught Tomron's approving expression.

Tomron shrugged. "Going against the Elders took courage."

Batumar nudged his gelding forward. "I am going to dislike it if I have to change my mind about the pup and start respecting him."

The column progressed up the road. He rode more easily with his arm healed. He felt easier too, knowing they had healers with them and they were seeing to the soldiers. Yet, he still very much wished that Tera was with them.

* * *

They fought but one small skirmish the following day. Thanks to the Shahala's help, they lost only six men.

They made quick work of the burial, with only one common grave and one prayer to the gods. The gods would have to understand. Perhaps they would not be offended by the haste, or by four of the Kerghi being buried without their armor and weapons.

Three of Batumar's soldiers put on the borrowed Kerghi armor, the fourth going to the Guardian of the Gate. The Kerghi had no uniform, but their preferred curved swords were distinct, their armor of black boiled leather often decorated with symbols of their nation: three peaks of a mountain with a curved sword over them.

The number of Kerghi soldiers they had met since returning to Dahru made it clear that the enemy troops were coming through the Gate at a rate that had to be stopped or the liberating army would stand no chance at all of succeeding against the invaders.

"Are you certain?" Batumar asked the young Guardian of the Gate who volunteered to return to the Gate and attempt to close it. "Infiltrating the

Kerghi troops is an endeavor most fraught with danger."

"Aye, my lord. I should be able to reach the Gate without being discovered."

"At least take more men."

The Guardian shook his head. "I do not need more than three guards. In truth, I do not even need the three. I expect to meet no enemy while cutting through the deep woods. The Kerghi have no reason to be that far in the forest. And when I do meet them near our Gate," he glanced down at his breastplate and curved Kerghi sword, "they will think that I am one of them."

"They discovered you the last time."

"I came through when they first opened Dahru's Gate. They were more vigilant then. Now troops are pouring through every day." He paused to look at the men selected to go with him. "You have greater need for soldiers here, my lord."

The three soldiers had additional orders once they arrived at the Gate. They were to look for Batumar's mother and daughters among the Kerghi's captives. And if they found the women, they were to protect them with their lives, as well as protecting the Guardian of the Gate. Although, Batumar hoped his daughters and mother were somewhere far inland, somewhere safe.

"I could not let you go alone," Batumar told the Guardian. "What would the Lady Tera say when I meet her?"

This reasoning, at last, the Guardian accepted with a quick smile.

"To victory, then." He raised his blade, probably drawing a sword for the first time in his life. After Batumar's nod, he sheathed it again—on the second try—and the four men walked into the woods, Batumar looking after them.

The road was bathed in sunlight, but the trees threw a deep shade. Within moments, the four men disappeared, darkness swallowing them.

The forward force Batumar led did not meet any more enemy that day and only a dozen Kerghi the day next. They were close to reaching Karamur—and ready to stop to wait for the rest of the army to catch up—when they encountered the first large force. The forward scouts rode back to warn them.

"A hundred soldiers and nearly fifty archers," the scout leader reported.

Batumar rolled his shoulders. "Makes me wish for the Landrian archers coming up behind us with their prince."

Tomron was riding by his side once again. "The weight of their large bows and quiversful of iron-tipped arrows make them heavier and slower," he said. "Our forward force needs to be light and fast."

Batumar looked ahead and drew a heavy breath. "I hate not the thought of another battle, but only that it will slow us down. This will be no quick clash, no petty skirmish. This will rob us of a day."

A hundred and fifty Kerghi, waiting in a large meadow the road bisected, was no small obstacle. The North Road had a steady rise, leading to the mountains. The enemy held higher ground—a distinct advantage.

Batumar considered everything he knew about this section of the road, the meadow, and the surrounding forest. None of it helped. By the gods, he missed Tera's quick mind and her counsel.

"It would have been better if we could have taken them by surprise," Tomron said, scratching his knee. "But if the Kerghi are lined up for battle, that means they have scouts in the woods too, and they have already seen us coming."

"We will make a show of calling a halt to the march for the day to camp here," Batumar told him, a plan forming. "We wait for darkness, then sneak into the forest in the dead of the night and pick them off one by one as they sleep."

"And if they decide to move forward and attack?"

"They will not give up the advantage of the high meadow. For them, the better position is worth waiting a day. They are unaware that we know that they are there."

He raised his arm to stop the column of soldiers, and called out. "We will camp here for the day. Pull off the road and into the woods."

Tomron called next, ordering four men to his side to look for a creek. He went off into the forest with them. Batumar did not expect them to return for a while, but they were back by the time the rest of the men unsaddled their horses and fully settled in.

"Found three scouts," Tomron reported with a satisfied grin. "They will not be returning to their commander."

Still, Batumar did not call his orders out loud. He went from group to group to explain their strategy, the most important point being that no Kerghi could be allowed to leave the battlefield. Khan Verik must not be alerted to how close they were to the fortress city.

The men ambled off one by one, as if going for water or looking for a place to relieve themselves. They left their horses and their supplies behind, each carrying only a single weapon.

Another enemy scout was found and killed.

As darkness fell, Batumar and his men spread out in the woods and filtered through the trees. Even when they were at the enemy's back, he did not give the order for an open attack. He, and his men, remained silent.

They did not charge with battle cries, but instead crawled through the meadow's tall grass. They cut down at least forty Kerghi mercenaries before the enemy even realized they were there. And *then* Batumar shouted the call to battle.

His men rose and attacked, none coming up the road, but all bursting through the forest. They were all suddenly among the Kerghi—the Kerghi archers useless.

Batumar lunged for the nearest man, pig faced and bowlegged. The snarling mercenary swung a double-bladed battle axe and swung it well. He had arms thick enough for a blacksmith, his steel missing Batumar's shoulder only by a tiger's whisker. Batumar felt the wind of the blow on his face.

He twisted out of the way, sword up as he completed his turn. The mighty battle axe swung high again by then, both of the man's arms in the air. Batumar's sword caught in him in a vulnerable moment. A great wet sound resulted as the blade slid across the mercenary's stomach, then a sickening splash as his intestines spilled and hit the ground. The man stared at the red pile with a disbelieving expression until his arms sagged at last and he staggered back, then stumbled and fell.

Batumar cut down enemy after enemy until a man rushed him from the back and knocked him to the ground. He managed to twist, but his blade was no use. He had to let go of his sword to wrestle his attacker. They rolled, then they rolled again, equally matched.

Batumar reached for the man's head, meaning to snap his spine, swearing when his hands slipped in the blood dripping from the mercenary's forehead. The man brought up his knee, hard, and Batumar thought he might have broken a rib. He swung his elbow in response and broke the man's nose. While the mercenary was temporarily dazed with pain, Batumar wrapped his arm around the man's neck and yanked hard enough to feel—if not hear in the din of the battle—the spine snap.

He wasted no time but released the man, then rolled out of the way of a hurtling lance, but was attacked again before he could gain his feet. His sword lay in the mud out of reach. He grabbed for the knife in his left boot and lost it immediately, stuck in the skull of an attacking Kerghi. The man screamed the whole time he collapsed.

Batumar rose to his feet, his second blade already in hand by the time the next attacker found him. The blade wedged between the foot soldier's ribs. The way the man twisted was pure bad luck, the knife breaking off between his ribs before the body fell forward, onto Batumar. He shoved the bleeding corpse off to the side, then lurched toward where he had last seen his sword.

"No enemy leaves the battlefield!" Tomron shouted a reminder somewhere nearby.

No sooner did the words ring out over the meadow than Batumar spotted two Kerghi breaking away from the battle and darting into the forest.

He wiped the blood from his eyes and ran after them barehanded.

CHAPTER TWENTY-SEVEN

TERA

The darkness felt thick and suffocating, complete, as if someone had thrown a blanket over my head. Or as if I had somehow traveled back to the beginning of the world, when all had been black, when the Great Mother had floated in the void, before she created light in the dark.

My stomach constricted into a tight fist. I packed up what little food I had left, then stumbled forward, holding my hands out in front of me, always thinking that in but a step, I would touch something truly fearful and horrible, but when my fingers did come against something, I felt naught but unyielding rock, a sign that I had to turn.

It's the right way, I told myself. It had to be. I had to find my way into the castle, and I had to find help to open the portcullis for Batumar when he reached the city.

I kept moving forward. I tried, as much as possible, at each new intersection to turn away from the direction where I once again smelled sulfur.

I went on blindly for an endless time before footsteps sounded behind me. I froze for a moment before swirling to face the danger, my heart pounding. I could see no light. Whoever was coming had no more torches left either. The footsteps neared.

"Lison?" I whispered. Then, "Fadden?"

The response came in Prince Graho's voice. "My lady?"

My muscles sagged with relief. I braced myself on the stones behind me as I searched the darkness for his face in vain. "How come you to find me? Why are you here?"

"I came to help," he said.

I would have thrown myself into his arms if I knew where his arms might be.

"And Batumar?"

"Fine well when last I saw him."

"Heading north on the road?"

"He was."

I wished I could see the prince's face. "Has your torch gone out?"

"I did not bring enough."

"Did you see Hartz and Atter at the foot of the cliff?"

"Aye."

"I lost Lison and Fadden. Have you seen them? I lost them a day back."

"I have not, my lady." He hesitated. "I know them for brave men, but this cave…this dark… Mayhap they turned around to flee."

I did not want to think that of the men.

I had many questions for Prince Graho, but I also feared to talk too much. I felt something sinister there in the darkness with us. Something watching and listening.

Perhaps Graho felt it too, because when he urged, "Let us hurry." He spoke the words in a whisper.

I did hurry, until the path forked and I walked into rock once again. "Stop."

I ran my palms along the wall until I felt the two openings.

I tried both, walking a little way in before returning to the prince. "The left fork is tighter, but it leads up. The right is wider and appears to be straight."

"This way." Prince Graho's voice came from the left branch.

He must have passed me while I was examining the passageway on the right.

"I smell fresh air," he whispered.

I followed after him, hope surging through me. Not being alone made all the difference. Having a voice to follow and hearing another draw breath next to me were a comfort in the darkness.

We passed a side tunnel. The smell of sulfur hit me again. I held my breath as I hurried past.

The smell was even stronger at the next passageway that bisected ours. I shuddered.

"I think this way," Prince Graho called, a few steps ahead of me. "We must turn here."

I trusted him. He was a sailor as much as a prince, possessing a keen sense of direction, which he had proved over and over, working with

Captain Temro to guide us through the hardstorms. I could only hope that his senses worked as well navigating underground. They must have. We were still going up. We would come out somewhere on the side of the mountain, even if not in Karamur.

I wanted to find the secret entrance to the fortress city, but more than anything, I wanted to be out in the light and fresh air. I followed Prince Graho, grateful to have him to lead me.

Yet I did balk at the next turn.

The tunnel the prince led me into was wider than the one we had just left, but somehow darker, the air thicker, damper, feeling like a touch on my skin. A cold shiver ran up my spine. My lungs constricted, and I had to struggle to draw air into them.

"This way. Hurry, my lady," Prince Graho urged.

Every instinct I had warned me away from the passage. I turned and scrambled back, did not draw an easy breath until I was back in the narrower tunnel. "Let us try another path."

Prince Graho did not respond.

"Graho?" I whispered. Then I shouted. "Prince Graho!"

No response came, not even an echo, as if the darkness in the wide tunnel ahead was so thick it swallowed my voice.

I hesitated, my heart trembling. *Do I push forward to find him?* I moved that way, but instinct pulled me back. "Graho!"

Nothing but silence. And in that silence, I sensed something unholy and unnatural. So I backed away, praying to the spirits to save Prince Graho, along with Fadden and Lison, to lead them out of here, to lead us all to the surface.

I stumbled forward on the uneven path in the narrow tunnel, alone once again.

Moisture ran down my face. I ducked my head. Vooren said his grandfather had gone blind in here because he had passed through a tunnel where the walls wept poison. But as I rubbed the back of my hand over my face, I realized that no poison was this but tears that my own eyes wept.

I kept going, always taking the path that led up, until my legs cramped, and I collapsed against the wall at last. I slid to the ground. I could rest here, sit a little. When my stomach growled, I took the bundle from my back to eat the last of my food. I tasted none of it. I drank the last of my water.

I closed my eyes, and it made no difference; I was so wholly surrounded by darkness. I did not know if it was day or night, or how long I had been in the belly of the mountain. *Two days? Three now?* The journey was taking much longer than the first time, as if everything was against me, as if I'd been led down the wrong path. How much longer could I walk before I would be too weak to go on? Mayhap another day or two. I had to find the exit before that.

Sitting in the dark, I said a heartfelt prayer to the spirits, then I pushed to my feet again. I had gone hungry many times in the past. I could walk with a cramping stomach. I would just have to stop to rest more often.

I walked what seemed like half a day when a dim light appeared ahead, a shuffling sound reaching my ears.

"Tera?" a familiar voice asked.

My heart leapt. "Batumar?" I ran toward the large shadow in the middle of the tunnel. "Thank the spirits! How did you find me?"

"Hurry." Without waiting for me to reach him, he turned and rushed back the way he had come.

I had to run to keep up with him.

When he turned, then turned again, I followed behind. I followed even when my muscles tired, even when my lungs burned, until we reached a widening of the tunnel and came out into a great cavern, the ceiling so high, I could not see it.

The ancient god's temple.

I froze to the spot as my gaze darted around, then darted back to Batumar. I forced my legs to move toward him. "Do not stop here! We must pass through as fast as we can!"

He did not move but waited for me now. I wanted nothing more than to throw myself into his arms, but as I reached him, his shadow remained just that. A large shadow. The body in front of me had no substance.

I lost my remaining breath as his torch disappeared, transforming into a dim, spreading light with no source. The shadow I had thought was Batumar grew, rose, and swirled like smoke. Batumar's beloved voice turned into the slithering, oily voice of Kratos. It felt like a hundred snakes crawling over my bare skin.

"Lady Tera, welcome back."

I turned to run, but I could see no opening that led out of there, could not even find the tunnel that I had just come through. Panic screamed in my mind. *How could I have been such a fool?*

Batumar had never found me, and neither had the prince. Both had been illusions to bring me to the god, after he had taken Fadden and Lison away from me. I hoped they yet lived and had found their way back out of the mountain.

"You pass through my domain once again," the ancient god said, his tone amused, and not unpleased. "You were meant to serve me. Accept my power and serve me, then, sorceress."

I was no sorceress. Nor was I Kratos's servant. "Never."

"Never is a very long time for your kind. Do you want to spend that time as an insect, easily crushed, or a woman with power enough to change her fate and the world?"

"I serve the light."

"Are you not aware that the greater the darkness, the brighter the light?" His words slithered around me and wrapped me up in their slick coils.

"You need power to save your people," he whispered. "Or will you let them perish? You have fought long and hard. Is this where you quit?"

Never. Never. Never. "Why would you help?"

"I want men to worship me again."

As his tone dipped cold, so did the air. I shivered and wrapped my arms around myself. I had slept in snow before and felt not half this chilled.

"The invaders worship their desert gods," he said, anger seeping through every syllable as his voice rose to the power of thunder. "My supplicants must return to me."

I thought of the bleached bones outside the Mouth of the Mountain and shuddered.

"Yesss," he hissed as if he could read my mind. "I demand blood sacrifice. I demand worshippers. I want their blood and their gold and their hearts. I demand a sorceress as my priestess. You, Tera, will bring the people to me. I made the same bargain with your great-grandmother not long ago. I am in your blood already, Tera of the Shahala. Your great-grandmother tried to serve me well, but she was too weak. She did not survive the attempt." He paused, then added in a smug whisper, "At least she did steal me your scrolls."

The god laughed as three scrolls floated above my head, then burst into flames, their ashes drifting down to me. "Seeing one's fate should not be granted to mere humans. All fools are the gods who make prophets." A sudden breeze blew the ashes away. "You will be mine, and I will write you a different fate. You are stronger than your great-grandmother. You will be able to carry the weight of my power. I can feel it. You will serve me well."

I had to work hard to push the single word through my tight, dry throat. "No."

My mind teemed with questions and revelations. No wonder the scrolls in the Sacred Cave held no answers when I had read them. The true prophecies had been here the whole time. How many lives would I have been able to save if I had read them? I asked the god nothing. I held still, awaiting death.

Instead of delivering a killing blow, the ancient god laughed. "Wonder you not why you keep returning to me? It is your destiny, sorceress."

"I am no sorceress."

"Not yet. You will be when I grant you power. What power do you wish for? The power over the wind to raise or calm great storms? The power over water to sink ships or to save them? The power over stones to build yourself castles? Or the power over fire to burn your enemies?"

So, he does have power over the sea, then. Boscor had been wrong about that. I shoved the thought away as it would not help me now.

"What if I want all four?" I asked, merely to stall for time. I was willing to die for my people, yet too much of a coward to hurry the moment.

"Then you would be a god." Kratos's dark laughter echoed off the rocks, going on longer than it should have.

The ancient god was a mad god, I thought, but did not dare say the words. He must have considered my silence to be submission, for the veil cleared from my eyes and I could see the enormous chamber truly. A raised, round platform stood in the middle, three giant, carved columns around it, holding up the ceiling. I could see the opening to the tunnels on one side of the chapel and a single doorway on the other.

Toward that opening I ran, and Kratos did not stop me. "Bring me blood," he called after me instead. "You took what was mine, in Rabeen. You freed them from the sacrifice holes. Those two were meant for me."

Ina and her daughter.

"I took your Fadden and Lison instead, but I am hungry yet. Bring me a new sacrifice," the god demanded. "Bring me offerings. If you do not, I will come for you. I will find you. I will fetch you back."

I kept going. If I but had a chance to save my people first, the ancient god could have me.

Nothing but darkness waited up ahead as I ran from Kratos. I moved forward as fast as I could, and soon found myself in a chamber that had a familiar feel. Instead of the uneven cave floor, I walked on smooth tile. I knew this place. If memory served right, the ceiling did not narrow here, no sharp turns. I kept my hands out in front of me anyway, so I would have warning of the opposite wall before I slammed into it. Then I did bump into something at last, and I felt the cold iron of the door that connected the caves to the palace.

Tears burned my eyes. *I made it. I am here.*

I ran my hands over the sheet of iron that blocked my way. When I had first seen the door, from the other side, it had been chained and padlocked. Vooren had the key. After seeing us through The Mouth of the Mountain, he had returned this way. Had he locked the door behind him?

My plan had been, that if I found the door locked, Fadden and Lison would lift it off its hinges. I wasted no time wishing they were here. Instead, I braced my feet and shoved my shoulder against the hard metal.

The door did not budge.

I tried again. And again, and again, and again.

Then, as I strained and strained, the iron scraped on the stone with a terrible screech, and an opening appeared, slowly growing to a hand's width. I stopped pushing and reached through into the darkness that waited there. I felt the silk of the flags that hid the door from the other side. Vooren must have restored everything the way it had been when we had first come down here.

I pulled my hand back and jammed my shoulder against the door again. I rocked it back and forth. Sweat rolled down my face. I grunted. I heaved. I was able to widen the opening another small measure, but there the door stuck, and I heard the chain snap tight.

Vooren had padlocked the door, but he had not been able to fully tighten the heavy chain. He was an old man, not much stronger than I. The slack in the chain allowed a gap, not enough to let through a warrior, but...

I had lost weight during the days I struggled my way through the caves—and before, while I had been held captive on that boat. I sucked in my flat belly and wedged myself into the opening. I shoved hard enough to scrape off skin. My hips fit, so did my shoulders, sideways, but my head held me stuck, held me prisoner of the caves.

I groaned my frustration into the darkness. I had not come this far to fail here. The castle was on the other side, the city of Karamur, and Batumar, heading toward the city gates.

I yanked harder, as hard as I could, holding my breath. I ignored the hair I lost and the pain, yanking so hard, I feared my skull would crack. I fought that door until I finally fell through to the other side, knocking over a pile of flags, then I lay there amongst them for a moment, every inch of my body sore, my scalp on fire.

A single torch burned at the very end of a long hallway. I had not seen its dim light before, with the flags between us, but now I gave thanks for that flickering flame to the spirits. No more stumbling around in darkness.

I was in the High Lord's palace. Filled with hope, I pushed to my feet and drew a ragged breath. I did not have the strength to close the door behind me, but I took care to hide it again with the flags, leaning the flagpoles against the wall, row over row until the opening was fully concealed.

As I moved forward, I did not bother with stealth. I was covered in sweat, dust, and blood, my clothes rent. I could easily pass for one of the unfortunate captives the Kerghi had pressed into service.

I needed to see Karamur. I wanted to learn as much as I could about the occupation and damage, about the enemy's plans, then find someone Kadar and get him out of the fortress city and to Batumar, with whatever information I gathered. Then I needed to find still more allies and a way to open the drawbridge in the middle of the night—once our troops arrived.

I limped down the hallway, then up the stairs. I thought I might find some Kadar in the dungeons there, but instead of men, I saw only wooden crates locked behind the bars.

Curiosity drew me closer. I reached through those bars and wedged my finger under the lid of the nearest crate to pry it open, but it would not budge. Iron nails held the wood in place. I tried another crate, then another.

The largest one of them all was the one that finally gave.

The lid opened with a creak, and I held my breath but heard no footsteps on the stairs. Nobody came. I lifted the lid a little higher and bent to peek inside.

A mass of gold coins glinted at me. *The khan's treasure.* Here hid the means to finance the empire of his dark dreams.

Kratos's voice echoed in my ears. *I demand blood sacrifice. I demand worshippers. I want their blood and their gold and their hearts.*

I shivered, then left the gold behind and went up the next set of stairs. Two Kerghi guards slept in the hallway, sitting up against the wall. I slipped past the men, careful not to kick or trip on the empty mead flasks scattered on the floor around them. Then I used the back hallways to find my way to the servants' quarters. There had to be at least a few Kadar servants left in the castle.

I was halfway to my destination when a dozen Kerghi soldiers passed me, hurrying down the hallway. They were young, no more than boys, with ill-fitting armor that looked like it might have been taken off corpses. They seemed intent on their purpose, as if a harsh commander was waiting for them somewhere. I pressed myself against the wall to let them by. They paid me no attention.

Around the corner, however, I ran into two more men, both well past their twentieth summers, and these slowed to give me a closer inspection. Their armor was decorated instead of plain leather. They wore well-made boots and carried better than average swords, the pommels engraved. *Captains?*

I stopped and bowed, as a servant might, letting them pass by.

They stopped in front of me instead.

"You had this one yet?" one asked the other, his gaze lingering on my chest. He licked his fleshy lips, then he sniffed at me, with a nose as bulbous as a chunk of ginger root. "Smells better than the rest. I don't mind sweat, but I'm growing tired of smelling half the army on a woman before I get my turn."

"Where are you going, girl?" The skinny one reached out to touch my hair. He had cruel eyes, his eyebrows touching each other to form a single straight line.

I bent my head again and kept it down this time. "To the kitchen."

He stepped forward until I backed all the way to the wall, and he still kept coming. His hips ground against mine. "The kitchen can wait. You come with us to the barracks first."

"I beg your pardon." I turned from his fetid breath. "But I was ordered—"

He eased back, then grabbed me by the shoulder, pulled me from the wall, and shoved me down the hall. "I'll be doing the ordering. When you talk to me, wench, all I want to hear is, *Yes, Captain.*" He snorted. "Do you understand me, you dim-witted bitch?"

"Yes, Captain." I gritted my teeth as I walked.

Could I outrun them? Probably not. I was weak with hunger. But if I could not run…at least I could walk faster.

Back here in this oldest part of the castle, the hallways were narrow and short with as many turns as a labyrinth. The castle had started as a keep, then rooms and entire wings were added on later. We would have to take a dozen turns in order to reach the barracks. If I got ahead of the men on one of those turns, I could quickly step into a room, then cut through to another and another. I sped up my steps. I had lived in this castle, and I knew its warrens. I could get away from the men.

"Look at the eager little slut go," Ginger Nose said behind me and laughed. "They all protest at the beginning. But at the end, they all spread themselves and beg for it."

His mean-eyed friend laughed with him and called after me, "Are you going to beg, wench?"

I was around the corner. A row of doors dotted the wall ahead. The third one led to the laundry. In the back of the laundry was another hallway, then stairs, back to the basement, to the room where the coal was kept. The coal chute would take me out of the castle.

I was at that third door and reaching for the handle when a servant woman came around the corner straight ahead.

Onra! My good friend.

When I'd left for the mainland with Batumar, Onra was her own mistress, living with her baker husband above their bakery on the main square of the city. Even now, having been forced into servitude at the palace, she wore a white baker's apron. The khan must have had her brought to the castle's kitchen.

As my heart leaped with joy that she was alive, she stopped. Then a shout burst from her, loud with excitement. "Lady Tera!" She ran forward. "Is Lord Batumar here? Are we liberated?"

The two soldiers came around the corner behind me just then.

"A lady, eh?" They had me the next moment.

"You get your filthy hands off her!" Onra recklessly grabbed the man to pull him away, even as tears welled in her eyes, her gaze hanging on my face. "You are back! Oh, thank the goddesses."

The soldier easily shook her off, but she was not deterred. She grabbed for my hand next.

She had lost weight since I had last seen her. A purple mark bloomed on her cheekbone, her blonde hair loose and disheveled. She gave up on moving the men away from me, but she did not step back. She stood there, looking at me with wonder as her tears spilled over. "You will help me find my Miko? They have taken him up the mountain. My lady…" Her voice broke. "We have seen dark days since you've left."

The two soldiers exchanged a calculating look. "Better see what Khan Verik says." Ginger Nose grabbed Onra by the arm. "You come with us, wench. If the khan takes your *lady* from us, you will take her place."

He grabbed me next and dragged the both of us forward, his fingers biting into my already bruised skin as we went. Away from the servants' quarters where I might yet find help. Away from any chance of being able to help Batumar. As the second soldier fell in step behind us, I wanted to scream with despair.

"Are there any other Kadar in the castle?" I whispered to Onra under my breath instead.

More tears rushed into her eyes. "The soldiers and castle guards were all slaughtered. Most of the women were raped, then taken up the mountain. The Kerghi kept a few dozen of us for serving wenches, but they said they'll take us too, next."

"I am glad your Miko survived. We will get him back. I swear."

"They let him live because he's a good baker. They kept the blacksmith too, and the fletcher. They said skilled men fetch a high price at the slave markets."

I thought of all the people of the castle that I knew and loved. Natta, the smiley servant girl who never failed to cheer me up. I grieved for her. I even grieved for Arnsha and the other concubines Batumar had inherited from his brother Gilrem. I grieved for our guards and the people of the city. I grieved for their children.

Then we walked by a window and the north tower caught my eye. The great tower lay in a charred ruin. I did not think the Kerghi had siege engines.

"What happened?" I asked in a whisper as we passed by.

"Lord Samtis sought to enlarge the tower. He thought he had time. He did not expect the Kerghi to come back down the mountain. The Kerghi fire arrows set the scaffolding on fire, but it hurt them more than us. When the enemy soldiers poured in, the tower collapsed on top of them. It killed nearly as many of them as our defending forces did." Onra's voice thickened. "In their fury, the Kerghi cut down a hundred captured men and women."

The mercenary marching us forward shook us. "Shut up, the both of you. Or I'll knock out your teeth."

I could not have spoken if he gave permission, for just then we passed by another window, one that looked out to the practice yard, and Onra's words became flesh. Rotting corpses decorated the walls, hung by the neck. Nearly all missed a body part or two, a foot, an arm, a nose. They had been tortured before they were killed.

In the middle of the practice yard stood the remains of a giant funeral pyre. All had not burned. I saw charred arms. I saw the blackened corpses of tiny suckling babes. I whispered the Last Blessing over them. The massacre of Rabeen haunted me still, and I knew I would never forget this courtyard either. I would see the dead for as long as I lived.

My heart broken, I turned to the man who held me captive. He would have taken part in the massacre. Which one of my friends had he killed?

"Release us at once! I *am* the Lady Tera, and I tell you true, you *will* regret this." I tried to yank my arm free, but I failed.

The two Kerghi captains were many times stronger than Onra and I, and fully armed. Fighting them had no chance of succeeding. And their khan... I had no illusions about what would happen when I was presented to him. Khan Verik had sent an assassin after me.

The plain truth was: the khan wanted me dead.

CHAPTER TWENTY-EIGHT
TERA

A dozen Kerghi guards stood around the perimeter of the Great Hall when we entered. Khan Verik himself sat straight ahead, scowling on a white throne made of bleached bones, shouting at one of his commanders in a language I did not understand. Nor could I truly focus on the words. A grisly sight on the wall behind the khan drew my attention.

On that wall above the throne, mounted like a hunting trophy, hung Lord Samtis's head.

He had been younger than Batumar, a born warrior, the man the warlords elected as High Lord of the Kadar when they thought Batumar had perished on the mainland. Samtis had been a good man, a strong man, even handsome. Now his dark hair was matted with blood. His eyes stared unseeing, his mouth hanging agape, his tongue black and shriveled.

He did not deserve to be mocked in death this way. Grief welled in my chest anew. Then that grief turned to anger. It turned to something hard and cold and determined.

As Khan Verik dismissed his commander, Onra and I were dragged forward by our arms. *Our turn.*

The new khan looked very much like his father, the man I had watched Batumar kill when Khan Woldrom had laid siege to the fortress city. Verik had the same hulking stature and the same red hair, the same flat nose, although, his small brown eyes were sharper and meaner. Black armor of boiled leather—from some rough and scaly animal—covered his body. He had two curved swords in his belt and daggers strapped to both thighs and both arms.

He barely glanced at us, irritation filling his voice as he spoke. "Have I no man left to beat servant girls into submission that you must bring them before me? Give them to the men, or give them to the dogs. I have more important affairs to attend to."

"Forgive me, Great Khan." Ginger Nose bowed his head. "But this one," he yanked Onra's arm up, "says that this one," he yanked my arm up next, "is the Lady Tera."

Verik's gaze snapped to me, his attention absolute and absolutely malevolent.

I straightened my spine and did not wait for permission to speak. "I am the Lady Tera. I have come to take back my island."

"You dare to look me in the eye and stand before me instead of falling to your knees?" he demanded, his cold voice whipping through the room like a north wind.

I apologized not. Neither did I lower my gaze.

"You imagine yourself my equal?" He scoffed, tapping his fingers on the arms of his throne—half a dozen thigh bones bundled together with iron chains—as he waited for my answer.

How many dead men had it taken to make that cursed throne? Were they Kadar warlords? I doubted they were simple servants.

The man liked his trophies. *If I fail here,* I wondered for a moment, *will my head be mounted next to Lord Samtis's, or will the khan have my bones made into some macabre scepter?*

"Tell me, then, Lady Tera, how do you find Khangar?" the khan asked with a dark smile when I remained silent. "Do you like the changes I have made?"

Khan-gar meant *the khan's seat.* He had renamed the city already.

Khangar. I despised the very word. So, the true name of our city was already erased. If Verik stayed in power, how long would it be before our people were erased as well, then even our memory disappeared?

"How do you like my throne room?" He glanced back pointedly at Lord Samtis's mounted head.

I hated his damned throne room, his throne, *and* the man. I was used to being in this room at the nightly feasts, sitting at the Lord's table on the dais at Batumar's side. I tucked those memories away until my mind cradled but a single thought: *I shall claim it all back, and I shall save my people.*

"Are you so great a sorceress as they say?" the khan demanded next. "I heard that when you first came to this city, you rode a manyinga beast. They say you called an army on the mainland with your power. You made them charge into battle and fear not the spilling of their blood. You have tigers fighting by your side. Rumor is, you brought Batumar back from death."

He leaned forward on his throne. "Do you deny the reports?"

The fingers gripping my arm tightened enough to hurt. The captain holding me did not like the khan's talk of sorcery. I remained silent.

"Speak!" the khan shouted. Then he calmed himself once again and taunted with a smirk, "Is your fear of me so great that you are struck dumb?"

"I stand alone and unarmed." I made sure my voice carried. "You sit there covered in blades, with a dozen guards, and still have me restrained. Which one of us is afraid of the other?"

Fury reddened his cheeks, but I was not yet finished. I held the khan's murderous gaze. "Withdraw from the city now. Leave the island with all your men, and you shall be spared."

"So, you do claim yourself to be a sorceress without equal?" His sharp gaze burned into mine, as if he was searching for the source of my power deep inside me. "I sent a Black Rock assassin for you. Yet you are here, and he is not. Which means when he offered you life in exchange for serving me, you killed him instead. You would have to be a great sorceress indeed to kill a Black Rock assassin."

"You may believe what you wish to believe."

He leaned forward in his seat. "I believe I am khan of the Kerghi, the founder of a new empire. I believe you will lose your head here today, sorceress, unless you pledge yourself to my throne."

At his words, the captain holding me shoved me down onto my knees. When Onra cried out, he roughly shoved her back at his friend standing behind us, who caught her and threw her to the floor. Then he stepped up and grabbed my free arm to help keep me down, the two men holding me between them.

They gripped me so hard that pain shot up my arms. They held me immobile, as if they thought I might need my hands to draw symbols in the air to work my sorcery. Tension poured off them, easing none even when one of the khan's guards strode to us and positioned himself next to me, drawing his curved sword with a menacing hiss.

Most people believed the only way to kill a sorceress was to boil her in tar. I was glad the khan did not hold with superstition. All in all, I preferred a clean death.

But not yet.

I *was* willing to die for my people, but not like this, not without gaining their freedom. I searched for the right words to say, anything that would delay my sudden and violent end here. *Help me, kind spirits!*

I opened my mouth, but before I could utter a single word, an oddly familiar sensation slammed into me, and I gasped instead of speaking. That odd sensation tugged at the edge of my consciousness. It had been tugging for a while, I realized, but until now, it had only whispered. Now it shouted.

Yet I sensed not a sound, but a strange, vast emptiness, a yawning dark hole that for some reason made me think of... *Batumar.*

My heart sped.

Is he here?

But no, this was not Batumar, I knew a heartbeat later. The strange feeling reminded me of the Hollow, the empty thing Batumar had once been, after the sorcerer of Ishaf had nearly ripped his spirit away from him.

My breath caught as understanding dawned on me at last. I was feeling the presence of a *sorcerer.* And since the sensation was strengthening, I was fair certain that the powerful sorcerer was drawing near.

Then he was right there. The khan's men held me fast so I could not turn, but I heard men rush in, weapons and armor rattling. A surprised expression flickered across the khan's face, then was quickly disguised.

I stared as golden-uniformed guards carried past me a frail old man reclining on a litter. He ignored Khan Verik and kept his gaze instead on the little golden dog that squirmed in the crook of his arm and licked his chin.

"Emperor," some of the men murmured, bowing deep.

The man was completely hairless, his skin painted gold, his shaved scalp studded with golden studs that ended in spikes. He resembled the carved images of the sun god, the desert god, I had seen on the mainland. He wore a robe richly embroidered with gold thread, the flower pattern running in stripes from his shoulders to his feet. Only when I looked closer did I realize that what I thought were flower heads were human heads instead.

The chopped-off heads depicted the way the men looked after their beheadings, blood running from their severed necks, eyes wide, faces distorted, but each individual and unique. Some wore crowns still.

"You were to hold her for me," the emperor I couldn't look away from told Verik in a mild tone, his voice ancient and redolent with power. Here was a man whose nonchalance was not faked. He had seen it all and owned it all. He was secure on his throne. He did not shout. He could afford to whisper. All men still listened to him.

Khan Verik drew deeper into his throne, his hands fastening onto the armrests. "Emperor Drakhar."

I no longer struggled to rise. My mouth dry, I drew myself instead as small as I could, wishing I could disappear. *Maybe I could.* Maybe they would forget about me. Maybe I could escape.

Then the sorcerer came into my line of sight at last, walking behind the emperor's litter, his long black hair decorated with a handful of thin braids, the end of each braid bound with silver wire. He was not much older than I—so young a man to hold all the power that emanated from him. He wore black leather as a warrior would. No palace sorcerer was this. He moved like a man who had seen battle.

On his belt, next to his sword, hung a hammered-iron war horn, covered with symbols I had never before seen. I heard much about that horn at Uramit. Its name was Tigerbane, created with magic so its sound would drive tigers mad, drive them off the battlefield.

As I looked up from the horn, I found the sorcerer's gaze on me. The amused glint in his eyes raised goose bumps on my skin. His eyes were blacker than his clothes. They were twin openings to a dark cave, and in that cave hid something watching and waiting.

When a cold shiver ran up my spine, he smiled.

Even the curve of his mouth was cruel. There was a sharpness to him, all lethal angles. Yet most women would find him handsome. He had the beauty of a well-forged blade. The foremost thought in *my* mind when I looked at him was: *deadly*.

I tore my gaze from him. I needed to send word to Batumar that the emperor and his sorcerer were in the city, but I could not fathom a way. I needed a distraction.

The emperor played with his little dog and gave no orders, yet two of his guards rushed to me and shoved Khan Verik's men away. One of the imperial guards helped me to my feet, respectfully avoiding my gaze and stepping away as soon as I was standing.

Then the emperor's imperial guards each moved to one of the khan's men, and this time, I did catch the slight flick of the emperor's fingers as he gave the order. The khan's men had their throats cut before they could rise from their kneeling positions. Blood spilled, then ran in rivulets to gather into pools. The emperor's little dog lifted its head and gave a few excited sniffs. The emperor petted him.

"You have no right!" Khan Verik sprang to his feet with a protesting snarl on his lips, his twin swords in hand. In but the blink of an eye, the imperial guards surrounded him. In another blink, he was disarmed. Then he was thrown down the steps, and he sprawled on his stomach in front of the emperor.

Verik scrambled to rise, cheeks reddened, blue veins popping out at his temples as he grabbed for his knives. "*I* have taken these lands. These islands are mine!"

Two of the imperial guards knocked him back down with the pommels of their swords, driving the metal hard into his back, then, as his knees bent, they drew their blades across the backs of his knees. The khan collapsed once again. This time, he did not rise.

The emperor barely looked at him, his gaze glassy and unfocused, as if his mind was somewhere else, as if he was merely passing through here, the people in the room not important enough to hold his full attention. "You are a mercenary, Verik. Your people sell their swords for gold and always have. Your father, Khan Woldrom, understood that. You do not. It is unfortunate."

"If you kill me, the Kerghi will rise against you." Verik spat the words as he struggled again, for the imperial guards now held him beneath their boots, pressing his chest against the stones.

"The Kerghi are not the rising kind." The emperor's gaze rested on him at last. "Your people are not organized enough. Never have been. You are a good scourge, a good mercenary army, good at sweeping through and killing without mercy. Your value has always been in knowing how to follow orders. Without that, you have nothing to offer me."

Another flick of his fingers, and the two guards yanked Verik to his knees, into the exact same position I had been in earlier.

Just the distraction I needed. I shifted on my feet, trying to ease back. I managed but one step before the sorcerer's attention snapped to me. His cruel lips flattened. He was not amused by my escape attempt.

While I silently cursed him, one of the imperial guard grabbed the khan by his red hair and jerked his head back, while the other cut his throat with a slim dagger, as quickly and easily as a cook killed a chicken for dinner. Blood sprayed, but only for a moment, then it gurgled and bubbled, flowing down the khan's chest. He was still trying to reach for his knives as he crashed forward.

As his executioners stepped back, leaving the khan's body to lie in the gathering pool of his own crimson blood, the emperor's glassy gaze turned to me. "I regret you had to witness all this unpleasantness, Lady Tera."

Whatever his mouth said, his tone told me he regretted nothing. Indeed, the khan's swift execution might have been for my benefit. The emperor was demonstrating how he treated resistance.

While he studied me, his imperial guards kicked the bone throne down the steps, then kicked it apart until it lay in pieces. Then they carried the emperor's litter up the three short steps to the dais. They set him down in the exact spot where the bone throne had sat moments earlier. The emperor remained reclining. He never stopped playing with his little golden pet.

The sorcerer did not join his master but drew closer to me instead. I did not move away. I did not want him to think that I feared him. I refused to look at the man, but I could swear I heard him chuckle under his breath.

The emperor cast a brief look at Khan Verik's body at last, then addressed the captain of the imperial guards, a big man with close-cropped blond hair. "Find someone to replace him at the head of the Kerghi. A man who knows his place."

He let his pet go, and the little dog ran down the stairs, straight to the khan's body to drink from the pool of crimson gathering by the man. The eager lapping sounds sounded unnaturally loud in the sudden silence.

The emperor's gaze returned to me once again. "I understand both

Verik and his father, Woldrom, have caused some harm to your people, the Shahala. That was not my intention nor did it happen on my orders. Have the Shahala lost a great number? I hope all have not perished."

"Not all," I told him. Whatever he was, whatever else he had done, he had stopped the khan from eradicating my people. Even if he saved them for his own evil purposes, I was grateful that many of the Shahala yet lived.

"I am glad to hear Verik was able to follow *some* of my direction. He did have orders to hold you safe and secure for me. Yet I have a feeling if we arrived but a moment later, you and I would not have met. A good thing I decided to visit a mooncrossing early. I have been looking forward to meeting you, Lady Tera."

"What do you want from me?"

"Ah, the impatience and directness of youth." He smiled, but the smile was far from indulgent. It was a cold smile that suggested further outbursts would not be tolerated.

"My empire is vast and war is constant," he went on. "I need healers. Since Woldrom and Verik managed to decimate the Shahala before I stopped them, I need their numbers increased again. I understand that you, proclaimed by many as the greatest of all healers, come from a Shahala mother and a Kadar father. It appears only one Shahala parent is necessary in a breeding pair."

Again, I remained silent.

"You do not protest?" he asked.

"Would anything I say stop you?"

He almost smiled at that. "You caused much upheaval on the mainland that cost me both men and coin. I thought you would be more obstinate, the type who refuses to acknowledge defeat. I am pleased to be mistaken. I have great plans for the world, and you have an important part in those plans."

His words brought to life a terrible suspicion in my mind. "You wish to breed me to make more healers?"

"Not quite. Your great-grandmother was a sorceress, was she not? Your grandfather and mother must have inherited the trait, yet never used it for anything but to enhance their healing. Unusual. Few with the power of sorcery are ever that restrained. Even you are not. You go to war. I have heard much about your exploits. I suspect most of your victories were achieved by the power of sorcery." He sounded almost like a proud parent.

His gaze flickered toward his sorcerer for a moment, but he kept addressing his words to me. "To rule the whole world, to become the Emperor of the Four Quarters, I need more power. My empire will need a faithful sorcerer or sorceress in each of the territories I hold. You are to breed with Drav."

Rage threatened to swallow me, but I refused to allow it to take over my heart. I saved that rage for later, for when I would be in a position to use it to destroy the man.

"Now, unlike healers," the emperor went on, "the most powerful sorcerers are bred from two sorcerers. Both mother and father must possess true powers. A sorcerer can gain power from killing another sorcerer and taking his power, but it is never as strong as power that is bred. *That* is what I want. Blood power."

This time when I remained silent, I did so because speech escaped me.

At last, the emperor smiled. "You probably think I will not live long enough for your children to serve me. But Drav assures me he knows how to make me live forever. Let us all plan together for that happy future. Can you not see it? Your descendants will stand next to my throne. The world will bow to them. They will have power you cannot yet imagine."

He reached out toward me, his emaciated arm slipping forth from the sleeve of his embroidered robe and sparkling. His skin was painted with gold even under his clothes. "Come, my Lady Tera, and take that power from my hand. Come pledge your allegiance."

CHAPTER TWENTY-NINE

TERA

I stared at the mad Emperor who wanted to live forever like a god, who expected me to drop to my knees before him and kiss his hand. I would *never* submit to him. He thought he knew me, but, in truth, he saw not me, only his illusions. In his madness, he had woven a tapestry of endless glory for himself. I was but a bright thread for him, in a color that he needed.

No, I thought then. He was weaving not a tapestry but a net, a net in which to capture all the world, every man and woman. I would not be part of such a trap.

"I wish for no power," I told him.

He retracted his gleaming arm, his expression turning puzzled as if he'd just heard his dog talk or seen a bird swim, something altogether unexpected. "What do you wish for?"

"Peace."

"Then serve me for peace. When the world is mine, when I'm Emperor of the Four Quarters, my peace will reign for a thousand years."

I shook my head. "A great empire, and not a free man or woman in it."

Kind spirits, show me the way.

The prayer I had said countless times in the past stopped me this time.

Was I really asking the spirits to show me the way, or did I still merely want to do everything *my* way?

Every time I thought about righting our world and all the war and pain and damage in it, I thought the world could be healed only with kindness and love. I was a healer. I believed with all my heart that kindness could survive in an unkind world. I believed in love of country and one's people, love of freedom, love of truth, love of service. If we were to make a better world, I could only see that world built on these values. Shahala values. Values my mother had taught me.

Yet my mother's last message, engraved on her tombstone for me to find long after her passing, said: *Spirit be strong, heart be brave.*

I was beginning to understand that message as I watched the emperor who sought to rule the Four Quarters. I must be kind and good in the world, but not only that. I also needed to have the strength and courage necessary to ensure that kindness and goodness survived.

Standing before the emperor even a year ago, I would have been filled with fear. But now I understood that while some powers were granted, others were claimed. After his father's death, Khan Verik had claimed his title by killing his own brothers. He had claimed our island by taking Karamur, the High Lord's seat. I was here to claim it back.

So I told the emperor what I had told the khan. "Withdraw from the city now. Leave the island with all your men, and you shall be spared."

"You may leave us for now," the emperor said as if I had not spoken.

I stood my ground. I could not allow him to dismiss me like that, not if I were to save my people. I had to try *something*. But what if the only thing I could think of was as evil as the man?

Not long after I had met Batumar, he'd asked me whether I could take life, the way I saved life. I had told him I would never try. Yet as I stood before the emperor... I reached toward him with my healing power for a reason that had nothing to do with healing, and sought out his heart. I listened to the rhythm. *Thump—thump—thump.*

Could I?

The sorcerer's cold hand descended on my shoulder. All my senses dampened. I could feel the emperor's heart no longer, could not hear it beat. All I could hear was his voice. The moment when I could have done something passed.

He was talking to the commander of his guard. "Troops do not like uncertainty, and they did not expect me here today. Neither did they expect the loss of Verik or to have a new leader. I will address the fighting men. Find a place large enough to hold as many of the Kerghi mercenaries as possible. The imperial guard can watch the city walls. I want as many Kerghi as possible to hear me. The siege-laying army that sailed from Uramit with Lord Batumar could be under these walls as early as..." He cast a questioning glace at his sorcerer for confirmation. "Tomorrow?"

"The last I have looked."

The emperor went on. "Our men must be ready. There can be no uncertainty, no division in the ranks. I shall have them swear allegiance today."

As many Kerghi mercenaries as possible… And Batumar with our men nearly here, only to be met with overwhelming force…

I had to get word to him, but how? And if I couldn't warn Batumar? If I couldn't open the portcullis and the city's gate? At the very least, I had to steal Drav's war horn away from him. We needed our battle tigers on the battlefield.

If only the sorcerer and the imperial army hadn't come. If only I could destroy the horn. If only I could even the odds.

A seed of an idea formed in my mind.

I needed time to think it over. I needed time to consider whether it could work. But time I had none.

I cleared my throat. "The courtyard outside the Great Hall will hold hundreds of soldiers. More can listen from the windows and the ramparts."

The emperor did not acknowledge me. He simply went on talking to the commander. "Make sure the Kerghi are assembled in the courtyard. If that is not large enough, have them up on the rooftops."

The captain nodded to his second, and the man hurried out.

The emperor was not finished. "Scour the fortress city for a catapult. If they have none, have one built overnight. I want it on the top of the outer wall, atop the portcullis, and as many barrels of pitch next to it as can be found in the city. Then gather up the servants. I want them bound and ready. When the enemy arrives on the morrow, I want every worthless peasant yet left within these walls to be dipped in pitch, then lit on fire, then lobbed at the enemy."

The horror of the images born of his words filled my veins with ice.

"I want a massacre that the world has not seen." He was so soft-spoken, so unconcerned, even relaxed. Yet it was as if death itself had whispered. "I want it to be known that any land I take, no rebel can liberate."

Think not of his evil. I could not despair. *Give not into hopelessness.* I could not surrender. *The tent pole must stand,* Tomron, my faithful general, had told me once in a difficult moment. *The tent pole must stand.*

I steeled my spine as I steeled my will.

Think of hope.

Batumar will be here by tomorrow.

Drav's gaze cut to me once again. Those dark, cavernous eyes threatened to suck me in and swallow me forever. I felt as if all the air had been squeezed out of my lungs. Cold menace emanated from him, but at the same time, I also felt curiosity and a dark amusement. I tore my gaze from him and gasped for air.

As I caught my breath, I straightened my spine. "I had a long journey. I shall retire."

"The sorceress should be there when you speak to the Kerghi,

Emperor," Drav told his master. "Having both a sorcerer and a sorceress by your side, especially a woman so famed, will distract the troops from Verik's beheading. They are simple soldiers. They need something to talk about in their barracks at night. Better to have the Lady Tera as the topic."

The emperor did not look at me, but, after a moment, he inclined his head ever so slightly.

"I will clean up, then meet you all in the courtyard." I began walking away, glancing at the door as if I was ready to flee. I had to draw Drav with me.

The sorcerer took the bait and seized me by the arm. "I shall personally make sure that she is prepared and ready."

His touch was cold, his fingers cuffs of ice. I looked up at him and felt once again as if my spirit was being sucked out of my body and into the twin black caves of his eyes.

As we left the room, I glanced back at the emperor one last time. His gaze flickered to the man who had cut the Kerghi khan's throat. The man bent down, used the same dagger to slice off the khan's ear, then held it out to the little dog. The emperor's pet snatched the ear away, then trotted back to his master, up the stairs, leaving tiny bloody paw prints in his wake.

CHAPTER THIRTY

TERA

Drav's hand slid from my arm to my wrist as we walked away from the
Great Hall. He would not release me, so we walked side by side, three of
the emperor's guards falling in step behind us. Onra trailed behind them,
wringing her hands. I flashed her a reassuring look before turning forward.

"I can change on my own." I knew the more I pushed him to leave, the
closer the sorcerer would stay to me. And he needed to be close if I were to
take that war horn away from him. "You must have matters of sorcery to
attend to, something more important than playing lady's maid."

"I assure you, my lady, as distasteful as your filthy clothes are, peeling
you out of them shall be a pleasure."

I did not respond, as a full unit of imperial guards appeared up ahead,
hurrying toward the Great Hall. They split into two columns and hugged
the sides of the hallway, allowing us to pass through the center. They would
not meet the sorcerer's gaze.

"Withdraw from the city now," I told them. "Tell all others who came
with you to leave the islands, and you shall be spared."

The guards ignored me, giving no sign that they even heard me. Drav
was the only one to react.

He shook his head with an amused smile. "You will not have a bad life
with me. We will stand together by the emperor's side. He does take care of
those who serve him well."

"I plan on serving him not at all." I mirrored his smile. "How times change," I said then. "When I was born, the emperor wanted me dead. He sent a man to kill me in my mother's womb, all because of an ancient prophecy."

"My father told him when and where you would be born." Drav's tone turned pensive. "And yet you lived. And now the emperor has changed his mind about you."

"Lucky for me."

Drav's smile returned, nearly reaching his bottomless eyes. "Lucky for the both of us, I think."

"I have no power of sorcery, as you must well know."

"You have something." He licked his upper lip. "I can taste it on the air. You have power in this place." He hesitated. "And there is another, darker power too, that clings here, a power very much to my liking."

My steps faltered for a moment. I could barely imagine what damage Kratos could wreak if he bound Drav—a true sorcerer—to his service.

Never.

"Why are you at the emperor's side?" I held the man's gaze as we walked. "What prize does he give you for your loyalty?"

"Maybe the prize is you, sorceress."

He said the words lightly, but something in his tone made me think the tale had more to it. I waited.

"My father assisted the emperor now and then, but he was not bound to Drakhar's service," he began in a bored tone, as if answering me only because he had nothing better to do at the moment. "He did, however, bind me to the emperor. I serve for life. As will my children and my children's children. Three generations were sworn. And a sorcerer's oath cannot be broken."

Neither his voice nor his expression betrayed the anger and resentment I would have felt in his place.

"It could be worse," he added, his smile now true and real. "The emperor could have selected a hundred-year-old crone for me to breed. Trust me, he would have expected me to make it work."

I did not know how to respond to that. I did not have to in any case, as we reached Pleasure Hall at last.

Under Kadar tradition, no man was ever allowed in a lord's Pleasure Hall but the lord himself—under punishment of death. Drav and the three imperial guards clearly did not understand the laws of Kadar Pleasure Halls, because not only did they come inside with Onra and me but stayed inside.

About twenty bruised and battered women cowered before us, all my age or younger. I did not know any of them.

"Do you know what happened to the concubines?" I asked Onra. I could not imagine they had met a kind fate when the Kerghi invaded.

"Lord Samtis spirited them away to the safety of his brother's keep before the enemy took the city," Onra whispered back.

I was most glad.

The new women, set aside to serve the khan, were beautiful, even under their bruises. Drav snapped at one to run and fetch food from the kitchen, then ordered the others to see to my needs. I imagined they had all been high-born ladies once, but they all rushed to obey like servants.

The common area of Pleasure Hall was a circle, doors opening from it in every direction to the concubines' chambers. In the middle stood a sunken pool that was usually steaming, heated from below, but now the water had been left cold. The walls were bare, the multitude of Kadar tapestries missing.

Drav let me go at last. "I think we can all agree that the first thing you need is a bath."

He stayed where he was. He did not send the guards away either.

If he thought he was going to cow me with as little as that, he was going to be disappointed. I was prepared to sacrifice a lot more than my modesty. I turned from him, stripped off my sweaty, dusty clothes and stepped into the cold water, suppressing a shiver. The women gathered to help.

At first, they tried to talk to me, but every time one said something, Drav shook his head. If a few words were exchanged regardless, one of the guards reached for his sword and stepped forward. Soon we all fell silent. I feared not the guards, but I did not want any of the women to come to harm.

"Wash her hair," Drav ordered.

I resisted nothing. I wanted the sorcerer to think that I was resigned to my fate. I followed all orders, while silently plotting.

The women washed and dressed me in one of my own fine gowns that I had left behind. When the platter arrived from the kitchen—with cold ham, bread, and cheese—I did not fall on the food. I would not show the sorcerer how desperate I was. Instead, I ate with ladylike restraint. And while I ate, Onra braided my hair.

Drav drew a handful of golden hairpins from his robe, each tipped with a black pearl, the metal decorated with swirls that seemed to form unfamiliar symbols.

"A wedding gift," he told me as he held them out on the palm of his hand.

My hands fisted at my sides.

Drav flashed an amused grin. "What a shame. History calls for a warrior, and here you are, a healer. Yet you have spirit. I do not think I shall break it, unless, of course, the emperor demands that you should be broken." His expression turned hard. "Now accept my gift."

I did not move.

"I told you," he bent to my ear to whisper, "I do not wish to break you,

Lady Tera."

"What if I wish to break *you*, Lord Drav?"

He laughed. "They did not tell me how truly magnificent you were. There is nothing a man like me loves more than a challenge." Then his tone hardened. "Take the pins."

They were likely imbued with some controlling magic. I wanted to throw them across the room. Yet what good would it do when Drav could make me pick them up? I nodded to Onra, and she took them from the man. As she slid them into my hair, I waited to feel the touch of his power, but I felt nothing. Perhaps he was that skilled—able to leave his victim unsuspecting.

I sat still while the women fussed with me, taking as much care as if I was still the High Lord's favorite concubine, on my way to Yullin's Feast. I let them do their work but paid them little attention. I was waiting for opportunity to pass Onra a message.

Drav watched me too closely, however.

When the women finished and stepped away, his dark eyes glinted with approval. "Makes me wish tonight could be our first night, but preparations must be made." His gaze roamed over me. "Still, the stars do align, so maybe as soon as tomorrow."

I stood straight and tall under his inspection, not bothering to hide how cold his words left me. Time to set the trap. "Tomorrow, Lord Batumar will be here."

Drav sneered. "Then he will perish. I heard the sorcerer of Ishaf was not up to the task. Let me assure you, *my* lady, when I rip a man's spirit from his chest, he dies and he remains dead."

"He will come for me. Soon we will be together again."

Drav turned thoughtful at my words. His dark eyes narrowed. "How come you to be here before your army? How did Khan Verik manage to capture you? I did not think the man clever enough."

I refused to look away from his probing gaze. "I came on my own to retake the city."

He laughed with delight. "Ambition is a fine thing in a sorceress. But watch out for delusion. Delusion is quicksand." He shook his head, his expression thoroughly amused. "You walked up the North Road and what? Banged your slim fist on the gate, demanding entrance?"

I matched his mocking tone. "Did you not see me come? I thought you foresaw our arrival at Rabeen after we sailed out of the hardstorms. Did you not foresee the rest?"

His lips flattened. "I saw you sail into Rabeen's harbor, but not what you did on the island. I saw you in the Shahala port city of Sheharree and then the Kadar port of Kaharta Reh, but too late to send men to intercept. I had to watch the fleet burn. Then I saw you in a boat on the water, with three of Verik's men, then rescued and sailing up along the coast, then nothing."

Most interesting.

Not on Rabeen, and not once I neared Barren Cove. *Why?* The only thing those two places had in common that I could think of was Kratos's presence. Could the sorcerer not see past the ancient god's power? Did Kratos's presence dampen the sorcerer's abilities? If so, I might be able to surprise him yet.

I thought hard about that. I thought about the collapsed north tower. I thought about Boscor's tales of the Wyrn wars, how a handful of rebels used trickery against armies a hundred times their size. The plan that had been slowly forming in my mind took a more solid shape, like a ship sailing out of a dense fog—a swirl of gray at first, then more clearly defined, with more and more detail.

CHAPTER THIRTY-ONE
TERA

The spirits provided me with the unguarded moment I needed.

An imperial guard arrived, and Drav walked to the door to talk with him. While the men conversed in hushed voices, I cast Onra a sideways glance. She understood, stepping up behind me and pretending to adjust the back of my collar.

I did not turn my head, only whispered to her under my breath. "Tell the servants to stay out of the north wing."

She gave no response but briefly rested her hand on my shoulder to reassure me that she would see my request fulfilled. Then she stepped aside once again, for the sorcerer was returning from the door, his gaze fixed on me.

"I ask you for the last time. How did you enter the fortress city?"

When I remained silent, he placed a hand on the back of my neck. The unnatural cold of his fingers seeped into my flesh. This time, I did feel his power buzz along my skin under his palm, and all across my scalp, under the pins I was now wearing in my hair.

"How?" he demanded.

I felt compelled to answer. I did not mind. I only feigned resistance, looking away, pretending some measure of fear as I turned to face him. "None will follow after me that way, I promise."

He held my gaze, his dark irises expanding. I did hold back then. I wanted to test how far his powers to compel me extended. I remained in control, but only just. The sorcerer *was* powerful. I knew only one power greater than his in Karamur—the ancient god of the caves.

When I remained silent, Drav nodded to the guards. "Start drowning the women, one by one, until the Lady Tera deigns to give us a straight answer. Start with this one." He pointed at Onra.

The nearest guard grabbed my friend and heaved her into the water without hesitation, then stepped in after her, boots and all.

"A tunnel!" I blurted.

"A tunnel where?"

Onra struggled to stand, but the guard put his hand on her head to hold her under the surface. The water churned as her arms flailed. I lurched toward her, but Drav caught me by the arm and held me back with an unnatural strength.

"A tunnel through the mountain!" I shouted, then rushed on. "I can tell you how to reach it, but you will not find any enemy hiding in there."

The guard let up, and Onra lunged away from him, collapsing against the side of the pool and gasping for air, water running down her face in rivulets. I watched her for only a moment, to make sure she did not need my help, then turned back to the sorcerer. He was lucky I was no true sorceress, or he would have felt my vengeance.

"I do not sense a tunnel." He watched me closely. "Have you the skill to hide it?" He paused. "Take us there."

A sorcerer's command—the words brimming with power.

I drew back and shook my head. "You can easily find it. Look for the iron door on the lowest level of the castle, below the dungeons."

He raised an eyebrow and grabbed me by the arm once again. "You shall lead us, and you shall enter first."

"After the emperor's speech, then." I bit my lip. "He wants both of us to be present."

Drav narrowed his eyes. "There is time yet."

He led me out of Pleasure Hall, ordering the guards, "Bring me a full unit of men and make it quick. If there is a secret entry into the castle, we must secure it. If this is a trap and enemy soldiers are waiting behind the door, they must be rooted out at once. Meet us at the dungeons."

As the men ran off, Drav nudged me forward. "Lead the way."

I did, but none too fast, allowing my every step to speak of reluctance. I stayed silent as we passed dispirited servants who scurried along, hugging the walls, avoiding our gazes. They were carrying water jars and food from the pantries toward the Great Hall. The emperor must have demanded a feast, a feast I did not plan on attending. If all went well, he would not be attending it either.

We kept going. By the time we reached the dungeons, my heart was beating so hard, I feared Drav might be able to hear it. Then boots slapping on stone drowned out all other sound as his unit of soldiers joined us, hurrying to his service and crowding the hallway.

I sighed with resignation. "Best light your torches here."

Then I led the men down the last set of stairs, into the long corridor that yawned darkly before us. The chill in the air made me rub my hands over my arms, but I did not slow. Neither did I allow the dread that threatened to overwhelm me deter me from my purpose. I filled my lungs with musty air and kept going, straight ahead.

Within a few more steps, the torches illuminated the dead end, the jumble of flags.

"If you think this is a jest—" Drav's voice hardened with implied threat.

"Behind the flags."

He waved his hand, and half a dozen soldiers rushed to clear the back wall, revealing the partially open and still-chained iron door that separated the castle from the cave.

Drav examined the narrow gap, then raised an eyebrow as he glanced back at me. His measuring gaze ran over my body. "You came through there?"

"With difficulty."

He fingered the padlock. "I take it you do not have the key?"

"Last I knew, Vooren, one of the stewards, had it."

The sorcerer laid his hands on the lock and mumbled something, barely a few words. The sight of melting metal was startling. It dripped to the stones little by little and sizzled as it hit the cold stone. The chains gave and clattered to the ground, the sound echoing in the corridor. A demonstration of power.

Does it weaken him like difficult healing weakens me? Is it enough to make a difference?

The men dragged the door wide open, the metal screeching and scraping, then Drav pushed me into the darkness ahead of him and waited for me to take several steps.

"I was not certain if you were lying, but there *is* a cave here. Where does it lead?" he asked when he finally moved up next to me.

"To a hidden harbor. The journey is long, over difficult terrain. Some of the passageways are too low to walk through, so whoever passes through them must crawl." I did not bother hiding the shiver that ran through me. "We should go back. We do not want to keep the emperor waiting."

Drav watched me closely. "Not yet. I want to see more. I want to see at least what is right here." He turned to the men. "Spread out. Torches raised."

Across the room, several doorways yawned black before us. I knew the one I wanted. I led the men forward, straight to Kratos's chapel, then stopped in the middle of the cold cavern where the air held a taint of sulfur.

I could better see now the three great columns that surrounded the low circular platform we stood on, their tops disappearing into darkness. The platform and columns were richly carved with black snakes twisted to form long-forgotten symbols. The snakes had legs—capped with talons.

"What is this place?" Drav raised his torch, but the light did not reach the ceiling.

I hoped he would not realize that somewhere above that ceiling was the Great Hall and part of the courtyard where the Kerghi would be by now gathering for the emperor's speech.

"We are in an ancient temple," I said. "We must offer a sacrifice here."

Indeed, we were in a place of sacrifice. With all the torches, I could see higher up now, could see the crevices—similar to the ones on the cliffs of Rabeen—with their metal bars hanging half rusted off their hinges. *Sacrifice holes.*

Far above us, a dark chuckle floated, softly echoing off the rock. "Sorceress, you serve me well."

"Who is there?" Drav raised his torch even higher and peered up, while his men pulled closer to us and formed a protective circle.

"I have brought you sacrifice," I shouted to Kratos.

The god responded with full-blown laughter, and the next I knew, a soldier floated up from among us, shouting "Help me!" and waving his sword at the air.

He soon rose past the light our torches provided, then came silence, and then a piercing scream.

The remaining soldiers ran for the doorway or, rather, for the spot where the doorway had been moments earlier, but the entry had disappeared. Real or imagined, we were surrounded by solid rock.

Drav tossed his torch and let me go so he could hold his sword two-handed. He set his feet apart in the stance of a warrior, ready to fight. I gaped at the blue light that glinted on his blade.

Some of the guards cowered with their backs to the walls, weapon in one hand, searching with the other for a hidden lever to open the doorway they knew to be there somewhere. Others hid themselves in the handful of sacrifice holes that stood close to the ground. Others still hid behind the columns that long-ago supplicants had carved from the stone of the mountain.

Drav and I alone remained in the middle of the temple. I eased out of reach, while his attention was fixed above, then I eased all the way to the wide column behind me.

Another soldier rose in the air, as if invisible talons gripped him around the middle. He struggled to no avail. As with the first man, this one too disappeared from sight, this one too screamed.

The ancient god gave a satisfied sigh. "A fine sacrifice. And you bring me a sorcerer too. I shall have a priest and a priestess. My temple will be rebuilt. I am well pleased."

"Then you will grant me power?" I called up into the darkness.

"Are you willing to pay the price?"

"I am. Grant me power, and I shall pledge you my life."

"For what power do you wish?" Kratos asked then. "The power over the wind to raise great storms? The power over water to sink ships? The power over stones to build yourself castles? Or the power over fire to burn your enemies?"

While he spoke, men kept rising in the air one by one, some dropping their weapons, some their torches, some both. All screamed.

I heard them but in a muted way, saw them but with my vision blurry, as if a veil had been raised between us, as if the god existed in two different worlds, talking with me in one while drinking the blood of his sacrifice in the other.

Drav too was shut away from me. The sorcerer, realizing he faced a more ancient power than he had first thought, tossed his bespelled sword and lifted both hands as he shouted an incantation. Lightning burst from his fingertips.

I had no time to think about him. I had a god to trick. "I wish for the power over stones. I want to raise all the cities my enemies demolished. I want to rebuild our islands."

Kratos was silent for a moment. When he did talk, he sounded pleased. "You will raise my temples again."

A statement, not a question.

My body tingled. And with each man sacrificed, the tingle became stronger. I felt as if I was growing, as if my body was expanding, yet when I looked, my limbs remained the same.

"I grant my sorceress the power to command stone," the god declared, his voice neither cold nor threatening now, almost as if he was drunk on the blood of his sacrifice.

Even I felt dizzy.

The men were rising faster now, two or three at a time. Then I saw the last of them rise into the air, the unit commander, wild-eyed and grunting, slashing uselessly with his sword.

A happy sigh sounded from above. "Royal blood is strong blood. It is a rare sacrifice." The god slurred his words.

I had no time to ponder whether the commander was one of the emperor's bastards or the son of some king the emperor had conquered. My moment had come. Time to fight.

All through this war, I had thought to save my people and triumph over our enemies with kindness and light. I sought to heal. But when I had stood before the emperor and saw his darkness, I did not know how to heal *that*.

His empire had spread through the world like a black cloud. Like the blackening caused by an infection as it spread through the body, the kind of illness that, if a healer did not cut it out, would end a man's life. For that reason had I cut the blackening out of Prince Graho—to save him.

Batumar did not go to war because he enjoyed the killing. The warlord went because keeping his people safe required that sacrifice. I understood that before with my mind, but not until now did I understand it with my heart. Batumar gave no thought to what he wanted, what he wished. He did, at great cost, what was required—for the sake of others. That was why he was a hero to men, a hero to me.

I loved the warlord with all my heart.

From love comes courage.

As mad laughter rumbled from Kratos, bouncing off the walls of his sanctuary, I turned and laid my hands on the great column behind me. "Help me, kind spirits, if you can hear me."

With my mind's eye, I could suddenly see the small fissures in the stone, as in the past I had been able to see the cracked bones of a man when healing him. When healing, before knitting the bones, I had to soften them. I knew how to do this. Now I softened the stone beneath my hands.

"Sorceress!" the god roared high above.

His thunderous voice deafened me. An invisible hand with claws tipping the fingers knocked me back, hard enough so I flew across the cavern and slammed into the rock wall at the far end.

I could not breathe. My chest was on fire. But even as I fought not to lose consciousness, the temple trembled around me. I saw double, but I did see the great stone column buckle, then crumple, large chunks of stone rolling on the ground, like the severed heads on the emperor's golden kaftan.

Before the rumble could quiet, other stones fell, these from the ceiling that remained shrouded in darkness. Some rolled close enough to me that I could see carvings on them, ancient letters I could not decipher. Another column shuddered. Then even more stones fell, and I could see no longer, for too much dust filled the air.

The sorcerer's pins in my hair turned into claws and dug into my skin. Drav knew what I was doing and tried to stop me. But what I had set into motion could not be stopped. I clutched my head as blood ran down my face. The pain was sharp—like nails being driven into my head. I could do nothing to stop it.

The ground shook beneath me. More stones fell from above. I dove into a low sacrifice hole, and not a moment too soon.

Kratos roared as the ceiling collapsed. Then something tinkled—metal on stone. *Ping-ping-ping.* The gold coins that had been stored in the dungeons were raining down on us. Kratos had wanted blood and gold. He

207

had his wish—he even had me.

I was buried.

Drav's hairpins stopped digging farther into my scalp but remained in place. My lungs labored for air. Every part of my body ached. I did not have a bone left unrattled, no patch of skin left unbruised. My nose bled. I was certain that something vital had been crushed inside me.

I hurt so much, my ears were ringing. Yet even over that, I could hear the screams and howls of hundreds of dying mercenaries far above me. I could feel the men's fear and pain. The north wing of the High Lord's palace was collapsing.

I felt the god's rage too, felt Kratos coming for me, but the blood of the dying drew him. His bloodthirst, after being denied sacrifice for too long, was even stronger than his need for vengeance. It did not matter. Whether at the tip of his invisible talons or from my injuries and lack of air—I faced certain death.

"I beg you, kind spirits, save Batumar and our people, our soldiers and our island," I prayed with my dying breath.

CHAPTER THIRTY-TWO

BATUMAR

The liberating army stood in the forest, out of sight, all four hundred and fifty remaining soldiers lined up behind their leaders—Batumar, Prince Graho, Lord Karnagh, and Tomron—with the archers at the front of the army, ready for attack. They had not yet been discovered; no alarm had sounded. What outlying Kerghi guards they had found in the woods, they killed.

Batumar hoped they were in time. He *had* managed to gain a day. He had marched his troops through the night. Now Karamur's walls towered before them.

In peacetime, huts and cottages crowded around the fortress city between the outer walls and the fields. Now only their rubble remained. The Kerghi had destroyed them the year before when they were on the outside and Batumar had been within.

The mercenary hordes had also destroyed last year's harvest in that siege, but the fields *had* been replanted in the spring. The wheat should have been waist-high by this time in the summer, the heads filled with grain the people of the city badly needed. Yet the fields were barren once again, the fall reaping trampled by the Kerghi army when they had taken the city in Batumar's absence.

Two lost harvests. He would have to find a way to stave off famine. But first, he had to take the city back. Impatience made his muscles twitch, bloodlust coursing through his veins as he watched the army outside the fortress walls, their golden uniforms a contrast to the Kerghi on the parapets in black.

"Freshly arrived, from the looks of them," Tomron said on Batumar's left. "No tents set up yet, no fires built."

"They must have just come through the Gate and down the mountain," Lord Karnagh agreed. "Imperial troops. Close to six hundred men."

And more within the walls. Batumar kept his gaze on the city.

"Do you think the Lady Tera is inside?" Prince Graho asked on his right.

"If she said she would pass through the mountain and into the city, she will do just that," Batumar said. "I doubt her not."

Lord Karnagh turned to him again. "You were present when Karamur's defenses were rebuilt. You know every stone in those walls. Any weaknesses?"

"We worked hard to ensure we had none." Batumar held the reins firmly to keep his horse still. "Had I expected to be outside the walls one day, wishing for a way in, I would have left a secret entry."

"How about tunneling in?" the prince suggested.

"The city is built on solid rock to ensure that the outer walls cannot be undermined by digging."

"We have no siege engines," Lord Karnagh said with regret. "Nor the time to build them. Do you think the emperor is inside the walls?"

"The imperial troops would not be here otherwise." Batumar looked toward the High Lord's castle, set on the highest point of the city. Kerghi soldiers were sitting on the rooftops, looking down at the courtyard outside the Great Hall. They appeared to be listening to something.

Batumar unsheathed his sword, then he nodded at each man by his side in turn. "May the gods be with us on this day and carry us to victory."

"To victory," Prince Graho, Lord Karnagh, and Tomron echoed him before pulling back to lead their men.

The first flight of arrows were loosed but a few moments later, flying over Batumar's head, breaking the morning's peace. The Landrian archers might be too far in the forest to hit the Kerghi on the parapets, but dozens of imperial troops fell, having been caught unprepared in the fields.

The archers shot off another volley, still from inside the tree line. Before the imperial troops could even line up for battle, a hundred of them were dead. But that was all the advantage Batumar's liberating army was able to steal. The imperial archers nocked their arrows at last, and they shot back.

"Attack!" Batumar raised his sword and broke from the tree line, the cavalry behind him.

The battle for Karamur commenced.

Another hundred men fell to arrows, on each side, before the two armies met in the middle of the open fields. Tigers roared. So did the manyinga. Swords clashed. Batumar issued no further commands. Nothing could be heard over the din of battle. And in any case, his army had all pledged to fight to the death. They fought with the understanding that there would be no call to retreat.

Batumar hacked at the enemy from horseback until a lance took the horse from under him. Then he hacked at the enemy on foot, picking the largest man he could reach. *Hold on, my Tera. I am here.*

The imperial soldiers were no barbarians, no riffraff who joined a mercenary army for the spoils. These were trained fighters, proper troops, true warriors. Sword clashed against sword. Muscles strained. Then Marga lunged to help. The tiger brought down the enemy soldier's horse, and Batumar cut down the rider at last.

He suffered a cut himself, a deep gash in his thigh. He bled. He refused to slow. Tera waited for him somewhere ahead. He would not consider any other possibility.

When he laid eyes on the commander of the imperial troops, at some distance, Batumar dispatched the line of golden-uniformed soldiers in his way and headed straight for the commander. Then tripped. No, not tripped, stumbled. The ground was shaking. His gaze snapped to Karamur, where, as the ground shook again, a great cloud of dust rose over the castle.

A terrible cold spread in Batumar's heart and gripped it hard enough to steal his breath. *Damn the imperial commander.* He changed direction, fighting his way to the portcullis.

Hold on, Tera, my heart. Hold on.

He cut down a great many more men before the dust cloud settled, and he could see at last that the north wing of the High Lord's palace had collapsed, the very place where Kerghi soldiers had been sitting on the rooftops earlier.

"Tera!" The desperate cry tore from his lips as he lunged forward.

Tera had made it through the cave. She was fighting for them from the inside. He knew it in his heart. And he knew well enough how quick she always was to sacrifice herself for others. *Not this time.* Not if he had to take apart the fortress walls with his bare hands. "Tera!"

Men around him picked up the shout. "For the Lady Tera!" And it spread, giving strength to the warriors, her name their rallying cry.

When Batumar reached the city wall, he climbed. Lances showered down on him, until Prince Graho's remaining Landrian archers used their last arrows to clear the top of the battlements and the climb became easier.

Others climbed next to him, scrambling for handholds. When Batumar went over the top of the wall, he was not alone. A dozen of his men had his back.

They fought their way to the portcullis with single-minded attention, cutting down anyone who would stand in their way. He raised the winch first and sheathed his sword to work the pulley. The rope snapped tight, the counterweight lifting. The metal grid gave a protesting screech, but up it went in its stone channel.

Tomron was the first man through, his most trusted men close behind him. The khan's mercenaries stationed between the outer walls and the inner walls attacked them. The palace collapse had to have killed at least a few hundred, but plenty remained—maybe as many as a thousand.

How many did the emperor's sorcerer send through the Gate of the World? The question floated into Batumar's mind, then disappeared. Numbers no longer mattered. He would not have turned back if the enemy numbered ten thousand.

"To the inner gate!" He drew his sword and threw himself back into the fight. The second wall had to be breached next. All around him, the battle raged, men falling, blood soaking the ground. He barely saw them.

He could not recount how he reached the inner wooden gate. Later, he could not recall bellowing over the din of the battle, "The manyinga! To me!"

His men brought the beasts. And then Batumar set the manyinga against the gate and had them push forward. Wood creaked. One of the beams splintered.

"Better than a siege engine!" Tomron grinned next to him.

They were both standing on the bodies of their enemies.

The thick gate did not give easily, but it did give. The manyinga, their heads blooded, surged forward, widening the gap, sweeping giant beams out of the way like tree trunks in a flash flood. The liberating army poured in.

"To the castle!" Batumar looked around for Marga, but he could not see the tiger in the chaos of the battle.

"Marga!" he called, but he did not wait for her to appear.

The doors to the castle would be the most heavily guarded entrance. He fought his way to the nearest castle wall with a window, then began to scale the stones straight up. In his mind, he saw the north wing collapsing, over and over. In his heart, he was certain Tera had been in the middle of that collapse.

He could not think past the walls crumbling, of that dust cloud rising. He could not think that Tera might have sacrificed herself to remove the leaders of the enemy army, to give the liberating forces a chance to win. He climbed, hand over hand, caring little that the rough stones scraped his fingertips bloody.

CHAPTER THIRTY-THREE

TERA

I expected to wake in the spirit world, but instead I woke to pain and darkness. The air felt different. The *world* felt different, as if some elemental power had shifted, as when after a great winter storm, the dark clouds depart, and the pressure clears from the air.

I coughed, one violent spasm after the other squeezing my lungs, my whole body battered, worse than when I had been thrown around in our small cabin by the hardstorms. My mouth was dry and full of dust that burned my tongue and throat. My eyes burned too. As I blinked, the dust stuck under my eyelids scraped my eyeballs. My scalp ached where Drav's metal claws were embedded in my head.

Perhaps I deserved no better. I had taken lives—with my own hands. I had broken the most sacred vow of my people.

I did not justify my actions by telling myself that I might have saved many more lives than I had taken. The Shahala believe that there are deeds for which a justification can never exist. I did not rail against being sealed in the rock, trapped in a sacrifice hole until I ran out of air.

I thought my end was just. I had pledged myself to the ancient god. Now my bones would be his forever.

And yet...

He did not call to me with rage. He did not call to me at all. I sniffed the air, but could not smell sulfur, only dust. Maybe he had overgorged himself on sacrifice, and sated, he rested.

I rested too, eyes closed, head bowed, my arms wrapped around my knees to keep me warm. I had fought for my people, and now my fight was over.

Or was it?

Had I not promised to lead?

How long a rest did a god require?

I coughed. Every joint aching, I struggled to rise, grateful to have room enough to stand, then I felt around the sacrifice hole. I was blocked in not by rubble but a single large boulder. My fingers found only the smallest gaps here and there around the edge of the huge stone. I could squeeze my hand through a few of them but nothing bigger than a hand. Had I turned all my bones soft, I still could not escape my rocky grave.

I reached up to work Drav's pins from my scalp. I could do little to improve my situation, but I could do at least that. None of the pins would easily budge, however. I had to rip. More blood trickled down my face before I had them.

I fed them through the nearest gap, not wanting anything with me that belonged to the sorcerer. If he was out there still, I did not want him to have any power over me.

To be in Kratos's power was terrible enough. His darkness had taken me. I was surrounded by it, swallowed by it. That darkness trapped me, the ancient god's last sacrifice—at least, at this temple.

Kind spirits, save Batumar, and our people, and our island.

I prayed for a good long time before my mind cleared and I remembered that I had been given power over stone. My heart quickened.

I lay my hand on the boulder and envisioned it rolling away. I pushed. Then I pushed harder. The boulder stubbornly stayed. I could not soften it, nor could I crack it. I could not see the small fissures as I had seen in the great column I had shattered.

"Be gone!" I pushed anyway.

Nothing happened.

I heaved against the boulder with all my strength then, but it still refused to budge. I tried and tried again, tendons popping, muscles screaming. *Nothing.* My power over stone was gone. Kratos had given, and Kratos had taken.

Yet I had some lingering sense, enough to know that beyond this boulder lay another, then another, the temple fully collapsed and the entire north wing of the palace with it. Mixed in with the ruins was the blood of our enemies and their broken bodies, like mortar among the great stones of the fortress's outer walls. I had succeeded. Hundreds of men from the Kerghi army, and very possibly Emperor Drakhar, were dead. I had increased our army's odds of victory.

Was Batumar here? Had the battle already been fought? I wished I knew how he and our people fared. The thought that he would never know what became of me twisted my heart. I prayed again to the spirits to grant him victory, to grant the islands peace. For myself, I asked nothing.

I brushed my tangled hair and the dust and blood from my face, then I rested my head on the rock behind me and thought about my mother. I wondered how soon my spirit would join hers. I hoped we would recognize each other at once and would soar over the tops of the numaba trees like a pair of knar eagles. *If* I was granted the privilege to reunite with her.

I had never feared passing over to the spirit world. But now... When I had been a child, I used to think the good spirits lived on top of the numaba trees on our hillside, while the bad spirits lived under the sea, always angry and cold, pulling down ships.

After what I had just done... I did not know how I would be judged. I shivered. And once I started, I could not stop.

I kept coughing too. The air remained thick with dust. I wiped my face again, but it helped little. The burning in my eyes did not lessen.

I coughed more and gasped for air, until I slid down onto the ground. I lost track of time. I soared, sometimes into the past. I talked with my mother who was still alive and not a spirit, relieved to tears when she embraced me with love, not a trace of disappointment in her eyes. I reached for her hand, but my fingers closed around air instead.

Next I was soaring into the future, high above, in a cloudless sky, looking down the emerald carpet of the forests, then flying over the fortress city. Below me lay not ruins, but Karamur rebuilt, Batumar once again High Lord of the city and protector of its people.

I soared over the sea and saw the other Middle Islands, everywhere men and women living in peace. I saw ships sail swiftly to trade. They carried many of my Shahala people to heal.

I saw the Outer Islands, all rebuilt, even Rabeen. I saw the mainland, then Uramit, and the Landrian islands to the south, Prince Graho on his throne with a queen who held the moon and the stars in her eyes when she looked at him.

Up north I flew, to the kingless kingdom of the Selorm, over the castles of the Selorm lords, their tigers patrolling their fortresses. I saw Lord Karnagh in the seat of honor on their war council and, by his side, his warrior queen.

I flew higher then, into pure bright white made up from millions of points of light. At long last, I was among the spirits.

"I do not belong here." I tried pulling back.

One of the points of lights that surrounded me pulsed. *Not yet.*

"I tried to win the world with kindness and light. I could not. I brought men to their deaths."

Darkness and light cannot live together in the same place, at the same time. There is no compromise with evil. Light drives out the darkness.

"The Guardians said I was born to a prophecy. I was supposed to be a hero. I failed."

All prophecies call for heroes, and the number of these prophecies is many, one light said gently.

All are born to be heroes, another light added.

None are born to be heroes, yet another responded, but they were not arguing.

Then: *The hero is the one who takes up the challenge to give whatever it takes to save others.*

"I could not save all," I protested.

The world is imperfect, and so are all heroes, for they are of the world. The hero is not always the one who succeeds. The hero is the one who tries, even at a great cost.

CHAPTER THIRTY-FOUR
TERA

The next moment, I was back in the darkness, sealed in rock.

My skin burned. My throat ached as if I had swallowed sharp blades. My eyes felt as if they were melting out of their sockets.

I tried to heal myself but could not.

Many mooncrossings before, in Ishaf, when I thought Batumar dead, my hope had died with him, and I had lost my healing powers for a time. Mayhap that had happened again. Or mayhap the spirits, seeing what I had done at Karamur, let me live but took back my powers.

I did not know how much time had passed since the collapse. I could only judge time by how weak I was from lack of food and water. I tried to struggle to my feet again, but I could no longer stand.

The earth trembled above me. Or did it? I was so shaky, I could not be certain.

Wanting to be with the spirits once again, I closed my eyes. But this time when I dreamed, the dreams were dark.

I was back at the Kerghi siege of Karamur the year before, when I plummeted from the wall into fire. I heard Batumar call, "Tera!" over the moans of the dying, saw the night sky and the flickering of the torches in the distance as the Kadar soldiers searched the bloody battlefield for me.

I wanted to remain in that dream. Back then, Batumar had found me.

The same thoughts filled my mind now that had filled my mind then.
He lives.

He will come.

He will find me.

When I revived some, I stopped repeating the words in my head. I had to accept that even the most powerful warlord of the land could not reach me here. This time, not even Batumar could save me.

Pain was an ocean, washing over me in waves. When I slept, I dreamed dreams of delirium—flying fish with feathery wings, red manyinga dancing, tigers with emerald frogs for eyes. Sometimes, wide awake, I hallucinated. I thought I heard Batumar right next to me, telling me how much he loved me.

The earth trembled again and again. *I am shaking from shock.* Or maybe not. Dust sifted over me. The rocks above me *were* moving. The dust burned my eyes more, made my skin itch, then that burned too wherever I scratched.

I thought of Vooren's tale, how his grandfather went blind in the caves, in a tunnel where the walls wept poison. Mayhap the stone of the caverns contained poisonous minerals, like the Desert of Sparkling Death that separated the Kadars' country from our Shahala lands.

I had a terrifying thought: What if I would not die, not for a long time to come? What if my body *was* healing itself, but as I was covered in poisonous minerals, they kept burning me over and over? How many days of agony before I finally wasted away from lack of nourishment?

Exhausted from pain, I slept again. Or maybe I had simply lost consciousness, for when I woke, I could remember no dreams.

"Tera!"

I smiled at Batumar's voice. I was in a dream, then, after all, back to the night after the Kerghi siege of Karamur.

He lives.

He will come.

He will find me.

I wanted to dream the part when he lifted me into his arms.

A roar sounded somewhere above me—a tiger. I recognized her distinct sound: Marga.

There you are, great mother.

Moments later, a deeper, more powerful, roar reached me. The rocks shook, as if that roar had the power to move them. I recognized that sound too—one of the manyinga beasts.

Then came yet a third roar, one that echoed in my heart. "Tera!" From Batumar.

My throat felt as if it had melted. I could not call out for him. This did not upset me. I was in a dream. The noise and trembling came nearer and nearer to me and went on for what seemed days.

Then the very boulder locking me in shifted a little. I wished I could push to my feet, but I could barely lift my hands to block my face from the dust that fell again to cover me.

Marga roared, so near now. Then I heard the crash of the boulder. Air moved around me as the space opened, but I could see nothing. Something large and soft nudged me in the darkness. *Marga's head.* I thought again that I must be dreaming. I had to be, for she did not lick my face in greeting, but whined like a kitten.

"She is here!" a man called out.

Then Batumar's torn cry: "Does she live?"

"I cannot tell, my lord."

A hand landed on my shoulder and was rapidly shoved aside.

Strong, familiar arms lifted me, and I curled against Batumar's wide chest. This part of the dream was my favorite. This part I did not want to end.

"I am here." His voice was a ragged whisper.

I did not know how he recognized me in the dark, or how he had brought the tiger and the manyinga to me. For I was lifted, lifted, then felt the beast's coarse fur against my leg as Batumar settled us into the saddle.

He whispered, "Tera, look at me. My heart, say something."

I turned my face up. How did he expect me to see in all this darkness? How did he expect me to talk through the pain with a tongue that was on fire?

"Why is her mouth bleeding?" he demanded in a harsh tone.

Then another familiar voice, the old Guardian of the Cave. "In parts of the cave, there is a vein of poisonous minerals, my lord."

"Send a runner to the healers," Batumar ordered someone. "And have water ready in my chamber. Warm. A tub filled, and a hundred more buckets, and—"

"Nay," the Guardian cut him off. "Water turns the dust into poison when the two mix. Her own sweat and saliva burned her, mixed with the dust. I should have found her sooner. Forgive me, Lord Batumar. But the ancient god's power rendered my senses fair blind."

"How will we wash off all this poisonous dust?" the warlord demanded. "If not with water?"

"Sand, my lord. Bathe her in fine, powderlike sand, then wipe every inch of her body. Then do it again. Then, perhaps, a good rinse. If I recall, that was done with Vooren's grandfather to save him back in the day."

Batumar was already wiping my face and hair with his sleeve. "Why is her hair white?"

"That too, happened to the old steward, my lord. His hair turned full white by the time he found his way out of the tunnels."

Vooren had told us. I remembered it now.

I coughed then blinked hard, straining my burning eyes.

"She is coming to," Batumar said above me, but my mind skipped back to what he had asked only moments ago. *Why is her hair white?*

How could he see my hair without any light?

Two realizations sliced into me at the same time. The reason I could not see the warlord was not because we were in the belly of darkness. I could not see him, because I was blind. And this was no dream.

CHAPTER THIRTY-FIVE

TERA

"Tera? Can you hear me?" Batumar's tone was as close to begging as I had ever heard him.

I nodded. I could hear, but nothing else about my body felt the same as before. I felt as if I had died in the ancient god's temple and now I was painfully reborn. *To be what new creature?*

Batumar insisted on carrying me into my new life.

We entered a room, then the door closed behind us. The warlord held me to his chest for a long moment before he laid me down onto something soft—a bed.

"You are in our old chamber," he said. "The Shahala healers are coming. They did join us, with Koro's help, at the end." He drew a ragged breath. "Can you tell me what happened?"

I tried to form words, but no sound could pass my burning throat.

The door scraped open. The healers came, and the warlord gave me over to their care. "She cannot speak, and she cannot see."

I drifted in and out as they bathed me in sand, again and again, until, free of the deadly minerals, they could bathe me in water at long last. My cuts were healed, my missing and burned skin renewed. I drank cup after cup of potions, then honeyed warm milk.

Someone cupped his hands over my eyes, then gently ran the pads of his thumbs over my eyelids. A long pause followed. Then my throat tingled, and I knew that next to me, a Shahala healer was drawing my injury into himself. I waited for the healing to work, to be able to speak.

Instead, the healer said, "My lord, I cannot. Nothing I do helps her. Not with her voice or her sight."

Then another healer tried, and another.

"Perhaps, once the shock passes, the Lady Tera can heal herself," one of them suggested.

"Try again." Batumar's tone was darker than a hardstorm at midnight.

They followed his order.

Half a day must have passed before the warlord finally allowed them to leave. He walked out behind them. The door closed and then silence.

I drew a deep, rattling breath. I wished I could fall asleep. Instead, dark thoughts chased each other in my mind. I had been removed from the sacrifice hole. What had Boscor said on Rabeen? Kratos did not suffer a sacrifice to be taken from him.

Would he come for me?

I waited in the darkness.

Then the door opened again. Boots scraped on stone. I recognized those footsteps.

The bed dipped under me, and in another breath, I was pulled onto Batumar's lap, his arms surrounding me and tucking me against his strong body, as a baby bird might be tucked into the nest.

"Tera."

I laid my head against his chest.

His voice roughened when he spoke next. "My Tera. Come back to me."

I wished I could speak to him, but I could not. I patted his chest to let him know I heard his words, and he spoke again.

"We were outside the city walls when the earth began to tremble. We saw dust rise up over the north wing of the palace. When the dust settled, half the palace was gone. I knew you were there. I raced straight for you." His voice broke.

And the others? What happened to them? Prince Graho, and Lord Karnagh, and Tomron, the young Guardian of the Gate, and all our men?

As if able to hear my thoughts, Batumar went on. "We lost many men in the fight, but none of the leaders. Tomron was grievously injured but is already healed. He has taken half the remaining army to clear out what Kerghi soldiers still roam the rest of the island."

I gave thanks to the spirits for that.

"Neither Khan Verik nor his war leaders came forth to organize the defense once our troops breached the city walls. Some said they all perished in the palace collapse. His men surrendered."

Batumar paused before continuing. "We found the khan's headless body in the ruins later. The emperor beheaded him, according to one of the captured men. We dug the emperor's broken body from the ruins when we were searching for you. But we did not find his sorcerer. He is said to have come to Karamur with Emperor Drakhar. It is too dangerous to keep digging. More of the palace might collapse. I would give the whole city for *you*, but if the sorcerer is down there under the rubble, he shall stay down there and good riddance."

The warlord lapsed into silence.

When I nudged his chest with my head to let him know I wanted to hear more, he drew a heavy breath.

"The Guardian of the Gate could not close Dahru's Gate," he said. "So he attempted to destroy the Gate. At this, he succeeded. He destroyed the Gate before any of our people were sent through." Silence stretched, a hard and painful pause. "He did not survive. He gave his life to save us, as his father had."

The news of the young Guardian's death slammed into my chest like a battle axe and stayed buried there. Grief washed over me while Batumar held me and comforted me with his murmured words of love, his lips pressing soft kisses onto my forehead.

"My heart," he said, his tone gruff. "Please heal yourself."

He did not understand that I had lost my healing powers. After the first siege of Karamur, when I had been injured, I had resisted healing. I had been heartsick from the violence of the battle and that I had aided in the deaths of men. I had taken my injuries as my atonement. Now Batumar thought I felt the same way again.

He was not entirely wrong. I had seen too much evil since this war had begun. I wanted to see no more. Yet I would have returned from my injuries to my people if I could have. But I could not. I could not even leave my bed. The Shahala healers healed my injuries, yet my strength did not return.

As we lay together, Batumar shifted us to wrap his great body around mine. He had a leg thrown across mine, an arm around my middle, my head tucked under his chin, as if he thought I might fly away in the night like a bird.

I finally slept.

Night after night, Batumar held me like that and rarely left me during the day. Each time he did leave and return, he told me everything he heard and saw while he was gone.

"The Forgotten City of the Guardians survived, protected by strong wards. The Kerghi never found their way in," he told me, and I sighed and patted his chest to let him know how happy the news made me.

After a moment, he went on, his tone growing heavier. "We still have no news of my mother. She never returned from her pilgrimage from the sacred springs of the godesses. I sent men to search for her, but they've come back empty-handed."

Tears welled in my eyes. Had the Kerghi captured Leena, then? We would find her, I silently swore. I knew Batumar would not rest until we had her back.

"My daughters survived the Kerghi invasion behind the stone walls of their remote fortresses," he added, and told me how glad he was that they had moved away from Karamur. He invited them for a visit as soon as our castle was repaired.

On the seventh day after my rescue, he told me that the surviving warlords sought to bestow an honor on me. As they had no high title for a woman, some suggested that instead of returning the name of the fortress city to Karamur from Khangar, the city would be named after me in the future.

I shook my head.

"I knew what you would say about that and told them so," Batumar said.

We were in bed once again, his arms around me. He tightened his embrace and kissed my closed eyes, one after the other. "I wish you could see the city. The stonemasons are working double time. The army we brought is helping them. Many of the men are learning masonry as their new trade. Others are training as roofers and replacing the roofs on the houses. A hundred went to the port to learn to be shipwrights. The Kadar fleet will be rebuilt."

A heavy sigh rattled up his chest. "I wish you could see, and I wish that our people could see you, my lady. I am stopped a hundred times a day and asked how you fare. Vooren frets like an old woman. I suppose the old steward saw his grandfather afflicted thus, so he knows what it is like, more than anyone else."

Vooren survived. That eased my mind a little. I smiled.

We slept.

I dreamt of my mother. She was nothing but light—a spirit. She embraced me. I missed her so much still.

I woke to moisture on my face. Had I been weeping in my dream? I reached up and found my eyes dry. I searched for Batumar's face, then brushed my fingertips lightly across his cheek.

The warlord was crying in his sleep.

I pressed my lips against his. Truly, against his stubbled jaw first, some searching necessary before I found his mouth. I kissed him until he kissed me back, slowly, tentatively, as if waking from a dream and unsure whether he was yet asleep or awake.

In another breath, his large hands bracketed my face, and he kissed me deeper. I braced against the onslaught of emotion by bracing my palms against his warm chest. At that slightest sign of resistance, he drew back.

"You *will* heal. You *will* rise from this bed."

He rested his lips against my forehead until someone knocked on the door and called him away.

* * *

"Some expect you to rise and become empress," the warlord told me when he returned that evening. "To lead an army to the mainland. You vanquished the emperor. Many think you should take his throne."

I shook my head. The countries of the mainland would have to work out how to govern themselves.

"Our people want you to be their queen," he said in a soft, cautious tone. "Some of the Kadar and Shahala are talking about forming one country. And the soldiers we recruited on the mainland have no wish to return. They have nothing to return to. They want to be part of what we will build here. They want to keep following you."

"The Kadar warlords will never agree to a Shahala queen."

I gasped. My voice was rusty, but what I thought I was saying in my head came out of my mouth. My heart clamored, and my spirit soared.

Batumar embraced me in a fierce hug. "You can speak."

Yet he denied me the opportunity to do so again by brushing his lips against mine. When I kissed him, he kissed me back. He kissed me senseless. He went about it for a good long time before he spoke again. "See? You are ready to be queen."

"The warlords will not take orders from a woman."

"Gods, I have missed your voice." He kissed me again before saying, "The remaining Kadar warlords will take orders from their own High Lord. This morning, they elected me to the post once again. But they will not object if I am your general at the same time."

"The Shahala will never agree to a Kadar king."

"I have no wish to be king. I do like leading the army. I am a warlord. But they can call me the queen's consort, or anything they please."

I liked the idea of one unified country. But… "If anyone should rule, it should be the Guardians. They hold ancient knowledge."

"The Guardians wish to be your advising body."

All that was too much for my mind to comprehend. "All I wished for was to establish a Hall of Healing in the city."

"And you can do that too. You can call it the Queen's Hall. I imagine it will be popular."

I could hear the smile in Batumar's voice. His words painted a picture I could see in my mind. Hope unfurled softly and quietly in the middle of my chest like a baby bird unfurling its fuzzy wings for the first time in the nest. Then I remembered I could no longer heal. I swallowed the sadness of the thought.

"When I saw the north wing collapse…" Batumar said in a ragged voice, close enough to me for his hair to brush my cheek as he shook his head. "How? And if you ever try to sacrifice yourself again, I swear on my ancestors, I… What happened after you came through the cave?"

"You must send someone to fetch Hartz and Atter from Barren Cove," I said first. I hoped Fadden and Lison were with them, having found their way out of the tunnels. I hoped the ancient god had not killed them.

Once Batumar shouted for a guard and issued the order to have the men collected, I gave him a full account of my journey through the mountain, then what came after—all about the khan, the emperor, and the sorcerer. He kept holding me closer and closer as I went on with the tale.

When I finished, Batumar touched his forehead against mine. "You are a hero to our people. You are the hero of my heart." He drew a deep breath. "Look at me, please."

He touched my chin and tilted my head up to his, brushed his lips over mine. "Open your eyes, my heart. I know the healing is there, inside you. Heal your sight."

I could not.

"If you heal your sight," he bargained, "I will allow the Shahala healers to heal me from Ishaf's scars."

"I will not be bribed."

Then he whispered, "I shall let you see my scars."

A smile tugged the corners of my lips. He kissed them, one after the other. He shifted next to me. "I am taking off my shirt."

I let my hands slip to his chest and drank in the warmth of his bare skin. My fingertips glided over the thick ridges of his old injuries. He went completely still. He ceased even to breathe.

"Did you know," he said after several heartbeats, "that your people gather every day outside the palace, hoping to catch a glimpse of you, so they can thank you? They need to see you. And you need to see them. They have lost so much. The sight of you would give them strength. Come back to us fully."

I opened my eyes and stared into unrelenting darkness. Batumar was right. So much work remained. The war was over. We had to rebuild. And I would help in any way I could. I could certainly not lie about in bed like a spoiled concubine while others worked outside.

Silently I prayed to the spirits, especially my mother's, and I felt her light inside me, spreading through me. I let her healing spirit flow through my body. The darkness in front of my eyes turned into fog, then the fog lifted, and little by little I could see Batumar.

His obsidian eyes swallowed me. When I smiled at him, holding his gaze, he breathed a ragged sigh of relief. As I shifted to see more of him, I caught sight of my own hair lying over his shoulder. The once-black locks were moonlight white. He had told me that when he found me. I had

226

forgotten. I could not help but stare.

"Now you really do look like a sorceress," he whispered, his voice thick with emotion. "Welcome back, healer, sorceress, queen. You can be anything you want, as long as you stay with me for the rest of our lives."

He claimed my lips. As he kissed me, he pulled me closer, his strong arms surrounding me. He kissed his way down the line of my jaw, then buried his face into my neck and kissed all the most sensitive spots until the entire surface of my skin tingled. The spirits help me, I had missed this. I felt my strength returning.

He caressed my arm, my side, my hip, then his hand reached the bottom of my shift, and he tugged up the thin material, gently, slowly. I twisted to help him pull it over my head.

His dark gaze focused on my body in the flickering light of the bedside candles. His breathing roughened. I knew I looked like I had been through a war. I had. We both had. I finally let my gaze drop to his chest and then the rest of his body. He had worn nothing but his shirt when he had come to bed, so he was now completely naked.

Tears sprang to my eyes and spilled down my cheeks.

"Tera." He cupped my face, searching my gaze. "All is fine well. Nothing hurts."

Oh, but those scars. Whip marks, claw marks, along with thin cuts that had come from a blade formed a crosshatch pattern over his skin. Gouges—he had been stabbed too—punctuated the chronicle of pain written on his body. Every hurt one man can inflict on another had been inflicted on him.

"I lost you," I whispered against the ragged white ridges as I began kissing them.

"We have lost each other more than once, but I promise you, we will always find each other."

I swallowed past the lump in my throat. "Call for the Shahala healers. You said you would let them heal you."

"Later." He growled and flipped me onto my back, trapped my hands above my head, and pinned me to the bed with his lower body, holding most of his weight off me.

His hips settled between my thighs. His hardness pressed against my swollen and aching center. He dipped his head and kissed my lips first, devoured them like a starving man before moving to my breasts.

I arched my body into the onslaught. For the first time in a long time, I felt pleasure instead of pain.

"Yes?" he whispered against a tortured nipple, his breath fanning my skin that was wet from his mouth.

I moaned with need. "Yes."

He raised his head, and his obsidian gaze pinned me. "You are well enough? Are you certain?"

"I am certain." I pulled my knees up to cradle his hips between my thighs.

He was at my opening. He held my gaze the entire time as he pushed into me slowly, gently, as if I were an untried maiden.

Pleasure washed over me. I could barely catch my breath. We were home. The war was over. We were one, joined.

I moved first, more impatient than he, and he smiled. Then he kissed me and began a mind-melting rhythm, rocking into me, taking me higher and higher.

We soared to the very heights of pleasure together.

Nothing else existed but love, warm and all-encompassing, filling the space all around us like the gentle waters of a hidden lagoon, rocking us to sleep.

The next morning, I woke to find Batumar already awake and watching me.

"How well are you healed?" were his first words instead of a morning greeting.

"All the way, my lord." I sat up. "I am ready to rise and inspect the castle."

In a blink, I was on my back again and Batumar over me, kissing me gently at first, and then with more and more passion. Heat flooded through me and need again. He was entering me, claiming me, and this time, he allowed his desperation to show, moving neither as gently nor as slowly as the night before. This was a thorough, warlordly claiming.

I reveled in his passion.

He would have kept me in bed all day if I had not finally pulled away—much, much later—reminding him that he had some healing waiting for him. Also, I had work to do. I had my people to see.

He did, however, talk me into not calling for a maid. He helped me dress, himself remaining naked the entire time—most distracting!—and kissing my neck and lips every chance he had.

Even when I was finally at the door, he was still trying to pull me back.

A brisk knocking had him halting his efforts at last.

He groaned with frustration, then called out, "What is it?"

"Your lady mother, my lord," came the respectful response from a servant. "The Lady Leena has returned to the castle."

* * *

With Leena back at the palace, the last of the shadows disappeared from Batumar's face. My heart also lifted. In some ways, Leena was like a mother to me too.

She did not return alone but arrived with Bevon, a Femian merchant she met at the sacred springs of the goddesses. He had escorted his daughters there on a pilgrimage. There had he and Leena fallen in love, and there had he taken her for his wife, a custom among the Femians if not among the Kadar. As the Kerghi had cut off the road to Karamur, he had taken Leena back to his estate to wait out our return to the island.

In the coming days, the three of us spent a lot of time together—overseeing the repairs to the north wing of the palace—while Batumar reorganized and trained the troops, sometimes riding off to root out small pockets of Kerghi who remained on the island and tried to hide. Hartz and Atter returned, but we lost Lison and Fadden forever to the mountain. At that news, my heart broke all over again.

"You should have more ships built, Lady Tera," Bevon said one night, the three of us—Bevon, Leena, and I—having a private dinner together. He was a portly man and boisterous, never without a smile on his face.

"How many more could we need?"

The shipwrights had been working nonstop and the Kadar fleet had been restored to its original size. Prince Graho had helped, giving advice on better and more modern design, before he sailed back home, taking with him Lord Karnagh and the Selorm.

"I talked to some of your merchants at the marketplace today," Bevon told me. He went every day, to secure connections and promote Femian trade. "Sea trade with the mainland might resume soon. They say passage across the wild ocean is easier than ever before. The hardstorms have greatly weakened."

The Guardian of the Scrolls told me the same thing when he came to visit the next day. He was my age, lanky in his long robe, the cut of his face severe. Despite his young age, he was a man most forbidding. Until he smiled at me. To me, he was like a brother. Having him by my side made me miss the Guardian of the Gate that much more, however.

"What think you about the weakening of the storms?" I asked him.

He was silent for a moment before saying, "I searched all the knowledge of the ancients."

"And?"

"Nothing there." He sounded hesitant.

"But?"

"The old Guardian of the Gate used to have a theory. He thought that when the ancients, the First People, created the Gates, they drew power from the world. This created the hardstorms." His tone said he believed the theory not, but now that he had begun, he went on regardless. "We know that in ancient times, the ocean could be sailed. We thought the hardstorms came, and then the ancients created the Gates to be able to travel between lands without risking the wild ocean. But when the Guardian of the Gates traveled the world to learn about the Gates, he found some indication that the ancients created the Gates, and then the imbalance of power the Gates caused in the natural order created the storms."

I held that thought in my mind, turned it around and around. "So when the Gate of the World was destroyed, its destruction restored the balance of power?"

"Something like that." He did not sound entirely sure.

"Yet we still have some storms, because there are yet some lesser Gates in existence."

He hesitated only another moment before saying, "It is possible."

"Dahru no longer has a Guardian of the Gate." Tears burned my eyes. "The young Guardian left no son behind."

"Dahru no longer has a Gate," the Guardian of the Scrolls said heavily. "Perhaps the spirits knew we no longer needed a Guardian of the Gate."

We were silent for a long time, each lost in our thoughts.

So many great men killed. My grief bubbled up again. "Can kindness not survive in an unkind world?"

The Guardian folded his hands behind his back and rocked on the balls of his feet as he considered my question. Then he stilled and nodded. "I do think our world is healing." He let that last word hang in the air for a moment before continuing, his expression suddenly lighter and brighter. "Which brings me to the reason I sought you out, my lady. Allow me to show you something."

He led and I followed, down the hallway, then down the stairs, then down again. Up ahead, a wall had collapsed, and rocks littered the hallway. I shuddered, even though I knew the Guardian was not taking me to the ancient god's temple. The temple no longer existed.

Two guards stood at the end of the hallway, for no discernible reason. They both bowed to me, and they bowed to the young Guardian as well, as if they knew him. They said not a word when he borrowed one of the burning torches from its wall sconce and began climbing over the rubble.

He was smiling, brimming with excitement suddenly. "Almost there, my lady."

I was curious enough to follow him, lifting the hem of my dress and ignoring the dust and dirt the blue sateen was collecting.

Past the collapsed wall waited another corridor, one I had never before seen, a plain wooden door at the end of it, dry and cracked with age, covered in ancient cobwebs, as if it hadn't been opened in centuries.

I paused. "Where are we?"

"When you collapsed the caves and the north wing of the palace collapsed with them, a secret chamber opened."

I stared at him.

His smile grew to the point of childish excitement. "Remember the Forum, my lady?"

"Of course, I remember." The Forum was at the center of the

Guardians' Forgotten City up the mountain. Its round dome held the map of the stars.

"Remember you the scrolls of the Forum?"

"They were lost ages ago, if ever they were real and not a myth."

The walls of the Forum were covered with honeycomb-like cubbyholes. People believed that once each held a scroll, and the myriad scrolls held all the knowledge of the ancient world.

"They are real for certain." The Guardian smiled wider. "And they have not been lost in one of the fabled wars. They were secreted away to be saved." He opened the door with effort, the wood scraping on stone, the doorframe shuddering.

A dark, cavernous space opened, the musty air making me shiver. Before I could ask any questions, the Guardian hurried down the middle of the space, next to a long trestle table covered with wax candles. One by one, he lit them.

Flames bloomed, illuminating the treasure before me. The secret chamber revealed was ridiculously crowded. Sagging shelves covered the walls from floor to ceiling. On these shelves, in disorderly piles, sat a treasure trove of ancient scrolls.

I stepped inside, dazed. I wondered if this might be a dream. Until the dust made me sneeze.

"How many?"

The Guardian laughed out loud. He threw his arms wide, looking from shelf to shelf. "I have not been able to count them all yet, my lady. But I believe this must be all of them."

My heart soared. "You are the true Guardian of the Scrolls again."

"Aye, my lady. But I am merely the *guardian* of the scrolls. Has it not been prophesied that *you* would be sent to read them?"

When I did not respond, he added, "If virtue and kindness cannot survive in this world, then we must gain new knowledge and we must make a new world."

He was young, yet no one could say he lacked wisdom.

I nodded slowly, carefully. "That is a great task."

"Which is why your people need you."

As I looked away from him and back to the scrolls, for a moment I wondered if Batumar had not put him up to this conversation. "I have no wish to be queen."

"Then be a Guardian of our island." His tone turned solemn. "We have need of a third Guardian."

The word "no" was on the tip of my tongue. But instead, I said, "Yes."

His smile bloomed wide again. "I thought for certain that you would protest."

The Tera who had gone into the mountain would have. But I had learned a great many things while I had been alone in the dark. I had listened closely to the spirits, and even closer to the whisperings of my heart.

"Our island has fallen apart," I said.

"The whole world has fallen apart."

"Even the ancient god could not rebuild his own temples. We cannot weld together the crumbled parts of what we once were. Only birth can triumph over death. Something new must be born."

He smiled with luminescent pleasure. "And you wish to be the midwife. You *are* a healer. You healed countless broken bones and fevers, coughs and stomach aches and burns and boils. And injuries worse than that. Some say you can bring back the dead."

I shook my head. "I lost my healing powers in the collapse."

Yet I *had* learned at my mother's knee how to bring health and balance back to a single person with little more than potions and herbs, without any great power. I wanted now—with the spirits' help—to do that for our country, for all our people.

EPILOGUE

"Mother! Chalee says she will be High Lady of the Kadar someday and lead the warriors to battle," Umar shouted from the garden gate. Judging by the look on my eldest son's face, he thought this the highest affront.

"That is not what I said!" Chalee, only a year younger, sailed into the sprawling herb garden behind him. "I shall be a warrior queen."

The two often tried to out-warrior each other, despite my best efforts. I consoled myself with the fact that my youngest child, Niag, showed great skill at healing. At the tender age of six, he was not allowed to use his skills on people, but injured animals were often brought to him from the city. Truly, he was already famed.

"You mean you will marry a warrior king," Umar taunted.

"I will do no such thing. Kings are old and grim." Chalee sent him a death glare.

"You cannot be a warrior."

Chalee's gaze turned truly menacing. "Father says I can be whatever I want to be." She looked at me for support. "Mother led an army."

At this, Umar grew uncertain. He thought, then thought some more before finally saying, "You are better with the arrow than I, but I am better with the sword." He thought again, then his face brightened with the pleasure of a solution found. "You can be my general."

This did not appease his sister. "*You* can be *my* general!"

Leena hurried in behind them. "Are they still at it? They got away from me in the kitchens. I was trying to teach them the history of all the proper dishes for our main feast days."

"An octopus could not keep these two in hand," I said with a sigh. The children did have a minder, but most of the time, Leena dismissed the girl to watch her grandchildren herself. "Where is Niag?"

"He should be right behind me. Found a sick bird on the path. He has the tiger with him."

"If you need rest, they can all help me here. I just finished a class on battlefield healing. The apprentices are gone to brew their potions and their tinctures."

Chalee poked at the feverfew I was clipping and remained unimpressed. "Can we go watch the warriors in battle training?"

I sighed. Both Chalee and Umar were too adventurous by far. Then again, they had me for a mother and Batumar for a father.

"How about I take you to the Forgotten City, and you can help me translate some scrolls?"

The thousands of scrolls found in the ruins of Karamur's castle were back in their rightful place in the honeycomb walls of the Forum. I both translated and taught them. All I had ever wanted was to become a healer of true power, but I had somehow become a teacher and librarian. And it felt right. I felt in my true place with my students.

Umar and Chalee, however, groaned in unison at the prospect of visiting the scrolls. Neither of them was inclined to scholarly work.

"You could read us the scroll you wrote about sailing the hardstorms." This from Umar. Half the time he wanted to be a High Lord, the other half an admiral.

"Mother!" Niag burst into the garden at full run. "Marga is going to have cubs again. A girl and a boy."

"Can I have a battle tiger?" Chalee and Umar cried out at exactly the same time.

"Are you Selorm, then?" Batumar's voice boomed from the garden gate.

"Can you make me a Selorm?" Umar asked him, at an age when children still thought their parents could do anything.

"I already made you perfect," Batumar said, obviously not given to modesty. "And what did your mother tell you to be?" he asked in a stricter tone.

"Aww…" Then two sheepish "Peacemakers."

"I want to be a peacemaker!" Niag jumped into my arms. "A peacemaker and a healer. I think Grandmother Leena's feet ache."

"No," I said at once, before he got it into his head to soften her bones. "I will see to it. I have the perfect poultice, already prepared." At his crestfallen expression, I added, "I heard from one of the guards that we have a manyinga with a bellyache in the stables."

Niag's face brightened. He was wiggling back down to the ground. "Oh, Mother, may I? Please?"

"You may. But if there is any trouble, you send for me."

"Yes, Mother!" He paused. "And after, can I go see Beco?"

Beco was Onra's youngest, the same age as Niag. The boys played together every day.

"All right. Tell Mistress Onra that I will be by at the bakery to visit her later."

"Thank you, Mother! I will be careful with the manyinga. I promise." He ran as if chased by the Kerghi horde, and his siblings were right behind him. No child would miss a chance to be around the giant beasts. They found the manyinga endlessly fascinating. Niag liked to pretend that he was talking to them, while Chalee and Umar liked to pretend that they were riding the beasts to battle.

"Do not forget to be back for your lessons!" I called after them.

"Mo-ther," they groaned in unison and stopped to see if I might yet lift that sentence.

I raised an eyebrow at my children. "Why do we have lessons?"

Niag responded. "To build a better world, we must become better people."

"And how do we become better people?" I asked, fixing the other two with a pointed motherly look.

"We learn," they mumbled.

When I nodded, they took off again.

Leena went after them.

"And your foot?" I called.

"It is nothing. It can wait."

In but a moment, Batumar and I were alone in the walled garden. The scent of hundreds of herbs sweetened the air, a dindin tree offering shade, the summer breeze perfect.

The warlord took my hand and pulled me to him. "A Shahala delegation arrived."

"All is well?"

"Better than well, my lady. They wish to honor you at the feast. They are granting you the title Tika Shahala."

My heart leapt. My mother had held that title, the most respected title among my people. My eyes suddenly swam with tears. "But I lost my healing powers."

"They say you are the greatest healer that ever lived. You healed our island and our people." He paused. "I have more good news," he said before he kissed me.

I could barely remember to ask "What?" by the time I was released.

"Word arrived from Lord Karnagh. He plans to visit us in the spring with his lady and the children. He might sail with King Graho and his queen."

"In the spring?"

He watched me. "Had you other plans? Wish you to take a trip of our own?"

"Not in the spring," I told him with a smile. "A young baby is not fit for a long journey."

His eyes flared. He scooped me into his arms, his smile so wide and carefree, it stole my breath away. "Am I to have another son?"

"Or daughter. *We* are having another child. I believe I shall have some small part in it."

The High Lord of the Kadar was whooping and shouting so hard, I do not think he heard me. He carried me to the palace roof and shouted all kinds of nonsense, loud enough to be heard by the guards, and then up went a great cheer. He would neither put me down, nor would he stop embarrassing me.

"You would think the High Lord had more decorum than to put on such a display."

"Who would think such foolishness?" He gave a wolfish grin and kissed me for everyone to see. "Certainly not our Guardian Queen. She is far too wise."

Neither of us could stop smiling.

Around us, the city brimmed with life, completely renewed since the war.

Kratos's temple had collapsed and filled with rubble, many of the cave tunnels collapsing with it. The rest, the Guardian of the Cave closed himself. No more caverns led through the mountain, no more Mouth of the Mountain. The ancient god was gone from the island. I felt no hint of his presence.

Lison and Fadden were never found. Kratos had them, as he'd said.

After the emperor died, his mainland empire soon fell apart under the squabbling of his hundred sons. The only remaining part, a small landlocked country held by one of his generals, was a threat to no one.

We did hear rumors of a powerful sorcerer roaming the far deserts of Nolek on the mainland, and at first I thought... But no, his name was not Drav.

Most of the army we had brought from the mainland remained on Dahru, the men taking wives from among our many widows. Our streets rang with the sound of laughter. The newcomers brought their traditions and beliefs. They brought new ideas and clever inventions. Karamur was no longer a Kadar city, but a city that belonged to many peoples and was stronger for it.

We had strong trade with not only the other Middle Islands and the Outer Islands, but the nations of the mainland. Ships sailed daily from our ports to Felep.

"Think you, my lord, that we can hold on to this peace?"

"If we were strong enough to win it, we shall be strong enough to hold it," he said with the full confidence of a warlord. "Truly, my lady, the tales of your great feats, of tumbling ancient temples and fortresses, of vanquishing emperors and even gods, are so great, I daresay no sane man would contemplate going against us."

I drew a cautious breath. "The spirits help us. What tales?"

"They say the gods journeyed through the mainland, collecting an army against Kratos himself. The god of death—that would be me," Batumar said, unashamedly pleased. "The goddess of life—that would be you. And the god of rebirth, the moment between death and life—which would be King Graho. They say more babes than ever were born after we passed. Each town where we spent a night is revered. The caravan yard has become a place of pilgrimage."

I gaped at him. "We are myth?"

He grinned. "Aye, we are."

I thought about it, then I decided I preferred it that way. I did not mind the credit to be given to the gods. I sought no glory.

"What about insane men?" I asked then, since he had said no sane man would contemplate going against us. Starting a war did not require sanity. Just the opposite.

"If some new darkness comes, we shall stand against it," Batumar declared.

Aye, I thought. We will stand against evil, and we will win. My people, Batumar, and I—Tera, Tika Shahala, Teacher, Guardian Queen.

From love comes courage.

Spirit be strong. Heart be brave.

--- THE END ---

A Quick Note from the Author

Thank you so much for sticking with me to the end! I hope with all my heart that I was able to do Tera's story justice and you enjoyed the books.

Writing the first book in the Hardstorm trilogy was easy. I was young and idealistic and thought I knew all about life. I thought kindness was what our world most needed, so I wrote a heroine who was kind. I didn't realize how rare this was, or that it could become controversial, until I started receiving notes from readers telling me how disappointed they were that Tera never got her revenge on Kumra. Kick-ass heroines are very much the trend, and revenge must be had. (I tried a kind heroine in one of my romantic suspense novels SILENT THREAT—about a deaf hero and an ecotherapist heroine—and received the same pushback.)

The second book in the Hardstorm trilogy was a surprise. When I started it, I planned on Tera losing Batumar and finding new love with Prince Graho. I began the first draft that way, but nothing about it felt right. It felt like the writer was forcing a plot on the story. So I deleted over a hundred pages and let the story be what it wanted to be. Batumar fought to come back from death for Tera. I couldn't stand in his way. The end result is much better than my first plan, and it feels true. This is it. This is their story.

The third book was murder. It was a hell of doubts and second thoughts. I started and stopped a dozen times. This book made me face that I'm not as good a writer as I thought I was. You see, this trilogy is my exploration of what is right, how a person should be in this world, what is the meaning of life... You know, all those easy questions.

Writing the first book back in 2003, I thought I knew it all. Writing the second book in 2014, I realized I didn't know anything, but would figure it out by the time I had to finish the third book. No pressure.

Me: *I don't know what the meaning of life is, but I'm sure it'll come to me in the next twelve months.*

Well, it didn't.

Yet I know this for sure: kindness matters, and the world needs it desperately. The more kindness we can put in the world, the better. And this is something we need to consciously do when responding to others. We must choose kindness over all the other options. But it's not enough.

I think it's equally important to stand up and fight for what's right. We can't just send thoughts and prayers. The massive amount of greed and evil in the world is real, and they have armies. So what do we do to push back their shadow that sits on the world? How do we create a new society where justice and truth and kindness can survive and thrive?

I wanted this trilogy to have the answer. It doesn't. Tera does the best she can, and she strives to learn to do better. But her story at least raises some of the right questions, and I think they are questions worth pondering.

I'd love to hear what you think. (Even if it's *'Oh, for love's sake, stop philosophizing and just write books.'*) Here is my personal email: danamarton@yahoo.com

I don't know if my Hardstorm Saga ended to your satisfaction, but please know that I gave the best that I had, from the bottom of my heart.

With the most heartfelt gratitude a writer could ever feel for her readers,
Dana

If you enjoyed GUARDIAN QUEEN, would you please leave an online review? Reviews make a huge difference for authors. They count toward special placement at the online stores. Some advertising venues will not accept a book for advertising unless it has a set number of reviews, etc. If you could leave even just a sentence, I would appreciate your kindness beyond words. Thank you! --Dana

If you would like to try some other books written by me, I also write romantic suspense. Here are the series names if you want to give them a try.

BROSLIN CREEK
MISSION RECOVERY
PERSONNEL RECOVERY
AGENTS UNDER FIRE

And if you are in the mood for a dragon:
https://danamarton.com/book/dragon-lord

You can find me on FaceBook here:
https://www.facebook.com/DanaMarton

I've been plotting a new fantasy series, while also thinking about giving some of the secondary characters in Hardstorm Saga their own books. (Lord Karnagh, Prince Graho, even perhaps Drav the sorcerer.) If you'd like me to let you know when I'm ready with the next project, please sign up for my newsletter here:
https://danamarton.com/hardstorm/fantasy/newsletter/signup

22956350R00151

Made in the USA
San Bernardino, CA
18 January 2019